YOUR KIND ARE EVIL

"He's a dirty wizard!" the big one shouted. "Get him!"

The rats charged, which forced Sullivan to take his hands out of his pockets. He easily dodged the first clumsy swing and slugged the hoodlum in the chest. Ribs cracked under Sullivan's hardened fist. That one gasped and collapsed. The next attacker slowed, confused, as the pull of gravity changed. It must have felt like he was trying to push his way through molasses. Sullivan's casual right hook broke the man's jaw.

The last rat skidded to a stop and dropped his brass knuckles in the snow. "Sorry. I'm sorry. I'm sorry!"

"Too late." Sullivan reversed gravity and the hood fell ten feet into the air, screaming, before gravity returned to normal. Sullivan didn't Spike very hard though, so the man probably didn't break too many bones when he hit the pavement.

The leader was the only one left standing. He let go of the woman and she sank to the ground, coughing. Sullivan looked down at her and as his eyes adjusted to the darkness was surprised to see it was the redhead from the library.

"Filthy wizard. You stay back!" The thug raised his knife. "Your kind are evil."

"You don't find nothing ironic about saying that?" Sullivan walked toward him. "Bunch of men mugging some poor lady and you're preaching to me about evil? Robbing better be all you had planned . . ."

Baen Books by Larry Correia

The Monster Hunter International Series

Monster Hunter International
Monster Hunter Vendetta
Monster Hunter Alpha
The Monster Hunters (omnibus)
Monster Hunter Legion

The Grimnoir Chronicles

Hard Magic: Book 1 of the Grimnoir Chronicles
Spellbound: Book 2 of the Grimnoir Chronicles
Warbound: Book 3 of the Grimnoir Chronicles (forthcoming)

with Mike Kupari

Dead Six

SPELLBOUND

Book II of the Grimnoir Chronicles

LARRY CORREIA

Spellbound: Book II of the Grimnoir Chronicles

This is a work of fiction. All the characters and events portrayed in this book are fictional, and any resemblance to real people or incidents is purely coincidental.

A Baen Books Original

Baen Publishing Enterprises
P.O. Box 1403
Riverdale, NY 10471
www.baen.com

ISBN: 978-1-4516-3859-2

Cover art by Alan Pollack
Interior art by Justin Otis, Aura Farwell, and Zachary Hill

First Baen paperback printing, January 2013

Distributed by Simon & Schuster
1230 Avenue of the Americas
New York, NY 10020

Library of Congress Cataloging-in-Publication Data:
2011035403

Printed in the United States of America

10 9 8 7 6 5 4 3 2

To Abby

Acknowledgments

Thanks to Reader Force Alpha for the comments, advice, and corrections; Mike Kupari for brainstorming Grimnoir into existence; Justin Otis and Aura Farwell for the glossary art; Zachary Hill for the interior artwork; and the awesome staff of Baen Books for all that they do.

Prologue

Yesterday, I was told the most marvelous tale. If it had not been repeated by a gentleman of such strict conscience, I would scarcely have believed. Another child with magical capabilities has been discovered, and in Chelmsford of all places. The young lady I witnessed in London could change the weather and they say this Chelmsford youth can heal the sick. Two miraculous beings have appeared in England this year and there are rumors of them appearing in other lands. It seems there are more of these wizards found amongst us every day! Will their numbers continue to grow? Is this the end of days? The mind reels at the possibilities.

—Sir John Fisher,
Personal correspondence, 1849

France, 1918

DURING THE DAY the sky to the east was black, but at night it burned red. For three days straight the thunder had never stopped. At first she had cringed at every distant rumble, and the noise had left her frightened and crying, but now the bombs were just background noise. The constant rattling of their small house had become almost normal. Father had told her the thunder was called artillery, and though it sounded scary, they needed to be brave. The tears did not come so often anymore, and then only at night, when the others couldn't see her.

Father said that the fighting was still many miles away and that they would be safe here. Mother had wanted to flee but Father insisted there was nowhere else for them to go. They had no money. The government had confiscated all of their crops and most of their animals to feed the army. There was no food in the refugee-packed cities either. They were safer staying on the farm, for at least there, should the Germans break through, they might be overlooked as unimportant and passed by on the soldiers' push to Paris.

She was the youngest of five children. The older ones could recall a time before the war, but to her, it seemed as if things had always been this way. As long as she could remember, the Germans had been coming to kill them all. Father had gone away for what had seemed like forever to fight, and the older children had tended the farm in his stead. Since she was seven, she had been in charge of gathering eggs from the chickens. Father had been sent home after he had gotten really sick and nearly died from breathing the Germans' poison gas. His voice was scratchy now and he grew tired very easily, but she was just happy to have him home.

The war had gone on for many years but never before had it been this close. Father had spoken of how the two sides had barely moved, pushing each other back and forth, neither one giving hardly any ground, but once the

Kaiser had started sending dead men to fight, things had changed. Father tried not to show it, but he was scared of the things everyone had started calling zombies, and that made her scared of them too. He had explained that there was going to be one last big fight, and whoever won it would probably win the war once and for all.

The rest of the world would come to call these days the Second Battle of the Somme, but to her, it would always be simply the Big Fight.

For weeks leading up to the Big Fight, soldiers had marched east on the road that meandered around their farm. It had seemed like an endless stream of men, horses pulling carts, and even hundreds of modern trucks, while overhead, fantastic airships cast huge shadows. Some of the soldiers were clean and their uniforms looked new. Others were dirty, and they seemed as tired as Father had been when he'd come home. The men wore grey, brown, and green, but their flags were colorful. Father would point at the different flags and the symbols painted on their vehicles as they went past. "Those are our countrymen from the south. Those are British. Those are Canadian. Ahh, that volunteer American brigade. I hear they all have magic," and he had patted her on the head. "Just like you."

That had made her very proud. She was the youngest, but she was special, and she had waved at the passing Americans. A giant American boy wearing a metal suit and carrying a huge gun had even seen her and waved back.

Three days after the Big Fight started, the war came to her farm and killed her entire family.

⋘⋙⋘⋙⋘

The girl hid in the cupboard. It was all that she could do. Everyone else was gone. All her brothers and sisters, Mother and Father, everyone. Hot tears dripped down her face and her nose was running, but she tried not to make a sound. *He* would hear her. *He* would kill her.

The man was in the kitchen. She could hear his boot soles stamping against the floorboards. There was a crash as he pulled open the pantry. Dishes broke and he cursed in a language she did not recognize. *Was he looking for her?* She pulled her knees up tight to her chest and tried not to breathe. He was searching for her with his terrible grey eyes.

The pump handle was worked and water splashed into the basin. A few seconds passed and then the killer let out a gasp of pain.

The cupboard door was loose. There was a sliver of light leaking around the edge. She put her eye close and found that she could see a narrow slice of the kitchen. A bloody shirt lay discarded on the floor. The man was at the sink, holding one of Mother's dishrags to his stomach. The cloth came away red, revealing a ragged gash. Thick rivulets of dark blood were trickling down his bronze skin and splattering about the kitchen. It was a terrible wound.

He must have been injured before he had mysteriously appeared in the middle of the yard, for certainly none of her family had time to defend themselves. When he had appeared, seemingly out of thin air, Father had addressed him first in French and then in German. The stranger had answered by stabbing Father in the heart. Then he had been *everywhere*. Killing. Her brothers and sisters had run but he had chased them all down. Mother had told her to hide, but as she'd fled, she'd heard Mother screaming on the steps and then it had been quiet.

She was all alone with the monster.

The man's long white hair was dirty and tangled. There were many other cuts and bleeding holes on his body besides the big one on his stomach, and she prayed that he might hurry and die soon. As she watched him trying to stop the bleeding, she realized that the man's torso was covered in some strange design, like he'd been crisscrossed in blackened scars. Mother appreciated books, so the girl knew how to read, but she did not recognize any of the strange letters carved into the killer's chest.

"I know you are there, little girl."

She gasped and pulled back deeper into the cupboard.

"Hiding does no good, for I can see you in my head." His French was rough. He was a foreigner. He spoke almost like an Englishman would speak French, but he was certainly no Englishman either. "Do not be afraid. It will be over soon."

"Why?" she squeaked.

"Why?" The stranger chuckled, and then it turned into a grunt of pain. "My enemies, put a hex on me and I was unable to Travel very far. How did they do that, I wonder? Please come out, girl. I am . . . *better* now. I do not like speaking to a door."

She scrunched back as far as she could. "No."

There was a long pause. "You have Power. You are far more valuable than the others. They were empty. You . . . You are what drew me here. I should have taken you first. Such is life."

Muddy boots struck the floor as he strolled over and ripped the cupboard door from its hinges. The girl screamed. He grabbed a handful of her long dark hair, dragged her out, and hurled her against the floor. She sobbed and begged for her life. She tried to use her own magic, but was too terrified and shaky to make it work.

"I am sorry," he said as he went over to the sink. He picked up a bloody knife and came toward her. "You don't understand what it is like. No one does. It's like a furnace. It demands to be fed."

The house began to vibrate again, but the source of this new rumble was closer than the bombs. It was a truck! The killer looked toward the window and she used the opportunity to scramble to her feet and run for her life.

The truck engine stopped and metal doors clanged open. Someone shouted from the yard, "There's nowhere left to run. Come out and finish this."

Panicked, she ran for the door and into the light. She tripped over her mother's outstretched arm and tumbled down the steps. Her leg twisted and she cried out as a terrible pain shot through her, but she was so scared that she got back up and limped as fast as she could until she found a space to hide behind the woodpile.

Seven men climbed off the truck. Most were wearing workers' clothing, but two were dressed like soldiers from her country, and one was even wearing the grey uniform of the Germans. All had guns. They spread out as the one in the center walked toward the house. "Your madness ends here!"

"So you are all that is left." The killer tottered outside, pale and close to death. He surveyed the strangers, then leaned against the wall to stay on his feet. "What did you start with? Twenty?"

"And you'll pay for every last one of them!" shouted one of the others.

"A waste! Imagine the mysteries I could learn, the answers I could find. Yet, you chased me away. The greatest expenditure of life in the shortest period of time in the history of man is happening right over *there*!" The killer pointed toward the east where the sky was a black wall of smoke. The gesture caused him to grimace and clutch his side. "The mysteries of the cosmos would have been laid bare."

"We knew this battle would attract you like a moth to the flame," replied the leader. He looked to his men. "Kill the Spellbound."

When it was over, the grey-eyed man that had killed her family was dead, but so were most of the strangers that had arrived to rescue her. Even near death, the murderer had been able to disappear and reappear in different places faster than she could comprehend, and he had inflicted many wounds on her saviors before succumbing to his own. There had been crackling lightning, freezing sheets of ice, and men moving faster than was humanly possible . . . and so much death. She had been unable to look away.

The leader of the strangers had lived, though he was bleeding and hurt. He spent a minute at the side of his last living friend, until he passed away as well. The survivor went to each of his fallen companions and collected a ring from their fingers. Then he found her, still hiding behind the woodpile, curled into a ball and crying. Older than

Father, the stranger seemed thin and tired. Kneeling, he offered her his hand. She took it, his hands were softer than expected, certainly not the hands of a farmer, and he was wearing a gold and black ring. "It is safe now." Her answer was too quiet to hear. "Are you hurt? Do you have anywhere to go?" His eyes were filled with gentle sadness.

She tried to answer again, but her voice didn't want to work anymore. Sobbing, she got up and hugged him. Awkwardly, the man held her close. "They are all gone? There is no one left? I'm so sorry," he said as he lifted her and carried her away. "I'll find someplace safe for you, I promise."

A group of soldiers had been marching up the road, heard the shooting, and come running. From the way they sounded as they shouted orders, they were Americans. Rifles were pointed their way, but the man that saved her life addressed the Americans with a dignified, commanding voice. "I am a commandant in the Gendarmerie on special assignment. Here are my orders."

The American officer was a large and frightening man with a huge mustache and sideburns, but he understood French and seemed impressed by the papers her savior had produced. "These are signed by Foch!" The American snapped rigid and gave a salute, even though her savior wasn't wearing a uniform. "Very well, sir. What can we do to assist?"

The guns were turned away as her rescuer gently placed her into the passenger seat of the truck. "See to it these people are given a decent Christian burial, except for him . . ." He pointed at the body of the grey-eyed man.

"Burn that corpse. Burn it to ash. Then I have a message for you to convey to General Pershing at AEF headquarters. He will understand. Tell him that the Warlock is dead."

Chapter 1

I swear before my God and these witnesses that I will stay true to the right and good, that my magic will be used to protect, not to enslave, that all my strength and wisdom must always shield the innocent. I swear to fight for liberty though it cost my life. The Society will be my blood and its knights my brothers, and that I will always heed the wisdom of the elders' council. I willingly pledge my magic, my knowledge, my resources, and my life to uphold these things.

—Oath of the Grimnoir Society,
original date unknown

Miami, Florida
1933

FRANKLIN ROOSEVELT MUST DIE.

The angel had said so. No matter what, the president had to be killed, but it hadn't told him what to do about the crowd that had gathered to see the new president. Giuseppe Zangara decided he'd best murder all of them too, just to play it safe. It would be easy, since it felt like the angel had given him magic sufficient to burn the whole world. Roosevelt first, though. The last thing he wanted to do was upset the angel.

Other than a generalized hate for all rich capitalists, Zangara didn't know much about the man who had been elected President of the United States. Hoover, Roosevelt, they were all the same to him. Names changed, but all were filthy capitalists, these American politicians, crushing the workers underfoot. He'd come to this country and they'd stolen his health, ruined his life, and destroyed his dreams. Some said that those failings were his own fault, his health problems were just bad luck, losing his job was because he wasn't a very good bricklayer, but he knew the truth . . . Oh no, Zangara was not to blame. The capitalists were to blame. Capitalists were always to blame.

Florida was warm, even in winter. He'd come here because the humidity was supposed to be good for his health. Now, packed into the crowd, it was too hot. Excited, the mob waited for their false savior to arrive. Many of them had made signs, painted on cardboard or sheets. He could not read the words, but he could guess what they said. *We need jobs. We are scared. We are pathetic. Protect us from magic.* When these fools had heard the new president was coming, they had painted signs. When Giuseppe Zangara had heard the new president was coming, he had begun daydreaming about how to kill the man.

Originally, he'd planned to shoot the president with a gun. Sure, he'd been born with magic, but not enough to make a difference. His connection to the Power was weak.

Zangara had just enough magic to be branded a freak, certainly not enough to kill a capitalist and the many guards he was sure to have.

Then the angel had come to him last night, and everything had changed.

It was as beautiful as only something that had escaped from heaven could be. The angel had heard his prayers and come to bless him because of the righteousness of his cause. Its magic touch had fixed the sickness in his guts. It had drawn a spell on him that had made his magic a hundred times stronger, and even given him a fancy piece of jewelry. All it wanted in return was for him to destroy a man whom he'd wanted to kill anyway. Only it had demanded that he do it in a spectacular fashion. It had been his lucky night.

Giuseppe Zangara was very short. All the stupid Americans in front of him were tall, making it difficult to see past them. As the bodies shifted, he caught brief glimpses between them of the president's big automobile arriving. He tried to push his way closer, but there were too many people shoving. There was a cheer and many began clapping as the president stood up from the back seat and waved. A group began chanting "Remember Mar Pacifica," over and over, but others shouted for them to be silent. Someone opened the car door for the president. Time was running out. If he let the president escape, the angel would be upset with him and take the magic away, and he'd just be a sick and weak nobody again.

Luckily, the president stopped to give a speech. Good thing politicians loved to hear themselves talk. Roosevelt raised his voice so that everyone could hear as he started yapping about how everything was going to get better and they just needed to be patient and have hope. More lies. Filthy capitalist lies.

Now there was a lady with a big flowery hat blocking Zangara's view. His first instinct was to blast her into pieces, but the president had to come first. A nearby father hoisted his son to sit on his shoulders in order to better see over the crowd. Zangara noticed that someone had left a wooden folding chair at the edge of the mob and that gave him an idea.

Chair in place, Zangara climbed up. Now he could see better over the crowd, but the chair was wobbly. It would make aiming his magic more difficult, but it didn't matter . . . for the first time in his life he had Power to spare. Before, he could make little pops of energy, not worth much more than firecrackers, but with the new design the angel had drawn on his chest, so fresh it burned, he'd show these capitalist pigs real fireworks.

As the new primary shareholder of United Blimp & Freight, Francis Cornelius Stuyvesant had only been a millionaire for a relatively short period of time, but he'd already grown accustomed to people not keeping him waiting. Time was money, and by that logic Francis' time was worth more money than damn near anyone. His grandfather had been the richest man in the world, but thanks to the UBF board's legal wrangling over Francis' unorthodox inheritance, and the splitting off of several subsidiaries, he was only something like the fifth richest. It would have to do. He checked his watch and sighed. Obviously, no matter how wealthy you were, when the

President of the United States wanted to stop and give an extemporaneous public speech, he got a pass.

The club windows had been cracked open enough to let in the refreshing ocean breeze, which also enabled Francis to hear the speech. He watched Franklin Roosevelt for a moment and had to admit that the man was a fine orator, very good at stirring up emotion, and that was what troubled Francis. Roosevelt's words may have sounded reassuring to the masses, but some of those words were frightening to every Active in the country.

Officially, it was a vacation that had brought Francis to Miami. The weather in New York had been dreadful, so Francis taking his new personal dirigible, *Cyclone*, south for a holiday had not struck anyone as odd. Franklin Roosevelt would also be vacationing in the area at the same time. Roosevelt would not be sworn in until March, and since they were both such important men they had agreed to meet for dinner.

Unofficially, he was here to gather information. Francis was a knight of the Grimnoir Society, and the Society was nervous about some of the things Roosevelt had said about Actives during his campaign. Unlike his father and grandfather, Francis had no stomach for politics, but since he was already acquainted with Mr. Roosevelt (both came from very wealthy New York families) the elders had asked Francis to try to get a feel for what the president intended to do. Other socially connected knights had already tried, but the man was a cipher on this particular topic.

"I do not trust politicians." His companion leaned over to whisper, "but I especially do not trust this one."

"How does that make him special? You don't trust anyone." Francis didn't bother to lower his voice. Nobody was going to hear them over the general racket of the crowd outside and the excited socialites inside.

Heinrich Koenig shrugged. "What can I say? He speaks like a Mouth."

"Your best friend is a Mouth."

In the Society, the two of them were knights of equal standing, but Francis had created public UBF cover jobs for everyone on his team. Heinrich was supposedly Francis' bodyguard, though Francis reasoned that since he himself was a skilled Mover, a bodyguard was superfluous. However, Heinrich, with his professional paranoia and scowling distrust of almost everyone, certainly looked the part of a convincing bodyguard. Plus, Heinrich was a Fade, and nobody wanted to get into a fight with a Fade.

"Chose your words carefully with him, Francis. That is all I am suggesting. This one is slippery. How can a man who walks only because of a Healer be such a hypocrite?"

There was a rumor that Roosevelt had once been saved from a paralytic disease by a Healer. "His family could certainly afford a good Mending."

"He's benefited from magic, but when it becomes expedient to get elected, he is all in favor of rounding us up in the name of security."

"Nobody is going to get *rounded up*." The public was jumpy since the Peace Ray obliteration of Mar Pacifica had been successfully pinned on rogue Actives, but the idea struck Francis as absurd.

"The people are frightened of us. Many in your government know it was the Imperium's doing, but they are not ready to risk war. Instead, they blame us, a home-grown and more easily managed problem. So now we get to be the cause of everything from anarchists to the economy. You heard him promise to keep us under *control*. What do you think control means?"

"Well, that's what I hope to find out."

"You control an unruly dog with a chain . . . or a cage. Never underestimate fear"—Heinrich gestured angrily at Roosevelt—"or the men who would capitalize on it to get what they want."

"You are such a pessimist. This is America. Nothing like that could ever happen here."

"We used to say something similar back home, before the Kaiser raised an army of the dead."

Shaking his head, Francis turned back to the window just as President Roosevelt finished his platitudes. The crowd erupted in cheers. The people were angry, their families were hungry, their jobs were gone. They needed something to believe in . . . or someone to blame. He watched the desperate faces and knew just how dangerous things could become for his kind, for all Actives everywhere, if the things the elders were worried about came to pass. Magicals had more freedom in America than any other nation, but if America were to follow in the footsteps of the Imperium or the Soviet Union, where Actives were seen as nothing more than property of the state . . .

We can't let that happen.

Francis understood that his inheritance had made him a very influential man. Between Stuyvesant riches, Black Jack Pershing's teachings, and the luck of being born with magic, Francis now found himself a sort of unofficial ambassador for the Active race. He felt that weight on his shoulders and knew that he had to do his best in order to sway the government from a destructive course. A servant came by with a silver tray full of glasses. Francis took one with a grunt of thanks and downed the drink, not really paying any attention to what it was. Unfortunately, it wasn't made of alcohol. Prohibition was rapidly going the way of the dodo, but appearances had to be kept in the meantime.

Roosevelt was waving to the people as he walked up the steps. The staff had opened the doors of the club for him and the management had lined up to shake hands. Flashbulbs popped as the press took their obligatory photographs.

Then there was a much larger flash and Francis' eyes closed involuntarily, but not before leaving him with a split-second afterimage of the crowd, bones visible through their skin, before they were washed away.

The explosion was deafening. He would surely have been killed by flying glass if Heinrich hadn't grabbed his arm and Faded them both out of existence. A wall of heat and energy rolled harmlessly through them. It was a strange, fuzzy feeling as hundreds of shrapnel bits pierced his body and flew out the other side. Heinrich let go and their bodies returned to normal, solid and unharmed.

Bomb!

It took a moment for his vision to clear. The front of the hotel had been ripped apart, paint stripped away and timbers blackened. The president's automobile was on its side, sputtering flames. The center of the crowd was gone. The edges collapsed as the injured fell or scattered.

Heinrich shouted something, but Francis couldn't hear him over the highpitched ringing in his ears. Then Heinrich turned grey and stepped cleanly through the wall, leaving Francis alone at the ruined window.

There was a lone figure standing in the center of the carnage. A man was walking along, his lips pursed like he was whistling a tune. He spread his hands wide and blue sparks fanned between his fingers. He swept one hand forward. The hotel shook from another massive impact, this time directly against the steps where the president had been.

Francis was flung to the floor by a wall of hot air. The bones in his forearm broke with a sick crack and his forehead bounced off the hardwood. People were running and screaming and plaster rained from the ceiling. Wincing, Francis pulled himself up with his uninjured arm and looked out the window just in time to see a third explosion rip through the scattering survivors. The pressure wave flung bodies through the air, and they spun helplessly back to Earth as the madman turned to face the hotel again. He was laughing hysterically, seemingly having the time of his life. His shirt was flapping open in the fiery wind, revealing the red glow of a magical brand across his chest.

That alien marking could only mean one thing. *Iron Guard!*

The killer saw Francis in the window and grinned. Sparks gathered in his hands.

Gathering his Power and blinking the blood from his eyes, Francis searched for a weapon. The waiter that had brought him a drink was on the floor nearby, burned and gasping. The silver serving tray was next to him, aerodynamic and solid . . . Francis concentrated, using his magic to reach out and lift the tray from the floor. It appeared to levitate, up, over the windowsill, and then Francis concentrated and used a mighty blast of Power to hurl it at his target.

Being a Mover of his caliber was just like having a bunch of invisible, long range, extremely strong hands. Not impeded by the frailty of human muscle, Francis was able to spin the tray through the air at a terrible velocity and guide it with precision. The improvised discus hit the assassin square in the throat. That eerie smile disappeared as the head rolled off into the street.

Los Angeles, California

FAYE SAT IN SILENCE while the film reel played. It was an amazing thing, and though she'd sat through dozens of motion pictures over the last several months—since she routinely rubbed elbows with high society now—the magic of a moving picture never seemed to wear off. The projector was a small one, as was the screen. The smoky hotel room was certainly no theater, the subject was depressing, and there was no music or narration, but despite that, even this movie was neat. Faye just plain liked going to the movies. They were . . . well . . . *magic.*

The newsreel was showing scenes of Japan. Faye had never visited the faraway lands of the Imperium in person. The closest she'd ever come to Imperium soil was standing on their flagship, however briefly, before it was blown to kingdom come by Tesla's Geo-Tel. The film made Japan seem nice, with cherry blossoms falling like snow, big wooden arches, and exotic ladies with big sandals and pretty dresses. If it wasn't all controlled by a bunch of evil crazy people who'd already tried to kill her a whole mess of times, the film would almost make her want to go for a visit.

The hotel suite was crowded. Most of the participants were using tobacco, and she could watch the smoke curling into loops and swirls in the flickering beam of the projector. Faye found that it was hard to breathe, but the others didn't seem to notice. These important-behind-closed-doors types all seemed to smoke. Their Healer, Jane, certainly disapproved, and despite the fact that Jane could actually see your lungs right through your chest and sense disease coming a mile away, nobody wanted to listen to her on *that* subject.

Some of the people here were powerful, and not just in the magical sense, either. Knights had come from all over the country, and a contingent of them had even come all the way from Europe, including two of the elders. Things had really been shaken up since Mar Pacifica and the Geo-Tel. It was a huge meeting by the standards of the Grimnoir Society, and she knew that was partly because they wanted to see her in person . . . the girl who had dared to face the Chairman.

The elders had spoken to her alone for a long time. Faye had given her report; she'd been grilled, quizzed, questioned, annoyed, and poked at, and now she was ready to go home. When it was time for the movie, they'd invited everybody else in.

On the screen, men in robes beat a rhythm on giant gongs. Children laughed and played in the perfectly clean streets.

"They skipped the part with the torture schools," the man at her side pointed out.

"Hush, Mr. Browning," Faye whispered. "I'm trying to listen."

"There is no sound accompanying it, my dear."

He had her there. "It isn't polite to talk in the theater anyway."

John Moses Browning chuckled, but decided not to take her advice. He spoke up so that all could hear. "Is it possible that this was filmed prior to the Tesla event?"

Much to Faye's consternation, the elder in charge of the secret gathering had no qualms about talking during the movie either. "We have confirmed that this was filmed recently. Here he comes. Watch carefully, please, Miss Vierra."

That was her. There were only three members of the Grimnoir Society that had ever spoken with the Chairman in person that were still alive, and Jane and Mr. Sullivan weren't here. Faye made sure to concentrate, a skill that came with great difficulty when your brain worked so much faster than everyone else's. The projector was showing a big army parade. Imperium soldiers were marching in wave after wave, their posture as straight as the long bayonets on the ends of their rifles. There was a man riding a giant black horse at the head of the column. The crowd of thousands bowed and stayed bowed as he rode past. He was familiar, handsome, intimidating, and far too alive to be who she thought he was.

The image looked exactly like him. "There has to be a mistake," Faye said. "The Chairman's dead."

One of the younger knights at the back of the room chimed in. "The Imperium insists he didn't perish aboard the *Tokugawa*."

"The Imperium also says the *Tokugawa* and the *Kaga* got wrecked in a storm, and we all know that's a bunch of bunk."

"How can you be so certain he is deceased?" a young English knight asked.

His accent—was that what English was *supposed* to sound like?—grated on Faye's ears. "Shucks, I don't know. Maybe because I cut his hands off and threw them in a propeller, is how. Then the whole ship got blown up. I was there, you weren't. Besides—" John Moses Browning reached over and placed one hand on her knee to try to quiet her, because he knew what she was going to say next was going to sound crazy, and she already had cultivated quite the reputation for crazy, but Browning was too late. "I talked to his ghost afterward."

Mr. Browning sighed.

"Preposterous," said one of the other knights.

"No. He was sad that he was dead. He told me a poem."

The knights all began speaking at once. The film ended. The loose end of the reel slapped rhythmically against the projector. The screen went white.

"The child is quite mad, Browning," said a Frenchman.

That made Faye angry. First, she wasn't a kid anymore, and second, she wasn't crazy. The Frenchman was lucky she didn't Travel his head someplace without the rest of his body.

Mr. Browning stuck up for her. "This *child* killed a hundred elite Imperium troops in combat, did battle with the most powerful wizard the world has ever known, and then Traveled an entire dirigible and its crew a thousand miles . . . I would watch your tone, sir."

There was a polite cough. "My apologies, madam."

Damn right, Faye thought to herself.

"That man in the film could be a double," one of the other Americans said. "Maybe a Ringer? Heaven knows the Imperium has enough Actives—they are bound to have a few of those."

"Not a Ringer. Their magic clouds the viewer's mind. It has no hold over recording technology," Mr. Browning said. He was one of the senior members present and as far as Faye was concerned, the smartest one there, but she was rather biased. "A skilled actor would be more likely."

"Then this thespian deserves one of those new academy awards for his performance." One of the two elders was British. The elders never left the shadows, as their identities were always kept secret, but he sounded fat. Even his shadow was fat. "Bravo. Excellent performance, I say."

Faye didn't know very many of their names, and that was on purpose, including the Americans that hadn't been Pershing's knights. It wouldn't be much of a secret society if you knew everyone else's name, now would it? Whenever the Imperium captured a knight, the first thing they did was torture them until they gave up everyone else they knew.

The fat Englishman continued. "Our spies insist that both the Imperial Council and the Emperor believe this man to be the real Chairman. His mission of purification continues unabated. The schools still churn out Active soldiers, more territory falls by the day, and Unit 731 continues their eugenic madness. So, even if deceased, the Chairman is having a rather fine year."

"I'm telling you, *I* killed the Chairman," Faye insisted.

A new voice came from the back. "If anything killed the Chairman, it was the cunning of Isaiah Rawls and Kristopher Harkeness."

The room grew deadly quiet.

"Who said that?" Faye asked sharply.

Through treachery, murder, and blackmail, those two Grimnoir had delivered a sabotaged Tesla superweapon into the Chairman's hands. Its firing had vaporized the *Tokugawa*, but in order to deceive the Chairman, Harkeness and Rawls had sacrificed many of their fellow Grimnoir. Their plan had worked, but it had cost lives. Some had been her friends, and one in particular had been her grandpa. Harkeness was dead. Rawls was missing, and if she knew what rock he was hiding under she'd kill him too. It was amazing that anyone here actually had the nerve to speak up for traitors. Faye stood and tried to pick out behind the gleaming beam of the projector which one of the shapes she needed to hurt. "Say that again."

Browning sensed the coming murder. "Faye, please . . ."

"Enough," the elder in charge of the meeting spoke. He was German, and sounded a bit like an older version of Heinrich when he talked. "Their actions were a blight on the Society and made a mockery of what we stand for. Regardless of how you personally feel, Pershing's knights were the ones bled by their actions. Those names will not be spoken here today."

Faye returned to her seat. She may have been the youngest there and the only girl, but she wasn't about to have somebody talking up the men responsible for killing Grandpa like they were heroes. Whoever it was who said that . . . well, she was going to have a little *talk* with them after.

The German elder stood to address the room. "Turn off that blasted machine." The projector was shut down. The only illumination was the bit of sunlight sneaking around the edge of the curtains. "Gentlemen, lady, the elders have much to discuss. Our American brothers are in trouble, with being blamed for the Peace Ray destruction of Mar Pacifica, and talk of a registration of Actives or worse . . . These are challenging times for our people everywhere. Thank you for coming all the way here. Your reports are valuable and your efforts, as always, are appreciated."

"And of my request?" Mr. Browning asked.

"We have discussed it. The American knights have taken terrible casualties over recent years. Some here have already volunteered to join your cause and will be returning with you."

"And of new recruits?"

The fat Englishman answered. "It appears General Pershing recruited against our counsel anyway." It was obvious he was looking directly at Faye as he said that. "I can only assume you plan on continuing that tradition. You Yanks tend to do what you want, regardless of the risks it exposes the rest of us to."

"We did what we had to," Mr. Browning said pointedly.

"Though it may have felt that way in the past, you have not been in this fight alone. Across the Orient, the

Imperium grows. The Soviets are enslaving every Active they can get their hands on. Both groups have agents and saboteurs in every single land, stirring the pot."

"I assure you, sir," Mr. Browning said as politely as possible, "that there is a significant measure of difference between pot-stirring and having Tesla superweapons fired at your cities."

The German elder just nodded. Faye had to remember that Germans knew all about what it was like to get blasted with a Peace Ray. "Very well. You have the authority to recruit as you see fit. You will report solely to the American elder, who, sadly, was unable to join us today. Pershing's knights are yours to command, Mr. Browning."

"They will continue to be called Pershing's knights. I do not consider myself worthy."

"As you wish, old friend. Do your best. Alive or dead, it seems the Chairman, or perhaps the idea of the Chairman, is still our greatest threat."

Faye had to speak up at that. "There's something worse." The two elders hadn't wanted to listen before when they were alone, but now that all the others were in the room, they had to know. "The hungry thing. The thing that's looking for the Power. Even the Chairman was scared—"

"That'll be all," the elder stopped her gently. "Do not worry. We will discuss what you and Mr. Sullivan told us, and make plans accordingly."

It was the politest way that she'd ever been told to shut up. These Europeans sure were fancy with the manners.

The meeting broke up. The elders shuffled out one door to be whisked off by their many bodyguards to some other secret hiding place. It was understandable. Even though there were something like twenty knights watching this place, their enemies would love to take a crack at them. Sometimes Faye wondered if doing everything so secretly for so long had made many of the old Grimnoir too timid.

"I don't think I did very good," Faye told Mr. Browning.

"You shook things up a bit," he answered with a gentle smile. "But I don't necessarily believe that to be a bad thing. It is easy for an organization led by old men such as myself to be a little hidebound. In fact, the only other person I know of that's ever been able to shake up this bunch was Black Jack himself."

That comment made Faye especially proud.

Once the elders were away, someone opened the curtains. Faye was surprised to discover that many of the regular knights wanted to talk to little old her. Some of them had come a very long way, and apparently the stories about her had caused quite a stir. She really wasn't used to the attention. She spent the next few minutes retelling the story about the fight aboard the *Tokugawa*. She didn't even have to exaggerate to make it sound amazing.

There was a sudden commotion at the rear of the room. Browning may have been an old man, but you wouldn't know it by the speed his hand landed on the butt of the .45 automatic inside his suit. Several other Grimnoir reacted in the same manner, which just went to show that they were a jumpy bunch. One of the elders' bodyguards was in the doorway, speaking rapidly in French. Someone else was asking him to slow down. "Just a messenger," Browning removed his hand from his pistol and listened, scowling.

"What is it?" Faye asked. The other Grimnoir were reacting with disbelief. The ones like her that didn't speak the language were all asking questions, and that was most of them.

Mr. Browning had gone as white as the movie screen. "An Active tried to murder President Roosevelt . . . It is unknown if he survived. Hundreds are dead." He turned to face her. "This is horrible."

Francis and Heinrich were supposed to have met with the president today. She had spoken to Francis by mirror just that morning. She *really* liked Francis, and the idea of him being in danger made her sick, but he was smart and brave, so surely he'd be okay. Well, maybe not, because if anybody could get himself into trouble, it was Francis. At least Heinrich would have protected him and kept him from doing anything stupid. Heinrich was the reliable one. Francis was the cute one.

"The Peace Ray and now this?" someone exclaimed. "The government will clamp down on Actives for sure!"

Faye was sickened by the idea. There had been talk . . . But that couldn't happen here. Could it?

"This is dire news," Mr. Browning told her.

"What's going to happen?"

Mr. Browning looked very tired. "War, Faye. I believe someone just declared war."

The elders of the Grimnoir Society had not gone very far, and they reconvened a few minutes later in a room several floors below. The two that had been in the prior meeting were joined through a communication spell to the five other elders around the world. All had been listening in secret to the interview with Faye and the meeting afterward. The matter at hand was so important that it needed the full wisdom of all the Society's leadership.

The seven skipped the pleasantries. They had much to discuss.

The prepared mirror gave the illusion of spinning to face the distant speaker. "Do we believe she's the one?"

"As mad as it seems, we have no reason to doubt her truthfulness," the Englishman said as he turned to his companion. "Klaus?"

"She's very difficult to Read. Her thoughts are different. She is not unintelligent, quite the opposite in fact. She's just uncomplicated . . . and *quick*. All I can say is that she certainly believes her own story."

"Could it be? Could the Chairman really be dead?" a woman asked.

"Pershing's knights are no fools, and their stories are consistent. The girl is extraordinarily gifted. Her connection to the Power is unrivaled," Klaus pointed out.

A French elder interjected, "It seems that she is not nearly as strong now, though. Transporting the *Tempest* nearly killed her. Yet that fits the pattern, and the events leading up to that certainly fit with what we are looking for. Harriet?"

"She is about the right age."

"The battle that killed the Warlock was fifteen years ago," Klaus said.

"I know. I was there."

"As was I, Jacques . . ." Klaus told the French elder. "Only on the Kaiser's side. Second Somme was a nightmare. I still wake up with chills."

"That poor Okie girl doesn't know her own birthday, but she's certainly older than fifteen," the American elder spoke for the first time.

"Yes, but if the Power connected to her when she was young, rather than at birth . . . Then, yes, it is possible. This has happened before."

Harriet broached the question that no one wished to ask. "Well, what do we do about it then?"

It was an awkward silence. The elders were used to making difficult decisions necessary to defend their people, but no one wanted to harm a child.

"For now . . . We keep a close eye on her. If she becomes corrupted by the spell as Warlock did, we must be prepared to strike her down."

"Jacques!"

"Don't look at me like that. If that happens, it is either her, or all of us."

"No!"

"You would have us risk the safety of the entire world for one person?"

The discussian descended into a general argument, spinning about wildly, as it often did when the elders disagreed.

"We will do nothing until we are certain."

"We can't—"

"We'll make sure first," a calm voice interjected. "I have just the knight for the job."

"Very well." The American sighed. "Watch her carefully.

Test her. Have your knight try to discover the truth . . . And if she is the Spellbound . . ."

"If she's the Spellbound, *then* we must decide on a course of action," Klaus insisted.

"I will arrange everything."

"Browning and his men cannot know. They would never stand for it. Their fondness for the girl could blind them to her true nature."

"You would have us sit on our arses and wait to see if the most dangerous piece of magic in history has chosen to bind itself to an unstable child?" the Englishman exclaimed.

Several of the elders replied at once, "Yes."

"And if she is the one?"

"We will do what we must to survive," Jacques stated.

That matter was settled.

"And what of the matter of this coming Enemy?" Klaus asked. "Faye and the new man, Sullivan, are both convinced it is real."

"The Chairman's mythical beast?" the American openly scoffed. "Coming to devour the Power and all of us along with it? A fairy tale, nothing more."

"I hope you are right." The Englishman shook his head. "If the legends of Dark Ocean are true . . . May God have mercy on us all."

Crazy Guy

Chapter 2

Dearest Devika. I have succeeded where all others have failed. They called me mad, but I have confirmed the truth. The Power is alive. What we call magic is the means by which it feeds. It grants a piece of itself to some few of us, and as we exercise that connection through every manipulation of the physical world, the magic grows. Upon our death, that increase returns to the Power. It is a symbiotic parasite. Grown fat upon us, the process repeats, more Actives are created, the cycle continues. The Power itself has a certain measure of awareness. Aware? Yes. I do not know yet if it knows that I have stolen from it, and if so, how it will react to my petty thievery. As the Power is using us, I intend to use it. I beg your forgiveness for what I must now become.

—Anand Sivaram,
Personal correspondence discovered in
Hyderabad, India, 1912

New York City, New York

THE LIBRARIAN WAS FRUSTRATED. He had finally gotten through every single document, report, study, and book about magic in the entire rare books collection of the main branch, and though he'd found some interesting trains of thought to pursue, he was no closer to what he was searching for than when he'd arrived in New York. It really shouldn't have come as a surprise. A sizable Stuyvesant grant had gotten him the title of visiting research librarian under an assumed name and free access to the entire Library of Congress. After months in D.C. devouring every work on magic in the largest library in the world, he hadn't found anything about the Enemy. Weeks spent at the extensive Carr Library, devoted exclusively to magic, at the University of Chicago had been just as fruitless.

His newfound title and more of Francis' dough had gotten him a peek at all of the good stuff at the second largest library in the country. He knew full well that if New York didn't pan out, the only other place that might have what he was looking for was in Europe, and he didn't think he had time to learn French. The library he really wanted to hit was in Tokyo, but he didn't think the Japanese would be particularly fond of him coming for a visit, since he'd recently sliced their First Iron Guard in half.

It had been stupid to get his hopes up here.

The idea was troublesome, but Jake Sullivan was beginning to think that maybe he was the expert. And that was just downright scary.

He'd started hitting various collections after he'd combed through all of the Grimnoir Society's collected *Rune Arcanium*. The Society was proud of the information they'd collected over the years, and they'd kept the things that they thought particularly dangerous a secret. Once he'd taken the oath he'd been able to learn the collected spells of the Society, and though it had been educational, their spells were nothing to worry about.

The Society didn't know much about the Enemy either, and it seemed the elders thought he was crazy for even suggesting its existence. Sullivan knew something else was out there, searching for the Power, and it would find them eventually. They had to be ready. The Chairman had understood that. Why couldn't anyone else?

Sullivan rubbed his tired eyes, shoved the latest useless research paper off to the side, and checked his watch. It was nearly closing time. Studying magic was hard work, but it beat breaking rocks. The library was quiet, as such places tended to be, but it was especially quiet tonight. February was late in the year for this much snow, but there had been a real cold snap over the last few days, and the city was blanketed in white. Everybody with any sense had already gone home.

"Hi. They told me you could help me."

He hadn't even heard her coming. Sullivan looked up to see a fancy mink coat snuggled around a pretty redhead. "Pardon me, ma'am?"

"They said you were a librarian and that you could help me find something." She had the build of a calendar girl, the voice of upper-crust Manhattan, and a face designed to turn men into easily malleable putty, and as she batted her big flirtatious eyelashes at him, he could tell that she was used to men usually doing what she asked, and quickly. "You don't look like a librarian, though."

That's because he was a square-jawed, thick-armed, solemn block of a man who had obviously lived a high-mileage life. "I'm not that kind of librarian."

"What kind are you then?"

"The kind that isn't much help. You need to head that way." He pointed down the stacks. "Ask the nice ladies at the big desk in the middle."

"Oh, I'm sure you can be helpful if you want. You strike me like a real chivalrous type."

Sullivan just wanted to be left alone. "Not really."

"What're you reading?" she asked, craning her head over his shoulder to read. "Oh . . . Powers? Are you an Active?"

"No," he lied as he pushed the book away. "Just an interesting topic is all."

"Too bad. I'm fascinated by Actives. Can you imagine being able to do such amazing things? Controlling weather, reading minds, changing gravity, healing the sick . . . Oh, how would it be?"

He gave a noncommittal grunt.

"You don't seem very talkative. What's your name?"

"Nobody important."

"Well, nice to meet you, Mr. Important."

Sullivan could feel a pounding headache coming on. It must have been the eyestrain from twelve hours of reading small print. "Sorry, lady. Been a long day. Place is about to close." He paused to rub his temples. "If you want to find something you'd best hurry along."

She regarded him curiously. Pretty girls weren't used to getting the shove-off like that. "Well then. Never mind. Good night." She walked off, heels clicking against the marble floor. He hadn't heard her come, but he heard her go.

Despite the sudden headache, Sullivan watched her appreciatively. There was a fine-looking woman, perfectly friendly, just needing a hand, and he had to go and run her off in a rude fashion. Nobody had ever accused him of being overly friendly, or friendly at all for that matter, but he'd become even more withdrawn over the last year. That was to be expected. Anyone close to him was in danger. He was a marked man.

Delilah had died because of him. There was just no going back from something like that.

Ten minutes later Sullivan had gotten all the day's books put back in place. There was no need to say any goodbyes to the staff. They didn't know his real name anyway. Tomorrow he'd leave town. Days would pass before anyone even noticed the big quiet man was gone.

The front steps were slick with fresh snow. Pulling his fedora down tight, his scarf up over most of his face, and hunching his broad shoulders against the wind, Sullivan set out for home. He passed between the two big stone lions, Lennox and Astor, which were well-known local landmarks. One of the mayoral candidates had suggested renaming them Patience and Fortitude, because since the economy had gone to hell and everybody was out of work, it was going to take patience and fortitude for New Yorkers to get out of this mess.

Little did all those New Yorkers realize that if it hadn't been for the sacrifice of a bunch of brave unknown Actives, this whole part of the country would be nothing more than a big pile of ash. Bitter cold always put Sullivan in a melancholy mood.

The city got rougher and older only a few blocks from the library. He'd picked a rundown place to lay his head. New York had been especially hard hit over the last few years, so there had been plenty of vacancies to choose from. Folks in the rough parts of town paid less attention to each other, which was exactly what he wanted.

At least the snow covered the trash. The city looked clean, briefly, when it snowed. A group of bums were huddled around a burn barrel, hands extended for warmth; residents of the local Hoover Town. The vacant lots were filled with shacks and huts assembled out of junk and old tires. They looked over, but it was too cold and Sullivan was too physically intimidating to even bother panhandling.

There was a scream from ahead. A woman, and it didn't sound like she was playing around. The noise came from a nearby alley. The woman screamed again. There was a bang as a trash can fell over and then a man gave a rough laugh. "Help me! Somebody help me!" The cries echoed down the brick walls.

The bums just lowered their heads and stared at their fire. There were only a few cars on the street. The local businesses were all boarded up. He was on his own. There wasn't even a decision to be made, since his nature was set in stone. Sullivan sighed and walked to the mouth of the alley.

There were six figures in the dark. One was obviously the victim, female, being held against the wall by the neck. The man holding her was nearly Sullivan's size, and his four buddies were lined up behind. They liked to run in packs, numbers made them tough, these typical urban rats, always thin, hungry, and mean. One of them was tearing through the woman's purse, looking for cash or anything they could trade for hooch or dope or whatever their game was.

It was dark, but light enough to fight. His magic was ready. He felt the Power built up inside his chest and used a tiny bit to see the nearby world as it really was. Everything was just matter, some of it was heavy, some light, but everything felt the tug of gravity, and gravity belonged to Jake Sullivan.

"Let her go." He didn't even raise his voice. He didn't have to. Part of him wanted the fight. It had been awhile, and he hated men like these.

"Ain't none of your business, buddy," sneered the big one. He turned enough that Sullivan could see the gleam of a little knife in his off hand. "Keep on walking."

He felt for the heavy spots that might indicate a weapon, but the only thing dense on these thugs were their thick heads. No guns. Blades, leather saps maybe, but those things were harder to pick out from the background matter. One solid pair of brass knuckles stood out like a beacon. Surprisingly, it felt like the woman might have a compact pistol hidden inside her coat, but she must not have been able to get to it in time, or maybe she'd lacked the nerve to pull it. The other possibility was that she was in on it, and this was all some elaborate attempt to rob him, but it didn't feel that way. The big jerk with the knife was enjoying himself too much.

"You get one warning, then I hurt you." Sullivan hadn't

even taken his hands out of his pockets. "You boys seem young and times are hard, so I'll try not to kill you, but I can't promise nothing."

"You know who you're talking at?" said the one with the purse.

"No, and frankly I don't give a shit."

"We run this—" Not wanting to hear any nonsense about how their group of criminal losers was tougher than some other group of criminal losers, Sullivan reached out with his magic and Spiked. A bit of space broke and the gravity around the gang member changed direction. Left was now down, and the kid suddenly flew sideways into the brick. He crashed hard under the force of several extra gravities, bones creaking, and stuck there until Sullivan cut his Power. The kid fell into the snow in a shower of red dust.

"I warned you."

"He's a dirty wizard!" the big one shouted. "Get him!"

The rats charged, which forced Sullivan to take his hands out of his pockets. He easily dodged the first clumsy swing and slugged the hoodlum in the chest. Ribs cracked under Sullivan's hardened fist. That one gasped and collapsed. The next attacker slowed, confused, as the pull of gravity changed. It must have felt like he was trying to push his way through molasses. Sullivan's casual right hook broke the man's jaw.

The last rat skidded to a stop and dropped his brass knuckles in the snow. "Sorry. I'm sorry. I'm sorry!"

"Too late." Sullivan reversed gravity and the hood fell ten feet into the air, screaming, before gravity returned to normal. Sullivan didn't Spike very hard though, so the man probably didn't break too many bones when he hit the pavement.

The leader was the only one left standing. He let go of the woman and she sank to the ground, coughing. Sullivan looked down at her and as his eyes adjusted to the darkness was surprised to see it was the redhead from the library.

"Filthy wizard. You stay back!" The thug raised his knife. "Your kind are evil."

"You don't find nothing ironic about saying that?" Sullivan walked toward him. "Bunch of men mugging some poor lady and you're preaching to me about evil? Robbing better be all you had planned . . ."

"You wouldn't be so tough without your magic."

"Well, ain't you lucky? I done used up all my magic on your crew," Sullivan lied. He had plenty of Power still, but he didn't need magic to handle the likes of this trash. "I'm fresh out. Try me."

The boss thug bellowed and charged. Sullivan let the knife flash back and forth wildly. Sullivan had grown up poor in a tough town and was no stranger to back-alley fights. He'd fought on docks, in rings, at war, and had gotten extremely good at avoiding shivs inside the brutal dog-eat-dog world of the Rockville State Penitentiary. This encounter barely qualified as exercise. He kept moving just ahead of the blade, and when there was the faintest glimmer of confidence from his adversary, Sullivan ruined his night.

He stepped past the swing and broke the thug's nose with one fast jab. Sullivan was surprisingly quick for such a large man. Before his opponent could even cry out, Sullivan had grabbed his knife hand and twisted it back until wrist bones snapped. Then Sullivan kicked one of the thug's knees backwards. He stepped back and let the man topple into the snow.

Sullivan paused to dust his coat off. Some nasal blood had splattered his sleeve. All of the gang were down, crying, whimpering, or unconscious. He'd broken something on each of them, so that was probably a sufficient lesson for the evening. Sullivan wasn't even breathing hard.

The woman was standing up, so he stepped over the thug with the shattered knee and extended a hand. "They hurt you?"

She took his hand and he helped her up. "No. I'm fine. Just shaken up."

"Let me see your neck." He gently lifted her chin. It was difficult to see. "That'll leave a bruise, there."

"Just a boo-boo," she insisted.

Sullivan let go and retrieved her purse. The goon that he'd Spiked into the wall cursed him, so Sullivan stepped on his fingers. That shut him up. "This ain't the part of town for somebody like you." He passed her purse over. "What're you doing here?"

She didn't answer his question. "I thought you said you were the kind of librarian that couldn't help people?"

"I'm better at some things than others. Come on. It stinks in here. Let's get you home."

There was far more light on the street. He could see that the woman was holding together well. Her expensive coat had been stained by alley grime, but her attitude was firm. Not a crier, this one. Remarkably, there was a cab coming around the corner, which was fortunate timing, since he had no idea where the nearest telephone booth was. He waved at the cab.

The redhead looked him square in the eye. "So, what you did back there . . . You're a Heavy, I'm guessing?"

She did know a thing or two about magic. "I prefer Gravity Spiker. It's more dignified."

The cab stopped before them.

"Who are you?"

"Just a guy who was in the right place at the right time." His headache was coming back. He opened her door for her. "You got cab fare?"

"I do. Thanks." She politely took his hand as he helped her in. "Thank you so much. Is there anything I can do for you? Do you need a lift?"

"I'm good. And listen, if you're going to carry that piece, you'd better be ready to use it next time."

"Oh, I will. I promise." The woman smiled at him, and she had a dazzling smile. "Thanks. You're a regular knight in shining armor."

Sullivan closed her door. "Oh, you've got no idea."

The cab pulled away. The driver peered into the center mirror to study his passenger.

"So, is that the Heavy?"

"That's our boy," she said before turning around and waving at Jake Sullivan out the back window. He was standing there, lighting a smoke, and raised one hand to wave awkwardly in response. She turned back around. "I'm positive."

Her Power hadn't been of much help earlier. Despite appearing to be a lout, he was too smart, and judging from the look on his face when she tried tipping the scales, he could feel the intrusion, so she'd been afraid to push.

She'd needed to see his magic in action to be sure, and just like the files said, he was one dangerously powerful Heavy. She waited until they were around the corner before removing the red wig. Her primary concern during the attack was that it might have gotten knocked loose, and that would have looked suspicious. "Radio the others. We'll pick him up tonight."

Miami, Florida

FRANCIS COULDN'T BELIEVE HIS EARS. He had made the policeman repeat himself, but the message stayed the same. Heinrich Koenig had been killed.

As a boy, armed only with his wits and Fade magic, Heinrich had survived on the streets of Dead City. He'd walked through the Berlin Wall, joined the Grimnoir, and been one of their bravest ever since. As a knight, he'd fought in dozens of battles, Soviets, Imperium, it didn't matter, he had a special hatred for anyone who would use magic for evil. Heinrich feared nothing. No matter what the odds, no matter what they faced, Heinrich was always the first to volunteer. He was brash, fearless, and utterly loyal.

And dead.

Francis had to lean against the wall as the world dropped out from under him. His forearm was broken and his head hurt, but the physical injuries were nothing compared to the swift kick in the gut he'd just caught. He could afford a Healer, but from what he'd heard, both of the Healers in Florida had exhausted all of their magic trying to save as many lives as possible. He could wait. The policeman said that Heinrich had been on the steps when one of the magical blasts had gotten him. He had helped carry the injured president toward safety when he'd been struck down. The cop told him that Heinrich had died a hero.

"Tell me something I don't know." Francis flopped onto a bench to stare off into space. *Dead. Holy shit, Heinrich is dead.* He had to tell the others.

"Can I get you anything, Mr. Stuyvesant?" the policeman asked as he handed Francis a paper cup filled with water.

"Bottle of whiskey?"

"That's illegal . . . Hell, I'll see what I can do."

They'd stuck him in a detective's office. There was a name stenciled on the glass of the door. It was backwards and Francis was too tired to try to read it. "How much longer do I need to sit here?"

"There are some other federal men that still want to ask you questions." The young officer turned to leave the room. He stopped on the way out, seemingly embarrassed. "You're a hero too, sir. Everybody is saying that you killed that assassin. Chopped his head clean off."

"I'm not feeling particularly heroic," Francis muttered.

"Just unexpected is all. I mean with you being a rich guy and all. Getting your hands dirty and being brave like that," the officer stammered. "And you're even a . . . a . . ."

"An Active?"

The policeman lowered his eyes. "Yeah. Well, I guess you folks aren't all bad, huh?" He retreated and closed the door behind him.

They had already questioned him repeatedly, what more did they want? Sure, he could have thrown his weight around and had an army of lawyers descend on the place if necessary, but he was still too numb. What was he going to tell the others? What was he going to tell Faye? She was really fond of Heinrich. And poor Dan. Heinrich was the closest friend Dan had, his partner on a multitude of missions, hell, even the best man at his wedding. Dan was going to take this hard.

Florida water always tasted vaguely swampy. Francis frowned at the cup, but no matter how hard he concentrated it wouldn't magically transform into proper mind-numbing alcohol. He was only telekinetic. There was only one person who had ever had the kind of Power useful enough to turn water into wine.

A few minutes later the door opened again, only instead of another local officer it was a man in a shirt, tie, and shoulder holster. The tie was undone and there was a big black automatic in the holster. He was of average height but with a torso like a heavyweight boxer, probably forty, with dark hair thinning on top, and thick, angry eyebrows. His chin was dark with stubble and his manner was cold. The stranger took in the stained remains of Francis' expensive Italian suit and the cast around his arm. "You Francis Stuyvesant?" He didn't offer to shake hands.

"And you are?"

He ignored the question and took a cigarette out of his shirt pocket. "Smoke?"

"No. Thank you. What's going on?"

He pulled the curtain down over the glass door. "I ask the questions. If you try to get all indignant and do some *don't you know who I am* rich asshole shtick, I'll personally shoot you in the head and get it ruled a suicide."

The stranger had said it so matter-of-factly that it took Francis' tired mind a moment to realize that he'd just been threatened. Francis was not used to being threatened. "Who are you?"

The man struck a match with his thumb on the first try. "The UBF heir . . . In the flesh." He lit his cigarette. "Why, lucky me. I'm just a poor old investigator for the OCI."

"So what's OCI?"

"Office of the Coordinator of Information."

"Is that supposed to sound intimidating?"

"Naw," the man chuckled. "It isn't the name that's intimidating. It's what I'm authorized to do that's intimidating. We take care of sensitive things. Like regulating magic, or questioning spoiled brats who suddenly became important because their rich grandpa kicked the bucket."

Francis had cultivated the public persona of being a useless fop, good for little more than attending social functions. It helped when your enemies underestimated you. The UBF board had thought that he would be an easily controlled figurehead because of that public persona, and he'd used that to his advantage to end up with actual control of the company. Despite that, most of the papers still thought of him as more a topic for the society pages than the business section.

Apparently that's what this mystery G-man believed about him as well, so there was no reason it couldn't work to his advantage. Might as well run with it. Francis played indignant. "You can't talk to me like that."

"I can and I will. You can call me Mr. Crow. So tell me, Francis . . . You mind if I call you Francis?"

"That's Mr. Stuyvesant to the likes of y—"

The man was quick. The fist slammed into the side of his head so hard that Francis was certain that if he hadn't flinched his eyes closed before impact they would have popped out of his skull. The world wobbled and then the floor tile came up to meet him.

Nobody slapped around the upper crust. This wasn't some collar off a crap-town speakeasy. Francis was somebody *important*. The surprise was worse than the pain. He knew how to take a punch, but he wasn't as used to taking an insult. Something was very wrong.

"Let's try that again."

Francis was dragged up by the shirt and placed on the bench. The blow had staggered him, but he'd felt worse. Francis' initial reaction was to use his Power. There were dozens of items scattered around the detective's office that would look better stuck through the G-man's ribs, but he needed to see what this was about first.

"Will you get a load of that bruise? You sure did get banged around during that attack, didn't you, boyo? Let's try this again." Crow returned to his seat, perched on the edge of the desk. "Normally I only get to beat confessions out of darkies or bohunks. I never thought I'd get to beat a confession out of a rich kid. If only mom could see me now."

"You can't do this."

"Yes. I. Can. State of emergency, OCI is now in charge of any investigations involving Actives. Things have changed. You just don't know how much yet. So tell me,

Francis, why is it that there have been two major acts of magical terrorism in the last year and you were a survivor of *both*?"

The Peace Ray had been aimed at his estate in Mar Pacifica because an Iron Guard wanted to blot a group of Grimnoir off the face of the Earth. *Today?* "Just lucky I guess."

Crow casually backhanded him. Francis' head snapped around.

"The assassin . . . Did you know him?"

"No."

"You sure?"

"I've never seen him before."

"Maybe you've seen this?" Crow held out his hand. In it was a familiar gold ring with a black stone. A Grimnoir ring.

This was very bad. "I don't know."

All knights received one when they took the oath. It was spellbound with a few minor wards, the insides engraved with designs of Power. They were useful tools and a symbol of the office. Francis didn't wear his in public. He was too famous, photographed too much, and the Society didn't need the exposure. He always kept his ring nearby though . . . Was that his? Had they searched his luggage? Did this OCI know about the Society?

"What's the ring for?"

"It's just a trinket. I don't know. Is that mine? Because I've got lots of rings."

Crow held it up to the light. "There's writing on the inside. Magic? Isn't it?"

"I wouldn't know," Francis said evenly.

"Funny. This was on what was left of your dead German friend . . ." Crow set the Grimnoir ring on the desk, then reached into his pants pocket to take something out. He placed an identical ring next to the first. "This one was on the man you decapitated. Or was it the other way around? Did I get them mixed up? Hard to tell, since they're *identical*, even down to the funny writing inside."

The killer had a Grimnoir ring? Had the killer been a member of the Society? *Impossible!*

Crow got tired of waiting. "What? No reaction?"

"I'm not a jeweler." Francis sniffed. "I'd like to talk to an attorney now. The lawsuits are going to be very impressive. I don't know what your agency pays, but I hope you like soup lines. I've got *butlers* with a bigger salary than you."

"Oh, I'm not in this for the money." Crow shook his head sadly. "Tsk tsk, young Francis. I'm trying to have an honest conversation here and you're trying to complicate matters with legal mumbo jumbo." He came off the desk in a flash. Francis barely had time to brace himself before Crow slugged him in the mouth. Francis saw stars. Crow stepped away, shaking his hand loose. "God, I love this job."

That's enough of that nonsense. The next time Crow got up, Francis was going to teach him a lesson in humility. There was a solid-looking paperweight sitting on the desk. Bouncing it off his teeth at fifty miles an hour ought to do the trick. He lifted his head with a groan and looked the G-man square in the eyes. "I don't know anything."

"Your bodyguard had a weird thing on his chest, half tattoo, half scar. What was that?"

Since Jake Sullivan had worked out the kinks, Heinrich had volunteered to be bound to a Healing spell a few months back. It had been painful and dangerous, and a fat lot of good it had done him. It helped you recover faster, but too much damage at once and you still died just like anybody else would. "Beats me. I don't know what my employees do off the clock."

"I know you don't have anything like that on you. I asked the doctor after he patched you up. But strangely enough, the man you gave the old guillotine treatment had something similar . . . Bigger and more complicated, but the same general idea. That strike you as odd?"

Francis' response was a stony silence. He couldn't think of anything else to say. Somebody had tried to kill the president and was pinning it on the Grimnoir.

The lack of response seemed to anger the man. "Was Zangara a loose end that needed tying? Was your job to kill your triggerman before he could talk? Was that why you were here, Francis, as cleanup for your little magical plot?" Crow shouted, spittle flying from his lips. "You thought you could get away with it! You people always think you can get away with it. Well, you aren't better than anyone else. I got you, Francis. You helped try to kill the president."

"That idea's got holes an imbecile could drive a blimp through. You must have come up with it yourself. You're quite the gumshoe."

Crow came off the desk, hand curling into a fist. Francis concentrated on the heavy paperweight, reached for his Power, and—

Nothing.

Crow knocked him silly. Francis hit the tile and Crow kicked him in the face. Francis got his arms up to protect himself as Crow kicked him repeatedly. "You tried to use magic on *me?*" Crow stomped him hard, again and again. One shoe caught the cast and ground the freshly broken bones. Francis cried out and curled into a ball. The door flew open with a bang. Several Miami cops spilled into the room. Crow was roughly pulled away and dragged from the room. shouting, "Magic won't work on an OCI man, asshole. You better warn your friends."

The cops were trying to help. Somebody asked him a question. His head was swimming and he couldn't remember what his answer had been. His Power had failed him. For the first time in his life, when he'd reached for it, the magic hadn't been there. They got him onto the bench. Somebody stuffed a towel against his nose to catch the blood. There was more commotion in the doorway. Francis recognized the man standing there waving a briefcase as a UBF attorney. How had his Power failed? Somehow he was on his feet, and weaving his way down the hall. The lawyer was talking to the police, rapid-fire legalese flying faster than bullets. They were heading for the exit.

Crow had been backed into a corner and blocked off by two cops. His face was red. "Everything's changed now, Francis. Your kind aren't untouchable anymore."

"This isn't over!" Francis shouted back.

"We're watching you." The cops had to hold Crow back. "Hunting season's coming! Opening day . . ." He stuck out his finger like a pretend gun. "Bang."

Francis made it outside. He hadn't realized how late it was. The darkness was a bit of a shock. He stumbled down the steps to a waiting car. Flashbulbs popped and photographs were taken. The attorney made sure that the press got plenty of shots. From how hot his face felt, he knew he had to look like a bad meatloaf. The driver came around and opened the door.

"Get us out of here. Snap to it," Francis ordered. The attorney barely had time to climb in before they were rolling. "Give me your pen."

"Huh?"

Francis reached over and snatched a golden ink pen from the lawyer's pocket. He held it in the palm of his hand and concentrated. The pen lifted, spun in a lazy circle just like he wanted it to, then fell back in place. His Power had returned. It felt perfectly normal, but when he'd tried it against the government man it was like his magic wasn't even there.

He tossed the pen back to the surprised attorney. "Crow's right," he mumbled.

"Excuse me, sir?"

Francis stared out the window. "Everything has changed . . . Driver, get us to the airfield."

The Miami Police detained Crow. Federal lawman or not, he had just assaulted a prisoner, and not just some prisoner off of the street, but an extremely important man, *and* the press knew. Heads were going to roll. The locals put calls in to contact Crow's superiors, but rapidly discovered that his superiors were very difficult to reach. Crow waited long enough for the cops to not have a direct eye on him and then easily made his escape. There was no cell that could hold him if he didn't feel like it. He even stopped long enough to pick up everything that had been confiscated: his fabricated identification papers, his .45, the Dymaxion nullifier, and his coat, before walking right out the door.

Later, the police would finally get through to somebody at the mysterious Office of the Coordinator of Information, only to be told that they had no officer by the name of Crow. The U.S. Attorney's office would be stymied as well. Eventually the whole thing would go away like these things tended to do.

His men picked him up on the corner. The automobile barely even slowed as he got into the back. "Status?" he asked in greeting.

"The President is going to live, but he might still lose the use of his legs."

"That's unfortunate news." Crow feigned sympathy rather well. "I don't know if the country is ready for a cripple to be in charge. What about the prisoner?"

"He's been secured, sedated, and sent with two Dymaxions to headquarters."

"Good news. Where is Stuyvesant now?"

"Heading for the air station like you predicted."

"Excellent." Crow's manner was completely different than when he'd been questioning Stuyvesant. Inside, he'd acted hot-headed, erratic, and violent. That had been necessary. He needed Stuyvesant rattled. Out here it was back to business, so Crow was collected and focused. Hot, cold, good, evil, friendly, vicious, it didn't matter, they were just modes. He picked the one he wanted and wore it like a suit. It was all about whatever it took to get the job done.

The brazen assault on Stuyvesant would raise questions as to why an investigator had been so angry with the rich kid and supposed hero of the hour—even though Stuyvesant's presence had been an unexpected development and certainly not one to be wasted—but with the press there, rumors would begin to spread about Stuyvesant's possible involvement. And all that would occur without the OCI having to say anything official at all.

"I rattled him. I want Stuyvesant's every move watched. I want to know who he talks to, who he calls, who he meets, where he goes. I want to know how his breakfast tastes and I want to know the temperature of his bathwater. The second he meets someone else on the list, do the same to them." He thought about it. "And I want two layers on that kid. Make one obvious but put our best men on the second. When Stuyvesant thinks he's lost the first, that's when he'll make contact with his conspirators. Don't underestimate him. He's sharper than he looks. Most importantly, watch out for that Traveler girl. The second she shows up to check on her boyfriend, I want her brought in."

"Yes, Mr. Crow," the OCI agents answered in unison.

"*Alive.*" The girl was the most valuable one in the bunch. If they lost her, the boss would be very upset. "What else have we got?"

The driver spoke. "The situation in New York has improved. That mercenary girl found the Heavy. Our men will snatch him shortly."

"No. I want a soft touch on that one. Play it easy. Check the reports. He's worked with the Bureau a bunch. Find somebody he doesn't hate, if there is such a thing, and use them to make contact. Borrow whoever we need to, but do *not* let the BI know what this is about."

There was a serious professional rivalry developing between the new OCI and the entrenched Bureau of Investigation. J. Edgar Hoover thought that Active criminals should be treated like any other type of criminals. He saw OCI's lumping of all undesirable Actives together as foolish. Hoover grumbled about violating civil liberties, but Crow figured he just didn't want to lose clout.

"Let the Heavy take the call and see what that's all about. Then we'll take him down." Crow didn't use the word arrest, because from what he'd heard about the Heavy, it would be a bloodbath. "Nothing flashy. There's no way we could take that one alive."

They only knew who a handful of these people were. Stuyvesant was one, but he was just a kid. The Mover was like a tree. You could shake a tree to see what fell out. Sullivan? That son of a bitch had strolled through Second Somme. The Heavy was a rock. You shake a rock and it was liable to just roll over and squish you.

"How do you want us to handle it?"

"Wait until he's done talking, then put a bullet in him . . . Make that lots of bullets. Don't let our boys take any lip from the military intel types that are there, either. Let the Heavy take the call, then pop him. I'll fill out the paperwork."

"Yes, Mr. Crow."

Crow wasn't his real name. He'd gone by dozens of names over the years, doing things outside the law for people too squeamish to do them through official channels. He'd worked for everyone from United Fruit to Woodrow

Wilson, though this was the first time he had an entire government agency at his disposal. Plus the laws were actually on his side for once, or would be soon at least. Those were being written now.

No, Crow wasn't his real name, but it was real enough to accomplish his current assignment.

Eliminate the Active group known as the Grimnoir Society.

Chapter 3

The more we progress the more we tend to progress. We advance not in arithmetical but in geometrical progression. We draw compound interest on the whole capital of knowledge and virtue which has been accumulated since the dawning of time. Some eighty thousand years are supposed to have existed between Paleolithic and Neolithic man. Yet in all that time he only learned to grind his flint stones instead of chipping them. But within our fathers' lives what changes have there not been? The railway and the telegraph, chloroform and applied electricity. All before the invention of magic. In the span of my own life what has man not accomplished? Telekinesis, teleportation, pyrokinesis, biological manipulation, communication with spirits. Ten years now go further than a thousand then, not so much on account of our finer intellects as because the light we have shows us the way to more. Primeval man stumbled along with peering eyes, and slow, uncertain footsteps. Now we walk briskly towards our unknown goal.

—Sir Arthur Conan Doyle,
The History of Wizards, 1926

New York City, New York

THERE WAS A KNOCK on the apartment door.

Sullivan was already awake and waiting by the time the visitor made his presence known. He'd been a light sleeper his whole life, a trait that had only been reinforced during the war. The deep sleepers hadn't lived through the nighttime poison gas barrages.

The echo of a man's footsteps in the hall had been enough to rouse him, and the fact that those footsteps had stopped at his door had been enough to clear his head and put his big Browning .45 automatic in his hand. There was a bit of yellow city light leaking in around the curtains, just enough for him to make out the hands on his watch. Nearly midnight.

Odd time for a caller, but if it had been the Imperium, they probably wouldn't have knocked.

The apartment was tiny, in a nondescript old building half a mile's walk from the library. He lived there under a false name. He associated with no one, had no friends, didn't even hit the bar downstairs. Nobody, not even the Society, knew where he was. He checked the black and gold ring on his finger, but its spells weren't warning him of anything. Flexing his Power, he let his senses adjust to the world of pulls, mass, and density to get a sense of the surroundings. There was only one man in the hall.

The knock came again. A muffled voice called out. "Sullivan? You in there?"

He always left his clothes where he could find them

in the dark. You never knew when you'd have to leave someplace in a hurry. "Who is it?"

"Sam Cowley. Can I come in?"

Cowley was from the Bureau of Investigation, one of Hoover's men. *Unexpected.* Technically, he had violated the terms of his parole by bailing out last year, but Pershing had set things in motion to clear Sullivan of his obligations and Francis' lawyers had made sure that everything had been signed, nice and legal. For all he knew, he should have been in the clear.

Besides, if the G-men had come to haul him in again, they would've known better than to send a lone agent. They would have sent a crack team and a whole lot of guns. Sullivan had cultivated a bit of reputation over the years. Throwing his shirt on, he kept the .45 behind his back and opened the door a crack.

He kept his voice flat. "What're you doing here, Sam?"

"Looking for you, obviously." Cowley stood there politely, hat in hand, obviously waiting for an invitation inside.

Sullivan stuck his head into the hall and looked around suspiciously. "How'd you find me?"

"Modern law enforcement has all sorts of scientific resources . . ." As in, none of your business. "We need to talk."

Agent Cowley was a soft-looking, plain-spoken, but hard-working cop. They had worked together on several cases and Cowley was about as scrupulous as a government employee could possibly be, but Sullivan had been burned by the BI before. The list of people he trusted was a very short one, and he wasn't about to start putting any of

J. Edgar's men on it anytime soon. "Time's served. Hoover's jobs are done. I'm square with the BI."

"The director didn't send me. Can I come in or not?"

Sullivan stepped out of the way. "Not much to look at, but have a seat." He gestured at one of the two ratty chairs beside the round table in the kitchen. There really wasn't much to the apartment other than the kitchen and a closet with a bed squeezed into it, but at least the rats were small, so he'd lived in worse. With Society money, he could certainly afford something nicer now, but nicer wasn't low profile.

They shook hands. Sullivan was careful not to squeeze too hard. Cowley was a paper pusher, and Sullivan had a grip that could make boilermakers flinch. The crumbling old building had been wired for power, but it seldom worked right, so Sullivan lit an oil lamp on the table. As expected from a criminal investigator, Cowley immediately took note of the several mirrors hung on the walls and the items on the table: a notebook, a package of marking pens, a bloodstained towel with several scalpels and picks arranged on it, and some corked vials filled with a black liquid. "Whatever have you been up to?"

Casting spells, something that nearly everyone thought was impossible. After he'd figured out how to carve a healing spell into his own chest last year, he'd had a few of his fellow knights volunteer for the same treatment. Since he'd managed not to kill Lance or Heinrich, he'd started experimenting with some of the other designs that he remembered from his viewing of the Power. Since this was uncharted territory, he had stuck to drawing them on himself. It was terribly painful, but since he hadn't died, he called that real progress. It was terrifying work, but the next time he went up against a magically augmented Iron Guard, he'd be ready.

"Nothing important." Sullivan swept the containers of demon smoke off to the side, covered them with the towel, and set his pistol on top.

Cowley pulled out a chair and sat down. He didn't bother removing his overcoat. Apparently he wasn't planning on staying long. "Well, Jake. Good to see you again. Been awhile."

"Since Chicago . . ." It had been after his initial encounter with the Grimnoir. Cowley and the other BI agents had been easily defeated by Dan Garrett's team, but Sullivan had tried to chase them down on his own. He'd managed to fight his way through most of them, thereby impressing Black Jack Pershing, and the rest was history. "When your boss chewed my ass for getting tossed off a blimp."

The G-man sighed. "You know, Mr. Hoover's not a bad man. He just has a very stressful job. We put a lot of bad characters away."

"He told me I was a slave." It was still a sore spot. Cowley had no response to that. "How do you think he'd react if he knew that you could do even a little bit of magic?"

"Got me there . . ." Cowley said slowly. He was a passive Torch, with just the barest glimmer of ability to create and control fire. Hoover's distrust of magic and dislike of its users was well known. It was a growing and popular sentiment in positions of authority, especially since the destruction of Mar Pacifica. "Times are changing.

Probably going to get even tougher on magicals too, I imagine, after what happened today."

Sullivan hadn't been close to a radio all day, hadn't seen the paper, and his only human contact had been beating the hell out of a gang of hoodlums, so he had no idea what Cowley was talking about. "What happened today?"

"You don't know? An Active tried to assassinate President-elect Roosevelt."

This was not what his people needed. "How bad?"

"I don't have any details yet. My superiors did send out a cable that he's alive. I hear it was bad. Big crowd of admirers there when it happened. The police in Florida are still collecting body parts, so they don't even know how many people died yet. It's a real mess down there."

"They sure it was magic?"

"Don't know what kind, but he was making the air explode with his bare hands."

"Hmmm . . ." That sounded like the descriptions of a Boomer, though he'd never actually met one. "Imperium, anarchist, communist, or nut on his own?"

"Nobody knows yet."

"This is a nightmare." Sullivan rubbed his face. "Absolute nightmare."

"Poor Roosevelt," Cowley agreed.

"Poor Roosevelt, hell. Poor us. I saw a mob try to lynch a little kid once because they thought his magic was *scary*. What's gonna happen when they've got a reason to be scared?"

Mar Pacifica had been his brother's doing. His big brother had been a genius, an evil genius, but a genius nonetheless. The Imperium had drawn first blood, weakened its enemy, and gotten away with it. That same attack had cost Delilah her life. *Matty, I hope you're slow-roasting in hell.*

"Whole place is going to blow up now. Good thing it's too cold to riot tonight," Sullivan muttered.

"Not down South it's not. I've heard some awful things have happened already. Business burned, random Actives gunned down . . ."

He'd have to get in contact with the Society quickly. They would be doing damage control, and hopefully, if the assassin belonged to some group, making the rest of them go away permanently. This kind of thing was exactly why the Grimnoir existed, protecting Actives from Normals, and vice versa. He'd gotten rather good at communication spells, and that was much cheaper than a telephone call, but first things first. He needed to get rid of Cowley. "So why the visit?"

"Listen, Jake, this isn't Bureau business. I'm on loan to another agency tonight. Things are a little chaotic right now. I can't talk about it. You need to come with me right now."

"Where?"

"New Jersey."

"Why?"

"A matter of national security."

As a straightforward man, he had no patience for evasion. "No."

"Look, I can't tell you until we get there. It's top secret."

"I'm going back to bed." Sullivan stood up.

"Well . . ." Cowley relented. "Fine. I don't know what's going on, exactly. I said I would ask you because I reasoned that you seemed to like me more than anyone else who works for the government."

"That's not saying much, Sam."

"This place is surrounded."

Sullivan went to the window and pulled back the curtains. Sure enough, there were police cars parked along the street. NYPD uniforms and plainclothes overcoats both, the men five stories below were huddling for warmth beneath the lamps. It was a modest show of force, but he wasn't impressed. Sullivan had fought through everything the German army could throw at him and the Chairman's personal Iron Guards. The hardest thing about getting through the bull's perimeter would be not accidentally hurting any of them. "Why all the law?"

"There are some new rumors about you . . . Things that made my . . . colleagues nervous. In particular something about you fighting the entire Japanese Navy by yourself."

How did the BI know about that? None of the Grimnoir would have talked, because they certainly knew how to keep a secret, but it could have come from one of Southunder's men or the UBF volunteers from the *Tempest*. "That's just crazy talk . . . It was one ship with a skeleton crew and there were about fifty of us." It had still been ten-to one-odds, but there was no need to exaggerate.

"Who is *us*?"

Cowley, being a man of integrity, would probably make an excellent Grimnoir knight. However, that wasn't Sullivan's place to decide, though he would suggest the possibility to John Browning the next time they spoke. "Just some friends of mine."

"I just know what I'm told. Orders are clear. You are to be driven to a certain location in New Jersey as soon as possible. You're not under arrest. This is not to send you back to Rockville or anything like that. You have my word. This is a request from your government, but you absolutely have to be in New Jersey by morning."

"And if I refuse, those cops down there pump my guts full of lead?"

"No. You have to be alive. That's orders. I volunteered to come up and talk, because I told them you can be hard-headed, but you're basically a decent sort. However, even if we have to shoot you down with tranquilizer darts and throw a net on you like some sort of wild jungle cat, you're going to Jersey."

Sullivan let the curtain fall. "Well, hell, Sam. Now you've got me all curious. And they do say that curiosity killed the wild jungle cat. Let me get my coat."

There was one of the new Ford V10 Hyperions waiting. The engine was running and the exhaust formed a cloud in the chilly winter air. Cowley opened the passenger door and gestured for Sullivan to climb in.

"Nice ride," Sullivan said as he sat down.

"That's why we're taking mine. Government cars are garbage scows in comparison," said the driver.

He looked over to see who it was. "Well, that figures."

"Evening, Mr. Important," the woman from the library said.

"You left off the Nobody."

This time she was wearing a cold-weather dress, and her hair was light brown rather than bright red and tied back neat and plain. "Let's take a ride."

"A wig . . . Too bad. I fancy redheads."

Cowley got into the backseat and closed the door behind him. The Hyperion featured a state of the art interior heater, and that made the night slightly more bearable. The girl put it into gear and took off entirely too fast. One police car got in front and turned on its siren while another pulled in behind and did the same. Wherever they were going, they were planning on getting there quick.

"How long you been following me?" Sullivan asked her.

"Found you yesterday. Watched you all day today," she answered, all business, eyes on the road. The socialite accent was gone, replaced with one that sounded vaguely East Texas, and he had no idea if it was real either. "It was easy to do, what with your nose in a book the whole time. You know normally men tend to notice me sooner when I'm all dolled up like that. It makes tailing men challenging."

"I can imagine. Sorry, been preoccupied. Miss?"

"Hammer."

"Nice to make your acquaintance, again. Miss Hammer." Which probably wasn't her real name either. There weren't any females that worked at the BI other than clerical staff, and judging by the way she had played him like a sucker earlier, she was no stenotyper. "I didn't know Hoover had started hiring lady agents."

"He doesn't," Cowley chimed in. "Miss Hammer's a—"

"Freelance consultant," she said. "I don't work for the government. I take care of odd jobs. I'm assuming you're not offended by a woman in the work force."

"Can't say I've given it much thought. The mugging?"

"Oh, nothing I couldn't handle, but I provoked those boys on purpose. Boys like that are rabbit dogs. They see something run, they're going to chase it. Can't help themselves, poor things. It's in their nature. So don't get feeling blue for hurting them. Only way a rabbit dog learns not to chase something is to beat the chase right out of it. You did them a favor. Maybe next time they smell fear, they'll think twice."

Got played again. "Did you get a good show?"

"I was fairly certain it was you from the descriptions, but I needed to make sure. My clients pay me to be thorough. I learned all about your history, Sullivan. Up until you dropped off the face of the Earth last year."

She knew quite a bit about him; he knew nothing about her, except for an impression that she was crafty, and therefore dangerous. "Why are you here?"

"I'm protecting my current employer's interest. You knew some mobsters . . . Well, the mob's got nothing on big companies when it comes to protecting what's theirs, and we can play pretty dirty too."

"The Bureau calls it industrial espionage," Cowley said.

"I would never participate in anything illegal like that, Agent Cowley," she said. Hammer was a superb liar. "Your name came up at my client's and it became very important to find you. That's why they called me. I tracked you down. My client had already asked a favor from the BI so they were looking too. My client suggested I work with them in order to expedite matters. So here we are."

Sullivan had done his best to cover his tracks, and his ring was spellbound against Finders and Summoners. Whatever Hammer was, she had talent. He should probably get her card and pass it on to Francis. UBF might be able to use her, and Francis certainly loved the industrial espionage angle of the business. "Your client must be an important man."

"Was. Passed away last year. I work for Edison General Electrical."

Thomas Edison? Why was EGE, founded by one of the greatest supergenius Cogs of all time, interested in him?

"Have you heard of the Shelved Projects Branch?" she asked. "We've managed to keep it out of the papers, but it's where we store . . . Well, you've probably never worked with a Cog before . . ." Actually, Sullivan had, and now considered two of them friends, but she didn't need to know about his Grimnoir associates. "Cogs are very rare. Heck, even low-level Fixers are hard to find. What most people don't realize is that sometimes those bursts of magical inspiration can take a Cog down some very strange paths. Shelved Projects is where EGE stored those experiments. Some of them are downright unnerving."

"What's this got to do with me?"

Hammer nearly left some of the Ford's paint on the bumper of a truck that hadn't heard the sirens. The driver honked and shook his fist at them. "It'll be easier to explain when we get there."

Menlo Park, New Jersey

THEY ARRIVED IN ONE PIECE, though there had been a few close shaves. Hammer drove like an unhinged maniac. The Hyperion was said to be the fastest factory car ever produced. Safety advocates had declared that the Cogs who had designed such an infernal machine must surely have been driven mad with a desire to kill other motorists. After this particular ride, Sullivan was inclined to agree. Hammer had decided that Cowley's police escort had been too slow, and had zipped past them once they got out of the city. It was the fastest that Sullivan had ever ridden in an automobile, and that was saying something, since there was an inch of snow on the ground.

There was a faded EGE sign and a *NO TRESPASSING* warning on the fence of the industrial park. "This is the place," Hammer said as they coasted through an open gate and came to a stop in front of a rather plain warehouse.

"Where'd you learn to drive like that?" Sullivan asked.

"Riding horses. Same fundamental principles."

"No. No, they're not," Cowley said, a little green around the edges and glad to be alive. "I can assure you."

"Sure. Give it the spurs when you want it to go faster; close your eyes and hang on for dear life when you need to stop in a hurry . . . same thing." She shoved her door open. "Come on."

Sullivan shrugged and followed the strange woman into the night.

The warehouse was bland and innocuous. For something that was supposed to be housing a bunch of wild Cog inventions, it didn't look like much. Maybe that was the best protection of all. There were a lot of automobiles parked under a nearby cover. The place was busy tonight.

There were two men in thick coats waiting at the entrance and both had new Pedersen auto-rifles slung over their shoulders. Their hard faces told him that they certainly weren't regular security guards. Cowley stopped. "This is as far as I go. I'm not cleared for this particular conversation . . . And believe me, I'm glad about it." He held out his hand and Sullivan shook it. "Good luck, Jake." The agent turned and walked away like a man who was very glad to be going.

That was ominous. The guards nodded at Hammer as she passed and gave Sullivan the once-over. "This the guy, Hammer?" one guard asked.

"That he is, Arthur."

"Thank goodness. Every time that thing rings, it scares the piss out of me." Arthur shivered. "I'm telling you, it's the work of the devil."

The other guard spoke. "Unnatural, I say. Mr. Edison should have burned the evil thing when he had the chance."

Hammer took a small automatic out of her coat and handed it to Arthur. "You packing, Mr. Sullivan?" she asked.

"Of course," Sullivan said.

"You'll have to leave it here. Company policy," Arthur said.

"Your policy stinks."

"Trust me, buddy. It's for your own safety. There are some things in Shelved Projects . . . Well, let's just say that you don't want to have any big metallic objects on you in case the alarm goes off. Some of our other guests disagreed, too, only they had fancy badges that told me to mind my own business."

"They're going to feel mighty stupid if the alarm goes off," Hammer stated.

"That's what I told them, but what do I know? I just work here. I'm not a top government man." Arthur snorted. "I promise I'm not just yanking your chain. It really is for your safety."

Sullivan pulled out the enchanted M1921 .45 that Browning had given him and passed it over. "Careful. It ain't loaded with sofa pillows."

Arthur put the pistols in a lockbox next to the door and closed it. "Well, come on in." Arthur opened the door for them. "You don't want to keep Satan waiting."

They entered the dark warehouse. The door closed behind them and locked. "What was that about?" Sullivan asked.

"You believe in ghosts, Sullivan?"

"I don't rightly know."

She groped around on the wall until she found a switch. "Well, apparently they believe in you."

"You're making me nervous."

"Good. Nervous is healthy. Nervous keeps you alive," Hammer said. The lights came on, revealing a wide space, filled with shelves covered in dust and cobwebs. "This way. We keep it hidden downstairs. Safer that way."

"I'm not moving another foot until you tell me what's going on."

She folded her arms. "Why, Mr. Sullivan, we both know that's not what's going to happen. You're an intensely curious man. You try to hide it. You may act like a palooka, but you just can't help yourself. You've got a dying need to know what's going on, so you're not fooling anyone. Now that we've lost our Bureau chaperone, I can give you the straight scoop." Hammer didn't even wait for his response before she started walking across the warehouse.

The EGE woman certainly had his number. Sullivan sighed and trailed along.

"Have you ever heard of Edison's spirit phone?"

"Who hasn't? He said something in passing once, some reporter took it out of context, so a bunch of spirit mediums and frauds started claiming to have one so they could swindle suckers into thinking they were talking to their dead relatives."

She just smiled and shook her head. "That's what we want the public to think." Hammer stopped at the back wall and opened an innocuous fuse box. "Now which one were you? Ahh, there you are." She played with a few switches and there was a loud click. She placed her hand on the wall and pushed. A secret door hinged smoothly open. "After you."

There was a flight of steep metal stairs disappearing into the floor. Sullivan climbed down until he found himself at the end of a plain concrete hallway. Two more men were stationed there, and they just nodded politely. Apparently the first guards had called ahead. He noted that these were only armed with wooden truncheons instead of firearms.

Hammer grabbed the rails, slid down like a sailor, and landed lightly.

"Lots of security around here."

"And you're only seeing the first layer. People would kill to get their hands on the things behind these doors." Hammer led the way down the hall. "Mr. Edison was a skeptical man, you know. It started as a lark, an experiment to silence the quacks and charlatans. The reasoning was that if he built a machine sensitive enough that a ghost could talk through it, then surely, if ghosts were real they'd make themselves known. Then that Cog magic got fired up while he was working on it, and he ended up fiddling with it for three straight weeks, hardly stopping for food, sleep, even water. When he finally dropped from exhaustion, it had nearly killed him, and his Power was burned out for a year afterward, but it worked."

"How?"

"Science isn't my area of expertise. The thing is, it worked, and we could call out, but nobody ever called in. It was a one-way street. EGE's best minds don't know why. We could make a call and occasionally get . . . something from the other side, but it usually didn't make any sense. Edison had done it. He'd found a way to contact ghosts."

"Ghosts? Not demons, like from a Finder? They're bringing in spirits from another dimension all the time."

"Nope. These were actual dead people from Earth. Many of them didn't even know they were dead and couldn't figure out who they were talking to. Edison brought in teams of interpreters and even a Babel, because obviously, just from pure statistics, most of the ghosts who picked up the other end of the line didn't speak English."

This was a lot of information to take in. Hammer kept talking as she took him down the hallway. They passed many heavy steel doors, each with a black Roman numeral painted on it. Uniformed security, workers in coveralls, and lab-coated staff passed them, all of them glancing suspiciously at Sullivan. The secret underground lab had far more workers than its outside appearance indicated. The tunnels went off in directions that showed that this facility was much bigger than the building above it.

"Lots of money and work went into running the spirit phone, but they never met George Washington or Julius Caesar or anyone interesting. It's not like there are switchboard operators in the afterlife. We were spending a million dollars a pop to make a call to some random somewhere, and most of the time nobody answered."

"Must be busy in heaven."

"That's the problem. I don't think we got heaven. When it did occasionally work, we weren't getting happy people, and there sure weren't any choirs of angels singing. After a bit, most people thought that Edison had built a phone line to hell."

"Oh . . ." Sullivan scowled. "That could be awkward."

"Try explaining that to the shareholders. We don't know where we connected to, just that the spirits of some dead people end up there. The conversations were usually screaming gibberish, angry ranting in Chinese, that kind of thing. It didn't help that a couple of researchers went crazy and there was a rash of suicides on the EGE team. Plus, it was sucking up too much of EGE's capital to keep it running and it wasn't like Edison could tell the board that calling hell was a sound investment. The Coolidge administration decided that it should be kept secret because news of the spirit phone could cause—what did he call it?—*anxiety* among the public."

The theological implications of such a device were . . . troubling. "I can see how people might get a little upset. Might get some folks to behave nicer though, if they thought they really would go to hell."

"Or have the public go ape-shit and bananas . . . Pardon my French. Coolidge played it safe. He asked that the project be shut down, so EGE powered down, quit making calls, and just gave it enough juice to keep the connection live in case we ever decided to fire it up again. They were worried that if we shut it down completely, we might not ever be able to reconnect." She stopped at a large steel door labeled XIII and removed a ring of keys from her coat pocket. Another guard stepped aside so she could unlock it. "Three weeks of Power-fueled Cog madness from the greatest mind of our time and"— the heavy door swung open—"we got this."

Sullivan stepped inside a room that was nearly as large as the warehouse above. A dozen men in laboratory coats were wandering about, checking panels of gauges and flashing lights, while in the very center of the room, cordoned off by protective railings and metal safety cages was a twenty-foot-by-twenty-foot glass box filled with crackling lines of electricity and another, slower, blue energy that could only be the visible manifestation of raw magic. It was a thousand lightning strikes imprisoned in a big fish tank. The air hummed with violence as fat power cables fed the hungry box.

It was frankly awe-inspiring.

"Impressive, isn't it?" Hammer asked, already knowing the answer. "A one-minute conversation uses more electricity than Newark does in a week. The big partition was left over from the elephant electrocuting days back when he was trying to prove that direct current was safer than alternating current. The room is reinforced, because if that containment was to break, it could flash-fry Menlo Park."

The last time he'd had anything to do with Cog super-science he'd nearly been vaporized by a Tesla weapon. He wasn't exactly fond of this sort of thing. "You know, the way you were talking, I was kind of expecting"—Sullivan held his hands out about a foot apart—"a telephone."

"The original hypothesis was that it needed to be sensitive. Turns out it just needed to be bigger. And it is like a phone; look closer." Hammer pointed at the base of the massive, flashing death-box, where there was an older two-piece telephone unit, with separated microphone and earphone, sitting on a small metal cradle next to a folding chair.

"Somebody has to sit *next* to that thing?" The amount of energy running through the machine was staggering. "What's in there?"

"All sorts of stuff." Hammer waved her hand dismissively. "Half the periodic table, including some things that are theoretically supposed to annihilate each other on contact. I don't know. It's way over my head."

"I thought you said that they'd barely kept it running?"

"It was on standby mode for years. This is not standby mode. After what happened a few days ago they restarted the project."

"What happened?"

"The phone rang."

Before Sullivan could digest that the crowd had seen them enter and was swarming. A man armed with a large clipboard reached them first. "Mr. Sullivan?"

"Yeah." He could hardly take his eyes away from the spirit phone. "That's me."

"Oh, thank goodness. We've been looking all over for you. Come right this way. He should be calling very soon. The check-ins have been exactly every seven hundred and seventy-four minutes. I have no idea how he can tell such precise time without any physical instrumentation."

Another man, this one in a uniform, pushed past the scientist and pumped Sullivan's hand. "Captain Ellis, Naval Intelligence. Thank you for coming. I just need to confirm that you are in fact, Sergeant Jake Sullivan, formerly of the 1st Volunteer Active Brigade." Sullivan nodded along. "Very well. If we had more time we'd conduct a proper security check, but as it stands the Navy appreciates your assistance in this matter. Your conversation will be recorded. Anything you can get him to say concerning the makeup of their forces would be greatly appreciated."

"Since this is the first time the dead have ever endeavored to speak with the living in a scientific environment, I'd suggest asking more valuable questions," interrupted another man in EGE coveralls. "This is a monumental occa—"

"That'll be all, Doctor," snapped the captain. "We've got no time for your frivolity. See if he'll divulge their attack plans in the Pacific, Sergeant."

The brain side of the group was eager. The military side of the group was nervous. There were four men that stood back a ways that didn't seem to fit with either side. They smelled like enforcers, and the way that they kept looking nervously at the spirit phone told him that they were also new here.

"Right this way, Mr. Sullivan," coaxed the first scientist as he glanced at his watch nervously. "We only have a few minutes. Please do hurry." He reached out and took Sullivan by the sleeve.

Sullivan smacked the hand aside. The EGE scientist put his fingers to his mouth and slinked away, surprised. "Who's calling?"

The crowd exchanged glances.

Hammer spoke. She seemed to be enjoying the general discomfort of the eggheads. "Three days ago the spirit phone rang and for the first time ever, the dead called us. The thing on the other end claimed to be the ghost of Baron Okubo Tokugawa, Chairman of the Imperial Japanese Council, and he asked to speak to you."

Machine Man

Chapter 4

Finders have proven the existence of disembodied spirits. Thus, I've had to revise my opinions on the nature of such spiritualist matters. If we can evolve an instrument so delicate as to be affected by our personality as it survives in the next life, such an instrument, when made available, ought to record something.

—Thomas Edison,
New York Times, 1921

Menlo Park, New Jersey

SULLIVAN TOOK A SEAT next to the electrical monstrosity and waited to receive a call from hell. The chair rested on a rubber mat, as if that would somehow help protect him if the energy inside the box escaped. The glass wasn't even warm, but that didn't make him feel any safer. The phone itself looked normal. Nothing else was.

Several different audio recording devices had been set around the table. Two film cameras were rolling, one electrical and one hand crank, just in case. Judging from the sheer amount of fingernail biting this was a momentous occasion for the EGE scientists. The Naval Intelligence people were having conniption fits. Sullivan had been given a typed list of questions to ask the Chairman's ghost. The connections did not usually hold for long. Time would be of the essence.

The longest that EGE had ever been able to keep a connection was five minutes. A team of six men were sitting at one console, fiddling with dials, wearing headphones and concerned expressions. The scientist that Sullivan had mentally christened Clipboard Man was watching the clock on the wall. He interrupted his nervous sweat dabbing long enough to begin a countdown. "Ten . . . nine . . . eight . . ."

Briiiiiiing.

The bell sounded like a perfectly normal telephone. It was sort of sad, that after all the labor of constructing this terrible abomination in the sight of God, Edison couldn't be bothered to come up with anything more impressive for the ringer.

"He's early!" Clipboard Man turned deathly pale. "Why is he early? Oh no. What do we do?"

Briiiiiiing.

Sullivan simply answered the phone. He put the earpiece against his head and the connection made an unpleasant hum. He leaned in closer to the microphone. "Hello?"

"Mr. Sullivan." The voice seemed to come from a billion miles away, and maybe it was. "It is I, Okubo Tokugawa."

It sounded like him, but it could be a trick. "Prove it."

"We spoke for the first time in the between place, where the dead go to dream, where the Power dwells. For you it is a haunted place of barbed wire and muddy bones." The voice grew stronger. Closer. Steady and calm. "The last time we met was aboard my flagship. After you fed your own brother a sword, I asked you to stand with me to watch an old world die as a new one was born."

"Chairman."

"I was. Am. It is hard to know. Things are . . . sluggish in this place. So cold. So very dark . . . It is hard to see and harder to think. *When* are you?"

"It's February sixteenth, nineteen thirty-three."

"I have not been gone long then . . . Does the world miss me yet?"

Perhaps it wasn't an odd question, coming from a dead man. "No."

"They will soon enough." The sound that came next might have been a sad chuckle.

"Your Imperium still thinks you're alive."

"Indeed? That is for the best. They will need to be strong for what is coming."

The Chairman had not pierced the veil to make small talk. "What's this about?"

"I cannot reach my followers, but a warning must be given. I can no longer find the dream of the Power. My sons can no longer hear my words. I despaired, for I saw what had come, yet had no one to give my message to. Until I found this light in the void. There is no marvelous device such as this in the Imperium. It is difficult, but in this cube, my words can be heard, even if only by my enemies."

Sullivan looked over at the glass nervously. The pulsating energy was eerily quiet. Was the Chairman's ghost actually *inside*?

"But we are no longer enemies. The dead have no enemies, only memories like fog and kingdoms are like dust. Japanese, American, it matters not. All will die if I cannot prepare them. Yet, who among you would heed my warning? And I knew . . . The strongest among my foes would understand."

The Chairman's entire doctrine had been based upon survival of the fittest, and Sullivan had been the one to defeat the Imperium's finest Iron Guard, but it had been a crazy little Okie girl that had done the impossible and crippled the Chairman himself. "You want the strongest?" It was probably a sin to goad the restless dead, but he couldn't resist. "I should go get Faye, then."

"Perhaps she will be someday. The Power has blessed her with a bond beyond anything I have ever seen. I do not understand why it chose her, but she has her own part to play in the events to come. You will have to do, for you have seen the Power as it really is."

"What do you want?"

"The Enemy has caught the scent of the Power. It will soon be on Earth."

Sullivan exhaled slowly. He was one of the only people in the world who understood what magic really was. It had traveled from world to world for who knew how long, bonding magic to intelligent creatures, letting their magic grow, and consuming that magic when they died. The abilities that had appeared in the last century weren't miracles, they were just manifestations of a being that could influence the natural world. It was a repetitive cycle.

Sadly, he'd also learned that the Power was not the top of its food chain. Something else fed on the Power, just as it fed on them. And the Power fleeing and leaving its hosts to be destroyed by its predator was just part of the cycle. "You're certain?"

"Yes."

"Tell me about the Enemy."

"It will consume the Power until the Power has no choice but to flee. When that happens, the Enemy will wreck this world like it has done so many times before. You must defeat it before it takes hold."

"How?"

"First there will come a scout. This is the Pathfinder. The enemy sends them ahead to many worlds, searching for prey, but the spaces between are vast and deep. The Pathfinder must gather enough energy to send a message back to the Enemy, and it *must* be destroyed before it can do that. I have done this myself, twice before."

"Where is it?"

Clipboard Man shouted, "The signal is breaking up."

The Chairman's voice had grown distant again. "The coming of the Pathfinder woke me from my sleep, and already I can feel myself drifting away. It will arrive soon. The time is short. It is . . . confusing. I can no longer think clearly. My children, my Iron Guard . . . I taught them how to search, but you must warn them. They will know what to do."

"How much time do we have?"

"Weeks, perhaps months. Certainly not years. Time is different here." The Chairman kept talking, but it was too faint. Sullivan didn't understand. The background noise was louder. It sounded like a crowd of thousands screaming, until it all coalesced into one hoarse buzz.

"We're losing the connection."

"Sullivan, ask the questions!" shouted the Navy captain, pointed madly at the papers on the table. "The questions!"

But the Navy questionnaire was forgotten. It was about things like who tried to assassinate the president and Imperium weapon systems. Those things meant nothing compared to this. "How do I kill the Pathfinder?"

"Each one is different, but each . . . So very powerful."

"Better than you were?"

"Yes." The word trailed off into a hiss. "I was the first of our kind. The Power learned on me, but there are others like me, almost as old . . . If you can find them, convince them, they can hel—"

The line was nothing but the empty wailing of the damned. "Get him back."

"We're trying," said Clipboard.

Suddenly, the Chairman's voice returned. "—d. I think it has found me. I do not know how. A piece of the Pathfinder is here to silence me. Listen carefully. You must warn my children, my Iron Guard. They will know what to do."

"Why would they trust me?"

"There is no time now. It is upon me. I leave you with a gift. Prepare your mind."

A terrible pain struck him in the temple. Sullivan flinched and dropped the phone. The lights flickered and the tank of Power flashed. Then just as quickly as the pain had come, it was gone. He picked up the earpiece.

The line was silent for a time. Sullivan could hear his own pulse.

"Dark Ocean is the key. You are on your own now, Mr. Sullivan. Farewell."

A horrible screeching noise came from the phone. Sullivan jerked it away from his ear.

Clipboard was running back and forth watching needles bounce and lights flash on the console. "The connection's back, but there's something—" A warning buzzer sounded. "Surge! We've got a surge. Oh no. Shut it down! Shut it down, now!" The lights flickered.

Pop.

Everyone in the room turned to look at the glass cube and the spider web of cracks spreading across its face. *Pop. Poppoppop.* The break grew wider. The Power contained inside licked the edges and tasted freedom.

POP.

"Run for your lives!" Clipboard screamed.

Knocking over the phone, Sullivan jumped from the table and followed the crowd toward the exit. An alarm Klaxon sounded. Red lights embedded in the ceiling began flashing. He had not noticed it before, but there was some sort of huge steel shield suspended over the door and it began to slide down on smooth hydraulics to seal the room.

He had been the closest to the cube and the furthest from safety. "Shit." Sullivan sprinted for the rapidly shortening doorway. The others were going through, and the last few had to duck, but Hammer was waiting for him. "Hurry!" The blast door was closing behind her. She looked at it, then back at him, then went to her hands and knees and scurried through.

CRACK. Flakes of glass struck him in the back. The room shook. Sullivan had played a lot of baseball as a boy, and he slid like he was trying for home plate. He barely made it through on his side. The fat lip of descending steel nicked the side of his head. He rolled into the hallway, knocking down Hammer as the blast door sealed shut.

The red lights were flashing. Sullivan stood up, wincing at the bump on his forehead. "Will that hold?" Then he realized that was a dumb question, since all of the technical types who knew better were still running. He grabbed Hammer's outstretched hand and pulled her up. "Come on!"

They had made it about twenty feet when the containment for the spirit phone failed. The release made a terrible *WHUMP*. The basement shook so hard that Sullivan and Hammer were knocked off their feet. Dust and concrete bits fell from the ceiling. The blast door had held, though it had been stretched and bowed like the edge of a steel bubble and the thick walls around it were cracked and steaming.

The alarm was still sounding. The lights in the hall were red as blood. Someone got on an intercom and told damage control teams to report to Room XIII and for everyone else to evacuate in an orderly fashion. Several scientists ran past screaming and crying. Hammer sat up and coughed. "Hope that isn't coming out of my paycheck."

Sullivan touched the cut on his scalp. It wasn't too bad, nothing the Healing spell on his chest couldn't handle. It would be just another beauty mark in no time. "I'd like to stay and shed a tear for your fancy phone, but I've got important business to attend to."

Hammer stood up and cringed when she put weight on one leg. "Thanks for clipping me there, buddy. It was like getting run over by a car."

"Sorry." Objects in motion tend to stay in motion, and

he was a very big object. "I need to go. You heard what the Chairman said."

"I didn't understand any of it, but come on. The alarm has sounded so the second layer of security will lock this place down tight."

Everyone else was ahead of them. He took one of Hammer's arms and helped her walk. His clumsy slide had managed to twist her ankle. They went back the way they'd come in, past the doors marked with Roman numerals. After seeing the terrible thing that was behind one of the doors, it made him wonder what was behind the rest. Despite being an intensely curious man, he decided that he really didn't want to know . . . right this minute, anyway.

The red emergency lighting was dim, so he had to do a double take when something huge and misshapen clanked past in the intersection of hallways ahead. It was only visible for a second, but it had been a foot taller than Sullivan and twice as big around. He pulled Hammer to the side and took cover in the shadow of door IV. He squeezed her tight and watched. "Shhh. Demon."

"That? It's okay," she reassured him. "That's part of the second layer of security I was telling you about."

He shook his head. "I don't like Summoned. Especially a big one like that. I can't believe you'd keep one of those things around." The intersection seemed clear. "Greater demons are aggressive. Way too dangerous outside of a war zone. You better have a master Summoner babysitting it nonstop."

Hammer chuckled. "Oh, Mr. Sullivan. That's no demon. That's a tele-automaton. EGE's board just isn't ready to unveil them to the public yet. They're still working the bugs out. Come on. It won't hurt us . . ." She looked up at him. "Seriously. Let go."

Sullivan released her. "Sorry."

"Thanks for trying to protect me from imaginary Summoned." She stepped into the hallway and adjusted her dress. "But you're rather rough with the ladies."

"My last girlfriend was a Brute." Sullivan grunted. He stepped out after her and froze. The four men that had been out of place at the spirit phone were heading their way. They had guns in their hands and the one in the lead was screwing something on to the end of his that could only be a sound muffler. They saw each other at the same time. They began running his way with murderous intent.

"You set me up," Sullivan said to Hammer. "Should have known."

"No wai—" Hammer began, but then she jumped back as a bullet struck the wall next to Sullivan. "Hell!" She ran the other way, but they weren't shooting at her. The gunmen were aiming for him.

The door marked IV was heavy and solid, but so was Sullivan. He flared his Power, increased his mass, and slammed his shoulder into it. The lock failed and he crashed inside. It was another large space, but so cloaked in shadow that he couldn't tell how big. There were only a few red emergency lights flashing above.

The floor was made of a metal grate. There were darker shapes on each side, tall units, shaped like standing coffins built to hold giants. They stretched into the distance. Pipes and cables stretched from the ceiling into the tops of the devices. He passed at least five of the things, before Sullivan ran to the side and took cover behind one of the units. He hid just as the feet of his pursuers hit the metal floor.

"Come on out, Heavy. We just want to talk."

And sell me a bridge in Brooklyn. Sullivan stayed mum. He'd let them all come inside, then he'd Spike them through the roof. Light beams flickered back and forth. Some of them had hand torches. He crept around the cold metal edge and spotted the four silhouettes. They were confident, but he'd see how confident they'd be when up became down. Sullivan focused and Spiked hard.

Gravity didn't change. He tried again. Nothing happened. Confused, Sullivan pulled back.

"You feel that?" one of the men asked.

"Yeah, I felt it." Their leader raised his voice. "You trying to use magic on us, Sullivan? It won't work. You might as well come out in the open and face us like a man. I want to get out of here before this place falls down on our heads."

It was rather unnerving to have his magic not work on demand like it always had, but Jake Sullivan wasn't the panicking type. He was, however, the analytical type. First he took inventory of the Power gathered in his chest. It was there, he could feel it, but it was like something was keeping him from using it. It was like a blindfold for his eyes or earplugs . . . Everything was where it should be, but muffled.

Concentrating, he felt the spells etched into his flesh. They were still alive with Power, but it was as if he couldn't access them. The laceration on his head should have been tingling with Healing magic, but it wasn't. Even his Grimnoir ring felt dead.

Interesting. Somehow these men were blocking his access to the Power. But that puzzle would have to wait. He had to get out alive first, which meant either taking out four armed men with just his hands or escaping. Smart money was on escaping.

Sullivan moved quietly down the grate. He had the wall to his right and the giant coffins to his left. If he was lucky there would be another door at the other end.

"We going to do this the hard way then, Sullivan? Your call."

Sullivan hit the far wall. It was a dead end. There was a heating vent he thought about trying, but who was he kidding? There was no way in the world that he would be able to fit in there, and he didn't want the indignity of getting shot in the ass while his shoulders were stuck in a duct. That meant fighting his way out. His hand landed on something leaning against the wall. It was a big spanner. Nice and long with all the weight at the end. Perfect for cracking skulls. Sullivan took the wrench in hand.

He risked a peek. The leader gave some hand signals. The four men spread out, one on each of the far walls, two in the center. Once they were formed up, they all started walking his way, torches bobbing along ahead of them. They were treating this like a pheasant hunt, walking the field, down the levies in a line, keeping an eye on each other so he couldn't sneak between them, until he had nowhere else to run. They intended to flush him out.

The gunmen were halfway down the room, nearing where Sullivan was clutching his spanner, when there was a loud rumble from the hallway. At first he thought that another part of the building had fallen down. The rumble came again and he realized it was a *footstep*.

"What the hell was that?" The flashlight approaching on his side bobbed away.

"Quiet!" snapped the leader.

Sullivan used the distraction to his advantage. He covered the distance between the coffins swiftly. The light came back around. Sullivan caught the man by the gun hand and swung him facefirst into the nearest metal coffin. He tried to fire his gun, but Sullivan blocked the hammer with his thumb. He tried to push away so Sullivan clubbed him on the back of the head with the wrench.

Lights flashed his way as Sullivan shoved the dazed man into the open. The others opened fire. His victim took a round in the chest and sprawled forward. Sullivan felt a bullet burn across the back of his hand. He dodged back around the coffin, but the pistol he'd hoped to secure went bouncing across the grate to disappear into the shadows.

The guns were quieter with the mufflers attached, but the bullets sure made a lot of racket as they punched holes in the sheet metal he was hiding behind. There was a lull as empty magazines were dropped and new ones slammed home.

"We got you now, Heavy. Nowhere for you to hide."

There were three of them left and they knew exactly where he was. He was pinned down. They'd fan out and soon enough one of them would have a clean shot . . . He had to get out of here. It was hard to hit something with a pistol in one hand and a flashlight in the other, which might give him a chance, but he'd probably still get ventilated. Sullivan prepared to run for it.

There was a metallic thud as something shook the grating. "Greetings, EGE guests. Allow me to help make your visit a pleasant one," a new voice boomed.

"What the hell is that?"

Sullivan peered around the corner. It was the thing he'd glimpsed in the hall. The flashlights gave him a better look at it this time. It was shaped like a man, mostly. The head was a disproportionately small oval ball with two rectangular glowing eyes. The torso was round too, like a pot-bellied stove. The arms and legs were too long and too thin, with bones of pipe encircled in metal skin. The feet were huge and splayed like a duck's, probably so that the mechanical oddity could keep its balance.

There was a scratching of a record, like an automated player making a new selection. "Due to the delicate nature of EGE scientific equipment, no weapons are permitted in EGE Shelved Projects areas. Please, place your weapons on the floor and wait for an EGE representative to secure them for you. Thank you for your cooperation."

"Well, ain't that something? It's one of those mechanical men I read about in *Popular Mechanics*. Welcome to the future, boys."

"We don't have time for this. Shoot it, Willis."

There was the muffled snap of a silenced pistol and a *ding* noise as the bullet bounced off the mechanical man's rounded torso. It barely even swayed.

The record player scratched and rattled as a new track was put on the turntable. "Warning. Please desist from damaging or defacing EGE property." Logically, Sullivan knew that it was impossible for the prerecorded voice to know, but he could have sworn the mechanical man sounded annoyed.

Willis shot the mechanical man four more times.

This time there was no warning. The mechanical man raised one arm. There was a loud *clack* that Sullivan recognized as the charging handle being worked on a Browning 1919. The thunder of the 30-caliber machine gun filled the room. Sullivan covered his ears.

The three men twitched and jerked as shell casings spilled from the machine's arm and fell through the floor grate. After a ten-second burst, the firing stopped, and the smoking metal arm was lowered. They were well past dead.

The mechanical man made a rumble as its torso swiveled toward the coffin Sullivan was hiding behind. The record player scratched. "Due to the delicate nature of EGE scientific equipment, no weapons are permitted in EGE Shelved Projects areas. Please, place your weapons on the floor and wait for an EGE representative to secure them for you. Thank you for your cooperation."

The wrench hit the floor immediately. Sullivan came out with his hands up.

Brief pause. "Thank you for your cooperation. EGE representatives will be along shortly. Please enjoy your visit to the Shelved Projects Branch."

"Thank you," Sullivan said. "You mind if I search those fellas?"

It took awhile for the mechanical man to pick the right record. "I'm sorry. I do not understand your question."

"Great. Just tell me if I start to do something against

the rules." He picked the one that had been acting as the leader. Sullivan checked his pockets, careful not to get blood on himself. There was a wallet and a badge holder, which he took, though he was careful not to pick up any of the perfectly good guns that were lying around.

The mechanical man lumbered closer to see what Sullivan was doing.

"What are you?"

"I am an EGE Tele-Automaton Mark Five. I ensure the safety of the EGE Shelved Projects Branch."

"How do you work?"

"Through a strategic partnership between Cseska Robotica and Edision General Electric, the EGE Mark Five series operates on a proprietary system combining state of the art scientific methods and ultramodern engineering."

"Uh huh . . ." Sullivan could see the lightly glowing carvings on various parts of the mechanical man's body. It was spellbound. Cog science had figured out a way to connect this thing directly to the Power. And thinking of Power . . . How had these guys been able to block his? Sullivan continued his pat-down and found something odd. One of the men had a small orange Bakelite box in his pocket. Sullivan opened it up and saw that it had some sort of gem inside. One fingertip set it spinning.

"Warning. Please desist from damaging or defacing EGE property."

Sullivan looked up at the mechanical man. "What?" The mechanical man shook as he lifted the box. "This thing hurting you?" The glowing spells seemed to flicker. Sullivan took a step closer and the mechanical man drooped. The arms fell with a grinding noise and hung limp. The lights behind the eye holes gradually went dark. He walked over and knocked on its chest. It was dead or asleep. Sullivan looked down at the mysterious box, shrugged, and shoved it in his pocket.

Picking up one of the hand torches, Sullivan inspected the coffins. Now with more light, he could see that there was a porthole in each one. A quick look inside revealed that there was a different type of mechanical man in each one. Some looked quite a bit like his new friend, bulbous and odd; others were rougher, like boxes with girders for limbs; while a few were much more streamlined, man-sized and looking like a knight in a suit of armor. All had been spellbound, though these seemed inactive. Too bad he didn't have more time to explore, but he had to get out of here.

He made his way out through the chaos. The facility had taken quite a blow from the collapsing spirit phone and the night shift was being evacuated. The power was out almost everywhere and from the smell, something had caught fire. At one point he saw some of the Navy people shouting his name, searching for him, but Sullivan kept his head down and ducked behind a fire truck. He didn't know how many other enemies he had here. There was no sign of Hammer either. He stopped at the front office, which was luckily deserted, broke open the lockbox with one solid kick and retrieved his pistol.

Hammer's giant Ford Hyperion was in the garage with the keys still in it. The starter turned over on the first try despite the cold. He didn't like stealing, but it was a question of priorities. Somebody was going to come looking for the men that had tried to kill him, so he wanted as much of a head start as possible. He'd leave the Hyperion someplace it could be found easily and even top off the tank, but it served her right for setting him up. He hit the road and gunned it in order to leave Jersey behind.

The night had raised a lot of questions and not very many answers. Dead men calling, presidential assassinations, Pathfinders, dark oceans, devices that could quell magic, and mechanical men . . . It was enough to make a poor Gravity Spiker's head swim. He needed help. It was time to call the Grimnoir.

Chapter 5

And how will the New Republic treat the inferior races? How will it deal with the black? How will it deal with the yellow man? How will it tackle that alleged termite in the civilized woodwork, the Jew? Certainly not as races at all. The world is a world, not a charitable institution, and I take it they will have to go. The whole tenor and meaning of the world, as I see it, is that they have to go. So far as they fail to develop sane, vigorous, and distinctive abilities for the great world of the future, it is their portion to die out and disappear. The world has a greater purpose than happiness; our lives are to serve God's purpose, and that purpose aims not at man as an end, but works through him to greater issues.

—H. G. Wells,
Anticipations of the Reaction of Magical and Scientific Progress Upon Human Life and Thought, 1901

UBF *Minotaur*
Somewhere over Nevada

IT WAS FRUSTRATING SOMETIMES. She seemed

to have a stronger natural attachment to the Power than anybody else around, though she wasn't nearly as strong as she'd somehow become on the *Tokugawa,* but she was mediocre at creating anything more than the most rudimentary of spells. Sure, she could Travel like it was nobody's business, which was supposed to be one of the hardest types of magic to master, what with all the possible ways of crashing into things and dying, so why couldn't she make this stupid communication spell work right? And now everybody was staring at her, wondering why the girl that had supposedly fought the Chairman couldn't even get a stupid little spell to take.

Faye, Mr. Browning, and the new volunteers had left L.A. a few hours ago, catching the first blimp heading east. They were rushing back to help, though nobody really had any idea what helping meant in this case. It wasn't like she could shoot or stab her way out of so many folks hating Actives. Moving made her feel like she was doing *something* though. Heck, on a blimp, even when they were sleeping they were moving. One nice thing about blimping was that the staterooms tended to have pretty comfy beds, which meant you could usually get a good night's sleep on one, at least until your Grimnoir ring tried to burn your finger off.

It had been about five minutes since Faye's ring had turned hot enough to wake her up. It wasn't just her, either. All of the assorted Grimnoir aboard the *Minotaur* had received the same signal and it had been a strong one. Somebody really wanted to talk. They had gathered in the observation bubble because it was quiet and they could lock the door to keep out snooping crew members.

Since Faye had gotten here first, she'd volunteered to cast, and now she was regretting it. It was starting to frazzle her nerves, but she wouldn't give the unfamiliar knights the satisfaction of seeing her fail. She redrew the design in the pile of salt and tried once again to concentrate on letting her own Power connect. Lance made it look so easy. *Focus*, he'd said, *the Active provides the juice. You're just a battery. The Power knows what to do based on what part of it you draw.*

There were many different material components that could be used for spells. The Grimnoir had learned them through trial and error. The most common was good old fashioned salt or fine sand, because you could try again if you screwed it up. Even dirt would work if you were good enough. It was harder to do, but a spell could be scratched onto a glass surface, though she'd never managed to get one of those right.

Four knights had joined them in Los Angeles and now they were all looking at her. It wasn't helping her nerves any. Faye had not had much time to get to know them, but *most* of them seemed like they would be okay.

The nice French girl didn't talk much, but when she did, she talked with a funny accent. It made her sound exotic. She'd introduced herself as Colleen Giraudoux, but everybody else just called her Whisper, so Faye did too. She was very refined and pretty, with dark, elaborately constructed hair that was way nicer than Faye's flat, straw-colored and constantly tangled mop. She even dressed fancy and wore a little bit of makeup around her eyes and on her lips and cheeks, which was a little scandalous in America even these days, but which was apparently perfectly acceptable in France. It seemed like all the young male passengers on the *Minotaur* kept looking Whisper's way, and she never so much as blushed or batted a perfect eyelash with all that attention.

Whisper didn't seem to look down at Faye just because she wasn't educated, fancy, or worldly, so since Whisper was only probably five or so years older, Faye hoped that they could be like sisters or something. Faye's only real sister had died of a fever back when she was really little, Delilah was dead, and Jane was hardly ever around, so it would be nice to make friends with another girl.

She hadn't gotten to speak to Mr. Bryce or Mr. Bolander nearly as much. Mr. Bryce seemed to treat talking like it was a contest to see who could say the least, and if that was the case, then he was the champion. He was a tall, bony, suspicious type who seemed to scowl a lot and was always watching people with shifty eyes that she could barely see under the edge of his bowler hat. He reminded her of the scarecrows they'd had back when she was kid, back when crops actually grew in Oklahoma. She didn't know what Mr. Bryce's Power was. Probably something sneaky.

Mr. Bolander was a broad man, with the big arms of somebody who had worked hard his whole life. He seemed really friendly, with an easy manner and a genuine smile, but Faye hadn't gotten to speak to him much at all. He was a Negro, which meant that his quarters were in a different part of the dirigible, and there were only certain hours when the coloreds aboard were allowed to eat in the galley. There hadn't been any Negroes where Faye had grown up, and in fact she had only spoken to a few in her whole life, so the whole thing about shooing them away from everybody else seemed odd to her. Why bother? With her Power, she could kill every single person on the *Minotaur* without even trying hard, but nobody treated her funny. Now *she* was different. But Mr. Bolander was the one that had to keep away from polite company because he was browner. If folks were that rude over looks, it was tough to imagine how they'd treat him if they knew he could shoot lightning bolts out his eyes.

If those three had been the only new knights, Faye would have been glad for the help, but there was one left, and Ian Wright made her skin crawl. He had come from the same group as Whisper that had been working in Europe, only he wasn't anything like her. Even now, while she was trying hard to make the stupid spell bind, he was watching her, acting like he was better than she was. Sure, he hadn't said anything specific, but she could see it on his smug face.

Ian was probably in his mid-twenties, but it wasn't his age that made her think he didn't deserve to be called *Mr. Wright*. He was decent looking enough, but Ian was moody and she found that turned him sort of ugly. They said he was English, but that he'd grown up here, so he didn't really sound different. Mr. Browning had said that Ian's Power was mightily impressive and that hardly anybody in the whole Society was better at making spells. He talked smart, but as it turned out, he was the knight that had stuck up for Harkeness and Rawls in the meeting, which automatically made Faye hate his guts.

Just thinking about those traitors made her slip up on one of the designs. Ian stepped forward. He was going to offer to do the spell for her, and he was going to play like he was being chivalrous for doing it, when in reality he was just being a big mean jerk, but because she was thinking about jerks instead of drawing her markings correctly, the spell fizzled again. She wanted to swear at the Power like it was an obstinate milk cow that wouldn't put its head through the stall, but that would just make her look dumber.

"Let me do it," Ian said as he nosed in. "It may be an emergency."

"We're in a blimp. If it's an emergency, what are we supposed to do about it?" she snapped.

"Well, I suppose you could just pop on down to wherever it is and easily take care of everything for us."

"Faye, he may be right," Mr. Browning said. "Let him do it."

Cheeks burning, Faye grudgingly got out of the way. Ian wet his fingers in a cup of water and drew a complicated design in the salt. He frowned at it, said the proper words, and the room seemed to shudder. The salt instantly flash-fused into a solid disk. The circle floated into the air until it was a bit higher than she was tall. It had only taken Ian thirty seconds and the view of the other side was clear as could be. *Damn it.* He was *way* better at spellbinding than she was.

"Whoever started this has alerted every Grimnoir within reach. There are a lot of people getting on. This will be very draining for him."

The circle floated and seemed to spin like a top as others made the connection. She recognized Lance Talon by the bottom of his bushy beard before his circle had even gotten into position to show his face. Others followed, some Grimnoir she didn't know, then Dan and Jane Garrett, who had curlers in her hair and was still throwing on a robe, more strangers, and then Mr. Sullivan, who from the background had built his circle using the rearview mirror of a moving automobile. Though he would never brag, Mr. Sullivan was remarkably good at spellbinding, which was especially surprising that somebody with a bruiser's hands could have such a delicate touch.

"So who called this conference?" Mr. Browning asked.

The circle spun. She recognized the disorderly stateroom of the new *Cyclone*. "Francis!" Faye exclaimed. "What happened to your face?" He looked like the losing fighter at the end of a long boxing match. One eye was swollen shut and purple and his lips were all puffy and cracked. "Are you all right?"

"I'm fine. Heinrich was killed in the assassination attempt." There were collective gasps. Jane cried out and Dan swore. Faye was too surprised to react. "I don't have much time. This link hurts to keep open and I'm not in good shape. You all know about Roosevelt? I think the assassin was an Iron Guard."

"No-good rotten bastards," Lance snapped.

Francis hurried and told them about the attack, and then his interrogation and beating at the hands of the mysterious Mr. Crow. The assembled Grimnoir shared an uneasy look when he told them about the assassin's ring, and Faye thought a few of them might have a fit when they heard about how Francis' magic had been blocked. She was still stunned about Heinrich, and by the time Francis finished, her knees had gone all wobbly and soft.

A deep voice cut in. "This is Sullivan." The mirror spun over to him. He was still driving, and from the lights zipping past, going *really* fast. He held a small orange box up to the mirror. "This is how they blocked your magic. I don't know how it works. There's one word stamped on the bottom, looks like Dymaxion. There's a stone inside, and while it's spinning it disrupts your connection to the Power."

"However did you get that?" Mr. Browning asked.

"Four men tried to kill me tonight. Didn't recognize them, but probably from the same outfit as the one that beat up Francis. One of them had this."

Faye realized that the bad men weren't that smart, since they had *only* sent *four* men to kill Mr. Sullivan. Obviously they hadn't known who they were dealing with.

"There's more, though. Francis, how long can you hold the line?"

"I'll do my best," Francis answered, through gritted teeth.

"I'll make it quick." Sullivan rattled off events like a military man giving a briefing, which in a way, was exactly what he was. "The Chairman's ghost called. EGE has a working spirit phone. And yes. It really was him. He said the Enemy's sent a scout. It'll be here sometime soon. We have to stop it before it sends a message home saying this is the place for dinner."

That cinched it. It was Faye's turn to smirk at Ian. "Told you so."

"Enemy? Wait—you mean the big *thing*?" Lance asked. "Hell, I was hoping you had imagined that."

"Me too. I've got an idea on how to find it, but we'll need to work fast."

Mr. Browning was the senior knight. "We have two problems then. It appears we are meant to take the fall for this assassin and this *being* has finally found us. Could the two be related?"

"Don't know . . . Maybe," Sullivan responded. "We don't know enough about it to guess. The Chairman said his Iron Guard had been trained to deal with it, but he can't reach them. I was led to understand this has happened before."

"I think I know where we can find an Iron Guard fast," Dan said. "Can you meet me in D.C.?" The view spun back to show Sullivan nodding. "Good, I can meet you there tomorrow afternoon . . . I'll help you talk to him on one condition." And when it came to a skilled Mouth like Mr. Garrett, *talking* took on a more sinister meaning.

"Yeah?"

"That when we're done, we kill the son of a bitch . . . for Heinrich."

The Grimnoir were quiet. Everyone knew that Heinrich had been Dan's best friend. Sullivan grunted in agreement. "Sounds swell."

"Count me in on that, too," Lance said. "This OCI will be watching so we'll need to keep a low profile. We don't know who else of us they know about."

"They sure know about me," Sullivan stated. "Won't be the first time I've been on a wanted poster."

"There are other resources to find out more about this new office. I will place some calls." Mr. Browning checked his pocket watch. "I have Faye and some volunteers. We will go directly to Florida to investigate. Francis, we must assume that you have been compromised and that they will be watching. Go about your business and stay out of contact."

"But, John, I can—"

"Lead a band of killers to our door? Yes. Indeed you could."

Francis obviously did not like Mr. Browning's directions. "Fine . . . I can't hold this link much longer."

Francis really didn't look very good. Faye wished that she could be there with him, but even a Traveler had limits. The last time she'd gone that far in one hop she'd spent a few weeks unconscious, though in her defense she had drug an entire dirigible along for the ride.

"Then good luck and Godspeed," Mr. Browning said. The magic circle fell and broke into hardened bits. Browning wasted no time giving the order to the assembled knights. "Contact everyone. We must warn them what is coming."

That meant more communication spells. Faye groaned. "Can I go borrow the radio?"

Menlo Park, New Jersey

IT HAD BEEN a real pain to get here so quickly.

Per Crow's instructions, the scene had not been disturbed after the bodies of his men had been removed. It had been roped off and chalk outlines applied, which had been difficult since the floor was a metal grate, but there was enough chalk and dried blood that he got the picture. Crow had seen so much violence in his life that reconstructing the event was easy. The Heavy had taken one by surprise, then the robot had gunned down the others. His men had been stupid. He should have dealt with it himself, but even he had his limitations.

Reconstructing this particular scene was easy. Dealing with the rest of these Grimnoir was going to be hard. His new office had money, but it was short on talent, which was why he'd made the trip from headquarters all the way to the EGE facility personally.

The building was a mess. They were still cleaning up the wreck of the spirit phone. They had been lucky that the entire building hadn't just fallen down. It was too bad about the phone. It would have been really nice to have the recordings of Sullivan's conversation, but the cameras had been destroyed when the phone had flashed out of existence. There were transcripts from the witnesses, but they had not been close enough to hear every word.

What he did have of the conversation was confusing, something about an enemy coming, but that was over Crow's pay grade. His job was to break the Grimnoir. His boss and the intelligence types could worry about the other stuff.

He'd thrown all of the EGE people out of the robot room except for the one he really wanted to talk to. The Coordinator's office had a thick file on her. She was flagged as a rare type of Active and a potential problem down the road. However, she had a rare talent he needed, and more importantly Crow knew what she really wanted, and that gave him leverage.

"Pemberly Hammer . . ." he said, playing it soft. "Pemberly. Sounds old-fashioned."

"Named after my grandmother." She stood back a bit, arms folded in the shadow of the deactivated robot. Crow knew she wouldn't expound, but it didn't matter. He knew all about her. She came from a proud old Texas line, even had a couple of ancestors at the Alamo. All his intel suggested that she was just as stubborn as all the ranchers, sheriffs, soldiers, and rangers that had come before her.

"Speaking of family, I heard about your pops. We're in the same line of work, me and him. Lawmen got to stick together."

"From what I saw from your boys last night, you're nothing like my father. He had honor."

"I heard he could track anybody or anything. I understand you inherited his abilities."

"I've got a rep and I earned it myself. All I know about you is that you flashed some special badge and real important people asked how high they needed to jump. Who are you supposed to be?"

"Crow. Office of the Coordinator of Information."

Hammer frowned. Of course, she automatically knew when people were lying to her. She could tell the name was fictional, but the office wasn't. "Never heard of it."

"You're not supposed to have . . . yet. We regulate magic."

"What?" She laughed at him. "You can't *regulate* magic."

He didn't care for her attitude. "We do now. I need your services."

"Listen, Agent Crow—"

"It's just Mister."

"Fine, *Mister* Crow, I'm not interested in working for your kind of outfit. Your boys just walked up to Sullivan and started shooting easy as saying hello."

"This job pays good. You can read minds, so you know when I say good, I mean real good."

"I'm no Reader, and I'm still not interested. Good thing I don't need your money."

"Well, I'd heard you worked for whoever paid the most. Turning down good money . . . You're not much of a mercenary then."

"Girl needs a job. Doesn't mean she has to take every one that comes along. Good day, Mr. Crow." She turned to leave.

He wasn't about to take any lip off a skirt. Crow knew he had a few options. Negotiation was a delicate dance. Sometimes you could threaten or bully, other times you could bribe or coerce. Cracking people was like cracking a safe: everyone had a combination that would open them right up, but sometimes it was just easier to dynamite the doors off. "I know what you want."

"And what would that be?"

"A badge."

She stopped in the doorway. "I already told you—"

"If my organization isn't to your taste, I can pull some strings. Anywhere you want, wherever you want." He could tell that he'd hooked her. "Come on, Hammer. Would I lie to you? Dig a little deeper."

She did. Crow could feel the pressure in his head. She couldn't Read him, but there was no lying to a Justice. He let her rummage through the top compartment, just enough to see that he wasn't bluffing. She wasn't even trying to be discreet. "Oh my . . ." she said slowly. As expected, what she found had shocked her. Crow wasn't offended. Fear was just another tool in the tool box. "What *are* you?"

Interesting. She'd gone deeper than expected. The girl was dangerous. "Somebody you can't afford to cross. You got a little peek at what I'm capable of. If you help me, I help you reach your goals. Badge anywhere you want one. If you don't help me, then what your Power does becomes public knowledge. I'm sure potential employers would love to know that their most closely-held secrets aren't safe when you're around. In fact, as much corruption as there is in this world, I could see how nobody would ever hire someone like you. Too risky, because everybody has secrets . . . Your call."

According to the OCI scientists' categories and rankings of known Actives, Crow had been born as a relatively common type, and they mistakenly still had him there. Only a handful of men knew about what he could do now. Which meant that when he was done with this Justice, she would have to be disposed of.

She was angry, afraid, and trying not to let it show. *Good.* That's right where he wanted her, and it was fine if she knew it. "You hook me up wherever I want, and all I have to do is this one job for you?"

"That's all I want."

Hesitantly, Hammer came back into the room. "What's the gig?"

"Find Jake Sullivan again. He'll have gone to ground and I want him found quick. OCI will pay double what you got to find him last time."

"Sullivan? You should have said so. He stole my new car. I'd have tracked him down for free."

He was pleased. Crow had learned all he could about Hammer first, about her abilities and her history. Despite the tough and cynical reputation she'd cultivated, she was basically an idealistic person, and nobody was easier to manipulate than an idealist.

Crow realized that he'd forgotten something. "One second." He walked over to the still robot and inspected the Cog craftsmanship. "Impressive. This thing tore my men to pieces." He put one finger in the dents where the pistol bullets had bounced off. "Your clients called it a *robot*. What's that mean?"

"Czech word for serf. One of their Cogs invented the first one awhile back. EGE improved on the design. Nobody is better at sticking spells on stuff than these boys. They bring bad things to life."

"I thought Edison didn't believe in building offensive weapons."

"Not since that debacle with the Navy ship that got all those sailors fused into the deck a few years back." Hammer shook her head. "He wouldn't do it, but Mr. Edison's body wasn't even cold before they'd figured out how to arm these. Each one has a 30-caliber machine gun, but they can take flamethrowers, antitank guns, you name it."

"Does it think for itself?"

"I think they can only follow orders."

"Huh . . . I like that. They pretty tough?"

"Very tough. This is the five series. The six just entered production. It's even better. Like a security guard that never sleeps or a soldier that never gets scared. Army procurement wants some if they can get the funding."

Crow seemed deep in thought. "That it?"

"Yeah. I'm done with you. You're going to want to get a move on before Sullivan gets too far away."

"Head starts don't matter with me."

"Good. Do me a favor and send in one of those eggheads on the way out. I've got a few questions."

Hammer was obviously relieved to be away from him. A minute later one of the EGE scientists came in, nervous. Crow tended to have that effect on most people.

"You needed help, sir?"

Crow pointed at the robot. "Are these expensive?"

"I'm no salesman, but I believe so. They're somewhere around seventy *thousand* dollars each. The machining is very precise."

"Hmmm . . ." Crow thought about it for a moment. That was an obscene amount of money, but OCI was about to have an even more obscene budget. "Does EGE offer a bulk discount?"

"I would have to ask."

"Hell with it. I'll take a dozen."

Chapter 6

After we lost the vote, they told us to go home, but most of us stayed. Summer got hotter. Tempers got shorter. So they sicced the Army on us. MacArthur was in front, chest full of ribbons, thumping a riding crop on his leg and giving orders like we was the Hun. Some of us met them on the way, waving white shirts like flags over our heads, begging for an hour to get the women and children out of the camp. The hotheads and the communists began throwing rocks and bottles so the Army threw gas bombs back. My head got split open with a club. I wanted to cut them so bad, just let my bones grow into claws and rip them to bits, like I was back in the war, but I didn't. My brother's boy turned blue and died the next morning from the gas. Nothing I could do. He was just too little . . . Folks wonder why we stayed. We were hungry and broke. Of course we stayed. We had nowhere else to go.

—Higby Yates,
Former member of the
1st Volunteer Active Brigade
and Bonus Marcher, 1933

Washington D.C.

THEIR CHOSEN MEETING PLACE had not been picked by chance, but rather because it seemed appropriate. The authorities hadn't even bothered to clean up the mess left over from last summer. The shacks and tents had been burned, but the remains still sat there in their orderly rows, tattered or rusting, while the sun went down over the Anacostia Flats. It was a place where trust had been betrayed.

As someone who understood what it felt like to get stabbed in the back, he had wanted to see the place for himself. Jake Sullivan sat on the grass and savored a smoke while he waited for the others to arrive.

Lance Talon got there next, *sort of.* A mangy stray dog came trotting up to Sullivan like it owned the place. That was his first clue. Normally a cur like that would have skulked around in the shadows until it decided it was worth the risk to try and mooch food. The dog was brown except for where it was pink and it smelled like it had been rolling on something dead.

"Evening, Lance," Sullivan said.

"Hey, Jake," the dog answered with a deep voice. A dripping tongue hung out, but the dog's mouth didn't move as Lance spoke through the animal. "I'm on my way up the road. Figured I'd sniff around first."

"How can you smell anything over that stink?" Sullivan pinched his nose. "Would you back up already? I'm dying here."

"Smells like perfume and roses to me right now." The dog trotted a few feet downwind. "Better?"

"Much. Why the mutt?"

"I'm guessing you haven't read the evening paper yet." The dog cocked its head at him and whined. "I was making sure this place wasn't swarming with coppers first."

"Haven't seen the paper in days."

"I've got one with me. You're famous. Or is it infamous? Nice to make your acquaintance, Mr. Dillinger."

"That bad?"

"You think I'm exaggerating . . . Hang on a second."

The dog's manner suddenly changed. It blinked stupidly, as if trying to figure out how it had woken up here. The last thing it remembered was whatever wonderful dead thing it had been playing with before Lance had taken over its brain. The mutt saw Sullivan, yipped in surprise, and took off into the ruins at a dead run.

A Ford box truck came to stop nearby and shut off its engine. Sullivan tossed the butt in the grass and stood. Lance Talon limped up, his cowboy boots crunching on the gravel. They shook hands, both of them knowing better by now than to try to out-squeeze the other guy.

Though short, Lance was a tough fellow with a lumberjack's beard and the shoulders to match. More comfortable in the outdoors than in the fake trappings of civilized society, the Beastie had adventured his way around the dark corners of the world, hunting exotic animals until the Grimnoir had put his skills to use hunting Imperium instead. "Nice view." Lance glanced at the Capitol in the distance. The dome could be seen over the trees.

"Formidable, even if it's packed with liars and thieves." He handed Sullivan a folded *Washington Herald*.

"What page?"

"Buddy, you're the headline."

DANGEROUS ACTIVE MURDERS
FEDERAL OFFICERS

The next line was even worse.

JAKE "HEAVY" SULLIVAN:
Possible Conspirator in Magical Assassination Plot?

The picture was his convict shot from Rockville—the one that made his eyes look small, black, and dead. These people certainly moved fast.

Lance tried and failed to peer over Sullivan's shoulder while he read the lies. Jake was nearly a foot taller, and it didn't help that Lance had taken on a sort of permanent bad-posture stoop because one of his legs was shorter than the other. A particularly nasty demon had taken a chunk out of him and there hadn't been a Healer around. "I heard talk you're going to be declared public enemy number one. I saw that movie. James Cagney is too pretty to play the likes of you."

Sullivan crumpled the newspaper in disgust and threw it on the ground. "Damn Hearst and his excuse for journalism. Whatever happened to reporters checking facts themselves? That man will print anything that makes an Active look like an animal."

"Us being animals seems to be the popular sentiment

over there today, too." Lance nodded at the Capitol. "The president is going to live, thank God, but all Actives are footing the bill. Dark times are coming, Jake."

"Well, let's go risk our lives finding this Pathfinder to protect all these ignorant bastards so they can sit around and bitch about our kind. You know this very spot should've been blown up by the Geo-Tel . . . what, twice now?"

"Last year and '08. Feeling bitter?"

Sullivan didn't respond for a long time as he surveyed the wreckage of the camp. "I'm not going back to Rockville. I'm done breaking rocks. I'm not going back in a cage. I'll die first."

"I'm rather disinclined toward tight spaces myself." Lance chuckled as he took a flask out of his pocket, unscrewed the lid, and took a swig. "Ahh . . . That's good stuff. Well, you could always put out to sea. Pirate Bob said you'd make a fine executive officer."

"Maybe I should. There's no law out there except for what a man makes himself." Sullivan took the offered flask and took a long pull of bootleg booze. It burned going down. He coughed. "You find that in a bathtub?"

"Turpentine gives it that special something."

He took another drink, wiped his mouth with the back of his hand, and passed the noxious swill back over. "What do you think I should do?"

"I don't rightly know that myself." Lance was one that understood sacrifice. He had been a self-made man, successful and respected, and he'd given that up to protect Magicals. He'd lost his entire family in the secret war against the Imperium, yet here he was, still fighting, and he would probably keep on fighting until the day he died. "Nobody would blame you if you took off. Not with that kind of heat on your neck."

Quitting was not a concept Sullivan was familiar with. "You know what this place is?"

Lance surveyed the ruins. "I took a look around through the eyes of that poor hungry beast. Tent stakes rusting away in the dirt, shacks in a nice grid all laid out with streets, latrines dug. Feels like a military camp."

"Sort of. Ten thousand men dragged their families here because they tried to collect early on what was promised them. A buck and a quarter for each day served in the war. They were out of work and stupid enough to think that they could get what was theirs before the notes came due. Should've known better."

"Ahh. The Bonus Army."

Sullivan's eyes wandered over the flats where a shanty town had been destroyed. A handful of the people here had been survivors of the 1st Volunteer Active Brigade, just like him. "An army." He snorted. "They were just desperate folks looking for help from a nation that didn't have two nickels to rub together. Congress said no. When the crowd didn't leave, the real Army forced them out with tear gas and tanks, then put the whole damn thing to the torch . . . People got hurt. Kids died."

"Sad day, that."

Sullivan kicked at a rock. "They should've left peacefully when they lost the vote."

"Would you have?"

They both knew Lance already had the answer to that. When a man like Sullivan set a course, it was seen through to the end. "They weren't expecting to be treated like that. I know what they were thinking, the marchers that is. After what they went through in the war, they figured it meant something."

"I was in the war. AEF," Lance said. "Dan was too. We were staff officers, though. That's how we met Pershing. I heard it was much worse for you 1st Volunteer boys."

Sullivan took the flask back and drank some more. It wasn't as awful this pass. "I can't speak for the others, but the 1st . . . We got gassed, burned, bombed, fought demons, undead . . . Jesus, wave after wave of the undead. Slept in the mud, lived in the mud, killed in the mud, froze and died in the mud. Then we had the biggest battle in history, Active on Active, gun, knife, and tooth. Fire in the fucking sky and rivers of blood hip deep for days. We killed a million Germans and scorched Berlin off the map with a Peace Ray. All that for a buck twenty-five a day. We were a hell of a deal."

Lanced helped him keep watch on the Flats as the sun fled. "You know, Jake, I do believe that's the most I've ever heard you say in one sitting. Melancholy renders you downright talkative."

Sullivan shrugged. "I'm Irish."

Headlights illuminated them and a horn buzzed. Dan Garrett had arrived.

"Well, I got a truck bed full of goodies. What do you say we go kidnap an Iron Guard and make a little mayhem?" Lance thumped him on the back. "That ought to cheer you up."

Sullivan took one last look at the remains. They had come looking for a fair shake and had got burned out for their troubles. Life was never fair. Only suckers bought that line. "Maybe you're right about going out to sea, joining Southunder's crew. I can make a new life, quit living under somebody else's boot. Fight the good fight as a free man."

"Sounds mighty tempting when you put it like that."

"Yeah, that's what I'll do . . . *after* we save these ungrateful fucks again."

Dan met them with a firm handshake. Their Mouth didn't look like much, late thirties, soft around the middle, losing his hair, and wearing thick glasses. In his case, looks really were deceiving because Dan Garrett was one dangerous operator. His magic lay in his voice.

"Evening, gentlemen," Dan greeted them.

The Mouths liked to call it Influence. The antimagic groups liked to call it mind control. Whatever it was, Sullivan was glad to have Dan on his team.

"How you feeling?" Lance asked.

"I'm fine." His dark expression gave evidence that he was anything but fine. That raised an interesting question: when a Mouth lied to himself, did he believe it? "Heinrich died fighting. That's how he would have wanted it."

"He wouldn't have had it any other way. Where's Jane?" Sullivan asked.

"She's fixing up the local safe house. It's been empty for a long time."

Lance and Sullivan exchanged a glance. It went unsaid, but they'd both been hoping for her to tag along. A Healer was a mighty valuable person to have around when you take on an Iron Guard. "She okay?"

"You mean, is she still having nightmares from being

kidnapped by Madi?" Dan shook his head. "My wife is far braver than folks give her credit for. No. She wanted to come. I didn't want her to."

"What?" Lance sputtered. "One of us catches a Jap sword and we're gonna be wishing she was here."

"I told her not to come. I lost her once. I didn't want to risk it. Something else maybe, but not when Iron Guards are involved. I put my foot down. I talked her out of coming."

"You talked, or you *talked*?"

That must have stung. "Go to hell, Lance. She's my wife. My decision was made. Briefly anyway. Then she told me to take a hike. She's going to meet us on the way. The woman's stubborn."

Lance grinned. "Looks like you married up in more ways than one."

"Yeah, I know. She's got more guts than I do. Still, I don't want her anywhere near an Iron Guard again, but she'll be tailing close in case one of us gets hurt." Dan pulled a folded paper out of his coat and passed it to Sullivan. "See if you recognize this."

He held the page up to catch the last bit of sun. The drawing was in charcoal. It was a complex spell, far beyond anything he'd been able to pull off. Sullivan was one of the only men alive who had seen the Power as it really was, a living creature shaped from alien geometries, and because of that he recognized a few of the spell's segments, the biological design of the Healer, the interlocking triangles of nuclear forces, even a touch of the hexagram shape of gravity, but as a whole its purposes were a mystery. "Can't say that I do."

"Is it Japanese?" Dan asked.

"Their kanji system is different. Sort of pretty. It's got style. This is . . . I don't know. Where'd you get it?"

"Somebody Browning knows. Turns out we've got a knight on the government payroll. He arranged a drop. I just picked this up from under a mailbox off Pennsylvania Avenue. This is what the assassin had etched on him."

"Bullshit." Sullivan couldn't imagine binding this to a human being without killing them. Even the few little spells he'd etched on himself had taken him to death's door, and he'd done that in secret to keep the others from worrying. His older brother had been one of the strongest men alive, able to wear thirteen Imperium kanji, but none of them had been this big. It would take a monster to survive this binding. "Was the killer Jack Johnson?"

"Radio called him a sickly little man."

"A Grimnoir ring and this *thing*." Lance whistled as he took the paper. He was one of the more talented knights when it came to spellbinding. "Something's fishy. If that's Imperium, and I can't think of anybody else good enough to pull this off, they've got some new toys to play with."

"Russian maybe?"

"Naw. Stalin's wizards are crude. Whoever designed this was an artist."

"Closest thing I've seen to this style was Indian writing. The British brought a few units of them over to fight in the war with us," Sullivan said. "Lance, would you hijack a bird and make sure Dan wasn't tailed."

"Good idea." There wasn't any flash or big show of Power when Lance did his thing. It was only as if he was distracted, like his mind was on something else, which in this case it was. "Got a pigeon. Gimme a minute . . . Looks clear to me."

"So I got a message to deliver. You got any ideas?" Sullivan said.

"Send them a polite letter? Jane's got nice calligraphy." replied Dan.

"I have to do this in person. I've got to convince them." Sullivan replied.

"The ambassador has a compound out in Virginia a ways. There are some mighty big guns in my truck," Lance said.

"I've been doing some poking around, trying to learn about their security and I've got an idea." Dan Garrett shoved his glasses back up his nose. "This may sound a little, well . . . Hear me out first. I think we should walk right in the front door."

Fairfax County, Virginia

DAN GARRETT'S PLAN WAS BRAZEN. They'd gone over it in detail and it still struck Sullivan as a fool's move. Yet, it also made a certain kind of sense. Stealth was out of the question. Maybe if they'd had a Traveler or a Fade, they could have snuck in, but Faye wasn't available for a few days and Heinrich was dead. He didn't know how much time they had, but waiting around for help seemed like a bad idea.

The timing worked. Their informants had said that the ambassador was having a meeting with a group of businessmen, lobbyists, and other various Imperium teat-suckers and hangers on. The folks raking in that fat Imperium money probably wanted to make sure the assassination attempt wasn't their benefactor's doing, and if it was, that it wouldn't hurt the bottom line. Security would be tight because of this, but it would also put a lot of westerners and potential witnesses on the property. That *might* keep things from turning ugly.

At least the Imperium wouldn't be expecting their most hated enemies to show up on the doorstep.

The compound was relatively isolated, and even though the county was crowded with over twenty thousand residents, the Japanese had bought up quite a bit of land to keep it that way. The ambassador's residence was an impressive new construction. Three stories tall, with no expense spared, and designed by some famous architect, it looked like a proper residence for the representative of a rich and growing empire. Surrounded by a twelve-foot brick wall, the property took up several acres, complete with its own small orchard, a fish pond, and a sandbox that it was said the ambassador liked to draw circles in for some odd reason.

Sullivan was riding shotgun while Dan drove the stolen Ford Hyperion. It had been the only vehicle they had access to that was swanky enough to fit in. They pulled onto the lane and rolled toward the gate. Lance was parked a quarter mile back in his truck. Lance was Plan B. Jane was waiting in another car on a different street. An extra getaway vehicle never hurt, plus she could put them back together, provided they lived that long.

Sullivan eyed the men at the gatehouse. They were

Americans, which surely made the neighbors more comfortable. Probably hired guns to keep out anti-Imperium protestors. The real protection would be inside. "You got this?"

"Easy as pie." Dan rolled down his window and applied the brakes. The gateman was dressed in a blue uniform with gold piping. "Good evening," Dan proclaimed. "We're here for the meeting with the ambassador. Please let us through."

Sullivan could feel the slight vibration in his head. The Mouth was pushing hard. Dan's Power wasn't even aimed at him, but the words made Sullivan feel like they were *supposed* to be here.

The gateman blinked a few times, confused. The smarter somebody was, the more difficult they were to Influence. "And you are?"

Dan turned it up, hard. "You've seen us a bunch of times. We're here constantly, real regular visitors. You like us because we tip generously. In fact, I'm tipping you now. You just stuck twenty whole dollars in your pocket. Aren't we swell? Now open the gate."

"Thank you, sir!" the gateman snapped to and hurried for the controls.

Dan rolled the window back up. Sullivan chuckled. "He'll be feeling dumb when he can't find that twenty-dollar bill later."

"He wants a tip? Don't work for the Imperium." The gate rolled open and Dan drove them through. "We think the ambassador was an Iron Guard once, and there should be at least one other one posted here."

"This reliable?"

"General Pershing seemed to think so before he passed away. We were told he was off limits, though. Diplomatic courtesy."

"Odd to be holding a war and still have things like *courtesy*."

"The general wasn't fond of the notion, but we couldn't start openly assassinating their diplomats or they'd start doing it to Americans overseas."

They pulled up in front of the mansion. Ten other cars were parked there already. Many of the nicer automobiles had curtains over the back windows to protect their valuable clients' privacy. Some folks loved taking Imperium money, but they sure didn't want the rest of the world to know about it.

There was something that had been nagging at Sullivan's mind. "Dan, I know you really want to get even for Heinrich, but—"

"I know, I know. Finding out about the Enemy is more important. These are Iron Guard we're talking about, though. What're the odds of us getting out of here without a fight?"

"We're about to find out." Two men approached Dan's window. These were Japanese, wearing black uniforms with the blue sash of the diplomatic corps. Young and fit, well-trained soldiers by the look of them. "Ready?"

"No, but too late now," Dan said. "Lance?"

There was a tiny squeak from inside Dan's shirt that sounded like an affirmative.

One of the guards opened Dan's door and he stepped out. The first guard bowed respectfully toward the Mouth. However there were other figures standing further back in the shadows with their hands inside their uniforms, and they sure as hell weren't bowing.

Dan cleared his throat. "We are here to speak to the ambassador."

The soldier's manner was politely suspicious as he looked Dan over. Daniel Garret didn't look like much of a threat. Then the soldier looked into the car and gave Sullivan the eye. Now *he* looked like a threat. The soldier turned back to Dan and asked, "Who are you, and what is your business here?"

Now came the dangerous part. They had talked it over. Dan's Power was immense, but the more wary the subject, the more difficult it was to Influence him. The goal was to get in to see an Iron Guard, so they'd decided to do something completely crazy.

"We're Grimnoir knights." The first soldier bellowed something in Japanese. A dozen pistols were drawn and pointed their way. Orders were shouted. Runners left to summon reinforcements. The guard at Sullivan's window tapped the glass with the square barrel of a 9mm Nambu. Sullivan took that as an invitation, so he slowly opened the door and climbed out with his hands raised. Dan waited for the commotion to die down before continuing. "We come in peace with a message for your Iron Guard."

"Grimnoir only speak in lies!"

"That's for your superiors to decide," Dan answered. "not you."

"Give me this *message*."

"No."

"I will convey it to them."

"I'll only speak with the ambassador or the Iron Guard."

"You will do as I say or die!"

"We die and your superiors are going to wonder what brought Grimnoir into this nest of snakes, and you won't be able to tell them. Besides, you're not going to shoot us with all those businessmen in there. The ambassador would lose face."

That obviously got under his skin. "I should cut your heads off and decorate the gates with them."

Sullivan decided to be direct. "That bullshit may fly in Manchuria when you're slicing up unarmed Chinamen, but you're in America now."

The first soldier snarled and jammed his pistol into Dan's gut.

"Whoa, easy, pal!" Dan exclaimed. "Jake, would you kindly let me do the talking?"

"When you crossed that gate you stepped onto Imperium soil. Your pathetic ways mean nothing in these walls. Once the Chairman leads us to victory—"

"I thought you said the blue sash meant they were diplomatic?" Sullivan was losing his patience, and there wasn't much to begin with. "Nothing diplomatic about a bunch of punks throwing their weight around."

The soldier left Dan and walked toward Sullivan. "You dare to speak to an Imperium marine in such a way?"

"Yeah, you boys are mighty impressive. I only managed to kill twenty or so onboard the *Tokugawa*, right before I killed my brother, the man you called Madi." There were gasps from the assembled guards. The muzzle of the soldier's gun was pushed against his neck. Sullivan didn't even flinch. "Get your boss. We didn't come here to waste time yakking with the help."

Some of the guards began to argue amongst themselves. Apparently there wasn't protocol in place for dealing with despised Grimnoir knights just showing up and announcing themselves.

"What are you doing, Jake?" Dan slowly asked.

"Diplomacy."

A larger figure appeared in the shadows of the ambassador's house. A harsh command was barked in Japanese. Sullivan didn't speak the language, but it had to be the equivalent to *stand down*, because the guns were immediately lowered. The first soldier stepped back and bowed his head, but kept his hate-filled eyes on Sullivan.

The new arrival stomped into the light. He was extremely tall for a Japanese, probably six foot, and every bit as muscular as Sullivan. Even his humorless face was square from the thick muscles of his jaw. Probably only in his late twenties, he was dressed like a westerner, in a black suit and tie, with the only Imperial affectation being the blue sash of the diplomatic corps. Too small for his face, his eyes were extremely dark and piercingly intelligent. Sullivan could sense the Power on this one. It seemed to hang in the air, dangerous.

The elite of the Imperium forces, each Iron Guard was an Active trained from their youth in brutal schools dedicated to war, then magically augmented with as many spells as their bodies could bear. Between magic, muscle, skill, and training, the Iron Guard were human tanks.

The Iron Guard stopped and gave Dan the once over, then moved on to Sullivan, whom he took the time to size up. "I trained with Madi once. It is obvious you are his blood."

"Folks always said we looked alike, before he lost half his face anyway."

"All of you Americans look the same to me, doughy and clumsy. No, I could tell because you share his loutishness, disrespect toward others, and lack of decorum." He turned to the guards. "Search them."

The pat-down was quick. He'd known that was probably coming and had left his piece with Lance. Thinking of . . . Sullivan looked over, but Dan seemed relatively calm. Lance had already made his move. *Good.*

"I'm Jake Sullivan."

"I know who you are. You are the Heavy that defeated Master Rokusaburo." The Iron Guard actually gave a small bow out of respect. "An impressive feat. He was one of my teachers and a skilled warrior. Nothing would please me more than to test your strength myself, but out of curiosity, I will honor your request for an audience. I am Toru of the Iron Guard, warrior of the Imperium, and servant of the Emperor of Nippon. Please come inside. I welcome you to our home as guests. We shall join the ambassador over tea."

Toru gave more orders in Japanese. The guards formed up, several in front, and several behind, guns still in hand. Toru motioned them toward the entrance. Dan fell in beside Sullivan and they followed.

"Seems like a polite sort," Dan whispered, "for an Imperium killing machine."

"One more thing." Toru paused at the door. "As guests, you need to be aware that if you filthy Grimnoir try anything, I will gladly stomp you like the vermin you are." He nodded politely. "For yes, I am an Imperium *killing machine*. Please do not forget it nor mistake my courtesy for patience. After you."

"Sincere too," Dan said.

The heavy door opened from the inside. It was thick enough to withstand a battering ram. Two more guards bowed to Toru, then stepped quickly out of the way.

Dan whistled. The home was one step below palace. Sullivan had never been to Japan, but could only assume that the ambassador's mansion had been decorated to match the styles of his homeland. Everything was very clean and simple, carved and darkly polished wood, starkly simple paintings, all illuminated by electric light fixtures designed to look like lanterns. He hated to admit that he liked it, as he didn't want to *like* anything from the culture that had spawned the likes of the Chairman and his eugenic evil.

If the goal was to impress visitors with the wealth of the Imperium, they'd certainly succeeded. The mansion was so large that there were rows of trees and an orderly garden planted in a giant room under a long skylight. The center of the place was like a little swath of peaceful forest. Guards watched them from every door and corner as their contingent walked by, many with Arisaka submachine guns slung over their shoulders.

"You sure got a lot of men here, Mr. Toru."

"The embassy is a busy place," their host replied. "Thus we require a sufficiently large diplomatic staff." There had to be at least a platoon of hardened "diplomatic staff" present. It would not have been surprising if it turned out there was an extensive armory somewhere on the property either. This many shock troops could cause quite the ruckus in the capital city if open war were to break out.

The sounds of a noisy dinner came from the other end of the mansion. Toru was leading them away from the ambassador's guests. That wasn't a good sign.

They reached the end of the interior orchard. "Through here."

It was a conference room. A long table was surrounded by plush chairs. The walls were covered with silk screens and images from the history of Japan. Sullivan was tempted to use his Power to feel what was hiding behind those screens, but he could safely assume that it was more men with guns pointed at them, and even the slightest tingle of magic might be enough to set them off. There was a map of the United States on the wall with red pins dotting it, but Toru quickly pulled a silk screen over to block it from view before Sullivan could memorize the locations. Toru gestured toward the table. "Be seated. The ambassador will arrive shortly."

The knights pulled out chairs at one end and sat quietly. Dan was sweating. Sullivan admired the paintings of samurai, funny looking-castles, maidens talking to skinny dragons, and waited. The Iron Guard and his men stood behind them.

The ambassador joined them a minute later. He was very old, thin to the point of being bony, with an impressive mustache that was deftly waxed into points. Since he'd been entertaining guests, the blue sash crossing his suit was covered in medals and ribbons. A guard pulled out the chair at the head of the table. The ambassador sat and placed his hands on the table, looking completely ambivalent about the knight's presence.

The two sides watched each other without speaking. Serving girls in kimonos appeared, set down cups, and filled them with steaming tea. Sullivan had been told the Imperium had a complicated ceremony for drinking tea, but apparently they were skipping the ceremony tonight. The girls fled behind the screens just as silently as they'd come in. Neither Grimnoir drank the tea.

"You are knights?" The ambassador's voice was surprisingly high pitched.

"We are," Dan answered.

"Are you here about the attempt against your president?"

"That depends. Was it you?"

"Your government has already decided that we were not involved."

"They decided the same thing about Mar Pacifica."

The ambassador gave a slight nod. "I have been told that the assassin was a Grimnoir."

"Then you were told wrong."

"You were among those that attacked the *Tokugawa*?"

"We were."

"I see . . ."

The ambassador didn't appear threatening in the least, but if the rumor was correct, then he was, or had been, an Iron Guard, which meant that he was exceedingly dangerous. Most people would have thought of Dan Garrett as innocuous too, but get him motivated and the Mouth could talk you into blowing your own brains out.

The reedy little ambassador probably had something similar up his baggy silk sleeves.

There. It was just the gentlest of nudges in his head. Sullivan could barely feel it, but there was another presence skimming the surface of his thoughts, just testing the waters. Somebody was subtly trying to Read them. The Active must have been behind the screens . . . No. Sullivan recognized the concentration hiding behind the nonchalant mask. The ambassador was a Reader, and he was *good.*

"You admit to attacking the Imperium flagship . . . Yet, you dare come *here*?" The ambassador stroked his moustache thoughtfully. "Tell me why I should not simply have you killed?"

"The Enemy has returned."

"Enemy?"

"The thing that pursues the Power across worlds. We understand the Chairman was something of an expert on it."

The ambassador paused to take a sip of tea. "I was not aware the Grimnoir held such superstitions."

Sullivan spoke. "The Chairman's ghost told me."

Gently, the ambassador set the tea cup down. "Such rumors . . . I'm afraid you are mistaken. The Chairman is in Edo, alive and well as only an immortal can be. It seems you have risked your lives for nothing."

"He told me the Pathfinder is almost here, and that Dark Ocean is the key to stopping it."

The ambassador would have been an excellent poker player. His eyes flicked over to the Iron Guard and then back to them. "How do you know of such things?"

"You're a Reader. See for yourself."

Caught, there was no point in being discreet, and the ambassador used more Power. Sullivan felt the intrusion, but rather than fighting it as instinct demanded, he concentrated on remembering the Chairman's phone call as clearly as possible.

The ambassador must have been well trained to not display any emotions, because he almost pulled it off, but now there was a hint of fear breaking through the mask. He looked to Toru and the guards. "Leave us, all of you." There was a rustling as the Iron Guard shifted nervously and asked something in Japanese. "That is unnecessary. *Leave*."

Toru was obviously distressed over this development, but he did as he was commanded. The Iron Guard gave the order and the troops filed out. Doors slid closed behind the screens.

Once the doors were closed, the ambassador wasted no time in dropping the polite act. "What is the meaning of this?" he demanded.

"You tell us," Dan said.

"I'll have none of your trickery, knight."

"I was there. Your Chairman was blown to kingdom come."

"You will not deceive me. Baron Tokugawa cannot die." He spoke with the fervor of a zealot. "Nothing can harm him."

"He knows," Sullivan said. "You know the Chairman's dead, don't you?"

"I know nothing of the sort."

Dan shook his head. Mouths tended to be good judges

of character, even when they weren't burning Power. "You suspected it, then . . . Look, I don't know what the Imperium's game is, but you need to alert your people or you need to tell us how to take care of this Pathfinder ourselves."

The ambassador may have known the truth, but he wasn't about to reveal weakness to his enemies. "How do you know of the Dark Ocean?"

You know how, Sullivan thought hard. *I'm telling you the truth.*

"The truth, and what is believed to be the truth are seldom the same thing."

"Deny it all you want, but I watched the *Tokugawa* explode myself. I don't need you to admit he's dead. No skin off my nose. But about the Enemy, if I'm wrong, I'm wrong, but if I'm right . . . Then we've got real trouble coming, and it is coming fast."

The ambassador did not speak for nearly a minute. He just glared at them, stroking his mustache and thinking hard. "Let us speak of this Enemy, then."

The Iron Guard closed the door to his chambers and immediately went to work preparing the spell. He had to move quickly.

Toru was not happy. Ambassador Hatori was his superior and as such, Toru was required to obey his orders without question. Even when it seemed the height of foolishness to leave him at the mercy of murderous Grimnoir, Toru had done as he was told, but the ambassador's ultimate welfare was Toru's responsibility and Toru took his responsibilities very seriously.

Grimnoir were foul assassins. Without honor, they chipped away at the Imperium's great mission of purification. They had killed many of his brothers, usually through ambush because they lacked the courage to fight face-to-face as befitted warriors. On several occasions they had even tried to hurt the Chairman himself, which was foolish, because everyone knew nothing could hurt the Chairman. Toru despised the Grimnoir and everything they stood for. Yet now, his friend and mentor was consorting with them as they spoke about the most forbidden of subjects.

He was loyal to the ambassador, but there were two people to whom he owed far greater allegiance: the Emperor, whom he had never even seen, and then the Emperor's advisor, Chairman of the Imperial Council, Baron Okubo Tokugawa, whom he'd had the incredible honor of meeting in person *twice*. Toru did not know what to do, but when the situation concerned the safety of the Imperium, there was no shame in seeking wisdom.

Spell completed, Toru took a step away from the mirror as it flashed with Power. The other side of the glass displayed the Edo Court. Incoming messages from the diplomatic corps always sounded an alarm so it did not take long to get a response. The servant that appeared was of lower standing than an Iron Guard, so Toru did not bother to address him other than to immediately state his report. The servant took the message and disappeared from view. Toru went to his knees and waited. A response could take some time. Hopefully it would not be too late.

Chapter 7

The Japanese troops are unflinching in their duty. Despite being outnumbered five to one, their elite corps of Actives assaulted the Russian fortifications with precise coordination. Never before have I seen men so willing to die to achieve a goal, and more importantly, so willing to die to atone for not achieving that goal. I witnessed a few soldiers who failed their compatriots during the assault, ask permission from a superior and then take their own lives in shame. The Imperial soldier looks upon death in the service of his lord as the singular purpose of his existence.

—Captain John J. Pershing,
Army Observation Report on the taking of Vladivostok, 1905

Fairfax County, Virginia

DAN GARRETT was sweating bullets. Sullivan didn't even look nervous, but then again, he was the tough guy with the Power that was useful for slugging it out inside a house full of Imperium. If Dan had known that one of the

Iron Guards was a Reader, he would never have gone through with this. It was damn near impossible to Influence a Reader. So much for sticking the idea in someone's head and then talking their way out. He was regretting having come up with this idea in the first place.

Though it did seem to be working.

The ambassador placed his hands flat on the table, as if to steady himself. "Tokugawa had long warned us of the coming of this menace. At first, many did not believe his talk of this *predator* from another world. In the years before he became the Chairman, before the emperor realized the greatness and wisdom of—"

"Before he took over Japan?" Sullivan asked.

It was obvious that the ambassador didn't like the Heavy's version of diplomacy. "He did not *take over*. The emperor came to embrace his counsel."

"Whatever."

"Long before he came to the Imperial Court, when the Chairman was merely a lone swordsman wandering the land, was when the first Pathfinder found us. Tokugawa battled it alone. He defeated the creature, but only after an epic struggle. Knowing that, in time, more scouts would come, he began to gather those that also understood the Power to his side. He was the first Active, but he found others nearly as powerful, those who, like him, were bound with the Power when magic was newly arrived to our world. Then he recruited soldiers. He taught us, hardened us, bound us to kanji, because only the strongest would be able to withstand the corrupting magic of the Enemy. A group such as ours was illegal by the Emperor's decree, so we trained in secret. We were few at first, and because

Okubo Tokugawa had been outcast because of his magic, he was only able to recruit from the basest elements—peasants, former samurai who wished to return to ways that the Emperor had outlawed, and even *yakuza.*"

"What's a yakuza?" Dan asked. He'd been practicing phrases in Japanese to use as magical weapons when fighting Imperium troops, but actually learning the complicated language had so far eluded him.

The ambassador pulled back one sleeve to reveal now-faded, once-colorful tattoos that began at the wrist and completely covered his arm. "I read your American newspapers and the talk of your criminals . . . Your *mob.* Let us say that I could have taught this Al Capone a thing or two." He covered the markings. "It is a shameful past to bear, but Okubo Tokugawa did not care about his soldiers' history, he cared only about our ability. You must understand, this was a very unorthodox idea at the time. We chose new names and swore fealty to him, allowing Lord Tokugawa to mold us as he saw fit."

"So the Chairman started a secret society," Dan mused. "Looks like we got more in common than I thought." Sullivan glanced over at him. The Heavy didn't seem to like that idea.

"We were called *Genyosha*. The Dark Ocean."

"Dark Ocean is the key . . ." Sullivan muttered under his breath.

"Another scout came. Dark Ocean lost many warriors, but we defeated the creature. This one had been even stronger than the last. Okubo Tokugawa knew that we had to be more prepared, and that Dark Ocean alone would not be enough. Eventually the Enemy would break through and consume the world. He did not need just one united organization, he needed a united nation, then an empire, and eventually a world. That was his vision. Only through that level of strength and purification could we hope to defeat the Enemy."

"You believe that?"

"Of course." The ambassador seemed honestly surprised at the question. "He was invincible and wise. I pledged my life to him. Most of us did. Dark Ocean became a tool of political manipulation. Many unfortunate things befell our enemies. In a short time, he controlled the Edo Court, and thus became the Chairman. The mission to purify the world began. We started at home, eliminating the weak and raising the strong. Next we took Korea, then China, where we built the schools and began the experiments. Millions have died so far, and millions more surely will follow, but in the end, the world will be strong."

Dan was astounded. "All of the evil things you've done—"

"Are *nothing* compared to what would happen if the Enemy wins. Do you not understand that yet, Grimnoir? Have you never looked into the eyes of a Summoned?"

Dan shook his head in the negative. The things had always made him a little uncomfortable, even the tame ones that Francis had owned. Sullivan leaned forward, intrigued.

"Those broken spirits, those damaged creatures, they are all that remain of the intelligences from the last world the Power inhabited before it fled to ours. They are refugees, dragged along with the Power. That will be the fate of man if the Enemy wins. The Chairman showed us a vision of the last world. It had been magnificent, far beyond our understanding, with cities made of coral, grown as tall as the clouds. But it was all ruined when the Power left them behind to be consumed by the Enemy. I would do anything the Chairman asked to spare us that fate."

Sullivan leaned back in his chair and folded his arms. "How's Dark Ocean the key?"

"I do not know. Dark Ocean is no more. When Okubo Tokugawa became the Chairman, there was no longer a need for us to hide. Dark Ocean was disbanded. We were placed in positions of trust and authority to continue to work on his behalf. It is no more. Our warriors became the first of the Iron Guard, our assassins the first Shadow Guard, those who could read minds or spin words became the diplomats. Few of us remain, and those who live are feeble old men serving as teachers, bureaucrats, or such as I."

"What about the other ones that were nearly as strong as the Chairman? He said they could help us."

"I will not speak of them . . . I have told you enough, Grimnoir. Your message has been delivered. I will communicate it to my superiors and action will be taken. Since you came under a flag of truce, the two of you will be allowed to leave."

"Do your superiors know the Chairman's dead, or does the hoax go all the way to the top?" Sullivan asked.

The ambassador's face turned red. "You try my patience, fool. Pray to your false god that the Chairman still lives, because without him to lead us against the Enemy, we are all doomed."

❖❖❖

Iron Guard Toru waited patiently before the mirror. The Power required to keep the link open was draining, but he would hold it as long as necessary. The Chairman had to be consulted. Toru owed the Chairman his life in more ways than one. It had been the Chairman's mercy that had spared him after his dishonorable actions in China. It had been the Chairman's wisdom that had dispatched Toru to America to learn at the side of the wise and noble Ambassador Hatori.

Most of all, it had been the Chairman who had given him life, for Toru was one of the thousand sons of Okubo Tokugawa. It was prestigious, but much was expected from a warrior who had the very blood of the Chairman pulsing in his heart.

It was a shock when the Chairman himself appeared in all his majesty in the mirror. *The greatest warrior of all time!* Toru nearly choked. It was only the third time he'd ever had the honor of speaking to his father in person. His forehead hit the floor.

"What is this?" the Chairman demanded.

Toru did not dare to lift his eyes as he stammered out his story.

"They said I was dead, did they? You are certain the Grimnoir spoke of Dark Ocean?"

"Yes, but I was not familiar with what they spoke of."

"Then you left them *alone* with Hatori?"

The Iron Guard died inside. He had displeased his father. "As Hatori commanded."

The Chairman was seething. "Listen carefully, Iron Guard Toru . . . Go immediately and kill the Grimnoir. Do not question them or capture them. Kill them."

"Yes, Chairman." He started to rise.

"Wait."

Toru finally dared lift his head a tiny bit. The Chairman was watching him with eyes of fire. Toru quickly looked back down. A small brown mouse was scurrying along the bedroom wall, surely sensing the Chairman's fury and trying to escape. Toru felt as low and pathetic as the rodent. The Chairman did not speak for some time, as if he was pondering a great riddle.

"If I have failed you I will—"

"*Seppuku*? You have a habit of making poor decisions, Iron Guard Toru, but no." Toru was filled with shame at the rebuke. "I have need of you still. Your actions are not what is troubling me. It is this matter before us, but I have made my decision. Your next task will be more difficult. We must assume that Hatori has been influenced by Grimnoir cunning. After you have disposed of them, Hatori must die."

Toru could not believe his ears. He must have heard wrong. "Chairman?"

"Ambassador Hatori is surely influenced by their magic and must be destroyed. Allow him to speak to none of the men. He is not to be trusted. Do you understand, Iron Guard?"

His stomach was sour. Hatori was his mentor. Killing him was unthinkable. "Yes, Chairman. I will do as you command."

"See to it. Summon some of your men."

Toru leapt to his feet. He flung the door open and called out. Within a moment he was joined by two marines. When they saw whom he was speaking to, they dropped to their knees and bowed as deeply as possible.

"You are witnesses to my will. Ambassador Hatori is relieved from command immediately. You will answer only to Iron Guard Toru."

Flustered by the honor of being spoken to directly by the Chairman, the men barely managed to sputter their confirmations.

"Report when it is finished."

The mirror flashed white and the spell was broken.

He had just been asked to kill his closest friend. It was madness. Hatori was a loyal warrior of the Imperium; he would never go over to the Grimnoir. Toru was consumed with doubt, just as he had been when he had last failed the Imperium. *An Iron Guard does not doubt. An Iron Guard acts.* There was no time for thought, no time for hesitation, not when the Chairman had personally given him an order. There was a rack by the door filled with weapons. He picked up his favorite, a steel tetsubo. Toru spun the spiked club through the air. "For the Imperium!"

It took a lot of practice to get the hang of steering a field mouse. The mouse-eye view of the world was radically different and hard to adapt to. Colors faded to a greyish-green; details were fuzzy while the smallest movements or lights became incredible beacons. The faintest smells were incredibly distracting, and his sensitive paws could feel the tiniest of vibrations or variations in the surface, but mostly it was hard to drive a mouse because everything was *huge*. The giant skyscrapers he was running between were small indoor trees. The jungle was a fern. It was hard for a human being to make the shift. It was a good thing that Lance Talon had a lot of practice.

He had picked up the mouse at the Bonus Army camp. Once it was under his control, which was a snap with an animal that had such an itty-bitty brain, he'd stuck the mouse in Dan's pocket. It had taken an amount of Power way out of proportion to the animal's size to keep control, but that was because of the distance involved more than anything.

Controlling an animal was sort of like driving an automobile. You didn't become the car, but you sat in the driver's seat and told it what to do. In Lance's case, he was a much-better-than-average Beastie, and could actually feel through all of the animal's senses. He'd followed his friends into the dragon's den with the goal of keeping an eye on things. When the one Iron Guard had been ordered out, Lance had decided to tail him, and it was a good thing that he had. It was also a good thing that the ambassador didn't own a cat.

The little animal's heart beat at an insane rate as Lance forced the little legs to keep moving. He could feel the rapid drumming as if it was his own.

Lance's conscious mind was in two places, and while the part that was in the mouse ran to warn Dan and Jake about the Iron Guard coming to club them to death, the rest of him was pulling the canvas cover off the new 5-inch Stokes mortar that had been bolted down in the bed of his truck.

"Maybe we should be going now . . ." Dan Garrett whispered to his friend.

But Sullivan still had questions. He was a man who collected questions like kids collected baseball cards. "I want to know more about how this Pathfinder creature works." It was obvious that the Heavy didn't trust the Imperium to take care of business.

"Do not trouble yourself with things beyond your comprehension." The ambassador was a crafty one. He'd told them much, but wasn't about to give up anything that would make the Grimnoir more capable foes. "I am done with you. I must return to dine with your countrymen who are more than willing to assist the Imperium's goals as long as there is gold involved. Your country rots from the inside out. Perhaps I have been a diplomat for too long and forgotten the ways of the Iron Guard, but because you came under a flag of truce, though it pains me, protocol demands that I *must* allow you to leave in peace."

Dan breathed a huge sigh of relief. It looked like he wasn't going to have to try to Talk their way out after all.

"That was a most difficult decision. When we meet again, I will not be merciful. In fact, now that I know that any of you somehow survived the *Tokugawa* means that you will be inevitably hunted down and exterminated." The ambassador stood. Though he was withered and aged, the old warrior still carried himself with pride. He clapped once. The doors opened and the soldiers filed back in. "See them out. Keep them away from the guests."

Dan was hauled roughly to his feet by the guards. It was degrading, but he was glad to be leaving. Avenging Heinrich could wait until they weren't outnumbered ten to one. When Sullivan didn't get up fast enough for them, one of the guards grabbed Sullivan's arm, but the Heavy just shrugged the man off. Subguns were leveled his way and bolts were retracted. Dan could appreciate his companion's stubbornness, but sure wished that he was better at knowing when to pick his fights.

Sullivan took his time standing up. "Make sure your superiors listen, ambassador. I'd hate to have to come back here."

"An Imperium man does not have fear . . . except for this Enemy. It will be done." The ambassador walked for the exit. The guards formed a protective line between him and the Grimnoir. "Farewell." He paused and looked down at his foot as something tiny and brown leapt across his shoe. "What's this?"

"Incoming!" the mouse shouted with a surprisingly loud voice.

Grabbing his Power, Dan opened his mouth to shout one of the Japanese phrases he'd been practicing, but before he could get the words out, Sullivan thrust one hand out and caught him by the wrist. Suddenly gravity *bent*. The table and chairs tumbled away and the room's occupants were airborne.

He had never been on the receiving end of one of Sullivan's gravity manipulating tricks before. Dan found himself dangling by one arm, only kept from being flung across the room by Sullivan's grasp. Down was *wrong*. Instead of being on the ground where it always was, it was somewhere behind him, where the Imperium marines were crashing through the silk screens. It was disorienting, like the most effective carnival fun house ever, only there wasn't anything funny about gravity being violated. It was frankly terrifying.

Sullivan released his Power and down returned to being down. Dan hit the floor at Sullivan's feet with a grunt. He'd done better than the Imperium men, who had been spread across the room. The Heavy wasted no time yanking him up. "Run for it."

Lance's mouse had an easier time disentangling himself than the humans. The little thing stopped in the doorway ahead of them. "Iron Guard headed your way. The Chairman ordered him to pop you. I've got—"

A polished dress shoe squished the mouse flat.

"You again," Sullivan said.

Dan looked up to see Toru standing in the doorway blocking their escape. The Iron Guard was holding a gigantic four-foot-long metal club in one hand. He surveyed the damage, said something in Japanese to the guards that had landed on the ambassador, then pointed his club at Sullivan's chest and shouted another order. He stepped forward, swinging, but Sullivan used his Power and the Iron Guard was hurled back. The club tore a big chunk out of the wall as Toru tried to catch himself, but then he spun through and disappeared from sight. Sullivan charged right after him.

"Jake!" The guards were getting up. Dan spied one of the weird Jap subguns and snatched it off the floor. He kicked the closest Imperium man in the face for good measure. "Shit!" Dan ran after the Heavy as a guard started firing pistol bullets right over his head.

Somebody had just stomped him and all his guts had exploded out his side. The pain was astounding, but it only lasted for a split second.

The real Lance Talon came back to consciousness lying on the cold bed of his truck, a mortar round still clutched in his hands. The sensation had overpowered both parts of him and put him flat on his back. There were certainly some disadvantages to being able to use *all* of the animal's senses. Luckily the feeling went away as soon as the link did, because it was something you never got used to.

Lance found his pocket watch and opened it. He'd inscribed the spell on the glass earlier. This wasn't taking too much Power because it was only to one other person, and she was nice and close. The glass showed nothing but black. "Jane! You there?"

She must have adjusted her mirror, because a pretty face swung into view. "I'm here."

"Your husband will be needing a ride right quick."

Jane started her car. "I'm on the way."

"Good. Be careful." He closed the watch and stuffed it back in his coat. "Because if you aren't, Dan's liable to come apart at the seams," Lance muttered to himself.

The Imperial compound was approximately five hundred yards away, on the other side of a copse of trees, out of sight, but well within range of the Stokes mortar. He'd carefully prepped the powder charges, preloading each of the rings at the base of the shells, and as long as he hadn't totally screwed up the aiming calculations (the instruction manual had told him 56 degrees for this range) the rounds should impact relatively close. At least the Imperium didn't have any neighbors he might accidentally hit.

The truck box was tall, and at his height he could move around in the back with just a slight crouch. Nobody passing by would realize this was anything more than just a regular old box truck. The instructions had warned that the recoil was *firm*, so he'd bolted the Stokes down, cut the truck box's roof off, and called it good. The Grimnoir now had field artillery.

Lance hadn't fired one of these things since the war. This new one didn't look too impressive, just a big pipe on a tripod, with a couple of gears for fine adjustments. *How bad could it be?* He dropped the shell down the tube, then covered his ears just in case. The recoil rocked the truck springs. The blast was impressive enough to knock his hat off. "Hot damn! That's the stuff!"

He reached for his Power and felt his surroundings for life. Living creatures stood out, like glowing blobs on a map that stretched for half a mile in every direction. The bigger animals were brighter, and the smaller ones faint, each kind with their own certain color. Some horses, cows . . . a dog . . . *There.* A bunch of fast movers. The blast had shocked a flock of blackbirds out of a nearby tree and into the air. Lance grabbed one. The simple animal's brain was shoved to the back, and then Lance was flying.

Gaining altitude, he pointed his beak toward the Imperium compound. One nice thing about birds was that they *always* had a good sense of direction. Amazing vision too. Lance couldn't explain the science behind their eyes, but they saw colors that he couldn't even explain to other people because man had never invented words for them. The mansion was easy to spot from a hundred yards up. He enjoyed the sensation of the wind and waited for the shell to hit.

A few more seconds passed before impact. There was a shower of sparks as the shell struck the outer wall of the compound and burst. A cloud of noxious chemical smoke began to belch forth. Lance let go of the bird so that he could have all of his brain to work with. He was a bit off, so he grabbed the elevation wheel and moved it two clicks. The smoke bombs had been made for laying down cover for the troops to advance across no-man's-land during the war, and they put out a lot of smoke, so Lance figured they should make a real good distraction for Jake and Dan.

But once he got sign that they were out, then he'd start tossing the *good* stuff.

Toru fell into the atrium. He was not worried, having trained against *Omosa* before, or Heavies as they were called in America, including the legendary Iron Guard Madi, and knew the key to defeating one was keeping your wits. As gravity changed direction, he would have to adapt quickly. Like now for example, he was *falling*, yet remained parallel to the ground, so he tried to keep his body oriented so that the inevitable return to normal would not cause injury or place himself in an indefensible position. A skilled Heavy often overwhelmed his foe through sheer confusion, but an Iron Guard with the proper mindset would not be fooled by such tricks. Toru reached the end of gravity's distortion and landed on his feet, skidding through the imported topsoil.

Several marines were running toward the commotion. Toru had not even come to a stop before he was shouting orders. "Bind the ambassador. He has been corrupted by Grimnoir magic." The men were confused by his command, but they would obey without question. Then the Heavy ran into the atrium, looking for a fight. The two warriors spotted each other and Sullivan charged. "The big Grimnoir is mine!"

Gravity changed again, hard to the side. It was not like being hurled by a Mover. There was no pushing, not even a sensation of being pulled, just that the thing you had understood as gravity your entire life was now aimed someplace else. Toru kept his mind clear and caught himself on one of Hatori's prized maples. He held on as dirt and leaves rushed past. The marines did not fare as well and hit the wall hard. One crashed through a window.

The Heavy was wasting his Power on tricks. Toru had yet to display his own Power. The tactical advantage was his. The Heavy would not know what to expect, and would probably be too slow to adapt. The Iron Guard's stomach lurched as gravity returned, and he landed in a crouch. The atrium was filled with a dusty cloud as the disturbed topsoil fell. Sullivan was coming his way with a determined look on his face. After such displays of magical prowess, it should take the Heavy a moment before he could distort gravity again. Toru activated his magic and felt his physical strength increase tenfold. With a roar, he launched himself out of the garden and across the space. He covered twenty feet in the blink of an eye and lifted the tetsubo overhead as he descended, prepared to crush the Heavy.

Sullivan did not so much as show surprise at the display. Gravity lurched and Sullivan dodged to the side as if he weighed nothing. The steel tetsubo smashed a gigantic hole in the hardwood floor. Gravity betrayed Toru again, and he found himself rolling across the floor.

The Heavy was catching his breath. "So you're a Brute."

"Yes." The Iron Guard rose. "You should not be able to use your Power so quickly."

"Lots of practice."

"Know that you face Iron Guard Toru, one of the thousand sons of Okubo Tokugawa!"

"That's gonna be nine hundred and ninety-nine sons if you don't get out of my face."

Toru came in swinging. His weapon was so heavy that most men would have a hard time even lifting it, yet he swung the steel tetsubo faster than most Iron Guard could wield a katana. It covered a vast arc with each movement, and anything it struck would be obliterated. Sullivan moved back, trying to stay ahead of the club. The Heavy had to be making himself lighter, because there was no way a man of that stature could be so quick—

Toru flinched as Sullivan threw a handful of soil into his eyes. Then a big fist caught him square in the nose. Sullivan had stepped inside the swing and actually *hit* him. Toru stepped back, blinking. Sullivan followed, and managed to strike him several more times. Toru's Power made his tissues incredibly resilient, but he felt each of the blows. It was like being hit with a sledgehammer. Toru ducked around the next attack. Years of training caused him to react without conscious thought, and he slammed one open palm into Sullivan's ribs. The shock up his forearm was like hitting a rock.

Sullivan sailed back, but somehow landed on his feet. Toru's Power-fueled strike should have shattered all of his ribs and pulped most of his internal organs, but the Heavy only grimaced and pressed his hand to his side. Only another Brute or a Massive could have taken such a blow. "Impossible. How do you live?"

"Like I said . . . practice."

Toru rubbed his eyes with the back of his hand, trying to clear his clouded vision. Seeing was very difficult, but no matter, he could see well enough to destroy this obnoxious Heavy. He lifted the tetsubo. This time he would not strike with reckless abandon, but rather he would break the Heavy with precision. Sullivan must have sensed the careful shift in strategy, because he turned and ran for the ambassador's garden. "Coward!" Toru followed.

But Sullivan was not trying to get away, and once between the trees, he stopped, raised his hands, and waited.

Clever. The Heavy was trying to neutralize the reach advantage of the tetsubo. However, it would not work. The biggest tree there was only as big around as Toru's leg. With a burst of Power, Toru cleaved his tetsubo through the growth. Trunks burst into splinters and barely slowed the club. Sullivan retreated as Toru destroyed everything in his path.

The ambassador's guests had been frightened by the noise and spilled out of the dining room to see what was going on. These men—business leaders and elected officials—were valuable assets for the Chairman's plans. Having them witness this spectacle was not beneficial at all. And worse, he spotted the other Grimnoir running right into the crowd of guests and yelling crazily at them. Toru could feel the impressive Power from here. "Seize the fat one!"

There was a noise as the glass ceiling of the atrium shattered. Something hit the far wall and coughed golden sparks. Grey smoke hissed out in a pressurized jet. *What?*

The distraction cost him. He looked away just as he cleaved a stout maple in half, and branches crashed down, temporarily entangling his tetsubo. Simultaneously, Sullivan surged his Power, and Toru found himself weightless. He had never experienced such a thing before. Surprised, he jerked on the trapped tetsubo to hold himself from floating away, except his Brute strength caused him to overcompensate. His legs flew into the air, then he was upside down and doing everything he could just to hang on.

Sullivan used the opportunity to nonchalantly pick up an entire fallen tree. The Heavy shouldered it like it was his own tetsubo and then he smashed the trunk into kindling against Toru's body. The Iron Guard barely had time to flare his Power to protect himself as he sailed across the atrium. He crashed into a support pillar hard enough to shake the entire mansion.

It took him a moment to clear his head. The atrium was filled with noxious smoke. Sullivan was nowhere to be seen, nor was the other Grimnoir. Toru ignored his injuries, knowing that his four Healing kanji would keep up, and surged to his feet. Many of the guests were throwing fits, even struggling against his marines.

An American congressman and a mine owner had wrestled one of his men to the ground and were shouting at the poor confused warrior.

"How dare you Nip bastards rip us off!"

"Take that!" The congressman began choking the marine.

Toru tried to be gentle as he booted the two Americans off. The congressman futilely tried to punch Toru, so Toru slapped some sense into him, then picked him up by the neck. "What is the meaning of this?"

"The Chairman was going to pay us with fake gold!"

Toru tossed the American into the garden. The other Grimnoir must have been a Mouth, and he'd gone right for this type of fool's biggest weaknesses, greed and fear. He did not have time to sort this out. "Try not to hurt them," he told the marine. "The magic will wear off soon."

The Iron Guard took up his tetsubo and ran for the front. The Grimnoir would be trying to escape. He might be able to cut them off. Toru turned to the side, flared his Power, and crashed through a window. The sharp glass slashed his clothing, but was unable to cut his magically toughened skin. He rolled across the lawn, then sprinted for the parking area with speed that only a Brute could muster. Thick smoke filled the entirety of the compound.

Luckily, the knight's automobile had not left yet. Toru reached it, stuck his hands into the wheel well, surged his Power hard, lifted the huge car and rolled it over onto its roof. They wouldn't be getting out that way.

"Iron Guard," a breathless marine ran up to him. "The Grimnoir have climbed over the back wall."

Another mortar round whistled in. This one hit the roof of the mansion. It must have been an incendiary because fire quickly spread across the shingles.

Toru roared in fury. *Damned Grimnoir!* "Put that fire out. Make sure the ambassador is secure. Lock him away and let no one speak to him. Get the guests under control, but do not hurt them . . ." The furious Iron Guard slammed his tetsubo into the upside-down car. The impact crushed the fender, threw one tire across the compound, and sent the whole vehicle slowly turning. "And retrieve my car!"

A blue Chrysler screeched to a halt on the road ahead. Jane had the window down. "Dan! Over here."

Dan Garrett was huffing and panting. Sullivan had pushed him over the back wall and then the two of them had hightailed it through the forest behind the Imperium's property. He had never been much for running. In college, he had been the football *announcer*. It was best to leave all that physical stuff to the boys that looked like Sullivan.

But at that moment, Jake wasn't looking too good either. He kept one hand pressed to his side and his breathing was labored. Dan knew that it had to be bad if *he* was easily outrunning Jake. "Come on. Almost there." They reached the automobile. "Honey, let me drive. Jake needs your help."

"Darn right he does. He's got a punctured lung!"

Sullivan fell into the back, Jane scrambled over the seat, and Dan got behind the wheel. He put it into gear and got them rolling. It would have been nice to keep that monster race car Sullivan had brought as their getaway car, but it was distinctive and would have stood out. It was ten o'clock at night, so there wasn't much traffic in this rural area—there were a lot more cleared lots than homes—but there would be more cars to blend in with the closer they got to town.

Dan concentrated on the curving country road while his wife took care of Sullivan. The rearview mirror suddenly filled with a squat bearded face. "Hey."

"Ah! Don't do that," Dan said.

"You deliver your message?" Lance asked.

"Sure did. Managed to wreck the place in the process. I convinced all those rich boys that the Chairman was swindling them. They must have had the possibility in the back of their minds because I didn't even have to push hard."

"Where's Sullivan?"

"Down here." Sullivan was lying on the back seat. "A Brute stomped a mud hole in me and walked it dry."

"Hush while I work, Jake," Jane ordered. "Good thing you've got that Healing spell on you or you'd be drowning in your own blood right now . . . Wait . . . *More* spells? Whatever have you been up to?"

Before Sullivan could answer, Lance shouted, "You got company!" Dan couldn't see anything. "Car is going to catch you at the next intersection. Turn it around." Lance must have grabbed an owl.

"You sure it's Imperium?"

"There's a guy riding on the running board with a machine gun. I don't recall Virginians being *that* inhospitable."

"Shoot," Dan hit the brakes. There was a ditch on one side and trees on the other. There was no good spot to turn around. He shifted into reverse. "Hang on."

"That Iron Guard didn't strike me as a quitter," Sullivan said.

Dan backed into the tree line, cranked the wheel, and then got them going back the way they came. He gunned it, but it would take a minute to get up to speed. There were headlights in the side mirror. "Here they come." He watched the speedometer climb too slowly and found himself wishing that they'd kept that Hyperion.

The back window shattered. The Imperium had opened fire. Dan took them around a long curve and out of view. The shooting let up momentarily. His wife reached over and picked up the Thompson that had been occupying the passenger seat. Dan's throat was tight. He had to get them out of here. He had to keep Jane safe.

The road straightened back out. The Imperium would be able to see them again. The Japanese machine gun opened up with a ponderous rate of fire. Red tracers flew past, and then another round hit. Stuffing flew from the passenger seat. Then the glass in front cracked. Jane answered and let the Thompson rip. The headlights behind them swerved side to side, but the flashes from that machine gun kept up. Then the side mirror exploded and Dan couldn't watch anymore.

"There's a fork ahead," Lance shouted through the magical link. "Bear left."

"That's the wrong way," Dan said.

"Do it!"

The road split into a *Y*. Dan swore and went left, which was taking them further out into the country, and even worse, into open farmland where they wouldn't be able to shake their pursuers. "You better know what you're doing, Lance!"

Iron Guard Toru pulled the spent magazine from the top of the Type-70 light machine gun and let it clatter down the road behind them. The marine in the passenger seat handed him another magazine of 8mm ammunition through the window. Toru rocked it into place and yanked back the bolt.

The car swerved as the Grimnoir returned fire. A normal man probably would have been thrown from the side, but all it did to Toru was upset his aim. That, the bumpy road, and the insects hitting him in the face were making this a challenge. "Hold steady!" Toru ordered.

The lights of the Grimnoir auto veered to the left, so he rested the Type-70 across the edge of the roof and squeezed the trigger, trying to walk the tracers into the moving target. One of the red taillights went out and his magically augmented hearing recorded the metallic clangs of puncturing metal.

The Grimnoir were fools. He had scouted the surrounding countryside during the construction of the ambassador's home. There was nowhere for them to hide in this direction. He would cut them to ribbons.

The Type-70 only had a 30-round magazine, and he burned through it in seconds. He tossed that mag and stuck his hand in the window for another. He'd barely finished reloading when he looked up to see a large black cow running into the road. It stopped, silhouetted in their headlights. He could have sworn that the cow looked right at them and *winked*.

The driver hit the brakes and tried to turn, but he was too late. They hit the cow at nearly sixty miles an hour. The front of their car crashed into the solid animal. Toru flared his Power to hold on, but the aluminum handrail he'd latched onto tore through the sheet metal like paper.

He hit the road nearly eighty feet away, traveling fast, and smashed against the asphalt, bounced a few times, then rolled. The Power draw was intense, and he did his best to keep it up, but there were limits to even Brute toughness and he felt bones break and muscles tear as he gradually flopped to a stop.

It took Toru nearly ten seconds to collect himself. His four Healing kanji were all burning Power, desperately trying to fix his ruined body. He groaned and got to his feet. The machine gun was gone. The Grimnoir's remaining taillight disappeared in the distance.

Toru muttered an oath that was far beneath the station of an Iron Guard.

Leaving a trail of blood from several deep lacerations, Toru weaved back to the wreck. One marine had been thrown through the window and into a field, and the driver had broken his skull against the steering wheel. Fluids were pouring from the engine. Their car was not going anywhere.

Somehow the accursed black cow was still alive, though not for long. All her legs were obviously broken, but she still managed to lift her bloody head to look at him with surprising intelligence. The farm animal then spoke to him with a voice like that of an American movie cowboy. "Didn't see that coming, did ya, asshole?"

They had a Beastie. "Damn your foul animal magic, Grimnoir."

"This link *really* hurts to keep up, but I just love to see the smug get wiped right off an Iron Guard's face." The cow laughed at him.

Iron Guard Toru limped over and punched the cow to death.

❖❖❖

The fire had been put out by the time Toru walked back to the compound. Someone must have reported the commotion because a fire truck and a police car were stopped at the main gate. He was glad that the guards had followed protocol and not let any of the local authorities through. The identity of their guests had to be protected at all costs. Having such American business luminaries show up in the newspapers as consorting with the Imperium would be an embarrassment to them and a blow to the Chairman's mission of infiltration and conquest.

Toru's clothing was mostly destroyed, and though his wounds had sealed on their own, he was covered in drying blood. To avoid any entanglements with the American authorities, Toru had simply leapt over the back wall. The men could handle the police. His mind was preoccupied, dwelling on the horrible duty that he had to confront.

The captain of the guard gave him a brief report. The man was still flustered from having actually been addressed by the Chairman. Now that the Mouth's Influence had finally worn off, the guests were regaining their composure. The American police had been told that the fire was an accident, everything was under control, and that attempting to investigate the ambassador's residence would cause an embarrassing diplomatic incident. Of course, they already had an agreement with the locals, so the predetermined amount of gold had exchanged hands. Ambassador Hatori had been secured as ordered. Toru inquired if anyone had spoken with the ambassador, and was told that the ambassador had not said a single word as they had led him away. Toru was glad to hear that, because he had not been looking forward to having to kill any other acquaintances tonight.

After dispatching the captain to gather the bodies from the scene of the *accident*, the Iron Guard went inside. The beautiful atrium was totally destroyed. Hatori's meticulously tended garden had been torn to pieces and spread across the entire building. It filled Toru's heart with sadness. Master Hatori had been very fond of this space. It had been his connection to their beloved homeland and favorite meditation area. The Heavy would die painfully for the slight.

Hatori had been secured in one of the unadorned rooms. Guards had been posted to keep watch, and they bowed as he approached. Toru paused at the door to steel his resolve and found himself staring at the tetsubo in his hand. He could not comprehend the reasoning behind the Chairman's command, but it was not the place for an Iron Guard to question his betters. The Chairman's word was absolute law. Whether his transgressions were real or imaginary, Hatori still had to die for them.

However, Hatori had been a good teacher, a fierce warrior, and in his old age a cunning diplomat, always representing the Imperium with honor. He deserved better than to be clubbed down like some nuisance peasant. Surely the Chairman would understand, since his teachings centered on the importance of honoring the strong. Decision made, Toru returned to his quarters to retrieve a few items. When he returned, he was able to enter Hatori's prison with head held high. This felt more like the correct path.

His teacher was kneeling on a mat, waiting patiently.

Toru did not address him. Hatori looked Toru over, saw the sword he was carrying and understood. "So this is how it ends, then?"

"As the Chairman commands."

"The thing you spoke to is not the Chairman. Okubo, my old friend, is dead."

Toru did not believe him. The Chairman was immortal. Perhaps Hatori had gone mad.

Hatori let out a long breath. "Am I allowed an explanation for my actions?"

"I am not allowed to hear."

"In the beginning, we fought the true Enemy. Then things changed . . . We changed. I fear that a false leader has taken control of the Imperium. I am afraid it is someone who does not understand what is truly at stake."

"Please stop."

"Very well. You always were a good student, Toru. I never had sons of my own. If I had, I'd have very much liked them to turn out like you."

Toru gently placed the silk package on the floor in front of Hatori's knees. "Know that I bear you no ill will. This way is better."

Hatori opened the silk to reveal the tanto knife. "Thank you." He seemed genuinely moved as he took up the blade and ran his thumb down the razor edge. "Would you be my second?"

Toru placed one hand on the wrapped hilt of the katana that had been presented to him upon achieving the rank of Iron Guard. "I would be honored."

The ambassador removed his shirt and set it aside. His chest was covered in layers of markings. The oldest layer was the faded tattoos of his criminal upbringing, next were his Iron Guard kanji, bestowed by the Chairman's Cogs, and the final layer was made of scars earned in countless battles on behalf of the Imperium. Hatori took the knife and placed the tip against this abdomen. "Please understand that I would never betray Okubo Tokugawa. I do not wish to be remembered as a traitor."

Toru drew his sword and took it in both hands. "Of course."

"I'm afraid you will understand what I speak of soon enough."

Hatori shoved the knife deep into his guts. The muscles of his face did not so much as twitch as he dragged it through his flesh. Blood poured from the wound. When the blade had cut all the way across, Hatori shuddered, his shoulders slumped, and his hand dropped the tanto into the spreading pool of red. Toru raised his katana overhead.

"No . . . I think you should understand *now*."

A spike of terrible agony ripped through Toru's head. Hatori used up all of his considerable Power in one mighty burst. Toru stumbled back, holding his head in his hands. It felt as if his brains were about to boil out his ears. Streams of information, strange memories, new images . . . They were crashing about, trying to make a new home in Iron Guard Toru's mind. "What have you done to me?"

"What . . . I had . . . to." Hatori bowed his head. "Forgive me. I am finished."

Already, his head had cleared. Toru moved in one fluid strike. It was considered shameful to remove the head completely from the body when serving as second, so he was careful to pull the stroke at the last instant, leaving just enough skin at the throat so that Hatori's head did not fly off. Instead, it rolled neatly into the ambassador's lap. The body remained kneeling as if in mediation.

It was a respectful end for a respected man.

Toru

Chapter 8

When Jack Johnson manhandled Tommy Burns and took the world heavyweight boxing championship back in '08, a cry went up across the land, for it was inconceivable that a Negro could hold such a prestigious title. Jack London made a desperate plea for a Great White Hope and for the next few years, every strapping, well-muscled white lad in the country was in danger of being shanghaied by desperate promoters to be thrown into the ring against the Galveston Giant. Johnson whipped them all. After he defeated former champ James Jeffries in the Fight of the Century two years later, we got real desperate. Brutes had been banned from boxing for twenty years, and for good reason since no mortal man could survive a punch from one of those Active savages. But for Johnson, out there lording it over us with his white women, we made an exception. Strings got pulled, money changed hands, officials looked the other way, and we snuck in our Brute assassin. The poor dumb Brute thought we were actually giving him a shot at the title. Hell, when he was sober, Bill Jones could lift a horse over his head. He crippled the champ for life thirty seconds into the first round. The referee stopped it when he saw our boy was magic, but

Jack Johnson's career was done for. We disqualified our stooge for using magic and kicked that freak of nature to the curb. We did what we had to do. Got to keep the sport pure, you know.

—Al Fitzsimmons,
New York State Commissioner of Boxing,
death bed confession, 1914

Dallas, Texas

THE WEATHER had not been in their favor and the UBF passenger dirigible had made lousy time. An hour before sunrise, they had finally landed at the biggest dirigible station in Texas, just in time to catch the local newspaper hot off the presses. The subject of the front page hadn't been surprising, but the other names mentioned in the article sure were. Faye had always thought it would be kind of fun to see her name in print in an actual big city newspaper. It turned out that it wasn't fun at all. Especially when your name was just there to say that the police were looking for you.

Faye could read and write pretty well now, she'd taken to it quick, but Mr. Browning read the interesting bits out loud for all of them while they waited for their breakfast. Mr. Sullivan was wanted for having shot down a bunch of policemen in New Jersey after they tried to question him about the plot to kill the president. *What a bunch of bunk.* Faye's name was on the list of people who might know something and were wanted for questioning, as was Mr. Garrett. She didn't recognize any of the other names, but could only assume that they were other knights she hadn't met yet. Next to each of the names was a brief description that was quick to mention what their Power was. The reporter didn't come out and say that a bunch of Actives were trying to take over the government, but he sure did manage to insinuate it.

Four of the knights were sitting around a table in the big diner inside the air station. The other two were sitting at opposite ends of the counter, with Mr. Bolander having to sit way over in the Coloreds section. That really bothered Faye, since Mr. Bolander was smart as anybody else and perfectly nice, but he seemed resigned to it.

Mr. Bryce sat by the door to keep an eye on who came and went, watching people over the top of his newspaper. That seemed smart. Faye decided that she'd better learn to start thinking like a fugitive. Those two men had come from the same group of East Coast Grimnoir, just as Whisper and Ian had come from the same group that worked somewhere in Europe.

"Anything else?" Ian asked.

"Only if you read between the lines," Mr. Browning answered patiently. "We know they're aware of Francis, but they fail to mention him here. They know more than they are releasing to the press. How much more is the question."

"Is this an attempt to rattle us?" Whisper asked. Faye loved how Whisper spoke English. It was like you took all the S sounds and held onto them just a little too long. It seemed rather *mysterious*. When she wasn't so busy trying to save the world, Faye decided she would have to go and visit Paris sometime.

"I believe so," Browning replied. "I recognize a few

of these other names. All knights, and all with some measure of public success. Dan Garrett, for example, is remembered by many from his radio days. Dr. Rosenstein is a prestigious surgeon in Chicago. Or they have a distinguishing physical feature, such as young Faye. In short, these are knights that will be recognized by the public."

The waitress brought their food. Faye immediately dug into her plate of hash browns and eggs. She was starving. Mr. Browning reached under the table and touched her knee gently. At first she'd thought that she'd had yet another breech of polite-folk manners—of which she was still trying to figure out all the many little details—but when she glanced up, Mr. Browning just looked her in the eye and tilted his head down slightly. *Huh?* Mr. Browning closed his eyes for just a moment too long, then nodded toward the door. A policeman had come into the cafe.

Her grey eyes . . . Of course. The newspaper had said she was a Traveler. Everybody knew Travelers had grey eyes, and since Travelers were so very rare anyways, a young female Traveler would stand out especially bad. Faye kept her head down, and went on eating in the most nonsuspicious way possible, which was more difficult than it sounded.

The policeman sat on a stool two seats over from Mr. Bryce and loudly ordered a coffee. Mr. Bryce, who struck Faye as a particularly dangerous man, subtly kept one eye on the policeman even while he appeared to be focused on eating his pancakes. The cafe was crowded enough that their table of four did not stand out, but Mr. Browning lowered his voice anyway. "Things are more complicated than we suspected."

"Somebody from the *Minotaur* is bound to remember her as soon as they read this," Ian suggested. "They'll be watching the air stations now. We need to get out of here."

Mr. Browning nodded. "You are correct, sir . . . Faye, there is really no need to inhale your food. Finish as you normally would."

"Sorry," she mumbled with a very full mouth.

"We will procure automobiles and split up. I shall continue on to Florida to research the identity of the assassin. Mr. Bryce will accompany me because he is a trained criminal investigator. The rest of you will rendezvous with Mr. Talon in Virginia."

That made Faye uncomfortable. She didn't know these new knights very well, and in particular really didn't like Ian much at all. That was an *awful* long time to be stuck in a car with somebody that thought Harkeness and Rawls were heroes . . . Not murdering Ian for that long might be *really* hard. "Me too?"

"Yes, my dear. I would love the pleasure of your company, but I believe that taking one of the individuals on the persons of interest list to the scene of the crime would be unwise. Besides, with all of these dealings with Iron Guards, your rather direct abilities will certainly be of much greater value to Mr. Sullivan and Mr. Talon."

That made her proud. Nobody was better at killing Imperium than Sally Faye Vierra.

"This should be pleasant." Whisper rummaged through her enormous purse for a moment until she found a pair of sunglasses. She passed the cheaters to Faye under the table. "I for one enjoy a good road trip."

Unknown Location

AS ALWAYS, his nightmares were of zombies.

The memories would haunt him forever. The death madness consumed even the best of men eventually, until they were nothing more than ravenous maniacs, driven only by pain that could not end and a hunger that could never be sated. His bad dreams were always of the chase, running through the crumbling alleys and broken buildings, hiding in sewers and crawl spaces, sleeping precariously on ledges where the undead could not cross without waking him, for if he was not careful in picking where to lay his head, then he would surely be awoken by teeth.

A boy had to be clever if he expected to survive for long in Dead City. He must be quick to decide and even quicker to act. Yet, his every move must be tempered with wisdom, because in the decaying hell that had been Berlin, one wrong choice would be your last. Always outnumbered, but never outwitted, he had grown to manhood in the festering pit. Only the smartest of the living lasted long inside the confines of the Berlin Wall, and the greatest compliment that could be given amongst them was *survivor.*

And Heinrich Koenig was a survivor.

He woke up chained to a wall but could not remember how he'd gotten there. Steel shackles encircled his wrists. Shackles meant nothing to a Fade, but when Heinrich tried to go grey, to drift the molecules of his body through his bindings, nothing happened. His Power was there, but it would not answer to him.

Curious.

Heinrich took stock of his surroundings. The room was windowless and constructed of crumbling brick. A single weak bulb hung from the low ceiling. It was very dark. There was a single door made of thick boards and the hinges were on the other side. There was no doorknob on his side. He tested the chains. They were substantial and went through holes that had been cut in the wall. When he tugged, there was no give. The chains were solidly anchored on the other side.

He was not afraid. It was not that he was fearless, but Heinrich was too methodical to spare the time necessary to dwell on fear.

Next, he took a physical inventory. His body ached, especially his head. The skin on his face and hands felt as if he had been sunburned. He was hungry, thirsty, and nauseous, as if he had been administered narcotics. His clothing smelled burned, and upon closer examination he could see where the grey fabric of his suit and trousers had been singed and blackened. His Grimnoir ring was missing. That ring meant a lot to him. Whoever had taken it would regret doing so.

Trying his Power again only succeeded in making his headache worse. He did not feel as if a ward of weakness had been drawn on him, so something else had to be going on. He tried to remember how he'd wound up shackled to a wall and drew a blank. The last thing he remembered was talking to Francis while waiting for the President to show up . . . Then there had been explosions. *Yes. Now I remember.* It had been a Boomer, stronger than any he had ever heard of, in the plaza killing many. Heinrich swore under his breath as it all came back. He had saved Francis by Fading through the shrapnel, then had run to save the President. He had reached the injured man, taken his hand, and dropped them both through the stairs. They had come out in the boiler room, but then there had been another flash of light . . . That was all he could recall.

There was a clank as the door was unlocked. A lone man. The door was closed behind him, and as he leaned in the shadows of the far wall, he removed a pack of cigarettes from his black suit coat. "You're awake. Good. Nice to finally meet you, Mr. Koenig. You can call me Crow."

Heinrich's throat was so dry that it hurt to speak. "Unchain me and I will gladly shake your hand."

"And wring my neck. Your reputation precedes you. You don't need magic to be dangerous. You were some sort of Dead City street urchin. You've fought zombies, Soviets, Cossacks, *and* Imperium, but somehow you're still around to talk about it. You got some mileage on you, kid. I seen it before. Old man's eyes in a young man's face. Being a Fade is like putting the cherry on top of a murder sundae. Those chains stay on."

"Why is my magic not working?"

"Well, I suppose it doesn't hurt to tell, since the sooner you realize you're stuck, the sooner you'll cooperate. This facility is protected by a device that nullifies magic. Strictly temporary of course. It only works while the machine is running. It makes it so that the Power can't hook up with you."

Crow seemed remarkably forthcoming, a sure sign that Heinrich would be killed as soon as he was no longer of use. "What do you want with me?"

"I want to talk to you about the Grimnoir Society."

"I do not know this thing you speak of."

"Spare me the lies, Fade. I'm familiar with your little club and my assignment is to destroy it."

This man knew much. "Torture me all you want, I have nothing to say."

"Too late. You already sang. Usually those truth serums don't work so good, but couple of sodium-thiopental drips, remarkable new invention that stuff is, with a few Readers picking through your brains for a whole day, and I got what I needed."

It was possible. He could not remember. "You are a liar."

All Heinrich could see of the man's face was the small bit illuminated by the striking of a match. Crow was smiling. His teeth were yellow. The teeth disappeared as he cupped his hand and lit his cigarette. "The Grimnoir play it close to the vest. We figure there are maybe three or four dozen of you in the country, but you only know the ones you work with. After you immigrated, you answered only to Black Jack Pershing. John Browning, who didn't have a fatal heart attack, was his number two. The remaining members of your group are that safari hunter, Lance Talon, Francis Stuyvesant the industrialist, Heavy Jake Sullivan, a Traveler named Faye Vierra, and Dan and Jane Garrett . . . You know I used to listen to his radio show? The man was good. He could do like a million voices. Amazing talent, that guy."

"Leave them be," Heinrich said, "or you will regret it."

"That's some big talk for a snitch. You gave up a few of the others outside your particular group, too. They're all out there, thinking they're doing the Lord's work or some such nonsense. I got twenty names out of you, mostly here in the states, and then you blabbed about your old pals in Germany. But they're not my problem. Twenty names . . . Twenty *living*, I should clarify. You gave us plenty of the dead ones. You boys have one *hell* of a casualty rate."

Heinrich saved his anger. He was examining his options and coming up with nothing. Killing this man would be very satisfying, but he could see no way to accomplish that in his current situation.

"You're probably wondering why I'm so interested in your friends."

"Not really. I assumed you were Imperium swine."

"Ha! That's a good one. I wouldn't work for the Yellow Peril. I bleed red, white, and blue. I even fought you tricky magic Krauts back in the Great War. No, see, me and my organization are supposed to clean up your kind. You Actives think you're so much better than regular folks. I'm the law. Things need to change and people like you would gum up the works. You Actives won't be happy until you take over. Some of our elected officials didn't have the guts to do what needed to be done. Except as soon as you Grimnoir tried to murder President Roosevelt, that all changed."

"That is ridiculous. I tried to save the man, not kill him."

"I know! You should be getting a medal, not rotting

under OCI headquarters. Heh, just between you and me, I know you Grimnoir didn't do it. We've already got conclusive evidence upstairs." Crow blew out a perfect smoke ring. It hung under the single light bulb. "But nobody in charge is going to see that evidence until I'm done cleaning house. I'm sure as hell not going to let a good crisis go to waste. My office just got a blank check to do whatever we needed to do to get you people under control. You know how rare that kind of pass is? In a little while, Congress will go back to getting cold feet and fretting about overstepping its bounds, but by then it'll be too late for your kind."

Heinrich had told Francis that Actives were going to end up caged like dangerous dogs. This was a terrible time to be proven right. He studied this new threat, trying to understand what he was up against. *Something* about Crow's eyes was wrong in the dark. The glow of the cigarette reflected in them a little too well. "You talk of controlling Actives . . . Yet you are one of us. No?"

The interrogator's posture changed the slightest bit. Crow's voice was imperceptibly different when he responded. "Me? Magical? I don't know what you're talking about."

"It makes you uncomfortable, this place? Not being in contact with the Power? I know that I do not like it already. Working here must be very challenging for you."

"You got all the answers, Kraut? You talk a lot for a man in chains."

"You speak of Actives as if we are a different species, but you know this is not true. You are very good at playing a part. I assume you wanted me to think of you as a true believer on a moral crusade. I wonder what you expected to gain from that."

The cigarette ash nodded up and down. "Oh, you're good."

"Yes, I am, and the good always win in the end. I would very much like for you to remember that as I choke the life from your body."

Crow banged on the door. It was opened for him a moment later. "I've enjoyed our conversation, Mr. Koenig. Be seeing you." The door closed behind him. Then the small light was shut off, leaving the prisoner in the dark.

Curious indeed. Heinrich went back to testing his chains.

Crow found the OCI's audio technician in the next room. "Did you get that?"

"It should sound nice and clear."

"Excellent. I want the tape to start at where I first mention the Grimnoir. Then cut it off right after I say that it'll be too late for his kind. Got it?"

"Yes, sir, Mr. Crow. I can do that."

So far these Grimnoir had impressed him; they were a tenacious bunch, but their loyalty to each other and their cause made them vulnerable. This was going to be like shooting fish in a barrel. "Call me when the recording is ready."

Bell Farm, Virginia

SULLIVAN WOKE UP SORE. Jane's magic was miraculous and all, but it would have been nice if the pain didn't linger on afterwards. There was no longer a rib sticking in his lung, but it sure felt like there was. That Iron Guard had damn near punched a hole *through* him. He had fallen through a train car once and it hadn't hurt that bad. He and that particular Brute son of a bitch were going to meet again, Sullivan was sure of it.

The two-story, eighty-year-old safe house was on an abandoned farm thirty miles southwest of the Imperium compound. It was in the middle of nowhere, didn't have electricity or indoor plumbing, and was frankly a dump, but Jane had bought plenty of groceries the day before; there was a pump, an outhouse, a wood stove, a barn to hide their cars in, spells carved into the walls to thwart Finders, and the beds didn't seem to have fleas.

Opening the moth-eaten curtains, Sullivan discovered that it was an overcast, grey day, and it was hard to estimate the time without the sun. His belly told him it felt like lunchtime, but burning Power that hard always made him extra hungry. He found his watch on the nightstand along with his holstered .45. Sure enough, it was nearly noon. It wasn't often that he got to sleep in. *Maybe I should get beat up by Brutes more often.*

There was a polite knock on the door. That told him who it was. Dan would have knocked with more authority and Lance probably wouldn't have bothered at all. Sullivan winced as he pulled his shirt on. "Coming, Jane."

Once he let her in, the Healer examined him critically. She folded her arms, tilted her head, and scowled at his lungs. Sullivan had to admit that Jane Garrett was one good-looking dame, blonde, tall, curvy, and somehow always incredibly *neat*. In their paint-peeling, dingy-as-sin surroundings, she was a ray of sunshine, though her bedside manner did leave something to be desired. She walked over and poked him hard in the side. "Hmmm . . . How does that feel?"

"Tender." He was not used to a beautiful woman staring at him that intently, but he had to remind himself that to Healers like Jane, everybody looked like see-through bags of skin filled with blood and guts. It was one downside to the most popular of all Powers, but Jane insisted that she was used to it. "So how do I look?"

"Like a translucent blood sausage. So . . . relatively normal." She closed the door behind her. "We need to talk, Jake."

This had been brewing since she'd laid hands on him last night and discovered the new spells. There were no chairs so he gestured at the bed. "Have a seat." Then he went over and leaned on the windowsill a respectful distance away. It wouldn't be polite to sit on a bed next to a married woman. Jake Sullivan, despite what some might say, always tried to be a gentleman to those that deserved it. "I figure I know why you're here. Let me say—"

"You are an idiot," Jane snapped. Sullivan nodded. He'd predicted that response. "A damn fool idiot. Do you have any idea how dangerous carving magic onto yourself is?"

"I believe I do."

"No. I don't think so." Jane was exasperated. She had been a child when the Harkeness family had come over from Eastern Europe, but the more excited she got, the more her heritage showed up in her pronunciation, accenting the wrong syllables. "The Society has been experimenting for decades, trying to get those horrid things to work right. Many foolish knights have died in horrible pain, while others became twisted and inhuman. Putting a spell onto metal or glass is one thing, putting one onto living flesh is different."

"Yeah." Sullivan chuckled. "The metal don't scream while you do it. They *really* hurt when you bind them on."

"Yes. I would imagine mutilating yourself with magic would . . . Why? Why would you risk that?"

He didn't answer because Jane already knew the answer.

She folded her arms and glared at him. "Are you trying to become our version of an Iron Guard then? You expect to beat them at their own game?"

"I do."

"Then you are an even bigger fool than I thought. The Iron Guard lose more of their humanity with each spell they take. They're weapons, not people. They're monsters!"

"My brother was a monster a real long time before he hooked up with the Japanese or got branded with a kanji, Jane. I ain't Madi."

"I . . . I did not mean . . ." Jane shut her mouth and turned red. Madi had soundly beaten them all and captured her. If they hadn't come after her, Jane would either be an Imperium slave or a Unit 731 experiment, and they both knew it. "Of course, you are nothing like your brother. He was a beast. You are a decent man."

"I wouldn't go that far . . . Look, I know what I've done is dangerous. So what? It's dangerous every time we face those bastards. I've seen the Power like nobody else has. That's how come I can make this work. That's why I have to make them work. Until we figure out how to match the Iron Guard, they're going to keep on beating us. The only reason we rescued you off the *Tokugawa* was because the Chairman was too *amused* watching us fight until it was too late."

"And I thank God every single day for what you all did for me, but—"

"But if I'd just been a little better before . . ." Sullivan trailed off. "Never mind."

"You're thinking of Delilah?"

He couldn't answer. Sullivan stood up and looked out the window at the dead grey fields. "Maybe."

"Jake! Her death was not your fault."

"Not a day goes by that I don't ask myself if I could've done something more."

Jane wouldn't let it go. "I don't think she'd want to see you killing yourself trying to avenge her."

"Delilah's dead. She don't get a vote."

"Risking your life won't bring her back."

"Of course it won't. It ain't like that . . . It's . . . Shit. Never mind." She could never understand. Her Power fixed people. His Power broke people. The only good thing he could accomplish in this world was breaking those that needed it, and one of the times he'd really needed it, he hadn't been strong enough to get the job done. "I'm not stupid, Jane."

"Could have fooled me. I see four working spells bound to your body, and two other attempts that did not stick. Grisly work."

"You can tell just by looking?"

Jane gave a resigned sigh. "Four are alive with magic.

Two are simply scar tissue. So which one of my over-exuberant and dangerously naive colleagues assisted you in this foolishness? Was it Heinrich? He was certainly crazy enough to try."

"No, but he wanted the same one for Healing that I figured out after Faye shot me in the heart. I've done a couple of those now. It's actually not too hard. No, I didn't have help. I carved these on my own."

"You did *what?*"

He had created them by himself with only a memory of the Power's geometries, a steady hand, a sharp knife, some Summoned smoke, whiskey to dull the pain, and a mirror so he could see his own chest while he worked. "You'd be surprised what a man can accomplish with a little motivation. Hard part is doing it backwards in the mirror."

"You're insane."

Sullivan laughed and returned to sitting on the windowsill. "Maybe. Not like there's a lot of sanity to spare in this outfit. Sane folks don't go around poking the Imperium in the eye. Look, Jane, something big is coming. I can feel it in my bones. Maybe it's this scout creature, maybe it's the big Enemy it serves, maybe it's just the winds of change blowing. Hell, I don't rightly know. But whatever it is, I'm going to be as ready as I can be."

Jane was staring at him again. "You're wearing three of those Healing spells."

"That's the first one I learned. Figured I'd practice it a few more times before trying it on anyone else. There seems to be a point of diminishing returns though. Each one of the same kind feels like it does a little less. Madi said he had five of these, so I'm assuming that's the max, but you saw how damn hard he was to put down."

"Cutting him in half seemed to do the trick." Jane actually gave a little smile. "Served him right. What's that other one?"

"This?" Sullivan touched a spot on his left side. "I don't rightly know. Found the design in a box of Cracker Jacks, figured I'd slap it on and see what happened."

"Jake!"

"I'm kidding." He opened his shirt and showed off the intricate scar. "That's what the area of the Power that affects gravitation looks like." Through years of determined practice, Sullivan already had a better connection to the Power than most, and had even blurred the lines between his abilities into other areas of the Power. The latest mark had been an experiment in pushing those boundaries even further. "It was an experiment. Seemed to increase my reserves, and I think it made my magic a little stronger."

"You think? That's reassuring."

His stomach rumbled. "You going to keep yelling at me? Because if you are we can do it over lunch just as easy."

"You Heavies are always hungry . . . Such large men with such rapid metabolisms, it is understandable." Jane shook her head sadly. "I know why you are doing this to yourself. Men like Madi cannot be allowed to win. If the rest of us are willing to risk our lives to stop that, then why should I expect less from you . . . Fine! Would you please just promise me that you won't do any more of these?"

"I never give my word when I don't intend to keep it,

so no. I'll do whatever I think is necessary. If that means more binding, then that's what I'll do."

Jane frowned. "Not that I want to encourage this madness, but how about you don't do any more stupid and potentially lethal experiments on yourself, without me, your Healer, there to keep your heart from exploding?"

"I can agree to that . . . If it's possible, you can help keep me from dying." Besides, Jane didn't need to know, but it had become increasingly difficult to come back from each new spell. He was nervous about trying any more without a Healer around anyway. "Do me a favor though. Don't tell anybody what I've done. The others don't need to know."

"You don't want them to worry? Why, I'm rather surprised."

"Not really. I don't want anybody to get stupid and try to copy me. Can you imagine Francis trying to give himself Brute strength?"

She laughed. "Or Faye, wanting to mind control milk cows or some such thing . . ." Jane got off the bed, strode over, and offered him her hand. "Shake on it."

He took her delicate hand in his big mitt. It was a soft hand, a Healer's hand, but she gave him a remarkably firm handshake. "Deal."

New York City, New York

THE OFFICE OF THE PRESIDENT of United Blimp & Freight was on the top floor of the Chrysler Building. The meeting that had been called was of the utmost secrecy. The palatial room had been carefully swept for listening devices, both magical and mechanical, and wards had been placed to chase away any Finders' spirits that might be lingering around. The only other man present was his single most trustworthy employee, mostly because of his opinionated and contrarian nature. They had spent the first ten minutes discussing mundane business matters, mostly so his secretary could type up some minutes before he dismissed her. He couldn't assume that OCI didn't have some means of getting into his papers. Francis wasn't taking any chances.

The UBF vice president of finance polished off the whiskey that his boss had poured for him, set the glass down on the antique executive desk nowhere near the coaster, and held up one hand in protest. "Hold on, Francis . . ." Then Mr. Chandler thought better of it, and pulled the glass back over to pour himself another from the bottle. The ice cubes hadn't even had a chance to melt from the first round. "You want me to do *what*?"

Francis leaned way back in his grandfather's stuffed leather chair and folded his hands behind his head. Experience had taught him that if he leaned back too far he'd find himself on the floor, but luckily he had never done that in front of witnesses. "I'm fairly sure you heard me the first time."

"I just hoped that I'd hallucinated the whole thing." Chandler swirled Kentucky's finest around in the glass and held it up to the sunlight streaming through the window. "You're talking about sabotaging a government agency during a time of national crisis."

"I'm not doing anything illegal, which is more than I

can say for them. Besides, I'm only asking for your help with the business part. The overall strategy . . . well, it's probably best if you've got no idea what I'm trying to do."

"When they're beating a confession out of me, I'll be sure to state that extra clearly. So, to make sure I've got this straight . . . You want me to find a secret company that makes a secret product, that nobody knows exists and has apparently never been publicized or advertised . . . and buy it. All while never letting anybody anywhere know that you're the one doing the buying or the snooping."

"That's a fair representation," Francis answered. He was rather proud of his idea. John had asked him to stay put and out of contact for everyone's safety, but he hadn't said anything about not helping out. "Think you can handle it?"

"I'm an accountant, not a detective." Chandler downed his second glass and sighed before continuing, "Though that is a fascinating career field. Hell, I do enjoy a challenge. I suppose I'm game."

Francis had figured his man would be in. Chandler wasn't Grimnoir, didn't have a lick of magic, and owed Francis no loyalty beyond his rather hefty salary. But it was a rare accountant who would volunteer for a gunfight on the Imperium flagship, so his volunteering to stick it to the OCI wasn't a surprise. "You can't let anyone find out what you're up to. They'll probably be watching." The OCI had been tailing him everywhere since he'd gotten back to New York, and doing an embarrassing job of it, since they were so easy to spot. "It could be dangerous."

"Dangerous? One of them sucker-punched a billionaire and got away with it."

"Millionaire," Francis corrected. Grandfather had been the billionaire. Between the board putting the screws to him and the UBF stock taking a hit because Francis had told the Imperium where to stick their gold, he was only a millionaire. Though to be fair, it was a *lot* of millions.

"Yeah, whatever. I prepare the financials, remember? Then this OCI guy waltzed out of jail, and your legion of lawyers can't even prove the man ever existed. Oh, believe me. I'll be *extra* careful." Chandler freed himself from the too-cushioned chair and headed straight for the door like a man on a mission. "I've got a few ideas to start with. Your grandfather liked to collect companies like they were stamps. We've got a couple small ones that aren't doing much of anything interesting. I think somebody is about to get a nice infusion of operating capital. Let me see what I can do."

"Thank you, Mr. Chandler," Francis said with all sincerity.

He smiled. "No, thank you, Mr. Stuyvesant. You somehow always manage to keep this job interesting."

After his accountant had left, Francis got up and walked to the window. The view of the city, from what had recently been his grandfather's office, was spectacular. The old man's guilty dying wish had installed Francis here, and he'd fought tooth and nail to keep it that way. Luckily, enough of the board had thought that it was easier to keep him around as a controllable figurehead than to fight, but he'd managed to surprise and outmaneuver most of them. Francis had worked hard for that view.

A considerable sum of money had brought a Healer in to repair his arm and his face, but his pride still stung from the beating Crow had administered. The whole thing was shameful. Not that Francis hadn't been hurt before, quite the contrary; he'd been shot, stabbed, crashed in a dirigible, and nearly drowned as a knight, but it was one thing to get manhandled by an Imperium warrior, it was something entirely different to be humiliated by a supposed public servant.

It wasn't enough that Crow had hurt him physically, it was the insinuation that he was some sort of traitor to his country. He had risked his life to keep his country from being destroyed by a Peace Ray! Who were *they* to accuse *him* of treason? Francis had cultivated a public persona of being a spoiled rich brat, but it irked him even more to have that lorded over him by some thug. Now he was reduced to hiding in his office behind a protective wall of lawyers when he should have been out there doing *something*. Black Jack would have expected more from him. Heinrich certainly wouldn't have sat around while the Grimnoir were being framed.

Several of his friends were wanted like common criminals. Even Faye had shown up in the papers. *Faye!* She was about the sweetest, kindest, most innocent, gentle . . . well, not really. She was about as gentle as a bag of agitated rattlesnakes, but he was really fond of her, and she certainly didn't deserve to have her name tarnished by a bunch of propaganda artists.

The whole thing made Francis very angry.

And there was nothing more dangerous that an angry millionaire with an ax to grind.

Fairfax County, Virginia

HIS NIGHTMARES were swift and violent, filled with disjointed images of flashing steel and spraying blood. The enemy scout was ruthless and cunning. Okubo, the legendary ronin, led the final charge against the beast and its created legions. Hundreds of their order had died, yet in the end, the warriors of Dark Ocean prevailed.

The sun had long since risen on a new day.

The Chairman had not yet responded. Iron Guard Toru had dutifully delivered his report concerning the death of Ambassador Hatori and the escape of the Grimnoir to one of the Chairman's personal staff. Before the link had been severed, Toru had been informed that the Chairman wished to give him further orders. So Toru had stayed on his knees, meditating in front of the mirror. Staying awake had been a struggle. Eventually the fatigue of his injuries and magic usage had finally rendered him unconscious. He woke up still on his knees, innocent blood on his hands, and Hatori's memories in his mind.

All Iron Guard were taught about their brothers' magical skills. A Reader had the ability not just to receive but to send messages and images through a mental link. Sending was very draining and took considerable Power. Considering the vast amount of memories that Hatori had shown him, it must have taken every last bit of Power his teacher had to accomplish such a feat, especially while ritually disemboweling himself. Toru's admiration for his mentor could not be higher.

The memories were centered around the secretive group known as Dark Ocean and their battle against the predator that had come for the Power. Dark Ocean had been a tight-knit group, and since they had been gathered during Okubo Tokugawa's wanderings, they were not all Japanese. Toru had not been taught that during his training.

However, the creature was just as wretched as he had been taught at the Iron Guard academy and the Chairman had been every bit as fearsome in mankind's defense. He was extremely thankful that his father was there to protect the world from such horrors. Truly, if it had not been for him, this would be a dead world. Once again, Toru was reminded what an honor it was to have been conceived by the greatest warrior of all time.

A few of Hatori's personal memories, his impoverished youth, and times with family, lovers, and friends, had come over as well, but Toru did his best to ignore those private things, though it was becoming increasingly difficult to separate his memories from Hatori's, they had become so fully meshed together.

It was a mystery why Hatori had seen fit to bestow these things to him. The glories were not his own, and he was therefore unworthy of having them. To further complicate matters, he also knew without a doubt that Hatori had been innocent. His love for the Chairman was unsurpassed. In one respect, Toru knew he had violated the Chairman's orders. He had been told not to speak to Hatori, yet his teacher had shared something more personal than mere words.

Toru decided that he would ask the Chairman for his

opinion on the matter, and if Toru had condemned himself through his foolishness, then so be it. He would have to die. Iron Guards did not fear death. They lived for death—or so it was taught, and Toru was careful never to admit to himself any doubts or unease about the philosophy. The best an Iron Guard could hope for was that when they met their inevitable end, it had somehow brought glory to the Imperium. Sadly, the Chairman would more than likely order his death for letting the Grimnoir escape, which was a shameful and embarrassing way to die.

The mirror remained silent.

Much time had passed. He was very hungry, yet dared not be away from the mirror. Iron Guards were familiar with fasting. He could do it for days if necessary. Toru attempted to meditate, but Dark Ocean kept intruding. There was something there, nagging at him. Something he was failing to grasp. His legs were impossibly cramped, but still he waited obediently.

A knock at his door broke his concentration. It was the captain of the guard.

"Any word from the Finder?" Perhaps if he could still destroy those Grimnoir, he could find redemption.

"No, Iron Guard. There has been no sign. There is a representative of the American government here to speak with you. As you commanded, I said that the ambassador had passed on due to a heart attack, but they are insistent."

"Send them away," Toru growled. He had no time for political games.

"It is concerning the events with the Grimnoir."

His leg muscles burned as he stood. "Stay here. Should a link be established, seek me out immediately."

"Yes, Iron Guard." The captain bowed.

The American was waiting at the gatehouse. He was surprised to see that it was a female. She was tall and bulky by the delicate standards set by Imperium women, but he could see how to a Westerner she could be attractive. The natural inclination of an Imperium man was to underestimate women, but Toru had worked in the West too long to make that mistake. The woman carried herself with the confidence of someone who had seen conflict. She was wearing a plain skirt, a white shirt, no jewelry or any other material affectations, and an overcoat large enough to easily conceal weapons. She looked very tired, as if she had not slept recently, and in normal times diplomatic etiquette would have demanded that he offer refreshment. These were not normal times, so he just wanted to get rid of her as quickly as possible.

"I am Toru Tokugawa of the Imperium Diplomatic Corps."

"Miss Hammer. I've been deputized by the Office of the Coordinator of Information."

Ah, their new secret police. But why come here, and alone? *No witnesses, of course.* Certainly, it was yet another American poking around, meddling uselessly in affairs beyond their understanding, eager to sell information. This was a relatively common occurrence, since it was common knowledge that the Imperium paid for information in large quantities of gold. Like swine, only rooting for bribes instead of food, Americans were obnoxiously quick to sell out their masters.

Yet, it would not hurt to develop another source within this new agency. "What do you want?"

"Information leading to the capture of Jake Sullivan."

That caught Toru off guard. "Who?"

"You know the name. Please don't lie to me. It's a waste of both our time. Sullivan came through this very gate less than twenty-four hours ago. Then it got ugly."

"How do you know that?"

"Intuition . . . and what looks like a big scorch mark on your wall over there, and the place still smells like smoke."

This was an intriguing development. "Please, come in, Miss Hammer."

The guards opened the gate for them. He led her along the gravel path toward the Imperium house. "I heard that your ambassador had a heart attack. My condolences."

"I heard that your president had been blown up. Now you have my condolences. As your people would say, we are even."

Hammer paused to study the obviously damaged roof of the mansion. "Lot of things going on this week. Is that Sullivan's work?"

"Why are you looking for this Sullivan?"

"He's a known member of a criminal organization known as the Grimnoir Society, wanted for questioning in relation to the assassination attempt on President Roosevelt, and a suspect in the shooting of four federal agents. A warrant has been issued for his arrest."

As a man of action rather than words, Toru had not liked his initial posting to the Diplomatic Corps, but he had learned Master Hatori's lessons well. Her discomfort and the way she looked away as she spoke suggested that she was lying, but not about searching for the Grimnoir. That much was true. "As you said, please do not lie to me. It is a waste of both our time. What are the real reasons you are looking for him?"

This Hammer obviously did not like being caught in her untruths. "He's a wanted man. Whether he did the things he's wanted for or not isn't my business. My business is finding him. That's all."

"What will happen when he is found?"

She sighed. "I imagine the OCI will kill him."

Toru would much have preferred to kill the Heavy himself, but anything that harried the Grimnoir was fine by him. "I can say nothing about what brought him here, or what transpired while he was on Imperium grounds. Yet, I assume that you have some sort of Power related to accomplishing your mission?"

"Maybe I do. Maybe I don't. Let's just say that I know he didn't leave by that front gate. Show me where he got out and I can pick it up from there."

The Grimnoir rings bore a spell that made tracking them with spirits very difficult. The spirit had to have them in visual contact, and even then, it took an extremely talented Finder or Summoner to bring in a spirit capable of accomplishing such a feat. "You do not strike me as a Summoner."

"I'm not. Just show me his trail."

If she was telling the truth, that meant that she probably would not be alerted if he were to have a spirit follow her. There was one Finder amongst the marines, but his creatures had thus far been unable to locate the Grimnoir. If this woman could somehow track them, though . . . The possibility was intriguing. "Very well. Come this way." They would walk around the property to the back wall. There was no need for her to see the shame of the damage.

Hammer had begun to ask another question, but froze, and then let out a shriek when she saw the front of the mansion. He followed her gaze to see what was the matter. The car that he had flipped was still on its roof. Of course, it was a very large car, and none of the men had even a fraction of his strength. They'd dragged it over so that it was no longer blocking the drive, but they'd need to have a truck come to remove it. He would have cleaned that up himself if he hadn't been waiting by the mirror. The captain would be reprimanded for Toru's displeasure, though to be fair, the captain had been left with quite the mess to repair. "I am sorry for the display."

The woman's hands curled into fists. She seemed to be experiencing difficulty controlling her emotions. "What? What the—that's—" Hammer was so livid that she was having a hard time forming the words. "That's my car!" She turned back to him. "Sullivan stole my car. That's *my* car!"

Toru found that humorous, but it would not have been fitting for an Iron Guard to display mirth before a stranger, so he restrained himself to just a polite nod. Even if his Finder could follow this woman to Sullivan, perhaps he should let her have the first crack at the Heavy. That would be especially amusing.

Chapter 9

The severity of the effects were unexpected, but we are certain that historical weather conditions will resume quickly. Our experts are certain that everything will return to normal in short order.

—William M. Jardine,
United States Secretary of Agriculture,
after the MWAB (Magical Weather Alteration Board)
backfired and resulted in record droughts
across the Midwest, 1927

Ada, Oklahoma

FAYE WATCHED THE FAMILIAR HILLS out the car window and got more and more uncomfortable with every passing mile. The last time she'd seen these hills she'd been a passenger in a car, only it had been nothing fancy like the Chrysler that Ian had purchased for several hundred dollars cash in Dallas. The last time, she had been in an old Model T, along with her Ma and Pa, all her brothers, and every single thing they owned that could fit inside or could be strapped down to the roof. It had been a long, hot, and dusty drive all the way to California, especially since they'd had to stop to steal food and gasoline along the way.

The land was still dead brown, maybe even browner and deader than she remembered, as if that was scarcely possible. Maybe it was because of the darkness of the sunglasses Whisper had given her. Her memories told her that this area had been green and pretty once, but that had been a long time ago. That had all changed one summer, and walls of dust, black as night, had blown up and covered the whole sky for days at a time. The crops had died. The pigs had died. Pa had gotten madder and meaner, and when he got like that he liked to blame her for having the devil in her, what with her scary grey eyes and her cursed magic. He used to yell a lot, always telling her that she had to be filled with all sorts of wickedness to end up with so much magic that you could see it right through her eyeballs.

Pa hadn't understood magic very well, but then again, most regular folks didn't.

The road was open and empty. Most of the houses they passed were abandoned and the fields were bare. The fences were falling down, but there weren't any animals left for the fences to hold in anyways. It had been four years since she'd left. It wasn't often that she thought about Oklahoma, because all her memories of living here were sad.

The others had debated and picked their route. It wasn't the most direct way, but they were trying to keep a low profile. And nobody liked to travel through the Oklahoma wastes if they could help it. Lots of places had bad drought, but there was a swath right up the middle where nothing grew anymore. When she'd heard they were going to drive straight through Ada, she'd kept her mouth shut. It seemed like an unfortunate coincidence. She had to keep reminding herself that this place wasn't her real home. She'd grown up here, but her real home would always be in El Nido, California, on the Vierra farm, where she'd been taken in and loved and treated nice, and even though the Vierra farm had been burned to the ground, it was still a million times better than here.

"Dreary," Mr. Bolander said. Faye snapped out of her funk and looked over at him. They were sharing the back seat. Ian was driving and Whisper was in the passenger seat. If anyone asked, she was supposed to remember that Ian was a businessman from New Mexico, on his way to buy a property in Virginia. Whisper was supposed to be his wife, which worked well since Ian was wearing a wedding band anyway and Whisper seemed to have an unending selection of rings available from inside her gigantic purse. Faye was Ian's young cousin along for the ride, and Mr. Bolander was Ian's hired man, which was funny to her, since in reality Mr. Bolander was the senior and most experienced knight, but he'd insisted that appearances had to be kept in case they found themselves in a Sundown Town. She had no idea what that meant, but everybody else seemed to, and she hadn't wanted to look ignorant.

"What?" It had been awhile since anyone had spoken. All that broken-down scenery made folks quiet.

"I meant the view. Dreary. Sad to see a place all shriveled up and dried out. They say that we're in hard times, but seeing this sure makes that sink in."

"It's ugly," Faye said quietly. It made her miss her green fields full of Holsteins.

"What was that?"

"I suppose I was just mumbling, Mr. Bolander."

"Call me George, please."

She turned to look at him. His eyes seemed a little sad as he studied the scene. "I've been told that this desert used to be fertile ground . . . until we ruined it."

Whisper chimed in. "I've heard about this. They spoke of it at university. The bowl of dust, was it not?"

"Dust bowl," Ian corrected. His need to constantly correct people annoyed Faye, but she bit her tongue.

"They were having a drought. Some bright boys in Washington recruited a mess of Weathermen to try and fix things. Biggest magical alteration of weather patterns in history, they said. Instead they made it a hundred times worse." George was still talking to her. The nice man had no idea that Faye knew all too well about what had happened. Maybe not about the decisions or the magic used, but she knew all about the awful results. "They tried to use magic like a hammer and ended up wrecking the natural order of things. It's barely rained here since and there's a hot wind that sucks the life out of everything."

"Magic's always got a price," Ian said. "Sooner people realize that and quit messing around with things over their heads, the better off we'll all be."

Faye turned away. "It's ugly . . . ugly and mean."

"Ugly maybe, but I wouldn't go so far as to call it mean."

George was wrong. She knew the truth. The darkness

of the dust storms that had ruined their skies were nothing compared to the darkness that lived in some men's hearts. The winds had just exposed that meanness for the rest of the world to see.

Steam was pouring out from the open hood of the Chrysler. George and Ian had their heads inside and they were poking at the engine. Faye had no idea what they were doing in there. Grandpa had always managed to fix the tractor when it had broken down, but she had never been much help at that except for fetching different-sized wrenches from his toolbox.

They had passed through Ada less than half an hour before, and Faye had been extremely glad when they had only stopped briefly to pump some gas at a weathered little station owned by a stern Chickasaw man. Faye had kept her head down, her glasses and big straw hat on, but even then it was doubtful that anybody would recognize her. Whisper had asked if they could stop for lunch, but everyone else had been eager to keep going. There was still plenty of daylight left, and even then the Chrysler had good headlights. Besides, they needed to get out of the bad zone before the night winds came. Faye was happy that they would be well away from her old home before they stopped to sleep.

But that wasn't looking too likely anymore.

"Doggone it." George mopped his sweaty face with his handkerchief. "I've got no idea. Plenty of fluid. No leaks. Radiator appears to be in good shape."

"None of you happen to be a Tinker?" Ian asked.

"Call them Fixers where I'm from. I'm a Crackler,"

George answered. "You want me to charge the battery, I can. Other than that"—he shrugged—"sorry."

"Traveler," Faye said, but everybody already knew all about her.

"Infernal thing." Ian stepped back and kicked the bumper. "Well, I sure as hell can't Summon a mechanic."

Whisper got out of the passenger side, scowled at the sun, then went back for her umbrella. She popped it open and walked over to examine the engine. "Is it broken?" Ian glared at her, as if the boiling steam cloud should have been explanation enough. Whisper, however, was either immune to his jerkiness or just plain didn't care enough to notice. "Well?"

"It overheated and died on us. Is there anything you can do?"

"I do not know much about automobiles." Whisper frowned at the engine. "I believe that touching it would soil my dress."

Ian sighed. "I meant magically."

"You would like for me to set it on fire?"

George laughed with genuine amusement. "Fine lot we are. Four powerful wizards and yet we're easily defeated by the internal combustion engine."

"Yeah, the Imperium best watch out for us . . ." Ian muttered. He glanced up and down the road. There wasn't another car in sight. "I saw a garage back in that town. It looked to still be open." Which was saying something since most everything else in Ada had been boarded up and abandoned.

"Everyone wore comfortable shoes, I hope," George said. "It's only a couple of miles."

"Lock the car up," Faye told Ian, and then to the others, "Anything you don't want stolen, take it with you."

"Is that necessary to—" Whisper began.

"Trust me." Faye got her .45 out of the car and stuck it into the special pocket in her traveling dress. The knife Lance had made for her went on the other side. Sure, *her* family had moved to California, but she knew how desperate folks around these parts could be. Other than Mr. Browning's pistol and Lance's knife, everything else was replaceable.

They set out for Ada, which put Faye into a very sour mood.

There was nothing but dirt for miles. The trees were all dead. The only other feature was the telephone poles running alongside the road, and it was so desolate that there weren't even any birds sitting on the wires. The afternoon wasn't too hot, but the wind was harsh and dry. She had to hold onto her hat to keep from losing it. Whisper's fancy umbrella got turned inside out in the first mile. She complained about that, called it her favorite *parasol*, and ended up chucking it into a ditch.

Ian made an attempt at conversation. "So, this telephone call that Jake Sullivan supposedly took . . ."

Faye was about worn out with this guy's attitude. "What do you mean 'supposedly'?"

"I'm not saying it didn't happen, just how do we know it was the Chairman's ghost?"

"Because Mr. Sullivan said so."

"Maybe it was a trick. I mean, Sullivan's a Heavy. Everybody knows Heavies aren't very bright."

George realized the hole that Ian was digging for

himself much faster than Ian did, and tried to intervene. "Normally, when I hear someone say 'everybody knows,' what follows shortly after tends to be wrong."

"Sullivan's only been in the Society for what, less than a year? But because he's had some dream about actually seeing the Power, we're all supposed to hop to when he tells us something crazy?"

"That's not true at all," Faye snapped. "Mr. Sullivan is super smart. He's just not a show-off about it like *some* folks."

"We're taking the fall for an assassination attempt, but instead of spending our time figuring out who set us up, we're spinning our wheels trying to talk to Iron Guards about some being that probably doesn't even exist."

Faye stopped abruptly. The others made it a few more steps before they realized she was no longer keeping up. She waited while they turned back to her. Faye put her hands on her hips and gave Ian the look normally reserved for people she was about to murder. "You better shut up."

"Hey, wait a sec—"

"No. You listen, and you listen good. This big critter is real and it isn't messing around. When it shows up, nothing else is going to matter. If you don't believe that, then you're the stupid one."

Ian's face turned red and he started to respond, but Whisper cut him off. "But how do you know this, Faye?"

How could she explain? "It's right there, right outside of the real world. It's pushing on the door, getting heavier and heavier, and pretty soon the hinges are going to give and then it's coming inside. When I listen, when it's real quiet, like when I'm trying to sleep . . . I can hear it."

Ian threw his hands in the air. "You're off your rocker."

George put one hand on Ian's arm to shush him. "Faye, how come you didn't say this to the elders?"

"I did . . . They didn't believe me either. I don't know how I know. I don't know how come my Power is different than yours. It just is. I just do. I can *feel* it, okay?"

"But—"

Faye was frustrated. She didn't want to argue with a bunch of people who just couldn't understand. She checked her head map and scouted the road for danger, *clear*, and Traveled. The soles of her shoes hit asphalt a hundred yards away. It was about as far as she could manage lately, a frustratingly useless little amount of distance compared to what she'd done before. She stood there in the dust and waited for the others to catch up. It gave her a chance to collect herself.

Of course the others didn't understand. Nobody else had a connection to the Power like she did. They got drips of water coming out of a faucet and she had a mighty river . . . or at least she had before. Now she was down to a small stream, but on the *Tokugawa*, it had been a river. She didn't know how she'd gotten so strong so fast, though the elders had kept poking and asking questions, trying to figure it out. They had seemed more worried about how she'd managed to Travel the entire *Tempest* than they were about the Enemy coming. They tried not to show it, but she could tell they didn't trust her. It was shaking Faye's confidence.

It was this place. Ada made her upset. Just being close to her old house made her feel like crying angry tears.

I'm stronger than that. I'm better than that. When she

was a little girl, she'd had to live inside her own head, because it was the only safe place. But she wasn't a scared little girl anymore, that nobody loved because they all thought she'd been possessed by the devil. She was Sally Faye Vierra, knight of the Grimnoir. She'd saved lives, battled the Imperium, and been a hero. She'd thought that she had put the miserable sad part of her life behind her, but apparently it was still there. It would always be there until she buried it once and for all.

She knew what she had to do.

Ian got to her first. "What's your deal?"

"Fix the car. I'll catch up." And then she Traveled away.

Ian Wright watched the Traveler blink out of existence. He looked around the wastes, but Faye was nowhere to be seen. "Well, damn it all to hell."

George and Whisper caught up a moment later. "Where did she run off to?"

"Personal business, I imagine," Whisper said. "You should not have insulted her."

Ian grunted. "Yeah, I was pretty dumb."

"You were rude," George pointed out.

"Not that. I wish I would've realized that she could've just Traveled back to town and saved us the walk."

It took many long hops to reach home.

The old homestead was smaller than she remembered. She hadn't realized it would seem so tiny. Maybe she'd just gotten used to being in cities with buildings that absolutely towered overhead, or maybe she'd spent too much time living in homes that made this place look like the shack it was . . . Or maybe she'd just gotten taller over the last four years.

The fences had been made out of scrap lumber and weaved-together branches. They'd been too poor to buy good wire even before the dust had come. The pigs had gotten loose all the time, but they had never wandered too far. Then they had all died when the air turned to poison and everyone had taken to wearing masks to protect their faces. The outhouse had collapsed into a heap of splinters.

The ground was a lifeless grey color and the entire yard had been smoothed perfectly flat by the constant wind. There were two metal poles in front of the old shack. Ma's clothesline had run between those. Faye remembered running and playing between the hanging clothes. Whenever she'd forget herself in the moment and accidentally Traveled, she'd receive a beating. Traveling had been so much fun, though, that it had still been worth it. Now, one of the clothes poles had fallen down. The other stuck out of the ground at an angle, like something had crashed into it.

The house itself was also at a slight angle. She'd like to say the wind had done that, but more than likely, Pa had been a little drunk when he'd built the place. The front door was missing. Probably taken by a neighbor to use for firewood. The doorway was a black, gaping hole. She couldn't do it. Faye told herself she was being silly. She'd fought the Chairman, why was this so difficult?

It took her nearly half an hour of standing in the yard before she screwed up enough courage to walk inside.

Beams of sunlight came through the tiny windows and

a few holes in the wall and roof. There was no glass in the windows, but then again, there never had been. In the winter they'd just hung old canvas over the narrow slits to hold in the heat. During the dust storms, they'd tried that, but nothing could keep out the choking silt. The floor was dirt. Faye remembered using her fingers and drawing pretty designs in that dirt. It used to make her mad when the others would walk on them, but since there was only the one room to share, it was to be expected.

It was empty except for spiderwebs and trash. Their cobbled together furniture was missing. She hadn't known why she'd expected otherwise.

There was lots of broken glass left over from Pa's bottles. She kicked those out of the way and made some space. Not worried about getting her sturdy dress dirty, Faye sat cross-legged in the middle of the room. She closed her eyes and sat still and quiet for a long time.

The memories came flooding back. When her eyes turned grey and her Power showed up, people had become scared of her and what she could do. Her pa had hated her for it. Her ma was always wringing her hands and crying. Life had already been mean and hard, and her becoming different had just made it worse for everyone. Any bad luck that happened, and there had been plenty, had been blamed on her.

She remembered listening in on one of her parents' whispered conversations late one night when they'd thought that everyone else had been asleep. They'd talked about maybe drowning her in the well. Ma said that nobody would ever have to know. Pa had said no, because murdering her would be a sin, besides, she'd probably just

Travel out of the water, and tattle on them to the sheriff. Ma had said that the sheriff would never believe a devil child. Pa had put his foot down and told her to go to sleep.

Not everyone had been like that, though. Some folks in town had been friendly. Nice as could be, and even interested in what she could do, except Ma always shooed her away from *those people* with their *crazy notions*. There had only been one other person with magic in Ada. He could make things freeze, until he got run over by a tractor and killed. Then she'd been the only cursed oddball around.

Good thing I'm not odd anymore. She had quit being odd the day that Pa had sold her for ten dollars to her new family.

Opening her eyes, Faye came to a very profound realization: This was an empty house. It didn't mean anything to her. The scared little Okie girl didn't exist anymore. She had important things to do, like solve a big crime and then save the world from a horrible monster from outer space. There was no time for moping.

Faye usually kept a packet of matches in her pocket. Unlike many of her associates, she didn't smoke, but you never knew when you might need to set something on fire. She pushed up all the garbage into one corner, found a piece of old newspaper, and struck the match. The trash pile quickly caught as she walked back into the sunshine.

The wood was so dry that it went right up. She marveled at how fast the place was consumed. It was like all that stored-up anger and sadness burned extra hot. Faye leaned on the fence and watched her old house burn to the ground.

OCI Headquarters

CROW WAS STUDYING a gigantic map of the country when the office phone rang. He let one of the men answer it. He was too busy puzzling over the logistical issues related to the overall mission of the OCI, and didn't want to interrupt his train of thought. Using the 1930 census data, there were approximately one hundred and twenty-five million Americans. The estimate was that about one in a hundred of those had some small measure of magical affinity, which put that at a staggering one and a quarter million people. Luckily, he didn't need to worry about them yet. They would come later, after the country was used to the idea of controlling magic. The boss was clever like that.

His current issue was the one in a thousand that was an actual Active, with access to magic capable of causing serious problems. One-hundred-and-twenty-five thousand people would need to register, and many of them wouldn't want to. Those holdouts would be his problem.

The law had not even been read in Congress yet, but the boss knew that it was going to pass. It was too early to begin implementing the plan, but it was common knowledge that some specific Actives would cause trouble. They were Crow's red flags, and there were a *lot* of red flags on that map. Too many of those flags had question marks drawn on them. The goal was to neutralize as many of those as possible to ensure a smooth transition. Then there were the gold flags. Those were the special cases.

There were very few gold flags on his map, but—the ones that the boss had big plans for.

The agent that had answered the phone called out to him. "Mr. Crow, we've got a trip wire in Ada, Oklahoma."

There were a few men under his command capable of drawing spells. He'd had them out tagging specific locations with magical wards. He didn't like having question marks on any of his flags. They'd warded homes, schools, friends, family, that sort of thing, and if a powerful enough Active got close, it would set off the alarm. It had been an expensive long shot, but a few of the trip wires had paid off so far. Crow checked the map. Gold flag. Question mark. "The Traveler?"

"Confirmed."

"Excellent." For her, he'd had trip wires placed at a burned dairy farm in California, the remains of the Stuyvesant mansion in Mar Pacifica, and what they believed was the shack she'd grown up in. This one was *very* important to the boss, probably in the top five most important Actives out there. She needed to be taken alive.

OCI was still a small agency. That would change soon enough, but for now his resources were rather limited. He had no men in Oklahoma City. He was hesitant to involve the locals: first, they could be untrustworthy and it was too early to risk developing a backlash against the OCI's authority; and second, from what his intelligence said about the Traveler, she would slaughter anyone that took her on without a nullifier. The team in Dallas had one of the precious Dymaxions, but he didn't want to risk letting her escape by the time they could get there.

"Dispatch the team in Dallas." On the other hand, she

was less than a thousand miles away from OCI headquarters as the crow flies. That turn of phrase made Crow chuckle. He could be there himself in a few hours, and have enough Power to spare to use his single greatest weapon. It would be incredibly draining, but if he caught the Traveler, it would be worth it. "They'll take care of detainment and transport. I'll handle the Traveler personally."

Ada, Oklahoma

FAYE WAS OFF doing who knew what. That was the hard part about being assigned to follow a Traveler. There really was no way to keep up. The other two Grimnoir had no idea what was really going on and were busy having the car towed into town for repairs. Volunteering to find their group lodging had given the final knight an opportunity to do some investigating.

The knight's orders had been simple: find out if Faye Vierra really was the Spellbound. How to do that had been left up to the knight's discretion. The original plan had been to observe Faye's behavior and abilities, but when they'd left the *Minotaur*, a new opportunity had presented itself.

Talking the others into taking this particular route had been easy enough. Luckily, Faye had kept her mouth shut about her connection to the area. All of the information that had been gathered by the elders had indicated that the girl was ashamed of her upbringing. The knight had hoped that stopping here would have agitated her enough to ascertain if she was, in fact, the one they were waiting for. When they had not stopped, the knight had been forced to sabotage their car. Perhaps if they were forced to stay for a while, Faye would provide some clues. Unfortunately, that's when the Traveler had run off like a spoiled brat.

Why do these assignments always have to be so difficult?

One of the signs seen along the walk back into Ada had given the knight an idea. As a rule of thumb, when an alternative method of investigation presented itself, it never hurt to check it out, even if it was a long shot. This time the knight had been in luck. There was only one doctor still residing in the dying town, but he had been there for a very long time.

Doctor Lincoln was an ancient man, who insisted on going by 'Doc.' He was a gregarious sort, and happy enough for pleasant company that he was not even slightly suspicious about the line of questioning. The knight had found him in his office, reading a big-city newspaper that was several days old. After purchasing some headache powders, the knight had struck up a conversation about Ada, and what, if any, interesting things the good doctor had seen during his many decades working there. A few interesting diseases, several horrific farm injuries, a large fire, and then the inevitable outbreaks of sickness as a result of the dust storms. The knight pretended to be interested until the subject could be turned back on point.

"Fascinating . . . Lucky for these people to have a doctor of your skill. You seem very experienced. Have you ever had any cases relating to magic?"

"Why, yes. A few. Back in oh-nine the Hickmans had a boy with superstrength. He ran off and joined the circus.

One of the Ebert kids was an Icebox. Amazing thing. Poor child was crushed in a farm accident. Then there was the McCullum girl around the same time."

The knight leaned forward until the chair creaked. "What did she do?"

"Oh, she was quite the rabble-rouser as she got older. Always managing to get into the oddest places and predicaments. Strangest and cutest little thing. She belonged to this backwards family, real poor, working scut land so nasty even the Indians didn't want it. They didn't come into town too often, had all their babies at home, too poor to hire a midwife, let alone having any trust in medicine, but the father came into my office one day, all shook up. He said that their daughter's eyes had turned funny all of a sudden."

"Funny?"

"Grey. They turned grey. They actually glowed a little in the dark if you looked at them just right. Turned out that the girl was a Traveler! Can you believe it?"

"Those are scarce," the knight agreed. Now they were getting somewhere.

"Indeed. I tried to comfort those poor parents, telling them what a miracle this was for them, but they'd have none of it, the superstitious fools. I especially remember, because I consulted a journal article about the physiological aspects of Actives when they brought her in, but since the entry on Travelers was incorrect, I had to write the journal a correction letter."

"What was so different?"

"It said that though Travelers didn't begin to exercise their abilities until their brains were more formed, all known Travelers had the grey eyes even at birth. This child had blue eyes, then one day—*bam*—grey and shiny as could be."

What luck! This could be it. "Do you happen to know what date this child's eyes changed?"

"That's an odd question," Doc Lincoln replied.

"I'm a student of astronomy," the knight answered quickly. "I would be curious if there would perhaps have been any peculiar alignments of the stars or planets that day that could have caused such a thing."

"Huh? Well . . . Hadn't ever given that much thought."

"It is a more recent line of thinking on the possible origins of magic," the knight lied.

"That's interesting. Makes about as much sense as anything else I've heard." Doc Lincoln got up from behind his desk and shuffled over to a bookshelf. He scanned down the spines. "I kept the issue they printed my response letter in. Only thing I've ever had published in anything more prestigious than the local paper, back before it folded up of course. Let's see . . ." He pulled out one of the thin journals and opened it to the front. "Here it is . . . Blah, blah, blah. I was long winded as a younger man. Let's see, the child's symptoms appeared on September 18, 1918."

It was a date that the knight could never forget. *There was the answer.*

"Oh, would you look at the time," the knight said without looking at any clock. "I really must be going. It was a pleasure, Doctor."

"Yes, yes, of course." He slid the journal back into

place. "And remember, don't take too much of that powder at once. With your delicate complexion it could cause blemishes."

The knight politely escaped the doctor's office and headed for the only boardinghouse still open in Ada. Rooms had already been rented for the evening. The proprietor greeted the knight politely, as there was far too little business these days. There was a single washroom with a full length mirror, but luckily the door had a lock. The communication spell was hastily prepared.

The elder that had given this particular assignment materialized on the other side of the glass. When the elder saw who was calling, deep lines of worry appeared on his face. "Is it so? Is she the one?"

The knight spoke carefully. Lives were at stake. "Yes, Jacques. I have confirmed that her eyes turned Traveler's grey on September 18, 1918." Only a handful of people knew about the dangers of the Spellbound, which was one of the reasons this knight in particular had been chosen. "During Second Somme."

"The day Warlock died . . ."

"As feared, it was not destroyed. The spell never left Earth. It chose her. I am certain Faye is the Spellbound."

"I prayed this day would never come." The elder looked away, distressed. There were some hard decisions to be made. "The other elders are hesitant. They wouldn't dream of hurting this girl. You and I however, we know better . . . We have seen what she is destined to become with our own eyes."

"I will do what I must. I understand the consequences far better than they can. What would you have me do?"

He hesitated. "For now, wait. Stay close to her. I will bring you new orders."

In other words, don't kill her—*Yet*.

Faye felt a whole lot better after burning down the house, like a great big weight had been lifted off her shoulders. Being careful to make sure nobody saw her Traveling, she popped back over to Ada and found their automobile being worked on in the shop. When she asked what was wrong, the nice mechanic said that it was the darndest thing he'd ever seen an engine do, and then he used a bunch of mechanical words that Faye didn't understand to try to explain why. She still didn't grasp it, so finally he explained that some important part had simply got real hot and melted, which it didn't normally do, but that he'd have it replaced in no time.

The mechanic told her that her friends had gone over to the local boardinghouse to get supper. He gave her directions, and said to tell them that they would be able to leave tonight if they wanted, but that they were probably better off sleeping here and leaving in the morning. The winds tended to get worse at night and that was a fool's time to try to drive across the wastes.

Faye decided to walk to the boardinghouse. It wasn't far. Ada had changed a lot, but not for the better. It was a ghost town, only some of the ghosts hadn't realized it yet. Most folks had given up and moved on, but the stubborn or desperate were still here, scraping out a living in a place that had been ruined by magic. There weren't very many businesses left either. The seed store had burned down, but it wasn't like anybody would miss it in a place where nothing could grow. The wind had eaten the paint off of the buildings, giving everything a worn-out and faded look. Only a few people were out and about, and there were only a handful of beat-up cars on the dusty street.

Some children were playing baseball in the road. They were all barefoot, the ball was a rock, and the bat was a stick. The pitcher was probably the oldest, maybe twelve, and judging from his broken front teeth he'd stopped a few flying rocks with his mouth. He quit smiling when he saw her. The game stopped and the players watched her as she walked by. She was an outsider, and therefore interesting and suspicious.

A woman was coming down her porch, wiping her hands on an apron. She shouted into the road. "Hey, you kids best get on home. Gonna be a real howler tonight." The kids scattered like she was somebody they were used to taking orders from. Then she saw Faye and smiled. "Well, howdy, missy."

"Ma'am," Faye dipped her straw hat in greeting. Faye realized that this woman was familiar. She was the schoolteacher, not that Faye had been allowed to go to school, but she had been jealous of the kids that had. The schoolteacher lady had always struck Faye as kind when she'd seen her around town. Faye was thankful for Whisper's big dark glasses, because surely the teacher wouldn't recognize her. "Evening."

"Good evening to you, stranger." The teacher cocked her head to the side. Like everybody that still lived in Ada, she looked dried out and sunburned. The wind was blowing her ponytail around. "We don't get many new folks in Ada."

"Our car broke down," Faye said, keeping her head down.

"Breaking down is the way of things around these parts." The teacher was curious, like Faye reasoned all good teachers probably were. "You look familiar. Have you been around before?"

Faye quickly shook her head no and started walking.

"Now hold on." Ingrained manners forced Faye to stop. "You got a place to stay, honey? Because I think it's gonna be a hard one. You don't want to get caught outside on a storm night. It's liable to peel your skin off."

"We're at the boardinghouse, ma'am."

"Oh, that's nice." The teacher was trying to get a better look at her face. "That's a nice place. You staying long?"

"Passin' through." Faye realized that the lady was trying to remember where she'd seen her before. In fact, she was trying to get a look at her eyes . . . Faye reminded herself that she needed to think like a proper fugitive. It was time to get out of here. "I best be going. Evening, ma'am."

"'Bye then." The teacher nervously put her hands together. Faye had made it nearly to the corner when the woman shouted after her. "You know not everybody here blames the wizards!"

Faye froze. *She knew.* "What was that?"

"I'm just saying . . . The wastes. The drought. Some of us know they were trying to help when they broke Mother Nature. The wizards were just doing what they were told. Not all magic people are bad."

"I hear most of them are regular folks," Faye answered.

"It wouldn't be right to be angry at somebody that

didn't do nothing wrong to begin with. Not right at all." Suddenly embarrassed at saying so much, the lady turned and walked quickly up her porch. "Have a safe journey, child."

Faye waved goodbye.

A block later, she found the address that the mechanic had given her. There was a sign in front of the old two-story home, but the wind had eaten all the words off. A nice old lady with blue hair answered the door. The way she squinted so hard told Faye that she was mostly blind, and by the way she shouted all her words and kept saying "Eh?" she was hard of hearing too, but she eventually ushered Faye inside. The other knights were eating supper in the plain dining room downstairs. There was a pot of stew in the middle of the table. The smell made Faye's stomach rumble embarrassingly loud.

"Look who decided to grace us with her presence," Ian said. "What've you been up to?"

"Burning something," Whisper suggested. *Of course*, Whisper was a Torch. Her strange fire magic had probably told her what Faye had doing. Whisper wrinkled her nose. "You smell like smoke." *Or maybe not.*

Faye was embarrassed. "I had some things to do. See, I grew up near here . . ." She crossed her arms nervously. Being recognized by a local made her feel stupid. "And, well . . ."

"It don't matter." George got up and pulled out a chair for her. "I've been doing this for twenty years now and I've yet to meet a knight that didn't have some things they didn't feel like sharing."

"Thank you." Faye sat down. The old lady brought her

a bowl and spoon, shouted a few questions about if the stew was good or not, said "Eh?" and cupped her hand over her ear when Ian tried to answer that everything was fine, and then shuffled back into the kitchen. "She seems nice."

"Anytime a proprietor is willing to serve me without making a scene," George said, "I'll take it."

"She's blind as a bat and deaf as a stone. She probably thinks you're white as snow. When everybody's equally blurry, you don't discriminate," Ian said. "On the bright side, that means we can talk business."

"The car is almost done. We can leave tonight if we want," Faye reported as she scooped herself some stew. "The winds get worse at night, and if it's bad you can't hardly see until you drive into a ditch."

"I say we leave in the morning then," George said. "Did he say what was wrong with it?"

"Some doohickey melted," Faye said between shoveling stew into her mouth. It was mostly potatoes and carrots, flavorless, like they'd been buried for quite a few seasons and then boiled until they were chewable. "What about Lance and them?"

Ian seemed cranky as usual. "Last we heard, they're hunkering down for a bit, so they won't miss us for another day. They made a real mess with the Iron Guard. Maybe if we're lucky we'll be asked to do something useful instead."

Faye was tired of his negative attitude. "You're not going to be happy until I Travel your tongue someplace without the rest of your head, are you? What is *your* problem?"

George tried to intercede. "Now, you two—"

"My problem?" Ian raised his voice slightly. "I think this is a wild goose chase. We don't know that this creature of yours is even real. Knights have stooped to consulting with Iron Guards! No good can come of that. Meanwhile, our organization is being slandered and our members arrested—"

"And what do you propose we should be doing about that?" George asked with the utmost calm.

"Find out who framed us!"

"Others are working on that. We're—"

Ian cut him off. "We're scared of what the answer is going to be if we poke too deep. Japan, Russia, and a dozen other nations have used every excuse in the book to enslave their Actives. You think America is different?"

George's expression barely changed, but a little bit of anger crept in. "My father was born a slave. You really want to get all preachy at me?"

"Are you nostalgic for the institution then?" Ian furiously pushed his chair away from the table and stood. "Because mark my words, Actives will be *property* if we don't fight back now. We have to assert our place before we're trampled into history."

"So, you're one of those," George grumbled. "Thinking that Actives are better than Normals, not equals. I should have known."

"I'm no Active supremacist. Don't you dare put words in my mouth, Bolander!"

"*That's* why you spoke up for Harkeness and Rawls," Faye said quietly.

"I'm sorry for what they did to General Pershing and

your friends," Ian said quickly. "But those two men struck the greatest blow against tyranny that any of our people have ever accomplished. Through killing the Chairman, how many millions of lives did they spare?"

Faye's voice was deadly. "That's easy to say when it wasn't your grandpa getting shot down like a dog."

"I didn't mean . . ." Ian's face turned red. "Fine. You know what? I'm one of the best Summoners the Society has ever seen. I should be using my Power to hunt our *real* enemies, not the imaginary ones." He stormed out in a huff.

"Can I kill him now?" Faye asked. "Pretty please?"

The look on George's face indicated that he couldn't tell if she was serious or not. Just in case, he said, "No."

Whisper had not spoken during the argument. She waited for a door to slam upstairs. "Ian and I have worked together for a long time. Please do not judge him too harshly. He has had to face some difficult things recently."

Faye had just burned down the horrible shack that she'd been raised in. She had a pretty high standard for what she considered *difficult*. "Whisper, I—"

"Ian's wife was taken by the Imperium."

"Oh . . . I didn't know that."

"I was very fond of her. Everyone was." Whisper stirred her stew absently. "Despite Ian's family's disapproval, they wed young. She was one of us, Grimnoir. In fact, that is how the two of them met. His family is rather wealthy, aristocrats even, and they saw her as unworthy, their love, scandalous. He was gladly disowned to be with her."

"How come?" Faye asked.

"She was a quadroon."

Faye didn't know what that meant, but George nodded in understanding. "She had a black grandparent, Faye. That can cause some . . . *legal* issues most places."

"Among other things. It did not matter. She was truly the light of Ian's life. Her name was Beatrice and they were everything to each other. Such love . . . it was like a story."

The French had a way of making things sound extra romantic. For the briefest second, Faye thought that sounded a bit like how she secretly hoped Francis felt about her, but then she decided she was just being silly. "What happened?"

"Several years ago . . . was it four, five now? How time flies when you're battling evil . . . She was pregnant with their first child, residing at home while Ian was away. We do not know how the Iron Guard found her, but they did, and they took her. Oh, how we chased them, but they eluded us. The trail was cold, but Ian would never give up. He went all the way to China, following even the vaguest hints from the spirits he could Summon, but he was too late . . . Beatrice had been given to Unit 731."

Just saying the name of the Imperium's experimentation unit made Faye's stomach turn.

"The bastards," George hissed. "I've seen their work."

"They did horrible, awful things to her. Ian could not save her, so instead he used his Summoned to end her life, to spare her any more indignities at the hands of the Chairman's Cogs."

"That's awful," Faye said quietly. That would sour anyone. "I didn't know."

"Of course not. He never talks about it, but I know it

changed him. He used to have the soul of an artist, even his Summoned were beautiful, graceful, heavenly things, yet now they are misshapen, cumbersome beasts. The form of a Summoned is a window into the soul of the man that commands them. He would certainly be upset to know I had told you of this"—Whisper leaned in conspiratorially— "but there is another thing you must know. I believe you have also met some of Beatrice's family."

"Really?" Faye hadn't met that many Grimnoir, and those that she knew well had confided to her about their losses. "Who?"

"It would have been brief. Just long enough to wring the secrets from you. I'm speaking of Isaiah Rawls . . ." Whisper seemed to enjoy the look of surprise that appeared on Faye's face. "Oh, close your mouth before you catch a bug. Do you think that those villainous conspirators came to trouble you on a whim? No? I believe Isaiah's granddaughter's death was what pushed him to such drastic measures to destroy the Imperium. Yet, by betraying the Society, he dishonored the name of all those who had followed him as well. As General Pershing was your leader here, Isaiah was ours."

"He was a traitor," Faye insisted.

"To some, and to others, a hero."

"And to you?" Faye liked Whisper, so dreaded the answer.

"There is no doubt to me that Isaiah was a traitor, but sometimes a trust must be betrayed to serve the greater good. Such distinctions can be difficult. However, it was no accident that Ian volunteered to join the American knights. Maybe he is seeking to atone for deeds done on his behalf . . . I do not know."

George was leaning back in his chair, appearing deep in thought. "And why did you volunteer?"

"Me?" Whisper's smile was mischievous. "I go where the excitement is."

Chapter 10

I don't believe I ever saw an Oklahoman who wouldn't fight at the drop of a hat—and frequently drop the hat himself.

—Robert E. "Heavy" Howard,
Letter to H.P. Lovecraft, 1932

Ada, Oklahoma

THE WIND WAS JUST as brutal as she remembered. The old house shook and rattled with every gust. The window panes flexed so much that the glass creaked like it was threatening to pop. The windows had been caulked shut to keep the dust out, and there were towels stuffed in the bottoms of the doors. The view out the window was a brown mass of blowing dust, interspaced with occasional soft blurs from a handful of lights, but around nine o'clock at night the power had gone out. After that, the dust provided its own sort of shadowed light, almost like it was infused with visible energy. Before he'd gone to bed, George had pointed out that there was static electricity in the dust, and had said that there was *lots* of it.

Power outages were a common enough occurrence, so the old lady that ran the boardinghouse had appeared and left them several candles and some matches so they could find their way to their room when they decided to retire for the evening. Whisper waited for her to leave, then simply lit the candles by thinking about it.

The winds continued to grow in intensity as Faye and Whisper sat in the dining room and watched the fury unfold.

"How can anyone live like this?" Whisper had finally asked.

"Most can't. The ones that are still here . . ." Faye thought of the teacher and those kids playing stickball. "Just tough I guess. Like human cactuses. Only more windproof. So, what's the word? Francis uses it for his fast blimps. *Aerodynamic* . . . So they're like aerodynamic cactuses."

"You have a strange way of looking at things, Faye."

"Thanks."

Whisper gathered up one of the candles. "I am going to bed. I do not know if I will be able to sleep, since the way this place is shaking, I'm worried it will fall down at any moment."

"Naw. This house is sturdy. All the flimsy places fell down a long time ago. You can get used to anything if you're tough enough."

"Have you ever heard of the principle of erosion?"

"Nope."

Whisper chuckled. "Goodnight, Faye."

Once Faye was sure she was alone, she snuck into the kitchen and got a box of table salt and a small glass of water. Using her Power, she took a look at the world around her. Faye called that particular trick her *head map*. With it she was able to get a basic view of everything in safe Traveling range. It didn't cover nearly as much area as it had last year. If she concentrated on one particular spot, she could instantly tell if there were any small things that could harm her if her body were to suddenly appear there. Her head map told her that Traveling anywhere out in the wind would be extremely dangerous. There were just too many things flying around, most were small enough that her passing would just shove them out of the way, but some of them were bigger and could get stuck in her. She knew from one particular incident involving a crunchy beetle fused into her heel that she never wanted to do that again.

But she wasn't checking her head map in order to Travel. It was also a handy tool for seeing where everyone else was when you wanted some privacy. The old lady was in her bed. All the other Grimnoir were in their own rooms. So she was safe.

She wasn't tired yet, and she was dying to talk to somebody she knew she could trust. The person she really wanted to see was Francis. He was good and honest, and she really liked him, and she knew that he liked her back. They had gone out on a few dates, even kissed, which had been super nice, but that was about it, because Faye was certainly not the *type* of girl that Francis had associated with before. At first she'd been worried that Francis would be embarrassed to be seen with her, since he was so very famous and rich, and she was just a nobody, and everywhere they went in public, people would take their picture, but Francis didn't care one whit about what folks thought about him. He did whatever he put his mind to, and Faye loved that. She missed his easy smile, his sense of humor, even the awkward way he tried to protect her though she was way tougher than he was. Basically, she missed him.

Plus she felt she should check in, just because she knew otherwise Francis might go and do something stupid on his own.

Faye made a circle of salt on the table and started to draw the communication spell from memory. This time she imagined that she was a little girl again, drawing pretty designs in the dirt floor of the McCullum shack, and when she thought of it that way, the strange geometries of the Power suddenly seemed to make a lot more sense. She used her Power, just a tiny bit, and thought hard about Francis to awaken the design. If it worked like it was supposed to, his ring would burn and get his attention. Remarkably, she managed to complete the spell on her very first try. The circle floated into the air and filled the room with white light.

There was a thump from the roof. It was pretty loud. Probably a flying branch or something. She would've checked her head map again, but didn't know if that would mess up the communication spell or not, and she didn't want to go through the effort of making another one.

It took a couple of minutes for Francis to get on. The background was his office in New York, which was good news because that meant that at least he had stayed put like he was supposed to. The circle spun around, showing windows full of New York lights, until the image filled with Francis' head. "Faye!"

"Hi. You got your face fixed."

"About as good as possible, but it wasn't particularly nice to start with."

Faye disagreed, but she'd feel foolish saying so. "Well, I think you look nice."

She could have sworn that Francis blushed. "Did you do this spell yourself?"

"I did."

"Very clear. This is your best one yet. You're quite the talented wizard." Now it was Faye's turn to blush. "So where are you? Wait, that's probably a secret."

"On account of them maybe coming to arrest you, yeah." Faye grinned.

"Don't worry, I'm cooking up something. Next time I meet the OCI, I'll be ready. You don't pick a fight with a Stuyvesant and expect to win."

"You picked a fight with a Stuyvesant and won," she pointed out.

"That's different. I . . ." There was a brief sound from behind her, like old canvas whipping in the wind. Francis' eyes widened in fear. "Behind you!"

Faye turned to see what Francis was looking at. She was surprised to find that there was a man in a black coat and hat standing in the shadows just outside the ring of white light. The hat dipped slightly in greeting. "Evening." His voice was low and deadly.

"Faye, that's him! That's the—"

"Man that's going to destroy the Grimnoir. You betcha. That's me. Don't worry, Francis. I'll be along for you shortly. Right now I need a moment with the Traveler." Hands loose and open at his sides, he took a step into the light. He was shorter than she was, but strong looking.

"Leave her alone, you son of—"

The man simply looked at the circle of salt and it shattered. Francis was silenced as the spell dissipated. The room was now lit by only a single flickering candle. Faye didn't mind. Her grey eyes could see much better in the dark than most folks', yet his eyes seemed to gleam a little too brightly as well, only red instead of grey.

"You know who I am?"

"Crow." Faye moved a bit so that the table was between them. Francis had said that he had a device that could block magic, though she could still feel her Power just fine, and she had a .45 hidden in the folds of her dress. Faye was calm. This was nothing she couldn't handle. "You're a very bad man."

"Simple, but sure. I'm the bad man and I'm placing you under arrest. I don't want to hurt you, though I will, and I'll enjoy it."

Faye checked her head map. "You're alone?" she asked incredulously.

"I don't need help."

She snorted. It was hard to intimidate somebody that had fought Iron Guards. "You ain't near as smart as you think you are then."

He circled around the table. She kept moving to keep it between them. "You first came to our attention after the *Tokugawa* incident. Some of the UBF survivors talked about you doing some mighty impressive things. Impressive enough to get my boss's attention. We started researching you, and what we figured out was amazing. What if I told you I know why your Power is so different? What if I could tell you exactly what you are?"

"I'd figure you were lying through your teeth."

"Aren't you even a little curious?"

"Oh, I'm plenty curious, but you can just keep on lying. You're alone but I've got friends."

Crow paused and crinkled his nose. "I know. I can smell them . . . a Crackler, a Torch, and a . . . Summoner? Well, I'll be. I know exactly what you are, kid. You're probably wondering how come your Power is so much weaker now than it was." That was a surprise. Not even all the Grimnoir knew about that. She tried not to let her surprise show, but Crow just smiled and went on. "Before, I bet it was like you could do anything, then you saved all your friends and nearly burned yourself out. You hadn't even been that strong for very long, but you got strong quicker and quicker."

"I practiced."

"And I bet Babe Ruth practiced too, but only a Brute could hit two hundred homers. You're no ordinary Active, kid. Come with me and all your questions will be answered. This whole thing is bigger than you and me, or your friends, or your Society. Sure, I'm a bad man, but I work for the good guys. You fight me, you're fighting against your country. Come on, Faye."

"My friends are innocent."

"Sure they are. Come with me then and help clear their names. I don't want to fight. I'm asking real nice here."

Faye stopped. "You should have thought of that before you beat up my boyfriend."

"You know what? Fuck it." Crow's teeth looked slightly sharp in the flickering light. "I was hoping you'd fight. I'm curious to see if you're as good as everybody made you out to be." He moved in a flash. The table came flipping end over end at her. It smashed against the wall as Faye Traveled to the side. Crow charged her, but Faye immediately appeared behind him. She pulled out the Colt .45, racked the slide, then raised it and pointed it at Crow's back.

"I've never shot a policeman before. You better leave before I start."

He looked back over his shoulder with an evil grin. "That's the spirit." Crow whirled toward her and Faye instinctively fired. The gun bucked in her hand. He kept coming, so she fired twice more, then Traveled back to where she'd started from. Crow passed right through where she'd been standing and crashed hard into the wall. He slid down and collapsed onto the floor, hands pressed against his chest.

Damn it! She really hadn't wanted to shoot any policemen. She was a *terrible* fugitive. Faye kept the pistol on him and shouted, "I warned you!"

"You killed me . . ." Crow's head fell forward. The hat covered his eyes.

George Bolander came hurtling down the stairs with a revolver in one hand and an oil lamp in the other. "What happened?" He saw Crow on the ground and aimed his gun at the man. "You all right, Faye?"

"That's the government man, Crow," Faye explained as Whisper and Ian ran down the stairs. Ian was shirtless and Whisper had on a blue silk robe with pretty flower designs on it. Both of them had handguns too. "He attacked me. I had to shoot him."

The four knights watched Crow's still form for a moment.

"Well, Ian, you wanted to take the fight to the other side," George said. "Looks like you're getting your wish."

A particularly nasty gust of wind shook the house. "Was he alone?" Whisper asked.

"Far as I can tell," Faye answered.

"There's something wrong here. This just feels . . . odd." Ian walked over, keeping his pistol trained on Crow the entire time, and kicked the G-man hard in the leg with one bare foot. There was no response. He moved Crow's hand away from the bullet wound. In the shadows it seemed almost as if the hole was *smoking*. "What the hell?"

"What's wrong?" George asked.

"I can feel it with my Power." Ian squatted down next to the body and used the muzzle of his pistol to lift the brim of Crow's hat, revealing four brightly glowing red eyes in a horizontal line across his face.

The G-man shoved Ian across the room so hard that the knight bounced off the far wall. Crow practically flew to his feet. "Just fooling with you."

Faye had four shots left in her pistol and she cranked them off so fast that they sounded like a machine gun. Whisper and George weren't too far behind. Crow was riddled with bullets and he jerked as they hit. Then it was quiet and the guns were empty. Crow was still standing, smoke drifting from the bullet holes. He slowly raised his glowing eyes and smiled at her. Now his teeth were *definitely* sharp, like rows of bone needles. Faye yelped and rummaged through her pockets for her other magazine. "Nice try, Grimmys. Now let's see if you're ready to play in the majors."

Crow moved incredibly fast and knocked George to the ground. The oil lantern shattered on the floor. Flames quickly spread across the wood. The oil hit Faye's feet and she Traveled back a split second ahead of the fire.

Whisper dropped her empty pistol and stretched her hands toward the flames. The circle of fire suddenly contracted tighter and tighter, until it was a ball of solid heat. She whipped one hand toward Crow. The oily ball of fire followed the trajectory and streaked right into his chest. There was a terrible flash and Crow was hurled into the living room.

Faye got her spare magazine into the pistol, yanked back the slide and let it slingshot forward, then Traveled after Crow. She landed behind a thick couch, raised her gun, and . . . Crow was gone.

"Watch out. He's really fast!" Faye shouted. "George?"

"I'm fine," George answered with just a hint of pain. "Ian?"

"He's a Summoned!"

That was impossible. Summoned were stupid. Crow was a person. But those eyes . . . They'd looked just like the terrible Bull King that they'd fought in Mar Pacifica. The only way they'd been able to beat the Bull King was because she had tracked down and killed its Summoner. Faye checked her head map. Where was—*There!*

The rooms of the first floor formed a ring around the main stairwell. Crow had circled back around and was coming through the kitchen and heading for her friends in the dining room. Moving like a freight train, he kicked the door into splinters and streaked toward Whisper. Faye appeared and swept her out of the way an instant before impact. Crow's momentum destroyed the next wall. Immediately, he turned with a roar, looking too big, twisted and inhuman. His clothing was stretching and tearing as he grew. *No* . . . that wasn't fabric. That was *skin*. Crow came out of the wall and roared with a noise that couldn't possibly come out of a human being.

George raised his hands. Blue light seemed to pour from his eyes, before it streaked down his arms and erupted from his fingertips. A blinding arc of electricity crashed into Crow. The noise was deafening. Thick black liquid sprayed out of Crow's chest and across the room, burning and smoking. Faye cried out as some hit her arm and sizzled.

The demon was hurled back, but kept thrashing and pushing against the energy. After several seconds of the Crackler's fury, George gasped and stumbled, dizzy. Crow took a step back toward them. His body was charred to ash and billowing smoke. "Not too shabby," he said around a mouthful of needle teeth.

"You shoulda been fried!" George bellowed.

"There's nothing worse than a nigger with magic." Crow seemed to shimmer as his body continued to change. "Time to learn your place, boy." His feet scorched the floor as he strode toward George.

"He's a Greater Summoned!" Ian grabbed George by the arm. "He's too strong. Up the stairs! Go! Go!" Ian fired his pistol repeatedly as George and Whisper ran past him.

Good idea! They were trying to funnel Crow so he wouldn't have room to maneuver, but he was too fast. They wouldn't make it. She needed to distract Crow away from her slower friends. "Hey!" Faye appeared directly behind the demon, shoved her pistol into his back and fired twice. He threw a backhand at her, but Faye appeared directly in front of him, extended her pistol and shot Crow squarely through the brain.

The blast of smoke from the wound blinded her. He lashed out and Faye gasped as a terrible burn crossed her stomach. Crow lifted one hand and showed her his newly formed claws. "Try to keep up, Toots."

She Traveled out of his sight and landed in the kitchen. The distraction had given her friends a moment, but it had cost her. Wincing, Faye lifted her blouse and discovered a mean cut dripping blood. "Darn it!" But like Mr. Sullivan always said, if it wasn't squirting then it wasn't a big deal. Faye grabbed the biggest kitchen knife she could out of a wooden block with one hand and a cast iron frying pan in her other. Now she was *mad*.

Faye appeared in the dining room. The curtains were on fire and the place was filling with smoke, natural and demon both. Crow was trying to push his way up the stairs, but was being simultaneously blasted with arcs of electricity and a stream of billowing fire. Whisper and George could only hold that kind of Power for so long and it gradually tapered off to nothing. Crow began climbing the stairs.

"Hey, stupid!" Faye shouted.

Crow slowly turned to look at her. At some point he had become seven feet tall and ram's horns were sprouting out the side of his head. He was charred like a piece of meat forgotten on a campfire spit. His skin was flaking off in gigantic burned chunks. Smoke was bleeding from dozens of holes. His voice had become deeper, the kind of voice you only hear in your nightmares. "You should have come along quietly, Faye. Your friends wouldn't have had to die."

She held up the butcher knife and frying pan. "Only person dying around here tonight is you!" She screamed and leapt. Crow surged toward her. Faye disappeared at the last second, came around, and clubbed him in one horn with the frying pan. The knife went through one of his gigantic legs. Faye Traveled back, breathing hard, but Crow was already following her. *Crap! He's faster than Delilah!*

Faye moved through the house, popping in and out as quick as her head map could determine it was safe. Crow followed her, swinging madly with fingers that had turned into black sickle claws. She continued to Travel in, striking and stabbing wildly, then getting out at the last second. The knife was slick with demon's ink. Her eyes and lungs stung. The house was wreathed in flames. Five jumps. Six jumps. Crow was still right behind. Seven. Eight. Nine.

She was getting tired. Her Power was flickering.

Crow followed her into the living room. He picked up one of the couches and hurled it at her. She barely had time to move before it shattered the window and flew into the night. The wind came howling in and brought the choking dust with it. Faye's head map screamed danger everywhere. Grit struck her in the eyes. The dust particles were too big to Travel in! *Upstairs!*

The demon lifted his hands to his four eyes as the dust

blinded him as well. Desperate, Faye leapt and landed at his feet. Shoes had been replaced with enormous goat's hooves. Lifting the knife, Faye screamed, and then drove the knife down as hard as she could through the hoof, pinning it to the floor. Crow emitted a horrific shriek and lifted his other foot to smash her through the boards, but Faye was already gone.

She hit the carpet on the second floor landing. The dust was billowing up the stairs, chasing her. Soon there would be nowhere safe for her to Travel. The neighboring houses were in range, but she wasn't about to abandon her friends. Below, Crow continued his demonic roar. Whisper was at the top of the stairs, moving her hands back and forth, gathering the fire roaring through the first floor together into another solid ball. The violent wind whipped her black hair around her head in a halo. George appeared, shoving a heavy dresser in front of Whisper to serve as a last-ditch barricade. Ian was sitting on the floor, looking calm as could be.

"What're you doing?"

Ian barely opened one eye a crack. "Calling in reinforcements."

"Poop." Faye checked her head map. The old lady was still sound asleep in her room. Faye couldn't just let some nice grandma get burned to death. This was going to take too much Power, but she had to do it. Faye popped into her room, took the woman by her arm, then picked a spot that seemed nice two houses down.

Faye appeared in the living room of a very surprised family. They had all been watching out their window the exploding, electrical light show coming from the flaming boardinghouse, and they screamed when they saw her. "Hey! Take care of her, would ya?" The father had been stuffing shells from a cardboard box into an old pump shotgun, but he yelped and dropped it when she scared him near to death. "Mind if I borrow this? Thanks!" Faye grabbed the shotgun and the box of buckshot, concentrated, and Traveled back.

She picked the furthest room from the stairs and barely beat the flooding dust. It stung her skin, but a moment later and it would have been *inside* her skin. Faye loaded the old Winchester the rest of the way as she walked down the hall. Her eyes were watering and she could barely breathe as poison smoke burned her lungs.

Crow was on fire and rumbling up the stairs. Whisper was continually whipping flames into the demon, over and over, her robe torn open and snapping in the wind around her. "Burn, demon!" The only reason they could breathe at all was that Whisper's magical skill was so great that she was causing the smoke to be funneled away from them. The black air coming from Crow's wounds was darker than the natural smoke roiling around him.

Faye leaned around Whisper, shouldered the shotgun and let Crow have it right in the face. The buckshot messed him up far worse than the pistol bullets. It kicked her good as she fed him four more rounds, but then the Winchester was empty and she was fumbling to reload from the box. Whisper fell back, Power exhausted, and George took her place.

Lightning crackled between his fingers. His eyes were pools of flashing blue. All of Faye's hair stood up. "This place is coming down. Get them outside, Faye. Now!"

"You can't stop him by yourself," she cried.

"Do it!"

Faye did as she was told. With Whisper's Power done, the smoke and dust was too much to bear. She couldn't breathe. Her head was spinning. She fell and the shotgun shells spilled down the carpet. The entire house shook and groaned as beams snapped. Faye crawled for the next room; she could at least breathe a little on the floor. She could feel Whisper behind her but couldn't see anything. She crashed into something soft. *Ian.* He seemed to be in a daze as she pulled him along.

The three of them fell into the bedroom.

"George?" Whisper asked.

There was an awful roar behind them and the crash of thunder. Blue light flickered through the smoke.

"Reinforcements?" Faye asked.

Ian was coughing. "On the way."

Faye made it to the window. It wouldn't open. Of course, everything was caulked shut because of the storm. She used the shotgun butt to smash the glass out. There were shingles below them. "Get outside!" Whisper went through the window and disappeared into the dust. She turned back and ran into Ian. "I'm going back for George."

"Can you Travel him?"

"Can't. Dust."

"You'll die!" he shouted.

"Probably." She started to push past, but Ian suddenly threw his weight against her. "Wait! Ian, no!" The next thing she knew he had used his weight advantage to shove her to the window, then he hoisted her up and through.

Faye rolled outside and landed on her shoulder on the shingles. Ian was visible for one last moment in the blue light above, a look of determination on his face, and then he was gone. “No!”

“Faye!” Whisper called. Faye looked down to see Whisper standing in the yard. It wasn’t too far to jump. The entire house shook violently and more timbers burst. Sparks swam past her as Faye kicked her legs over the edge and let herself drop. Whisper tried to catch her but they both ended up hitting the dirt hard. “Come on. Hurry.” Whisper grabbed her by the hand and pulled her along.

They made it out into the road. Crow’s demonic wail could be heard even over the wind. Behind them the house rumbled as half of it collapsed. Faye screamed in frustration. George and Ian were going to die and there was nothing she could do.

“What is that?” Whisper pointed at something gigantic moving through the fire. At first Faye thought that it was Crow, but unless he had changed even more drastically than before, this was something entirely different. The thing glowed with a calm pale light, but then it disappeared behind the flaming timbers. “It cannot be.”

“What?”

Whisper grabbed her hand and held it tight.

The pale light reappeared, this time coming through the front door. It had the red eyes of a Summoned, and was just as fearsome as Crow or the Bull King, only different, and Faye knew that this was what they spoke of when they said that a Summoned could appear as an angel.

It was eight feet tall and broad. Except for four small

eyes, its features were formless and soft. Its hands were simple and far too large. Its torso was disproportionately bigger than its stubby legs. It was carrying a burden in each hand. One of them coughed.

Ian and George! Faye squealed with delight.

The mighty Summoned dropped the knights at the edge of the yard, then turned back toward the flames just as the house fell down with a awful crash. A cyclone of fiery debris was sucked up into the sky. Faye ran up, grabbed the first body and started dragging him away. She couldn't even tell who it was because he was so filthy with soot.

The roof of the boardinghouse hit the ground last, coming to rest almost perfectly level as if the house had merely sunk evenly into the ground below. Faye felt a twinge of hope. Surely, Crow couldn't have survived that. No matter how great of a demon he was, that had to have—

A bubble formed in the roof. One claw ruptured through the shingles. Crow shoved his way through and clambered into the open. He was twisted and broken, but somehow still alive. "I'm not done with you yet, little girl." Crow freed himself and leapt through the debris to land in the yard.

Ian's pale Summoned stood, blocking its way. The two huge things faced each other for a moment. Crow cocked his horned head to the side. He was obviously weakened, parts of his body withering and deflating as the unnatural smoke that served as Summoned's blood was spilled. The pale Summoned was an unknown quantity. It did not move.

Flashlights and lanterns bobbed around the street. People had been drawn toward the commotion. Faye could only imagine what they were thinking as they saw the two titanic Summoned facing each other through the storm.

Crow ran toward Ian's Summoned. They collided. The pale thing's elephantlike feet slid back through the dirt as Crow struck furiously. Then the pale fists began to fall, striking with monotonous thunder, each one hitting like a piece of construction equipment.

The two monsters were entirely obscured as smoke poured from their wounds, but the blows could still be heard. *THUD. THUD. THUD.*

Faye realized the person she'd been dragging was Ian. His eyes were squeezed tight and he was grinding his teeth as he tried to control his Summoned. Suddenly, Ian screamed and every muscle in his body clenched tight.

The smoke cleared. The pale Summoned stumbled back as Crow drove his fist deep into its body. Crow ripped his hand free in a shower of flaming ink. The creature sank to the ground and began to melt into smoke. Banished.

"You idiots. You don't know what you're dealing with. I'm the greatest Summoner that's ever lived. Demons don't possess people! I possess them! You kill this body and I'll be back tomorrow. I can't die. I can't be beaten!" The surviving demon was falling apart, its body withering and blowing away on the wind. It was not long for this world, but it would be enough.

Faye could barely breathe. There was no way she could Travel. Crow's four red eyes locked onto her as he approached. The smoke solidified into massive wings, stretching from Crow's shoulders across the entire road. He was coming to take her away. She had nothing left to fight him with. Faye found the knife Lance had made for her, drew it, and held it out in front of her. She was not going without a fight. Whisper appeared at her side. The fire in her hands was weak and sputtering. Ian seemed to be unconscious, overwhelmed by the destruction of his Summoned.

Crow stopped twenty feet away and pointed at her. His red eyes were filled with madness. Crow's voice boomed across the town. "Sally Faye McCullum, alias Faye Vierra, poor white trash from a pigsty shack in Ada, Oklahoma, member of the illicit Grimnoir terrorist organization, by the authority granted to me by the Office of the Coordinator of Information, you are under arrest for illegal magic." The demon cackled as he turned toward the witnesses that had gathered by the commotion. "You see this? You all see this! Let this be a lesson to anybody that crosses us!" Crow shouted at the witnesses. Faye knew that somehow being inside that Greater Summoned had driven him crazy.

A single shape tottered through the dust on the opposite side of the demon. George was battered, burned, and bleeding, but he still managed to raise his voice nearly as loud as Crow had. "Demon! I'm George Bolander, knight of the Grimnoir." He raised his fists high into the air. "And I'm sending you back to hell!"

The air felt *wrong*.

Lightning flashed through the swirling dust above. The entire sky turned blue. It was almost like a smaller version of the Geo-Tel.

"What's he doing?" Faye shouted.

"He's using up all his Power at once, drawing on the energy of the storm." Whisper cried. "He will surely die!"

Crow swiveled his horns and studied the sky, then looked back at George and roared, "Show me what you got, boy!"

George roared as the storm ripped the life right out of him. Blinding lightning consumed the entire sky, a hundred strikes in a second, dragged to Earth by one man's Power. Thunder shook the whole world. A wall of white electricity descended and everyone in town screamed as it surged down to engulf them.

A hundred feet above the ground all the lightning stopped, rolling and twisting, as if held fast by the hand of God. Then it all flashed inward at once into one brilliant point directly over the demon. The arc burned their eyes for a moment, a pillar of blindness, then it struck with a concussion that took the whole town off its feet and shattered every window on the block.

It took Faye a moment to collect herself. When she came to, the wind had stopped blowing, leaving the night eerily calm. All she could see was a white streak. Gradually it turned purple and she could sort of see around it. The dust was falling from the sky and settling over them like peaceful snow. Ears ringing, she got to her feet and stumbled toward where George had been standing.

There was a deep hole scorched through the road where Crow had been. The road had been melted into tar and the sand was cooling into glass, but outside of a pinpoint circle, there was no damage. The demon was completely *gone*, blown into smoking ash and scattered.

George was flat on his back, arms spread wide. His eyes were open and collecting the falling dust. She landed on her knees next to him and took his head in her hands. He almost looked like he was smiling. "George?"

But her friend was dead.

The Power had torn the life right out of his body.

The ringing in her eyes began to subside. Folks were screaming, crying, praying . . . Somebody was banging the bell at the church and the burning wood of the boardinghouse hissed and popped.

George was dead. Another friend . . . Another knight . . . How many people had to die? *Not again. Not again. Damn it, not again.* Faye looked up at the sky and screamed until it hurt.

And then it started to rain.

Whisper

Chapter 11

The female half of the population of this nation are utterly powerless to strike an unjust law from the statute books. It is difficult to justify the notion that women are inferior, and thus incapable of voting rationally, when some of us can move objects with our minds, while others have displayed the constitution of ten strong men. Can you display any such feats, Your Honor? Do not tell me I am out of order! I already know you cannot, because I can read your thoughts.

—Elizabeth D. Carlyle,
Trial on the Charge of Illegal Voting, 1873

Bell Farm, Virginia

THE FARMHOUSE was quieter with Jane and Lance gone. Too quiet, and that just made him restless. Sullivan poked sullenly at his breakfast and wished that he could be doing something useful, but that was difficult when you were Public Enemy Number One.

Their rings had woken them up in the middle of the night. Francis had been hysterical. Then another call had come from a young knight that none of them had met before named Whisper. She'd told them about the battle in Oklahoma. One knight killed and two injured, including Faye.

Francis had wanted to fly down there himself, but Lance had talked him down. Since the OCI had seen him talking to Faye, that meant that there was now no doubt as to his membership in the Society. Francis needed to lose his tail and go to ground before he got rolled up too. Francis hadn't liked that at all, but the kid was smart, and knew that Lance was talking sense.

Faye's group was on the run and heading east, but that left about thirty-plus hours of driving ahead of them. Jane had volunteered to go and meet them halfway. They could certainly use her Power. Faye had some cuts and had been scalded by demon smoke, and another knight named Ian had been burned and inhaled too much smoke. Of course, Dan wasn't about to let his wife go do something potentially dangerous without him, and though his name had shown up in the papers, Sullivan wasn't about to try and talk him out of going. He let Jane do that. Their Healer was hard to argue with when she set her mind to something, and she really didn't want Dan getting arrested.

Since Grimnoir always tried to work with backup, Lance had volunteered to go with her. He'd promised Dan not to flirt with his pretty young wife, and had gotten out of there before Dan had a chance to turn too red.

That had left Dan Garrett and Jake Sullivan to come up with their next move. Dan, being the much less recognizable of the two, had taken Lance's truck into town to pick up the morning papers, and Sullivan read while he ate. His picture was on page one again, the dangerous public face of the Active menace. They'd put his picture right next to one of the assassin, like they were best buddies or something. Sullivan almost threw the paper down in disgust, but he forced himself to keep reading. Questions were being raised about how someone so obviously dangerous had been given an early release from Rockville. J. Edgar Hoover had been unavailable for comment.

There was nothing about Oklahoma yet, though a high profile Active battle against a Greater Summoned in front of witnesses surely wouldn't help their case very much. Roosevelt had been Healed, though he hadn't made a public statement yet. The inauguration was still on schedule. The people were up in arms. Active businesses had been put to the torch and many had been hurt. Some Shard kid had killed a few mobbers in Brooklyn, in what read to Sullivan like a clear-cut case of self-defense, but the editorials were screaming for his blood. Hearings were being convened about addressing the "Active problem." Antimagic groups were holding a gigantic march on Washington.

The real bad news was an article six pages in, so small he almost missed it.

Dan came into the kitchen. "Hey, pass me the funny pages if you don't mind . . ." He trailed off when he saw the look on Sullivan's face. "Oh no. What's wrong now?"

"Imperium ambassador dies of heart attack."

"Heart attack? Let me see that." Dan adjusted his glasses and read. "They killed him! They killed him to keep quiet about the fake Chairman."

"Looks like it."

"You think they'll spread the word to the Iron Guards about being on the lookout for this Pathfinder? They have to . . . Even they couldn't be that stupid."

Their effort had been for nothing. Taking his warning seriously meant that the real Chairman was dead. Whoever was leading the Imperium now would kill their own and risk the coming of the Enemy to stay in power. Sullivan put the paper down and walked outside without another word.

They were on their own. He would have to stop the Enemy himself.

Deep in thought, he wandered for a bit. There was a woodpile behind the house. Physical activity helped him think. He found an ax in the shed. It would be like breaking rocks. Just like old times.

Sullivan pondered over their predicament while he methodically split the logs. The Enemy was coming, but they didn't know how much time they had. They'd failed to alert the one government that did believe in the creature, and they were fugitives from their own. The ax rose and fell, and then Sullivan would drag over another log. The process repeated itself. He worked until his shirt was damp with sweat and the pile of split wood had grown large.

There were three possibilities. Defeat the Pathfinder themselves, or convince either the Imperium or the U.S. to do it for them.

First off, he didn't know if they could defeat the Pathfinder. The Chairman had been scared of the damn thing, and the Grimnoir had spent decades trying to kill the Chairman. It was only through treachery and luck that they'd finally taken him down. They didn't know enough about this thing to trick it, and they sure as hell couldn't count on getting lucky.

The Imperium . . . Somebody was playing Chairman, and doing a fine job of it from all accounts, but he wasn't the real Chairman, and that meant he could die. If the false Chairman was killed, then they'd have no choice but to believe. The issue then became traveling to the other side of the world and murdering a head of state, who was surely protected by a legion of Iron Guard, demons, and ninjas.

There were other Grimnoir in that part of the world, though . . . Something could be arranged. *Ironic*. This had begun with an accusation of them being assassins, yet their best chance to save the world would make that label a reality.

Sullivan smashed the ax cleanly through a gigantic log.

The last possibility was getting his own nation to pay attention. Sure, this Pathfinder was tough, but it couldn't possibly be a match for the entire might of the U.S. military. Sullivan was no politician. He had no idea how to get the powers-that-be involved. That was way over his head. After Mar Pacifica, the Grimnoir had tried to get the truth in front of the right people. Some had believed, some hadn't, but nobody had acted on it because to do so meant war. And though many could tell it was coming, no one was ready for war with the Imperium.

The Enemy was even more dangerous than the Imperium. The people running the U.S. government had to know. He had to figure out how to make them believe.

It would be difficult, even more so because Actives were so hated and feared right now, which was partially understandable considering what had happened over the last few years. The Grimnoir in particular were being cast as criminals, and the OCI was out to destroy them . . .

Why?

Sullivan paused mid-swing. Why was the OCI so motivated? Who'd created them? What was their purpose? The Grimnoir's only contact with that shadowy organization had been violent. The Society had sources that he was unaware of, they were a large group after all, and those knights were trying to figure those questions out. As long as the OCI was hunting them like animals, then they'd never stop the Enemy. Why had the secret police fixated on the Society? He smashed the next log into splinters without thinking.

The Grimnoir had to clear their names first. Only then would the government listen.

"Jake, come here for a minute," Dan shouted from the edge of the barn. Sullivan stuck the ax into a log and walked over. Dan was sitting in the truck with the door open, listening to the radio. "It's about you."

The newscaster was just finishing up. "—tor of the Bureau of Investigation, J. Edgar Hoover, denies that Heavy Jake Sullivan ever worked for, and was in fact paroled specifically on behalf of, the Bureau. Mr. Hoover has stated that these lies are simply slander against his brave agents."

That made Sullivan smile. Hoover always had hated bad publicity. He had berated and punished his men after the Maplethorpe case in Detroit and the time they'd let

Delilah get away in Springfield. And then it clicked . . . "The OCI screwed Hoover. They're who put my name in the papers and connected us." Hoover never would have done anything that could have splashed muck on his precious bureau.

"Former Illinois senator, Bradford Carr, is demanding a full investigation to find out if the Bureau inadvertently released a member of an Activist anarchist group. Senator Carr's close friend and mayor of Chicago, Anton Cermak, was one of the murdered in Friday's attack. Mr. Hoover will be holding a press conference this afternoon at the Department of Justice building."

They weren't that far away. "You thinking what I'm thinking?"

Dan frowned. "Apparently not, but you've got that crafty look."

"Hey, I trusted your last plan. I just want to go say hi to an old pal."

OCI Headquarters

"YOU FOOL. You incompetent! What in the hell were you thinking?"

Crow kept his eyes down. Partly to avoid his superior's rage, and partly because he was so exhausted he could barely lift his head. He wasn't allowed to bring one of his better bodies into the inner sanctum, so he was stuck with the weak one he'd been born with. "The Traveler is one of our prime targets. Intelligence suggested that she's—"

"Not that, imbecile. I know how important the girl is. I'm aware of the Warlock's handiwork. I saw his body with my own eyes," his superior shouted.

"When word came, I decided to capture her myself."

"That would have been splendid if you had. Instead you lost her and caused a spectacle." He placed a telegram in the center of the desk and slid it over. "*This* is going to make the evening papers."

Crow took it and read. Crow swallowed hard when he got to the part where the witnesses reported that the demon had said it was from the government. "Is there any way we can squash this in time?"

"Squash it? That Crackler blasted you so hard it ended a *drought*. They've got more rain today than they've had in the last six years. Six years! That part of the country has been suffering because of magical *government* meddling since '27, and as far as the people there are concerned it was ended by someone who proclaimed himself a Grimnoir, who then sacrificed himself to stop a *government* demon."

"I'm sorry, sir."

"Congratulations, Mr. Crow. You've single-handedly made our enemies into folk heroes. Squash it? No . . . A few days ago, the only time the public had heard the name Grimnoir was as a criminal cabal. Now they fight demons and make it rain."

"Maybe it's just temporary?" Crow asked hopefully.

The boss shook his head. "A Weatherman's already checked and said that it feels like the patterns there have returned to normal. There was only a magical blight there before, but it was too strong to break, and nobody was willing to kill themselves trying to drain it. Until you came along."

"I apologize for my actions. Things got . . . out of hand."

"Explain yourself."

Crow placed the telegram back on the table. He knew that he had to tread carefully. If his superior realized how close he was to the edge, he could easily end up in Rockville. "It's the Summoned. When I take them over, their minds are still inside. Usually that's no problem, I just push them out of the way, but some are stronger than others. Their personality can start to seep through." He didn't mention that it was getting worse all the time. "The Greater Summoned especially . . . I needed something strong that could travel fast. That particular one was . . . aggressive."

In reality, its rage had consumed him. When he'd forced the form to appear as a man, it hadn't been too hard, but when he'd let its form free . . . His mind had still been intact, but the demon had taken over his personality. He'd wanted to eat the Grimnoir that had dared to fight him, and he'd wanted to gloat about it.

"Show me your spell," his superior commanded.

Crow reluctantly opened his shirt to show off the intricate design tattooed on his chest.

The boss shook his head. "My work is perfect. The spell seems to be intact."

"Of course," Crow said. Before he'd received that magnifying mark he'd been an ordinary Summoner. It was frightening to think that the boss might have wanted to take that away from him. Being able to put his consciousness right into the body of a Summoned and being truly free was intoxicating. He quickly buttoned his shirt back up.

"Do you think the Dymaxion nullifiers here are affecting you?"

"I can't Summon while they're running, but if I'm already in the body of one, I can come and go as I please." The nullifiers did seem to make his control a bit more tenuous, but the boss didn't need to know that. The devices were an integral part of their security. He was careful only to be around the Dymaxions while in the body of one of his weaker Summoned, and even then it made it hard to separate himself from the weak creatures. It was hard enough to use one of his powerful demons; possessing one with a nullifier working could be disastrous.

"Fine, fine . . . I would reprimand you but I fear it would do more harm than good. You're my most effective man. I expect better from you. I'll overlook this, but I want you to be more careful in the future. Understood?"

"Yes, sir." Crow had figured he would be all right. He was an integral part of this new operation. Even before the boss had gifted him with such an epic spell, Crow had been a useful clandestine operative, going clear back to making war protestors disappear for the Wilson administration. His talents, ability to keep a secret, and complete lack of moral compunction made him a valuable asset.

"What's your next move?"

"Francis Stuyvesant ran, as expected. I put two layers on him. He's lost the first, but doesn't suspect we're still tracking him. We'll see what he gets up to. Otherwise I'm prepared to begin phase two."

The boss stroked his mustache. "I see . . . So you plan to take them in one fell swoop?"

"I do."

"Very well. Carry on and keep me apprised of your progress. Meanwhile, I have newsmen to talk to. There's damage control to be done. Dismissed."

Crow rolled his chair away from the desk. "I apologize again for my behavior."

The boss waved him away. "No need, Mr. Crow. Epic changes take epic work and sometimes lead to epic mistakes. Once every Grimnoir is imprisoned or dead, we'll look back on this day and laugh."

Fairfax County, Virginia

TORU HAD FINALLY RELENTED to the nagging of his men and eaten. They had brought him rice and fish. Then he'd dismissed them to return to his brooding. The more that Hatori's memories found their place and became clear, the more concerned he had become.

The final year of Hatori's life had been troubled. The ambassador had been privy to reports that a mere Iron Guard had not been allowed to see. The destruction of the flagship *Tokugawa* had come as a complete surprise. There had been no word from the Chairman. Some had begun to question . . . Was it possible that a Tesla weapon could destroy even the Chairman?

This was a great cause for concern. There was still an organization in place, but why would an immortal need to choose a successor? Even in the council there were factions vying for different outcomes. If the Chairman was truly gone, there would be a battle between them for supremacy. The matter was discussed. Lots were drawn and sides were chosen, and for one brief instant the future of the Imperium stood balanced on the edge of chaos.

But in the end, it had not mattered, because the Chairman had come back. Three days after the *Tokugawa,* he had walked right into the council chambers and taken his customary place to the right of the empty chair that was always left for the emperor, as if nothing had happened. He had gently chided his questioners for their lack of faith, but there was no doubt from his answers that he was truly the Chairman. A direct hit from the most powerful of all Tesla weapons had been but a temporary inconvenience. The Imperium had continued on its mission of purification.

Yet a few men had retained their doubts. Hatori had been one of them. He was one of Okubo Tokugawa's oldest friends, and something had seemed *off* about the returned Chairman. Their few conversations had been strange, as if the Chairman had all of the information, but was processing different conclusions from it than he had in the past. Hatori was stationed in a distant land, and thought that perhaps he had just been away from home far too long. He had never spoken about his doubts to anyone, for the good of the Imperium.

Until the Grimnoir came, and then Hatori had been forced to face the truth. He could no longer afford to ignore what he'd secretly believed himself for some time. The danger presented by the Pathfinder was far too great. Hatori knew that he had been a coward, unable to face his doubts until it was too late.

And now his shame had fallen onto Toru.

The young Iron Guard had just finished his rice when the mirror flexed and the glass rippled like water. The time was at hand. He put his bowl aside, adjusted his uniform, and prepared himself. Toru was mindful of his duty in all things and despite the doubts that Master Hatori had cursed him with, Toru would conduct himself as an Iron Guard should. He went to his knees and put his head to the floor, fully expecting that his death would be ordered.

The Chairman appeared before him. "I have heard your report, Iron Guard Toru. I am displeased that the Grimnoir escaped, but they are crafty foes. However, you did as I expected with Ambassador Hatori?"

"No. I have failed in that as well, Chairman."

"I see." He sounded very displeased. "In what manner?"

"I was commanded not to speak with him. However, he used his Power to send information directly into my mind. He took me by surprise and I was unable to stop him. There is no excuse for my failure."

"What did he show you?"

"Memories of his time with you in Dark Ocean . . ." Toru could not help himself. He glanced up in order to see the Chairman's face. "And his more recent doubts as to whether you were really alive."

The Chairman gave a little smile. "And did he think *me* an imposter?"

"He was unsure."

"A waste of a good man, demented in his old age. What of you, Iron Guard? What do you think of this tale?"

His next few words would determine if he lived or died. "His doubts have damaged my faith, Chairman. I do not know the answer."

The smile died. "I see . . . You are a brave one, aren't you, Toru?"

"No, Chairman, but I am honest."

"Have you spoken of these doubts with anyone else?"

"No."

There was a long, painful silence. "I am moved by your sincerity, Iron Guard. You are one of my finest warriors. You were once considered a possibility to be First Iron Guard. However, you have failed me too many times, first in Manchuria and now in America. Your martial skill is unmatched, but your spirit is weak. Some of your brethren have been dispatched from New York to assume your command. You are to remand yourself into the custody of the captain of your guard until then."

"Am I to die then?"

"Yes. I give you permission to take your own life. That would be for the best. Should you not, your brothers will do it for you."

Toru's ears flushed hot. The shame was greater than his fear of death. "Yes, Chairman."

"Farewell, Iron Guard Toru."

Teeth clenched so tight that his jaw ached, a sudden unexpected anger bubbled up from deep within. It was as if the spirit of Hatori was inside, shouting, demanding to be heard. "Father, wait."

"Yes?"

"So that both Hatori and my spirit may go easily into death, restore my faith, that I may know it is truly you."

"For your courage, I grant you this last wish."

The real Chairman would know the words of Dark Ocean, from the time shortly after the defeat of the second Pathfinder, while they were all so devoted to taking power by any means necessary. They'd been forced to work in secret, recognizing other conspirators only through codes and tricks, often in the form of poems personally written by Okubo Tokugawa.

"The life of an echo.

"Perfect sky and mountain firm.

"Fires of purity burn,"

"On a dark ocean," the Chairman finished automatically. "I wrote that myself, a very long time ago."

That was correct. "But what does it *mean*?"

"I . . ." The briefest look of consternation crossed his handsome face. "It means . . ." For the briefest of instants, the Chairman looked away, thinking, and then Toru knew the truth. "We were an image of the warriors that came before, as pure as air yet unyielding as rock, together we would make the empire pure."

Toru touched his head to the floor. His father, the poet samurai, would never debase himself by explaining one of his poems. The poem's meaning had to reveal itself. To explain it was to make it impure. The Chairman had told Toru that himself the very first time they'd met.

His real father was dead.

"Thank you, Chairman. I am at peace with what I must do."

•

Prince William County, Virginia

SULLIVAN WAS SO CLOSE that Hammer could smell him.

Not literally. Though that certainly would've been a strange Power to have been born with. She'd been compared to a bloodhound a few times, thankfully for skill rather than looks, but what she did was really much different than just following a trail. As a Justice, Pemberly Hammer could see the real truth of things.

She'd been exhausted after driving straight through from New Jersey and using her Power almost nonstop. Having picked up the spot where Sullivan had left the ambassador's house, it had either been stop and rest or fall asleep at the wheel and crash.

The little roadside motel was quiet by the time she woke up late in the afternoon. A few hours of sleep and a bath worked wonders for her. Soon the chase would be on again, but Hammer needed some quiet time to relax. She really didn't want to finish this job, but didn't see much choice in the matter.

Luckily for her, Sullivan had tended to pick a road and stay on it. You could learn a lot about a man by observing his path. Sullivan was straightforward. When she'd first started looking for him to take the call on the spirit phone, some folks had told her that the Heavy was dumb. They'd mistaken his directness for simplicity, and they couldn't have been more wrong.

A few times she'd driven right past a choice that he'd made and not realized it because she was tired and giving her Power a rest. Then she'd had to backtrack and try again. It wasn't an easy trick, but it was why she got paid the big money. Sullivan's choices had led her to some strange places, the spot where the Bonus Army had been driven out, and then out to the country to what she'd quickly realized was an Imperium-owned compound.

Toru Tokugawa had been remarkably truthful for an Imperial. That made her distrust him even more, especially since there was no way that he could have known that she could tell the instant he lied. She couldn't read thoughts, though she could try to push people into spilling the truth. The man had struck her as so particularly dangerous that she hadn't dared try. She got the distinct impression that he was someone who could take a human life as easily as a slaughterhouse butcher could plug a steer between the eyes.

Sadly, the Jap was only the second most unnerving person she'd met in the last few days, with Crow taking the grand prize for creepiness. She'd tried to tip the scales to be absolutely certain he was telling the truth, and instead she'd found something alien. Crow was a human shell filled with something nasty, like a rotten egg that looked edible until you cracked it.

But he also had leverage on her.

It was difficult enough to become a real professional peace officer as a woman. If word got out about how her Power worked, then that would be the end of her dreams. Considering the level of corruption in the world right now, no real department was going to hire somebody who could sense the internal rot.

As one who'd made a life out of figuring out the truth, being blackmailed to keep her secrets safe was particularly galling. So now she was hunting somebody who she had a distinct impression was a completely innocent man, on behalf of somebody who, near as she could figure, was completely evil. Daddy would be ashamed. He wouldn't have let some Yankee thug bully him into dishonest work.

Hammer sighed and got back to her job. She might not have inherited her father's integrity, but she had certainly inherited his work ethic. Used to living on the road, packing her bags only took a few minutes. She made a little ritual of checking each of her handguns before stashing them about her person. As somebody who knew just how dishonest the world was, she never went anywhere without protection.

There was another choice. Hammer pulled her car off to the shoulder and got out. Pretty country here, all farms, fields, and patches of trees wherever it was too bumpy to cultivate. It was greener than where she'd grown up in Texas. There was no traffic, which made her job easier. She walked to the middle of the crossroads.

Sometimes when her quarry had to make a choice, she didn't even have to use her Power to tell which was the true way. Some roads passed by, but there had been no real choice to make there, so her quarry had just kept on going. Sometimes she just knew, because she understood the people she was hunting. Other times, when it wasn't clear, where there were a few possible paths, that was when her Power came in.

Hammer slowly turned in a circle. West, south, east. She'd come from the north. She pushed her Power, and could feel it inside her chest, ready to hunt. It was like she could hear her daddy's words, clear and true as the day he'd taught her. *Know the outlaw. Know his mind. Know what he wants. Then your magic will show you the truth.*

She opened her eyes and knew that Sullivan had gone south. Hammer started walking back to her car.

There was a sudden noise, like the rustle of a vulture's wings.

She turned to see a man in black standing behind her. The Bisley Colt came out of her coat in a flash.

Crow tipped his hat in greeting. "Hammer."

She didn't lower the gun. "Where'd you come from?"

"I was born in Philly," he lied. He saw her frown. "Just testing you. Put that away before you hurt somebody."

Reluctantly, Hammer lowered the revolver, though she kept it in her hand. There were no cars in view. He had come out of nowhere. *How had he found her?* "You scared me."

"That's my job." That time he was telling the truth.

"Are you a Traveler or something?"

"Or something." *Truth,* and Hammer cursed herself for wasting it on a stupid question. "Your current assignment can wait. I'm assuming you can pick up the trail later."

Truth was harder to see, the older it got, but he didn't need to know her limitations. "Sure."

"I need you to meet me at the courthouse in Alexandria. I want you to listen to something."

"Can't you just tell me here and save us the trouble?"

"I need your professional opinion. Can you tell if somebody is lying from a recording?"

"Usually . . . How did you find me?"

"Trade secret. Meet me there in an hour."

Hammer turned and gestured at her car. "How're you—" but by the time she'd turned back, Crow had disappeared. She turned in a quick circle, but he was nowhere to be seen. Feeling stupid, she put the Colt away.

"Well . . . Looks like I'm working for Old Scratch," she muttered.

Daddy would not be proud.

The OCI agent manning the courthouse door knew right away who she was and led her to a small room by the judge's chambers. Crow had been there waiting for her with an audio tape already threaded into a complicated player. He didn't bother to greet her and she didn't bother asking how he'd gotten there so quickly. There were already four fresh cigarette butts in the ashtray. "Close the door." Crow gestured for her to pull up a chair, then he flipped a lever and started his machine.

Hammer had to tilt her head closer to the speaker horn. She could recognize Crow's voice. *"I want to talk to you about the Grimnoir Society."*

"I do not know this thing you speak of."

"Spare me the lies, Fade. I'm familiar with your little club and my assignment is to destroy it."

"Torture me all you want, I have nothing to say."

Crow turned a knob and stopped the player. "This is one of the Grimnoir we captured, a German immigrant by the name of Heinrich Koenig. He was there at the assassination attempt. The rest of his gang think he's dead. I want you to tell me when he's lying." Crow turned the knob and the tape began to turn.

Hammer listened carefully. Detecting lies was the easiest use of her Power. She'd practiced it so much that it was automatic, unconscious, and barely even drew on her supply of magic. The Grimnoir was truthful. He was scared for his friends and loyal, but she didn't need magic to tell her that. Crow, as usual, was a bundle of deceit.

"That is ridiculous. I tried to save the man, not kill him."

Crow's voice came on next, but the man quickly turned the knob and stopped the tape before she could hear what he had to say in response to that. "So, professional opinion?"

"Magic evidence isn't admissible in court, but this man's innocent. That's plain as day."

Crow took out another cigarette and a matchbook. "I'll pass that along."

"So what are you going to do with him?"

"He'll get a fair trial." *Another lie.* Crow sighed, "All right, you got me . . . Can't lie to a Justice . . . The German is to be executed as soon as my superiors are certain that he's outlived his usefulness. National security matter. It's out of my hands." He struck a match with his thumb and lit up. He shook the match out and tossed it in a waste pail. When he returned the pack of cigarettes to his pocket, he made a big show of finding something inside. "Reminds me . . . While you're looking for these Grimnoir, watch for these." He produced a ring and handed it over.

Hammer tried not to let her surprise show when the gold and obsidian ring landed in her palm. She'd seen this exact type of ring before.

"This was found on the assassin. The German wore one of these, too. All the Grimnoir have one. Even if they don't have it on, they'll have it nearby. Keep an eye out for anyone wearing one of these. If they've got this ring, they're the enemy."

Reluctantly, she gave the ring back.

There was a hard knock on the door. "Come in," Crow ordered.

One of the OCI men stuck his head in. "Mr. Crow, you've got an important call from headquarters."

"Got to take this . . ." Crow muttered. "This might take awhile." He walked out of the room and closed the door behind him. He'd left the ring on the table.

Hammer stared at it. There was no mistake. Though he had never worn one himself, her father had told her about the men that wore these.

She picked the ring up. It had carvings all along the inside. Crow had said that it was the assassin's ring, so she pushed her Power a bit to see if that was true. The impression she got was that Giuseppe Zangara had been the last man to wear it . . . only he hadn't worn it for very long at all. Before Zangara, another man had died wearing that ring. She pushed harder, trying to see the true history of the ring. The image was fuzzy. The actors were strange. The ring's true owner had been shot in the back and the ring had been stolen off his dead hand. It had been on so long that they'd broken the finger prying it off.

The truth faded and she put the ring back on the table.

She had to let Crow know the assassin was not a member of the Grimnoir Society.

But Crow was made of lies. Hell, he was a lie. Whatever he really was, he was certainly no normal man. He couldn't be trusted either . . . Hammer's gaze turned to the tape player. He had been in a mighty hurry to stop it. The door was still closed. The machine was still running. Hammer turned the knob.

"I know! You should be getting a medal, not rotting under OCI headquarters. Heh, just between you and me, I know you Grimnoir didn't do it. We've already got conclusive evidence upstairs. But nobody in charge is going to see that evidence until I'm done cleaning house. I'm sure as hell not going to let a good crisis go to waste. My office just got a blank check to do whatever we needed to do to get you people under control. You know how rare that kind of pass is? In a little while, Congress will go back to getting cold feet and fretting about overstepping its bounds, but by then it'll be too late for your kind."

For once, everything Crow had said there was completely true. He knew these people were innocent and he had the evidence to prove it . . . *the rat bastard*. Hammer heard a noise from the hall so she quickly stopped the tape.

Crow came back in, shaking his head. "Politicians riding my ass . . ." He looked at her suspiciously. "Why the long face?"

"Nothing. Ready to get back on the case is all. You need me for anything else, Mr. Crow?" She wanted to get out of there as fast as possible.

"Naw. We're good here . . . You know, Hammer, I think maybe we got off on the wrong foot. You're one hell of an investigator and you've got a rare gift. We're both professionals here. Once you've found Sullivan, maybe you should think about coming to work for OCI as a full agent. We're not the BI. That was your original goal, wasn't it? No place for girls there though. OCI don't care. Looks, brains, Power, somebody like you could go far with us."

Snowflake's chance in hell of that. "I'll keep it in mind."

❖❖❖

After Hammer left, Crow checked the player. Sure enough, she'd played the rest of the tape. People with integrity were *so* easy to manipulate. They were like reading an open book. Especially when, because of the rarity of their Power, the OCI had been gathering information on them for years. Even with somebody you couldn't lie to, you just had to figure out which truths you wanted told, and then steer them into filling in the blanks themselves.

One of the men reported in a while later. Just as expected, after getting away from the courthouse, Hammer had pulled her car over and spent twenty minutes searching through it and her bags. *Perfect*. He had wanted her unnerved and thinking about how he'd been able to find her in the middle of nowhere so easily. She'd found the tracking rune that he'd had scratched into the paint just under the bumper and destroyed it. He had specified that it shouldn't be made too hard to find. That would make her feel like she'd won, like she'd outsmarted him. A small victory would make her more confident that he could be outwitted, and that would make Hammer brave enough to make a hard decision.

Which was right where he wanted her.

Hammer found herself back at the crossroads.

Her father had taught her how to track, magical or otherwise, how to defend herself, how to listen to her magic, and all of the other useful skills that she'd used to make a good living. He'd also taught her about right and wrong, and how sometimes the truth can be somewhere between the two.

If the OCI's mission wasn't evil, then it was damn close. An innocent man was going to die for a crime he'd tried to prevent, and if Crow had his way there would be many more to follow.

She thought of the ring. She'd been a little girl then, gone to her father's office to bring him a lunch basket. A stranger had been there, wearing that same ring, and so she'd waited outside. Her curiosity had gotten the better of her and she'd listened through the crack as the stranger talked about trying to find someone that was using magic to commit crimes, and how he wanted to catch the criminal before it drew too much attention to *their* kind.

Afterwards, her father had talked to her. Of course he knew that she'd been spying. You can't lie to a Justice. He told her that such men were a force for good, and that though their existence was to be kept a secret, they were on the side of truth.

She knew that he'd helped them a few times. He'd done things over the years that were outside the scope of his duty as a marshal, dangerous things, and when he'd come home he'd never spoken about them. In a family where lying to your children was impossible, sometimes you just had to say nothing at all.

Lee Hammer had been a good man. Tough, quiet, hard as rawhide, but always kind to his family, fair to his people, and unyielding to his enemies. She'd grown up knowing that her father's reputation as an impossibly dedicated lawman had been well earned. He was the one to call when there was a dangerous fugitive that absolutely had to be found. She knew that it was because he could always see the truth of things, but that had been their secret, one Active to another. He was careful to teach her to only use her Power for good, to serve others and not just herself. She'd never been as good at that as he'd been, though.

Then he'd been gunned down by a gang and carried home on a plank. She still wore his star on a chain around her neck. Her dream had been to follow in her father's footsteps, but nobody was going to hire a young lady for that kind of work. Marshalls said no. Rangers hadn't wanted her. The BI had laughed at her. The only places that had female police relegated them to pushing paper as glorified secretaries.

So instead she'd used her skills in other ways, greedy ways, helping anyone that could pay her enough to get an edge over those that couldn't. Corporate espionage wasn't the same as catching crooks, but it had some of the same thrill and it certainly paid better than working for the law, but it had always felt hollow.

So, trying to follow her dreams again had roped her into something even worse.

Jake Sullivan had turned south here.

If she found him, she'd be rewarded. If she betrayed the OCI, then Crow would ruin her life, or from what she'd seen, probably end it. She knew she was being manipulated, but Crow's oddness kept her from getting a good reading as to what his endgame was.

When surrounded by lies, what would her father have done?

She went south.

Chapter 12

Dear Miss Etiquette,
If I think that an acquaintance might be a Mouth and using the power of suggestion on me, is it polite to speak up?

Signed, Befuddled in Buffalo.

Dear Befuddled,
It depends on the social situation. It is never polite to use mind control on anyone, however to suggest something aloud during a party could be very offensive. He may simply be a real charmer. If he is an Active, that is why a proper young lady always is certain that there are chaperones present.

—Miss Etiquette,
Newspaper column, 1933

Washington, D.C.

J. EDGAR HOOVER slid into the backseat of the waiting automobile with a grunt. "What an awful day." He sighed and pinched the bridge of his nose. "Take me home." The car pulled out of the garage and onto the busy avenue. "Damned bothersome reporters." He made special note of remembering the names of each of the newsmen that had asked the difficult questions and put him on the spot. He'd be certain to make their lives as miserable as possible. "They're like sharks when they smell blood."

"I know. Dreadful business," the driver said. Hoover was startled. He was not used to his driver talking back. The agents that rotated through the assignment all knew to just let him talk, and to only speak when asked a direct question. "Right?"

Hoover sat forward, glad to have someone to rip into. Berating underlings always made him feel better after a hard day at the office. "What's your name, Agent?"

"Garrett, sir. Daniel Garrett." He reached up and tipped the edge of his hat so that Hoover could see his face in the mirror. "I'm really pleased to meet you. This is such an honor. I can tell that we're going to get along really well. I feel like I've known you forever."

The unfamiliar agent had a soothing voice. Hoover relaxed. "Where's my regular driver?"

"In the trunk." The driver laughed. Hoover laughed as well. "No . . . Seriously. He's in the trunk."

Hoover laughed again. "Splendid!" This new agent had a marvelous sense of humor.

"Don't worry. He's alive, just gagged and tied up is all." The automobile pulled over at the corner. "Well, here's our other passenger. Isn't this great? It's like a party."

"Indeed." He was suddenly feeling very agreeable. His door opened and he had to scoot his bulk across the seat to make room for the new arrival, who was an extremely tall and thickset individual. He slammed the door behind him and the automobile immediately roared away from the curb.

"Afternoon, Mr. Hoover," Heavy Jake Sullivan said. "Long time, no see."

Suddenly J. Edgar Hoover wasn't feeling quite so agreeable anymore.

They'd picked a quiet spot, a condemned warehouse that probably dated back to the Civil War. It was a wide open space and quite a bit of light came in through the broken windows. Pigeons cooed in the rafters. Trash and bottles were strewn around, and from the old dirty blankets, it looked like quite a few hobos slept here. They'd found one busted up chair for their guest and Sullivan sat on an old cable spool.

Dan had gone to bring the truck around. Sullivan had figured it was for the best to remove the Mouth from the equation. He needed Hoover to make the deal of his own free will. He hadn't bothered to tie him up either. That would've been insulting to them both. Sullivan had given his pitch. Now he sat, arms folded, and waited for the Director's response.

"You want me to help you clear your name?" Hoover was incredulous.

Sullivan nodded. "Yep. 'Cause I'm innocent."

"You kidnapped the Director of the Bureau of Investigation!"

"I didn't think you'd return my calls."

"You should be under arrest!"

Sullivan looked around the empty warehouse. "You and what army?"

Being alone and defenseless only made him slightly more humble than when he was surrounded by armed agents. "I used to *own* you!"

Sullivan did not respond to that.

"Do you have any idea how much trouble you're in?"

"I didn't think I could go much higher than Public Enemy Number One."

"Yes, which is frankly an embarrassment." Hoover rubbed his face with both hands. "They corrupted my own system and used it to embarrass me."

"The Office of the Coordinator of Information, you mean?" Sullivan chuckled. "How's the power struggle going?"

Hoover looked at him funny. "You're well-informed."

"Very." Actually, it had been a guess, but it looked like he was right. "OCI used my parole to hang you out to dry. Way I see it, you either messed up and let a dangerous homicidal Active loose on society to serve as your personal hit man, or the OCI's got this all wrong, and me and my friends have nothing to do with this plot."

"You're rather clever for a Heavy, Mr. Sullivan."

"Gravity Spiker, and you knew that when you sprung me from Rockville. We're innocent, by the way."

"The evidence against your group is damning."

"What evidence? A mad Boomer wearing a spell and a ring makes hundreds of people guilty? That wouldn't hold up in any court. We're scapegoats. Patsies. And you know it. That evidence came from the OCI, didn't it?"

"Of course . . . Let me go, and I'll be sure to bring that to light."

Sullivan pointed. "Door's thataway. Your car is waiting."

He tossed the keys to Hoover, who, surprised, barely managed to flinch and catch them between his knees. "Don't forget your man in the trunk. That can't be comfy."

Hoover took the keys. "Just like that?"

"I'm here to make you an offer, Hoover, not hold you for ransom. The OCI is a problem for both of us. I can help fix it."

The Director stood and hurriedly fled across the space, shoes echoing on the hard floor. Pigeons scattered to get out of his way. Sullivan stayed in place, but he figured he wouldn't have to wait long. He had known men like J. Edgar Hoover before. Though they weren't nearly as powerful, they were of similar makeup. Everything was about *them*. Any twist of fate that didn't go their way was a personal slight. In a military officer, any positive report about a subordinate was felt as if they'd received a reprimand. In business, if the other guy made a buck, then they felt like they'd lost a buck, like there were only so many to go around. Everything was a competition, and no matter how successful they were, they were always bitter, petty men, who couldn't stand being shamed.

Hoover came back a minute later, his curiosity having gotten the better of him. "What are you proposing?"

"You want to protect the institution you've built. I want to protect my people. Neither one of us likes seeing the innocent taking a fall while the guilty get away."

"Of course not," Hoover snapped. "I know you hate me, but everything I've done has been to defend this great nation from our enemies."

Sullivan gave a sad little smile. Hoover was lecturing

one of the most decorated veterans of the Great War about defending the country. "I believe you. Despite what I think of you, you sure do like putting the bad guys in jail. I respect that. Have a seat." He waited for the pudgy man to return to the broken chair. "I'm assuming you know the truth about Mar Pacifica?"

"Anarchist Actives—"

"It was the Imperium."

Hoover scowled. "That's classified."

"I was there. Don't tell me about defending this nation, when I personally killed the man responsible for taking over the Peace Ray. I cut his head in half with a Jap sword. The *Tokugawa?* That was us too . . . We're on the same side here, Hoover, and you know it. I know you've got your hooks in everything. I'd like to share information."

"You have been busy. Very well. You go first."

That was expected. "I just did. Now you've got a confirmation about who killed the Chairman and saved New York from being vaporized by a Tesla weapon."

"And the Geo-Tel?"

Sullivan was impressed. Hoover was just as well informed as everyone said he was. "Destroyed."

"Hmmm . . . I don't know what to say about that . . ."

Thank you would be nice for once. "Tell me about the OCI."

It was obvious Hoover didn't like being manipulated, but he was a man who liked to explore his options. "A very secret, very minor, unimportant agency started by President Wilson, specifically to study magic and gather intelligence on known Actives."

"Isn't that illegal?"

"As I said—secret. They were authorized emergency police powers after Pacifica."

"I thought monitoring Active criminals was the BI's responsibility."

It was obvious this part put Hoover in a sour mood. "It was. OCI was to monitor Actives in general. After the Peace Ray, some . . . confidence was lost in the Bureau's abilities. OCI had already laid the groundwork and was prepared to step in. They've capitalized on recent events to increase their authority."

When he put it that way, government infighting didn't sound much different than the mobs jockeying to control different rackets. Another gang shows weakness, you make a move. "Why are they framing the Grimnoir?"

Hoover paused, as if thinking about how much precious information he was willing to part with. "Perhaps they think you really are responsible?"

"I was a detective, remember? They can't be that stupid. They're not trying to conduct an investigation. This is an extermination."

The top G-man in the country gave him a bit of a smile. "Very good, Mr. Sullivan. A lone killer, no matter how dangerous, the country deals with them and moves on. It doesn't require any great changes to the system. Now a conspiracy . . . that requires action to root out. That requires men, material, money, and management. Since things are changing so rapidly in these dark times, some parties may see this as their opportunity to insinuate themselves into the fabric of power. Your group is but the means to an end."

"And from the way the BI's been thrown under the train, too, I'm guessing you're in the way of that end, and it's probably not because you're such a fan of civil liberties for Actives."

"You might not think so, seeing as how you're a *convict*, but compared to my opposite number in the OCI, I am a saint. This may come as a surprise, but I've been against their agenda the entire time. I think it goes entirely too far and the American people will not stand for it."

"What's the agenda?"

The Director was surprised. "You don't know?" Sullivan cursed himself for the slip. "Perhaps you are not as well informed as I'd thought. Forget that I said anything. I'm not in the habit of divulging classified information." Hoover had scored a point.

"So what are we going to do about it?"

"We? I'll follow the will of the people through the instructions of their duly elected representatives."

"Sure. And if I bring you proof that OCI is rotten?"

"Then I bury them," Hoover answered maliciously. "If you are innocent as you claim, then my Bureau never made any mistakes at all, and that will simply have to be made public, that the OCI was barking up the wrong tree. I can see how an exchange of information could be mutually beneficial for both of us. I believe that we can come to an agreement . . . though if questioned, this meeting never occurred."

Sullivan extended one big hand. Hoover looked at it distastefully, then finally shook on it. Sullivan had to resist the urge to break all his fingers. "Welcome to the conspiracy, Mr. Hoover."

Fairfax County, Virginia

ALL ASPIRING IRON GUARDS had to read Okubo Tokugawa's personal history. He was their leader and their inspiration. An Iron Guard was to emulate the Chairman in all aspects of their life. Whether it was courage on the battlefield, artistry on the canvas, or cunning in the courts, Okubo Tokugawa was all that an Iron Guard should aspire to be.

He had also been a ronin, Toru reasoned.

The Chairman had been born into one of the greatest families in Nippon, but when the Power had chosen the young man to be the first Active, his sudden manifestation of magical abilities had been a great cause of confusion. This was before man understood anything about magic, and the young samurai's miraculous skills were frightening to the unenlightened. There could only be one Child of Heaven. The Shogunate was shamed by this development, and political rivals used his uniqueness as an excuse for war.

Seppuku was not an option for someone who could not seem to die, so he had been exiled for the good of the empire. Thus he had become a wave man, a ronin, carried about by the dark ocean of fate. It was only through this wandering time that the man who would go on to become the Chairman would learn true wisdom.

Toru clung to that idea. He was following in the footsteps of his father.

He would not obey the false Chairman's orders. The

imposter deserved no loyalty. He did not speak for the Imperium. In fact, by disregarding Okubo Tokugawa's final message from beyond the grave, the imposter was putting the entire Imperium in jeopardy.

If the imposter would not fill the Chairman's final order, then Toru would. He did not yet know how, but once the Pathfinder was defeated, then Toru would turn his attention to the imposter. Until then, however, pursuit was inevitable. No Iron Guard had ever forsaken his place before. Hatori should have fled, but he had been old, tired, and afraid. Toru would atone for his mentor's mistakes as well.

The marines were still unaware of what was coming. He had gathered his belongings, a bag of gold coins, a supply of American money, along with his favorite weapons, and then gone to the garden to meditate and to wait for the Iron Guards that were supposed to take his life. He could have just run, but then they would have given immediate chase. He would need time to plan his next move, and that would be difficult while being hounded by his tenacious brothers.

In winter the garden was as grey as his soul. The chill wind kept his mind sharp as he waited. He did not yet know how he would fulfill the real Chairman's command. He was not strong enough by himself to destroy a Pathfinder. He prayed to his father's spirit for guidance. He would need the wisdom of the Chairman to accomplish this mission.

One of the men disturbed his mediation. "Iron Guard, I have news." It was the Finder and he had a map in hand. The wind was whipping it about. He bowed deeply. "As you ordered, the spirits have followed the American woman. She has located the Grimnoir. They are hiding in a farmhouse not far from here."

Toru stood and took the map. There was an *X* drawn on it to the south of them. "Was the large one there? Sullivan?"

"Yes, Iron Guard. It was the same two that came here. She arrived as they were leaving in a red pickup truck. The spirit was not strong enough to follow them because of their ring wards. But from the looks of it, I believe they will be returning shortly. The woman is hiding, watching the place now."

The flash of inspiration was so clear that he had no doubt it was divine. The marine was not nearly as big as Toru, but he was rather tall. "Have you told any of the others?"

"No, Iron Guard."

Toru carefully folded the map and put it inside his clothing. "What is your name?"

"Okada Hiroshi," he answered proudly.

"You have done a great service to the Imperium today, Okada Hiroshi," Toru said solemnly, and then he bowed. The marine was shocked at the display. It was rare to receive a compliment from one of the mighty Iron Guard. "Thank you."

"Thank you, Iron Guard," Hiroshi stammered.

Toru drew his sword and struck so quickly that the marine never even saw death coming. It was completely painless. Toru had already cleaned the blood from his sword and put it back in the sheath before the body toppled. He gently carried the body into the garden and hid it. He then put on his most distinctive kimono and went back to the house. He made sure to greet a few of the staff, and then snuck to the basement to carry up a crate of explosives.

After returning to the garden, he dressed Hiroshi in his kimono and set the body next to the bomb. It was enough to make a mess, but would still leave plenty of big pieces. Toru bore eight kanji, Hiroshi only bore one. A careful inspection of the body parts would reveal what he'd done, but they probably wouldn't even check until they realized Hiroshi was also missing. His brothers would not search for him if they thought he was dead, and by the time they realized the truth, his trail would be cold.

Fuse lit, Toru escaped over the back wall into the woods. His Brute speed had gotten him a quarter mile away by the time the explosives detonated and thunder rolled through the trees. He turned for one last look at what had been his home and watched the smoke rising from the garden. For the first time in his life, he was truly alone.

The life of an echo.
Perfect sky and mountain firm.
Fires of purity burn.
On a dark ocean.

The Iron Guard understood it now. The meaning had become clear.

New York City, New York

"BUCKMINSTER FULLER. Heard of him?"

"Nope." Francis looked up from his drink, and then suspiciously down the bar. None of the other customers seemed to be paying attention to Francis and Chandler. It was a low-rent speakeasy and since technically *nobody* was supposed to be here, customers pretty much minded their own business. For whatever reason, Chandler seemed to be the expert on out-of-the-way dives like this around the city. Francis kept his hat pulled low and his overcoat collar up so no one would recognize him. Luckily, it was cold out, and every time the door opened another blast of cold air would come shooting into the dark bar, so at least he wasn't the only one dressed that way.

Chandler looked around the room, then lowered his voice conspiratorially. "I'm enjoying this detective thing. Much more interesting than accounting. Fuller's a Cog. He's got a little shop in Greenwich Village."

That wasn't particularly fancy for a Cog. "What's his magical brilliance in? Musical theater?"

"For a rich guy, you sure do look down your nose at the arts."

"Hey, I've donated piles of money to . . . stuff." Francis wasn't in the mood for witty banter. He'd told his secretary to hold his calls and then he'd slipped out through the UBF mail room and had run for his life. He'd gone from millionaire to fugitive in less than five minutes. Which was about as fast as he'd gone from nobody to millionaire in the first place. He sighed. "So what's his deal, Ray?"

"Fuller's a big idea man, but his thing is domes."

"Domes?" UBF employed several Cogs who specialized in useful things like engines, electronics, or aerodynamics.

"No wonder I've never heard of him. Who'd pay good money for a *dome*? Eskimos?"

Chandler finished his drink and then signaled the bartender for a refill. "The Office of the Coordinator of Information."

"Fuller owns Dymaxion?"

"One and the same. Fuller's come up with some sort of geometric design that chases away magic. Ten minutes after he announced it, OCI swooped in and told him to shut his trap. They have been buying everything he's turned out since."

Finally, some good news. "We need to buy him out."

"Already done, chief. Congratulations. You own a company that makes domes and a funny-shaped car."

"Just what I needed. When can I talk to this guy?"

"I told him to meet us here at seven p.m." Chandler looked at his watch. "So about three minutes."

"Anybody ever tell you that you're the best accountant ever?"

"My mom did once, but I think she was lying to make me feel good about myself." A cold wind struck as the door opened. Chandler leaned around Francis to see. "I do believe that's our Cog."

He was a handsome fellow in his late thirties, wearing a brown wool suit and a dark vest. Chandler waved and he came over to greet them. Confident, he looked Francis over. "Good evening, Mr. Stuyvesant," he said. "A pleasure to make your acquaintance." Francis shook his hand, a little perturbed that Chandler had let slip his name.

Chandler caught the look. "I didn't tell him."

"I recognize you from the papers." Fuller took the

barstool next to him. Francis noted that he was wearing multiple wristwatches. *Sheesh, Cogs and their odd habits* . . . Francis was thankful that Browning was relatively normal compared to most of them, and he was a wizard when it came to guns, so that was saying something.

Fuller continued. "The transference of such a massive sum of funds occurred so rapidly that I'm not entirely surprised to see that it was a company with as many resources and as well-informed as United Blimp and Freight, that would be so interested in my spheroidal research."

"What?"

Chandler interpreted. "We paid a lot of money, very quickly."

"Indeed," Fuller replied, happy as a calm. "A truly accommodative sum."

"How *much* money, Ray?"

"More than I'll ever make." Chandler grinned. "Let me get you two a table."

Francis' head hurt. He'd dealt with many Cogs in his relatively short life. They were all geniuses, even before their brains were boosted by magic. He'd heard about a few people that the Power had come upon later in life, and they'd gone from relatively normal communication to absolute incomprehensibility as a result. He was guessing Fuller was one of those. Cogs tended to be eccentric, but this man was either the smartest or the densest one of the bunch. "Wait . . . Wait, I need you to try to explain that again."

Fuller was very proud of his Dymaxion nullifier.

"Tensional integrity, or as I call it, tensegrity, is a structural relationship principle in which structural shape is guaranteed by the finitely closed, comprehensively continuous, tensional behaviors of the system and not by the discontinuous and exclusively local compressional member behaviors! The nullifier is based on tensegrity. The Power, itself existing omni simultaneously as a geometric construction, is driven from the area of spheroidal influence upon operation of the nullifier."

"Jesus . . ." Francis rubbed his temples. "Okay, let's try this. If somebody had a nullifier, and an Active wanted to be able to use their Power around it, how would they beat it?"

"Beat it?"

"Say I'm telekinetic, and that guy over there"—Francis pointed at a random drunk—"was about to shoot me with a gun. He's got a nullifier though, so my Power doesn't work. So, how can I pick up this glass"—Francis lifted his scotch—"and hit him in the face with it?"

"Hmmm . . . You could throw it."

Francis sighed. "I'd prefer to throw it with my *brain*."

"Magic as weaponry? Mr. Stuyvesant, I'll have you know my life's work has been based in livingry, not killingry."

"Are those even real words?"

Fuller seemed offended. "Absolutely. They are now."

The Cog seemed like a decent enough sort, his brain was just running on a different track than Francis'. "Let me level with you, Mr. Fuller. You've already sold some of these to a group called the OCI, correct?"

"Why, yes. I've created and sold a total of seven of the devices."

"Really?" Francis was surprised. "That's it?"

"Each one takes months of effort. The interaccommodative housing is simple enough, but the geodesic device is rather complex in its manufacture. Currently, I am the only individual capable of crafting the nullifiers, though I have tried to train others; their crafting requires almost an individual artistic touch rather than a replicatable construction methodology."

"It's hard, so you're the only one that can make them?"

"That is what I said."

I'm getting better at this. "Okay. The OCI has been using your inventions to do some very *bad* things. Like depowering Actives so they can assault them."

"Why would they do such a terrible thing?"

"I don't know. Every time we've met they're too busy trying to kill us to ask."

Fuller was confused. "Us?"

"Us . . . Actives." Francis concentrated on his glass. It rose off the table, hung there for a moment, and then floated gently back down. "I don't know about you, but I'd like to be able to use my God given magical Power to make this glass go up and down without asking the government's permission first."

Fuller corrected him. "*Up* and *down* are archaic terms, when in reality you mean *in* and *out* based upon the object's relation to the gravitational center of the Earth . . ."

"I bet you and my buddy Jake would get along swell."

"But I can see what you mean. I did not know my inventions were being used to cause harm. I do not approve."

"Well, first and foremost, now that you work for me, you're not making any more of them for the OCI. Will the other ones break or wear out?"

"They are very resilient and as long as the interaccommodative housing is unharmed and the spheroidal nullifier is in motion, then it will retain magical cohesion, even with minor maintenance. The first one I created was large enough to be motorized for continual operation and had a greater range, while the later six were portable but had to be spun by hand, which gives them only a few minutes of usage at a time, and a limited range."

"Gotcha. So smash it or stop it from moving. So getting back to my original question, how do I get around a nullifier?"

"As in the theoretical application of your glass of alcohol against that individual's face?" Fuller pointed at the same man Francis had.

"What'cha looking at, asshole?" the drunken construction worker growled. "Got a problem?"

"Nothing, sir," Francis answered happily. "Let me buy you a drink." Chandler was sitting at the bar near the entrance and had caught the exchange. He signaled the bartender to send the big fellow another round. *Good man.* "Lower your voice. Are you trying to get us beat up?"

"Sorry, Mr. Stuyvesant. There is one hypothetical answer to your question." Fuller produced a pencil and a notepad from his coat. "The Power is made up of thousands of individual geometric constructs." He quickly scribbled a complex design onto the paper. "This is what yours, as a Mover, looks like."

Francis took the pad. It was the design for a spell, only much more complex than anything the Society had cobbled together in the *Rune Arcanium*. This was closer to some of the things that Sullivan was playing with. He had never seen what his own looked like before. It was strangely familiar, like a half-remembered dream. "Where'd you learn this?"

"Learn it?"

"Who taught you this spell?"

"I'm looking at it right now," Fuller explained. "I can see the Power. I can always see magic and its many complex connections. That was how I was able to design the spheroid's repellent omnialternative correlation for the nullifier."

That blew him away. "You can *see* the Power? All the time?"

"Why, yes. Of course."

However much money Chandler had spent to pick this guy up was well worth it. Sullivan's few minutes dead and hanging around the Power had given them several new spells, and Fuller could see *everything right now!* Francis was going to be rich . . . well, richer. "Wow. I really wish I had more time. Back to the business of beating your nullifier . . ."

"In my travels I've come across two types of connections to the Power: those that are chosen by the Power directly, and those that man has created through his own experimentation. Their appearance is drastically different, as if the original was created by a master sculptor and the others are a copy done in chalk on a bumpy sidewalk by a fat-fingered child. The nullifier will repel either. However . . ."

Fuller took back the notepad and flipped to a new page. This drawing was much more complicated. It was shape on top of shape, using various points as starting areas for new lines and circles, until half the page was filled with a garbled mess. "This is the one Power-related geometry that not only resists the repulsion of the nullifier, but will actually destroy the omnialternative correlation."

"So if this spell comes close to a nullifier?"

"A catastrophic release of energy," Fuller answered. "Far greater than the interaccommodative housing can—"

"Boom?"

Fuller sighed like he was talking to a particularly idiotic subject. "Yes. Boom."

"Big or little? We talking hand grenade or Peace Ray?"

"Well . . . maybe grenade. Probably smaller than that. I would assume more like a very large firecracker . . . except perhaps for Dymaxion Nullifier Number One, which would be roughly equivalent to ten pounds of TNT."

That could ruin someone's day. Francis took the notepad. "Can I have this?"

"You have paid me a sum of money sufficient to guarantee the financial freedom necessary to pursue my life's work."

"So . . . yeah?"

"Yes, Mr. Stuyvesant. You may have my notepad."

The spell would be remarkably hard to get right. "Where did you see this one?"

"Only once. Several years ago I was taking the train to Chicago. A young man boarded and rode for a time. This particular geometry was bonded to him. I have not seen its like since, and I have seen many Actives."

Francis put the sheet representing his Mover abilities next to the mystery Power. The new one had ten times the lines. He had no idea how that translated into real world use, but he sure hoped that guy was on their side. "What does it do?"

"I have no idea. Are you familiar with the principles relating to the creation of a geometry on a solid plane of—"

"Yeah, I can spellbind."

"Spellbind . . . Spellbound . . ." Fuller smiled. "An interesting portmanteau. Would you mind terribly if I were to use that?"

"Why not? You seem to like sticking words together. So if I create this near a nullifier, it'll blow it up?"

"It is the one geometry that I am aware of which, in theory, would do so. However, I have never attempted to activate this particular geometry myself in order to see what would happen."

"Why not?"

"Because, Mr. Stuyvesant. That spell *frightens* me. I can extrapolate no possible explanation of what it may do. It is beyond my comprehension and has troubled my sleep at night." There was a sudden chill wind as the door opened. "I would urge the utmost caution in its creation."

There was a sudden shout from the bar. "Hey, watch it, jerk!" It was Chandler.

Francis looked up to see what the commotion was. His accountant had gotten up and shoved the construction worker. The big man was getting up with a look on his face that suggested Chandler was about to get pasted. "What in the world is he doing?" And then Francis realized that there were two men standing in the doorway, hands in their coat pockets, with a look that just screamed G-men.

"What's your deal?"

"That's right! I said your wife's fat *and* ugly!" Chandler raised his fists in an exaggeratedly drunken manner, then blundered backwards into the new arrivals, distracting them. One G-man shoved Chandler, who then slugged the construction worker in the mouth. The big man hit a table and took down a pair of dockworkers. Several other toughs took the opportunity to jump in. The UBF vice president of finance began shouting, "Raid! Raid!" Which caused everyone else in the place to stand up to see what was going on. The construction worker got up, charged Chandler, missed and took one of the feds to the ground.

Most of the patrons who were sober enough to not want to get arrested ran for it. Francis stashed the notebook. "Come on, Fuller." He got up, grabbed the Cog by the arm, and dragged him straight for the back. These places always had multiple exits in case of a police raid. The whole front of the bar had descended into a free-for-all. Francis looked back just long enough to make eye contact with Chandler, who winked, and then hit a sailor with a chair.

The speakeasy was in a basement. There was a brick hallway that went past the toilets, up some old metal stairs, and ended at a wooden door. Francis pushed hard and hit somebody with the door. The alley was even darker than the bar. Before his eyes could adjust, the man he'd struck took hold of Francis' sleeve. "Stop in the name of the law!"

Francis threw out a wild surge of Power. The G-man was slammed back off of his feet, and from the racket, into a bunch of trash cans. Still pulling Fuller along, Francis ran toward the light of the street. More bar patrons were coming out behind them and there was enough noise now that the downed G-man wouldn't be able to pick them out of the crowd. Francis turned right on the busy sidewalk and slowed to a walk.

Fuller seemed really excited. "That was interesting."

"You've never seen me. You've never met me. You weren't here. They're after me, got it? And they can't know we've talked. It's for your own safety. Go home. Understand?" Fuller nodded. "Good. Keep on walking like everything is normal. I'll be in touch." Francis veered to the side, saw a break in traffic, and ran across two lanes of traffic. It was an obvious move, but he couldn't let the OCI know that he'd met the man building their Dymaxions.

Sure enough, he was spotted. There was a shout as someone gave chase, then the squeal of brakes and the honking of a horn. An OCI man went sliding across the hood of a cab. Reaching the other side, Francis picked out a nearby restaurant and ran for the door. He collided with some customers that were leaving and knocked a well-dressed lady on her ass. "Sorry!" Then he was through the doors, past the surprised hostess, and running between the tables of startled diners.

There was more shouting as the OCI men followed. "There he is!"

Francis spotted the swinging doors of the kitchen and barged through. Food was sizzling and fire leapt from around a pan. Several members of the staff looked at him. "Hey, you can't be in here," a man in a white apron shouted.

"Where's the back door?" Francis asked.

The cook picked up a meat cleaver and pointed it at him. "Beat it!"

Francis concentrated his Power and jerked the meat cleaver from the cook's hand. It stuck hard into the ceiling. "Exit?" The frightened cook pointed to the left. "Thanks." Francis could see the OCI men heading his way through a porthole in the door. He ran for it, but on the way noticed several big bottles of olive oil on a shelf. He focused his Power and hurled the bottles hard against the floor. The jugs exploded into a slick mess. Francis made it to the back door just as the OCI came into the kitchen, slipping and crashing. *Suckers.*

He found himself in the second alley of the night. The door closed behind him, and luckily it was metal. Francis threw a bunch of Power against the frame. It was a strain, but he twisted the metal until it creaked and bent. They wouldn't be following him out that way.

Francis paused to catch his breath. Pershing had taught him how to keep a cool head in situations like this. *How many of them were there? Which way would they be coming from?* They'd be watching the streets. They'd have cars and radios. He had to give them the slip somehow. He had to maximize his advantages. *There.*

There was a sliding fire escape ladder leading to the apartments above. It was well out of reach . . . for those poor saps that weren't born Movers. Francis reached out with his Power, grasped the bottom rung and pulled hard.

It came sliding down. He quickly scrambled up the ladder as the OCI began beating on the kitchen door. The metal rungs were rusty and cold, and he was panting by the time he made it to the second story landing. He could almost hear Faye's voice chiding him. *Too much drinking and not enough healthy exercise.*

He tried to use his Power to yank up the ladder behind him, but nothing happened. *Nullifier!* "Shit." He pulled up the ladder by hand and then hit the stairs as fast as he could. He needed to get out of sight fast.

The OCI in the kitchen started shooting holes in the door trying to break the lock. It wouldn't work, but it told him these guys were not messing around. A bullet ricocheted off the wall below and made a terrible whine as it zinged off into the night.

The building was eight stories tall. He'd never make it over the top before the OCI got to the alley. Luckily the apartment window on the fourth floor was open a tiny crack. He pushed it up, climbed through and fell onto the carpet just as headlights illuminated the alley below. He risked a peek over the edge to see several men with guns fanning out across the alley, kicking over trash cans and poking through the dumpsters. One looked up, but Francis pulled back in what he hoped was the nick of time. There were all sorts of clotheslines leading from this fire escape to the building on the other side of the alley. With any luck the fed would just think the movement he saw was some of the lines swaying in the breeze.

He was in a plain bedroom. The lights were out, nobody was inside, and the door was closed. The sound of a radio could be heard coming from the other side of the wall. He breathed and listened to the crashing and shouting below. They wouldn't give up that easy. They'd canvas the neighborhood. Normally his Power would make a real mess of his enemies in a fight, but if they found him, that damnable nullifier would give them the advantage. He pulled out the notepad, craned it enough so that he could see the pencil lines from the reflected light, and tried to figure it out. He was fairly decent at drawing spells. He could make this work . . .

The doorknob turned. Francis hurried and crawled behind the bed. He tried to duck down as low as possible, but it wasn't a very tall bed. The door opened and a hand reached for the light switch. Francis reached out with his Power to pop the light bulb, but forgot that it wasn't going to work. The light came on. *Shit.*

"What's going on down there?" It was a girl's voice. Footsteps on the carpet. Francis had to shut her up and fast. She went to the window and looked down at the OCI. She was young, probably his age, but short and built thick like a fire hydrant. Francis prepared to grab her. He'd have to cover her mouth so she couldn't scream, and then try to calm her down. "Who left this open?" and then she looked over and saw Francis coming her way.

Like a good New Yorker, she did two things without even thinking about it. First, she screamed, and second, she kicked him right between the legs. Francis cried out and stumbled to the side as the girl kept on screaming. He fell over the edge of the bed and hit the floor.

"Up there!" one of the OCI shouted.

That really hurt. He just wanted to puke and die, maybe even in that order, but he got up and lurched for the door. The girl hit him with a vase and threw a shoe after him, all while screaming for help. Francis made it through the living room, found the door, and spilled out into the hall.

That was rather embarrassing. He'd fought a dojo full of Imperial Iron Guards once, and now he'd just been bested by a swift kick from a portly girl. The hall stretched in both directions. He limped toward the elevator. *No, they'd expect that.* "Stairs," he gasped. *Now is not a good time for stairs.*

He found the stairwell and clambered down a floor. The girl had been barefoot but he felt like she'd been wearing steel-toed boots. There was a noise below as the door to the stairwell banged open. It was too late. Francis turned and went up, or as Buckminster Fuller had suggested, *out* from the center of gravity. *Damned Cogs.*

Francis could hear the heavy footfalls below. He yanked open the fifth floor door as loudly as possible and then tried to move quietly toward the sixth, hopefully they'd veer off to check that. He had to think fast. He could either hide, run, or fight. His magic wasn't working, but he had a .45 auto and two mags inside his coat. However there were at least eight of them, maybe more. If he hid, they'd find him eventually. That left running. The buildings in this part of town were packed right on top of each other. Maybe if he made it to the roof he could jump to the next one. It was his best bet, so Francis ignored the pain and kept on running.

He was sweating profusely by the time he got to the roof. Luckily, the door was unlocked. There was a pigeon coop, some antennas, and a dried-out roof garden. Francis ran over to the edge. *Too far.* A Brute couldn't have leapt to the next building. Francis scrambled to the other side, but it was even worse over there. There was only a twelve-foot gap between walls, but he hadn't realized that he'd climbed up the *shortest* building on the block. Francis found one spot where there was a fire escape on the opposite building. It was far, but using his downward momentum he could . . . what? Rip his arms off on impact? He wasn't Jake Sullivan.

Francis pulled the Colt .45 from his shoulder holster and thumbed off the safety. He was going to have to fight his way back to the street. He'd probably get plugged in the process. He should've gotten one of those vitality spells bound to him when Heinrich had, but he'd been too scared. It was one thing to risk your life on the fly, it was another thing to do it by going under a slow knife and hoping to come back out of a magical coma. If he lived through this, though, he promised himself that he'd get one for sure.

He checked his Power. Still nothing. Whoever had a Dymaxion had to be in the building below. If he had his magic, he could easily blast past these bozos . . . Francis pulled out the notepad and studied the design as he moved over and hid behind the pigeon coop. Fuller's spell was his only hope.

Trying to burn the lines into his memory, Francis almost didn't even hear the deep rustle of wings over the cooing of the pigeons. He looked up just as a black shape passed overhead. *What now?* The shape landed softly on the other side of the coop.

"Come on out, Francis. It's over."

It was Crow.

Whisper had said he was some sort of demon, which meant without his magic he wouldn't have a chance, and if Crow was using a Greater Summoned, he was toast no matter what. Francis took one last desperate look at Fuller's design. He might have it memorized enough to produce it later, but he didn't have time to draw it now and he couldn't let it fall into Crow's hands. Tearing the little page out, he stuffed it in his mouth and chewed. He almost choked on the dry paper but he managed to swallow it.

Crow's footsteps could be heard coming around the pigeon coop. His presence was scaring the hell out of the birds. "I thought about killing you. You have no idea how tempting it is to just toss you off this building and say that you got scared and jumped."

Francis circled, keeping the little structure between them. He got glimpses of Crow's black coat through the wire. "Who said I'm scared?"

"Guilt then. Maybe a rich kid got in over his head in an Active plot and was afraid of doing hard time. I don't know. Whatever plays better in the press. You're scared though, Francis. I can smell your fear. Your sweet little girlfriend was braver than you are. Pert little thing, that. When this is over, maybe I'll keep her for myself. Show her what a real man can do."

"You're no man." Francis took two steps back from the coop, raised his gun and fired repeatedly. The flashes obscured his vision, but as Crow moved to the side, Francis tracked him and kept on shooting. He knew that he'd hit Crow several times. Pistol empty, Francis took another magazine from the pouch on the off side of his shoulder holster. Feathers were floating in the air. He got the mag into the well just as two massive hands landed on his shoulders.

"True," Crow hissed. Francis looked up into four glowing red eyes. "I'm no man. I'm better than that. You should get to know the *real* me." The great black head dipped hard, and a curled ram's horn, hard as rock, slammed into Francis' face.

Head swimming, Francis found himself on his back, staring at grey clouds stained pink by the city lights. Blood was running into his eyes. The demon stood over him, smoke leaking from several bullet holes. He seemed to ripple, like a pebble tossed in a puddle. Francis tried to blink away the blood, and when he opened his eyes, Crow appeared human again.

Crow's voice seemed to come from very far away as other feet crunched on the gravel around him. "Put this fink in the hole with the other. We're not done with him yet." A black leather shoe rose over his head, descended fast, and everything went black.

Chapter 13

You do not comprehend what we are facing. I have lived in both worlds, West and East. The Imperium is more than just another country and the Chairman is more than some mere politician to be bargained with. To illustrate, one of our most popular legends tells of forty-seven warriors whose master was disgraced by an enemy lord, and thus had to take his own life. Though revenge was forbidden by decree, they swore a secret oath. These ronin spent years plotting. They debased themselves, laying drunken in the street, beaten and spit upon by peasants, all so that their foe would underestimate them. But as soon as he let down his guard, they struck the castle, slaughtered his retainers, and sawed the lord's head off with the dagger their master had used to gut himself. Having made their point, every single one of them committed ritual suicide together. That is not the attitude of men you take lightly.

—Toyotomi Makoto,
knight of the Grimnoir,
testimony to the elders' council,
1908

Unknown Location

IT BEGAN IN THE RAIN, *holding George's dead head in her hands. A gigantic black bird spread its wings and blocked the rain. It spoke with Crow's voice. "You can't stop me, Faye. Don't even try."*

The demon was killing her friends, picking them off one by one. She'd Travel to their side, only to arrive a second too late. She'd appear, but they were already gone. She'd just find bits and pieces. Jane's favorite white dress, soaked red. Dan's broken glasses. Heinrich's coat was smoldering in a charred pit. Mr. Browning's workbench was empty, tools scattered. Lance's cowboy hat was ripped in half and there were bits of meat and hair stuck to it. Whisper's fancy umbrella was rolling in the wind down an empty street. She kept on Traveling, faster and faster, trying to catch up to the demon.

She was with Delilah again, like she'd been at the very end, missing half of her face. "Hurry, Faye. He's killing everyone!"

"I can't. He's too fast."

The pretty side of Delilah's face laughed at her. "Or you're too slow. What's it going to be, kid?"

"Why can't I get stronger again?"

"You must not want it bad enough."

Mr. Sullivan was the strongest. Surely, he could beat the demon. But by the time she got there he was holding his guts in his lap and trying to stuff them back inside. "Damn it, girl. I was counting on you. Look what you've done. You killed me again."

Grandpa. She found him at the haystacks, just like before. Dying from Madi's bullet, he whispered something that she couldn't hear, but she knew that it was something about how she hadn't been there to save him. Bitter sadness ripped her heart in two.

One last Travel put her onto the roof of a tall building. Francis was dangling from the edge. He called out for her to help, but she moved like molasses. As Francis' fingers slipped from the edge, a massive black shape climbed over the side of the skyscraper. It towered over her. The demon was a hundred feet tall, made of smoke and death, and it tore Francis from the ledge and flung him down before it came for her.

Faye woke up screaming.

She was in a car. It was dark out.

"Calm down. It was just a nightmare." Whisper was driving fast, squinting against the oncoming headlights. "Everything is fine."

It took Faye a moment to remember where she was and how she'd gotten there. *No. Things are not fine at all.* She cracked her neck. Her head had been hanging at a weird angle while she'd been sleeping. Her lungs and eyes hurt, and she was glad that it was too dark to see where the Summoned's blood had burned her. It throbbed with a dull ache.

There was an awful cough from the backseat. Faye looked over to see Ian stretched out. "Is he going to be all right?"

"I don't know," she answered truthfully. "I think he has some injuries we can't see. He's been getting worse. If I take him to a hospital, we will doubtlessly be arrested. I have good news, though."

"Huh?" Faye was still dizzy and it was hard to think. Something to do with the demon oil she'd breathed. It was messing with her head.

"Your friend the Healer is on the way. We're going to meet her in Knoxville."

Jane? She can fix anything. "Is that far?"

"You have been asleep for a very long time. We'll be there soon. Don't worry."

Faye nodded and rested her head back against the window. She'd been slipping in and out. The last thing she could remember it had been daytime and Whisper had said they'd been in Arkansas. "Are you okay?"

"Tired . . . I'll be fine."

Faye looked over again. Whisper was still wearing her torn nightgown. Of course, all of their luggage had burned in the fire. She caught Faye looking and smiled. "Yes. I look quite the mess. I've gotten some odd looks when we've stopped for gas, but luckily the attendants have all been boys. I flirt with them for a minute, say a few nice things, make an excuse about coming from a wild bonfire party, and that's either so scandalous or so exciting that they don't even notice you two."

"What are you going to do if it's a girl that fills up our gas?"

Whisper winked. "That is not an issue. I can flirt with girls too if necessary."

"Huh?" Faye didn't get it. French people were weird.

"Never mind that. Do you feel well enough to talk? I need to talk or I won't be able to stay awake."

Faye just grunted. She felt like she'd been run over by an angry Holstein. She was running a fever and her brain was working slower than normal, which probably put her around regular person speed. She didn't know how they could stand being so *sluggish*.

"How does your magic feel?"

What an odd question. "Why?"

"Well . . . You're a fugitive. If we come across a police roadblock I need to know what our options are."

That made sense. Faye checked her Power. It was there, and feeling surprisingly strong. It must have recharged better than her body. *Wait a second* . . . Faye checked her head map. It stretched much further than anticipated. Twice as far as it had when she'd been bouncing around fighting the demon. "It's . . . it's better. More like before."

Whisper looked temporarily distressed, but then tried to laugh it off. "Like when you Traveled the *Tempest*, because if you could have just taken us directly to Knoxville and saved me this horrendous trip I would have appreciated knowing that ten hours ago."

"No." Faye stopped to cough. "Not that much. But it's better than yesterday by a bunch." It was more like how she'd been before Madi had blown up Francis' house with the Peace Ray. It was like she'd first started growing stronger when Grandpa had gotten shot, and it had just kept growing and growing all the way until she'd gone toe to toe against the Chairman. Then she'd used it all up doing something that should have been impossible.

"You are stronger, but do you *feel* different?"

"Whisper, you sound scared. What's wrong?"

"Nothing . . . I . . . I am just concerned for you is all."

"I'm just tired." She'd been weaker after the *Tokugawa* fight, and though she'd gotten better again with practice, she hadn't come close to the energy she'd been able to muster before. *Why now?* That was really strange. Would the stronger connection to the Power stick around again, or would she lose it like last time?

If she hadn't been so darn tired and out of it, she probably would've pondered on that particular mystery for a while. Instead she drifted off and was snoring in a few minutes.

She didn't hear Whisper mutter to herself, "I wish that I had been wrong."

Bell Farm, Virginia

THEY MADE IT HOME LATE. Home, being a dilapidated farmhouse just itching to fall down, was a relative term, but it was a place to lay his weary head. Sullivan was tired. Playing mental games against somebody like J. Edgar Hoover was more tiring than breaking rocks. Plus, his body still ached from the fight with the Imperium Brute. Magical Mending could fix the wound, but the pain managed to stick around.

They parked the truck in the barn and walked to the house. Sullivan felt it first. The wartime instincts never really went away. The woods were too quiet. "We're being watched," he whispered. Dan started to turn his head. "Play it cool." The other knight pretended to relax, but he kept one hand close to his piece.

Sullivan exercised his Power to feel the world around him. The metal bits were so much denser than their surroundings that they stuck out like beacons. Fifteen yards. One person in the bushes. Armed.

The noise of a revolver being cocked was very distinctive. After that came a woman's voice. "Don't move."

He didn't need to move to bend the hell out of gravity, so Sullivan prepared to Spike their new guest halfway across Virginia.

"Easy, Sullivan. I just want to talk."

"Hammer . . ."

Dan had one hand on his pistol. "Who?"

"The lady who served me up to the OCI on a plate."

She came walking out of the shadows, gun trained on them. "I didn't know it was a setup. I was just supposed to get you to answer the phone. I didn't know they meant to kill you."

"I'm more inclined to believe folks who aren't pointing heaters at me."

"I'm just being careful. You've got a reputation for tossing people around."

Sullivan scanned the trees. The range that he could check with his Power was limited. She could have an army out there. "You alone?"

"Just me and Mr. Colt here."

"That's stupid."

"Only if I was here to fight, which I'm not. I'll put this down, but give me your word that you won't use magic on me first or start anything unless it is self-defense."

"Are you serious?"

"Promise."

That was an odd request. Sullivan looked at Dan, who just shrugged. "Okay. Fine. I promise I won't attack you unless you attack me."

"No tricks. Just hear me out. Then we part ways."

"Agreed."

"You're telling the truth." Hammer lowered the revolver. "You have no idea how *refreshing* that is."

"This your fake redhead, Jake?" Dan asked, the subtle edge of magic in his words. "Because I've got to say, she might've bragged to you about how good she was at finding folks, but she sure didn't exaggerate her talents. You certainly didn't exaggerate about her being pretty either. She's just as lovely in person. Very nice to meet you."

"Save the flattery for a chump, Mouth. Your Power won't work on me."

Dan smiled. "Can't blame a man for trying."

"You here to arrest me?" Sullivan asked. "Because I've really got more important things to worry about right now."

"Originally, I was. Now, I'm probably going to regret this. Hell, never mind, I *know* I'm going to regret this." Hammer paused. "I'm here to help you."

This woman was trouble. Sullivan shook his head. "No thanks. Got all the help I need."

"You know a man by the name of Heinrich Koenig?"

"What about him?" Dan asked, positively dripping suspicion over the use of his dead friend's name.

"He's being held captive by the OCI, until they get tired of him. Then they'll execute him even though they know he's innocent, which is frankly an idea I find bothersome."

"Impossible! Heinrich . . ." Dan looked to Sullivan. "Francis never got to see his body." Then he grinned as he latched onto some hope. "I knew that stubborn son of a gun wouldn't die that easy!" Dan went to unlock the door.

"So, you boys ready to talk yet? You know you want to."

It might be an elaborate trick, but he was always a sucker for a mystery, and Hammer knew that about him. Sullivan gestured to the door of the farmhouse. "Come in."

Hammer followed. "Not to be rude or anything, but you got anything to eat in here? I've been hiding in the bushes all afternoon, and spying is terribly famishing work."

As they entered the house, Dan had already positioned himself off to the side, .45 in hand. He cracked the slide over the top of her head, hard enough to lay her out. Hammer hit the floor and her gun slid away.

"Damn it, Dan." Sullivan looked down at the dazed woman. "What'd you do that for?"

"You gave your word, not mine." Dan opened Hammer's coat and discovered a gun belt. He removed another revolver and set it aside. "I don't know what her Power is, but I can tell it's something crafty. I bounced right off of her. Definitely a mental-type Active from what you said before, and she's just oozing Power. If she's going to start playing mind control or something, I want the deck stacked in our favor first."

It wasn't a bad idea at all. "That's reasonable. I just hope you didn't hit her too hard."

"That was a love tap. I was a perfect gentlemen. It'll just leave a goose egg."

Hammer was cursing them. She rolled over and put her hands on her head. "Oh, you filthy rotten—" Then she got really nasty.

"Lady's got a mouth on her. You believe that stuff about Heinrich?"

"Not really."

"Think it's a trap?"

"More than likely," Sullivan agreed.

"Help me tie her up?"

"Well, I said I'd play nice. So you do it. I'll get dinner started."

Dinner consisted of opening a few cans of vegetables and one that was filled with a congealed meatlike substance, mixing them together in a pot, and heating it all on the stove until it was hot enough to distract them from the taste. Sullivan never claimed to be a very good cook.

Hammer was tied to a chair with some baling wire that Dan had found in the barn. In the spirit of fairness, Dan had just tied her ankles and one wrist to the chair, leaving her left hand free so that she could still eat. After sampling the noxious sludge Sullivan had prepared, she'd said that they weren't doing her any favors.

"Being the fat one, you must be Dan Garrett. So, Mr. Garrett, you like hitting women?"

"Far from it. I work in an environment where it isn't terribly uncommon to have the supposedly weaker sex bend steel beams with their bare hands. I treat all of my threats equally. Hell, I'm practically a suffragist."

She poked at the baling wire with her free hand. "This isn't necessary."

"Nothing personal," Dan explained, "but a lot of very powerful people are trying to kill us right about now, so we can't be too careful."

"So you buffaloed me," Hammer muttered. "You're a real class act."

"If it's any consolation, my wife will Mend that bump when she gets back . . . Unless of course, she decides not to because you were rudely pointing a gun at her husband."

"And if I'd just walked up and been friendly as can be?"

"You'd probably still be tied to that chair, but wouldn't have the headache."

Sullivan chuckled. "First time I met Dan, I got tossed off a blimp. So in comparison, you got off easy."

Hammer glared at him. "You're a bastard."

"So I been told. Start talking."

She did. Hammer told them about being recruited to find him because she was a Justice. That piqued Sullivan's scholarly interest, since he'd never actually had a confirmation that such Actives were real. Hopefully, if they ended up on speaking terms after this he'd have to interview her for his notes. She insisted that she'd been as surprised as he was about how the OCI had tried to shoot him, and how afterward she'd then been recruited by Crow.

"Why, after seeing what a shyster bunch they were, did you go along with that?"

"None of your damn business."

Dan started to ask another question, but Sullivan held up one hand. He'd been forced to chose between working for J. Edgar Hoover or staying in Rockville. It wouldn't surprise him in the least to see G-men using dirt on another Active to get their job done. Blackmail, threats, whatever, it was one more reason to tread extra carefully around Hammer. "It don't matter. Go on."

She told them a bit about how her Power worked, how she could follow someone and know which path they'd taken, and how that had led her to the ambassador's mansion.

"Lucky that Brute didn't eat you for breakfast."

"Are you kidding? Toru was polite compared to you two. That's a sad state of affairs when the Imperium are the hospitable ones of the bunch."

"Oh, they're all sorts of polite, until he found out you had a rare Power and kidnapped you for Unit 731 to experiment on." Dan sounded bitter, the memory of Madi taking Jane still fresh in his mind.

"I didn't say I wanted to start palling around with them. After that I tracked you into the country. Then Crow appeared out of thin air. I still haven't figured out how he does that."

"Near as we can figure, he's a Summoner that possesses demons, like a Beastie controls animals." Which was a fascinating concept, one that he'd never heard of before, or even considered possible. It was too bad he was probably going to have to kill Crow, because he would love to know how he'd accomplished such a feat.

Hammer appeared deep in thought. "That makes sense. He's like a big bag of lies, and when I get a glimpse of the truth, it's been too . . ."

"Weird?" Dan suggested.

"Alien. I've only talked to him a few times now, but each time it's like talking to a different person."

Sullivan's guess was that was the different demons he was wearing. He'd have to update his notes on Actives, preferably after they'd put Crow in the ground. Whatever the hell he was, he was a danger first and foremost. "How'd he find you?"

"They carved a spell onto my car. I found it and wrecked it."

Sullivan got up and went to the kitchen window. The woods were still and dark. "That could've been a decoy. There might be another."

"Yeah, so I ditched that car and boosted a different one."

He closed the curtain. "That's not very nice."

"You stole my new Ford!" Hammer sputtered.

"I left it someplace it would be found."

"On its roof!"

Dan laughed at him. Sullivan folded his arms defensively and scowled at Dan. "It was on its wheels when I left it. My apologies. I'll make it up to you and get you another. Those Hyperions are pricey though. It might take me awhile."

"I can't believe it." She shook her head. "You're telling the truth. You're a real piece of work, aren't you, Sullivan? Every lawman in the country has your picture on the wall and you're worried about how you're going to replace my car. We've got more important things to worry about."

"So it's *we* now?" Dan asked. "Lady, I don't trust you as far as Jake could throw you. Why should I start now?"

She told them about the recording of Heinrich and Crow's admission that he had proof, and how both were at OCI headquarters. That sounded a little too *convenient* for Sullivan. Yet, as Hammer talked, he studied her. She was tough, and she had an attitude about her, but if this was a trap it wasn't her creation. Hammer seemed sincere . . . but then again, she'd played him like a fool the very first time they'd met. When she was done, she looked him square in the eye, and asked, "You believe me now?"

"I believed you were a redhead. Look where that got me."

"That was business." Hammer glowered at him. "It got you some exercise and a chance to talk to a ghost. Admit it, you'd do it again."

She had him there. "All right. If you want me to trust you, why the change of heart?"

"It isn't enough that I don't want to see an innocent man hang? I'm putting myself in jeopardy by even talking to you! What do you think he's going to do to me when Crow finds out? I'm risking my life. Isn't that good enough?"

Sullivan shook his head.

"Fine . . ." Hammer hesitated. "Tell me about your rings."

Dan covered his with his off hand. "What about them?"

"My father had a lot of respect for the men that wore those."

"He was Grimnoir?" Sullivan asked.

"I don't think so."

"Hammer?" Dan leaned forward. "Married or maiden name?"

"Born with it. I'm single . . ." she answered. Sullivan looked at her funny. "What?"

"I was just going to say I could see why." Hammer

made an amusing face when she was angry. "You're kind of pushy."

Dan paid them no mind. "You're a Texan?" Hammer nodded. "I've got an ear for accents. Was your father Lee Hammer?"

"You knew him?" Without another word, Dan stood up, pushed down Hammer's free hand and twisted it down with wire. He then took Sullivan by the arm and guided him out of the kitchen. "Wait! What do you know?"

Once they were out of earshot in the hall, Dan began pacing and rubbing his face. "Hell, this is complicated."

"What's the deal, Dan?"

"Keep your voice *down*. Lee Hammer never took the oath. Lord knows Pershing asked him enough times. Said he'd already taken one as a marshal and didn't ever want to have to choose between the two in case there was a conflict. But he helped us quite a few times. Pershing was a friend of his. They went after Pancho Villa together. I've heard stories about him, but never met the man."

"So, she's legit?"

"Maybe. Apples don't fall far from the tree, but sometimes they bounce when they hit and roll a ways."

Sullivan shrugged. His parents had been decent enough folks, but he had one brother that had been a murderous lunatic. "Yeah, I guess. So do you think she's leading us into a trap or not?"

"Her? Maybe . . . Crow, definitely. I wish we had that tape so we could see if it's really Heinrich's voice or not."

"If she's a Justice, then she'd have known if it wasn't him."

"Only if she's telling us the truth, which she might not be. I wish we had a Reader handy . . . This is complicated."

"You've said that. What's so complicated about it? She's either on our side or she's not."

"Because she'd be right to hold a grudge." Dan looked pained. "Look, I'll explain later. She can't force the truth out of you if you don't know it." He started to walk back to the kitchen but Sullivan stepped in front of him.

"I happen to be a fan of the truth."

Dan shook his head sadly. "He died helping us. We got him killed."

They hadn't twisted the wire down too hard. Dan Garrett talked tough, but he hadn't even let it cut into her skin. Hammer knew she could wiggle a hand free and get herself out of this in no time. They had gone around the corner to talk privately. It would only take a second. Her guns were sitting on the counter. They'd never see it coming.

This was stupid. They didn't trust her, and why should they? Sullivan was honorable enough to not put a bullet in her head and dump her body in the woods, but she couldn't tell about Garrett. Since Mouths were so good at twisting their words, their lies didn't even register. She hated Mouths because they were one of the only types that she couldn't judge. He'd sucker-punched her and she'd walked right into it. As a professional, that was flat-out embarrassing.

She could skip out the back, run for the car. By the time she could contact the OCI the Grimnoir would be long gone. Crow would be suspicious, but she could just say that they'd surprised her and tied her up. It wasn't too far from the truth. The wire wasn't that tight. She probably wouldn't even leave much skin behind . . .

Hell with it. As her daddy used to say, in for a penny, in for a pound. She left the wire alone and waited for the Grimnoir to finish their conference. Besides, they could come back around the corner any second and it would look real suspicious if she was in the process of untying herself.

The walls were thin. She could hear voices but couldn't quite make out what they were saying. When they came back in she would try to convince them that she was telling the truth. She had to watch herself, though. The normal alarm bells that would be going off when somebody lied to her simply didn't work with Garrett.

Sullivan raised his voice. Something had ticked him off. The conversation tapered off again and she didn't get to hear anything else. They came back a minute later, looking glum. Sullivan untwisted the wires around her wrists. "Sorry about this." He knelt down and freed her ankles. He was surprisingly gentle about it. "And I'm real sorry about the whack on the head."

She rubbed the circulation back into her hands. "And the general indignity of it all?"

"That too."

"And my car?"

"Don't push it." Sullivan went over and took a seat. Garrett stayed leaning against the wall.

"You've put us between a rock and a hard place," the Mouth said. "There's layers here, and we've got to figure out which ones are legit and which ones are a scheme, and

I don't have your advantage in that department, so you're just going to have to forgive my rudeness while we sort this out."

"That's okay. I hear Sullivan likes puzzles."

Garrett suddenly flinched and jerked his hand back as if it had been shocked. "Huh?"

Hammer noticed that Sullivan had clenched one hand into a fist and was studying his ring. "Incoming message," he said. "Lance."

"I got it. If you'll excuse me," Garrett said, and he hurried from the room, leaving her alone with Sullivan.

"What's that all about?" she asked.

"We can use these to set up communication spells," he explained patiently. "Probably a lot neater before they invented the telephone and all, but as you can see, not a lot of lines around here . . . And I probably shouldn't be telling you anything else."

"That's interesting." Hammer had always been intrigued by all the mysteries of the Power. She'd pieced together several useful tricks over the years, but according to her investigation, Sullivan was supposed to be a wealth of knowledge. "You remember the first time we spoke. I wasn't lying about one thing. I do find Actives a fascinating topic."

"Well, you came to the right place. Once we get this sorted out and if I'm not in the electric chair or Rockville, I'd love to talk about what it is you do. I've been cataloging as much as I can about how the Power works."

"So I did have you pegged, Mr. Librarian. Mind of a scholar in the body of an ox."

"Scholar? Maybe if circumstances had been different.

Here in the real world I'm just too damn good at fighting. It keeps cutting into my reading time." He chuckled. "Listen, Hammer—"

"Pemberly." She decided then that she liked this big, honest, tough guy. On first impressions, some people might mistake Sullivan for simple, but he was anything but. "That's my name." Sullivan nodded slowly, as if analyzing if she was trying to con him again. "Friends call me Pem."

"I'm sure they do, but I'm not there yet. I'm going to explain some things to you. Dan's going to explain some more. The Grimnoir are a good bunch. The folks running it are secretive sometimes to the point of stupid, but with the way things are going now I can maybe see why they're like that. We do good things and we defend a lot of folks who can't defend themselves."

That sounded a lot like her father. "You trying to sell me something?"

"I save the fancy talk for the Mouth. What I'm trying to say—" Sullivan stopped and jerked his head toward the front of the house. "You hear that?"

Someone was shouting.

Sullivan swept back his jacket and pulled a big automatic from a holster on his hip. "Hang on." He walked quickly down the hall. Hammer ran over and picked up her guns. If Crow had somehow followed her here . . . That was too horrible to think about. She followed Sullivan into the front room. He got behind the wall and peeked out one corner of the window. "Aw, hell."

"What is it?" She moved up on the other side of the window and looked out.

It was dark, but she could make out a lone figure standing in front of the farmhouse. He raised his voice and bellowed. *"Jake Sullivan! Come out and face me!"*

"That's the Imperium diplomat I talked to."

"Diplomat, my ass. Iron Guard," Sullivan said through clenched teeth. "Tough bastards. Remember earlier when Dan mentioned Unit 731?"

"Yeah?"

"You got a rare Power. Trust me, you do not want to get captured by the Imperium." Sullivan moved to the other side of the door and picked up a large, strange-looking rifle. He pulled the bolt back with a *clack*. A bandoleer of magazine pouches went over one shoulder. "Go get Dan."

"Jake Sullivan! I am Toru. Are you a coward? Face me, Heavy!"

Sullivan put one hand on the latch and took a deep breath.

"What're you going to do?"

"I'll hold them off and kill as many as possible. We're probably surrounded. I'll cause a ruckus and distract them. Once they're concentrating on me, then you two run for your lives."

"I'm a good shot." She hoisted the Bisley. "I can help."

He grabbed her hard by the arm and pulled her around. "Listen to me. Iron Guards don't die easy." Sullivan glared at her. "Don't be stupid. Get out of here. I'll catch up."

I'll catch up. It was the first time he'd actually lied to her tonight.

❖❖❖

Sullivan threw open the door, kept as much of his body behind concealment as possible, and aimed his bullpup BAR at the Iron Guard. It was dark, and the only illumination was from the lantern light leaking through the doorway, but the Iron Guard was only ten yards away. It was an easy shot. "Evening, Toru."

"Mr. Sullivan," the Iron Guard responded politely.

He had to keep Toru talking, let him gloat to buy the others time to escape. This place was flimsy. A machine gun in the trees would shred the farmhouse. Toru wouldn't have announced himself unless his men were already in position. That honor-bound son of a bitch probably wanted to fight him one on one to make up for last time. That seemed like the Iron Guard thing to do. *Good.* He'd use his Power to make a mess of things and hopefully Dan and Pemberly could make it out the back. There would be more Imperium in the fields, but hopefully Dan's Japanese language practice would finally pay off. "Nice night for a fight to the death."

"Most nights are."

"How'd you find me?" He said *me* instead of *us* on purpose. Hopefully the Imperium didn't know about the others.

"I had a Finder put a spirit on the woman looking for you. She struck me as someone who would not give up the chase easily."

So much for protecting the others. "That was clever."

Toru gave the slightest bow. "Thank you."

Sullivan never could understand these Imperium elites. They were unfailingly polite up until the moment they ended your life.

Knoxville, Tennessee

FAYE WOKE UP to the unnatural warmth of a Healer's touch. "Jane?"

"Yes, I'm here. Just relax."

Faye looked around. She was on a bed and couldn't remember if she'd walked to it or been carried. They were probably in a motel from the way it was decorated all simple and beige. Whisper was asleep in a big chair. Ian was on the other bed, and from the look of him, Jane had got to him first. His breathing was normal for the first time since the fire. She heard a rough and familiar voice. Lance was talking to somebody just out of view, and from the white light reflecting on the walls, she knew it was through a spell.

Jane's glowing hands were on her stomach. The deep scratches Crow had given her were burning. Globs of black oil rose up out of her skin and rolled until gravity dripped them to the blankets. She coughed hard and a bit of black smoke puffed out of her mouth and floated away. Her whole body was burning up, and then it was over and she could breathe. The recently fused bits of skin were hot spots, like when they used to heat rocks on the stove to stick in bed to stay warm during the winter, but everything else was cool. Her body was damp with sweat and sleepy.

"I've never seen anything like that before," Jane said. She was sitting on the edge of the bed and laid one gentle and freezing cold hand on Faye's forehead. "Believe it or not, Summoned are usually very clean. Rarely do their wounds turn septic so quickly. Everything about this one screams corruption."

"He's a real jerk, too. Thanks, Jane."

"It was nothing."

Ian had sat up the other bed, leaned over, and picked up something from Faye's bed. The Summoned ink that had come out of Faye's arm had formed into little balls of tar. "I've been dealing with Summoned since I was a child, and I've never seen one like that before."

"How so?" Jane asked.

Ian rubbed the goo between his fingers. "A few things. Obviously, having a human steering it being the biggest, but besides that, it changed shape and mass too quickly. When you draw in a Summoned, it takes a physical form and that's it. They don't change until they're destroyed or dismissed. The more powerful the Summoner, the greater the Summoned you can bring, but this thing was very different. Our friend Crow is playing in some uncharted ground."

"Good to see you're still alive, too, Ian. Thanks for asking," Faye said.

Ian looked around the room. "Where's George?" Faye shook her head sadly. He got her meaning. "Oh . . . I didn't know." Ian lowered his eyes. "I'm sorry."

"Don't be sorry. The people in Ada aren't." Jane patted Faye's arm. "We all die eventually, and very few of us will do it as bravely as he did."

"It was terrible, Jane." Faye's eyes suddenly felt really wet. "He was a really nice man."

"All over the country, people are calling him a hero. They're talking about him on every radio show, George

Bolander, the man that hit a demon so hard he ended the drought. Even if they've already gotten the story all wrong, they'll never forget him. All of the horrible things they've been blaming on Actives in general and us knights in particular were just washed away in one moment of courage."

Jane always did have a different way of looking at things that made Faye feel a little bit better.

"What're you doing up still, Dan? Don't you guys ever sleep?" Lance asked.

She could hear Dan Garrett's voice over the spell. "Busy day. Kidnapped J. Edgar Hoover and now Sullivan's questioning an OCI bounty hunter downstairs."

"Hello, honey," Jane called.

"That's your idea of staying *out* of trouble? Suppose that's what I get for leaving you two unattended." Lance scratched his beard. "From that stupid grin, I can tell you're enjoying yourself entirely too much. We picked up the other three. Jane got them Mended."

"That's great—"

There was the sound of a door crashing open. A woman shouted. "Iron Guards!" Faye popped off the bed in a flash. Even Whisper woke up instantly at the words. Someone shouting "Iron Guards" would always get a Grimnoir to jump, but the voice was coming through the spell. Faye ran to look over Lance's shoulder.

The view in the mirror showed Dan Garrett, a look of shock on his face. A pretty lady was standing in the doorway behind him. "Sullivan said we've got to run for it. He's going to hold them off."

"Oh no." Mr. Garrett turned back. "Gotta go."

"Wait!" Faye shouted. Her brain seemed to be working at its normal pace again, and she had an idea. Traveling safely wasn't based on how great the distance was, she'd proven that before. It was like space was a big sheet and she could just pick up two spots and smoosh them together, even when it was a *big* sheet. The dangerous part was that her head map could only see so far, a tiny percentage of how far she could actually go, and Traveling beyond that safe zone risked getting her stuck in something.

"No time, Faye."

"Just hang on!" A quick check showed that her Power was feeling especially feisty still. They were like a thousand miles away, but it didn't matter. She had a perfectly clear view through the mirror. She checked her head map, and as it came flooding in nice and clear, she redirected it. Instead of looking at a big circle around the motel room, she gathered all of that map up and shoved it against the spell.

"Whoa!" Dan and Lance both said at the same time, since it was their respective Powers that were holding the link together.

Instead of a big circle, her head map pierced through the mirror in a narrow beam, like light coming through a keyhole.

Clear.

"I can do this."

"Faye, wait! It is too dangerous!" Whisper cried.

"I have to." Nobody was better at killing Iron Guards than Sally Faye Vierra! She stuck out one hand. "Lance, gun!" They'd been through a lot together, so he didn't even bother wasting time questioning Faye when she got spun up. Lance drew his big revolver and gave it to her. "Hang on, Dan, I'm on the way!"

Bell Farm, Virginia

TORU TOOK A FEW STEPS closer to the lantern light, revealing that the Iron Guard was carrying so much gear that only a Brute or a Spiker could possibly walk. He had one of the strange Imperium light machine guns with the magazine on top in one hand and that gigantic metal-spiked club in the other. On his belt was that traditional long-sword, short-sword combo that the Iron Guard seemed to love, two pistols, and a hand grenade. He was wearing a big vest covered in pouches, and had a large backpack which, from the feel of gravity, was stuffed. Toru had packed heavy.

"You brought everything and the kitchen sink."

"I do not understand the reference."

"Kind of hard to fight carrying all that crap, isn't it?"

Toru set the machine gun down on its bipod and unslung the backpack and set it aside. He did, however, keep the big club. "I packed for a long journey."

"Hell's not that far."

"Perhaps, but I have a mission to attend to first."

Now we're getting somewhere. Sullivan tightened his grip on the BAR. The others had better be ready to run when the shooting started. "How many men did you bring, Toru? I want to know if you've got a sporting chance."

"I am alone."

"That's the second time I got that dumb answer tonight." Sullivan put the front sight right between Toru's eyes. "Bullshit."

"Master Hatori showed me your conversation. In fact, he gave me many of his memories. That is why I have come alone."

Black Jack Pershing had done the same thing to him once.

"The final instructions my honored Chairman ever gave . . . were to you, one of our most despised foes. Yet Master Hatori believed you were telling the truth, and that you really are the last man to ever speak to the Chairman."

Where was he going with this? "I was."

"Do you believe you are worthy to defeat the Pathfinder?"

"Doesn't matter if I am or not, I have to try."

"Good answer." The spiked club was placed on top of the backpack. "A wise answer. I know much of the Pathfinder. I am now the keeper of Master Hatori's sacred firsthand knowledge of the way of the Dark Ocean." The pistol belt was set down next.

"That's useful."

"That is why I have come here." Toru removed the two swords, still in their sheaths. He put the smaller one down, but kept the longer one in both hands. "If you are worthy of my father's legacy, then I will teach you how to find and destroy the beast. If you are unworthy, then I will kill you and do it myself."

"What happened to the rest of the Iron Guard taking care of it?"

"My brothers have been led astray. I am afraid they will not understand until it is too late for us all."

"By the fake Chairman?"

"Yes."

"You're on your own . . ." Sullivan was stunned. He'd never realized that an Iron Guard would or even could do something like disobey orders. "What's to keep me from gunning you down where you stand?"

"Your desire to defeat the Pathfinder." Toru slowly drew the sword. It was nearly three feet of menacing razor steel. Sullivan had used one to cut a man in half once, and even with the BAR in hand, was wise enough to fear one in the hands of a trained Brute. "My father, the real Okubo Tokugawa, was wise beyond measure. Even in death, he would not have chosen to speak to you, among all of our many enemies, unless he thought you had the strength to do what was necessary. I have prayed for his guidance and the way has been shown to me. I am doing what I know my father would have me do. Do you see this blade?"

"Kind of hard to miss."

"This katana represents what it means to be Iron Guard. It was presented to me when I proved worthy to bear the sacred kanji. This blade represents sacrifice and pain. It is my soul." He twisted it back and forth, studying the reflections of the lamplight. Toru knelt and held the sword before him. "Yet the blade has become tarnished." Sullivan could see that the steel was clearly without blemish. "It is stained, rusted, and chipped. This katana—" Toru had to choke back the emotion to continue. "It is flawed."

Sullivan slowly lowered the BAR.

Toru took the hilt in his right and the sharpened end in his left. With a surge of Brute force he bent the sword. It bowed, resilient, but even the finest steel will break eventually.

SNAP.

The noise made Sullivan flinch.

Toru placed the two pieces on the grass. Blood was streaming between the fingers of one hand. He bowed his head.

"I am Iron Guard no longer . . . I, Toru, son of Okubo Tokugawa, pledge to help you defeat the Pathfinder. That is my mission. My father chose you. It is my obligation to him to assist you until this mission has been completed and the Pathfinder has been defeated. I will not help you against my people or my Imperium unless it is necessary to battle the Enemy. I will teach you the ways of Dark Ocean, then we will destroy the creature or die trying."

Sullivan didn't know what to say. There was movement behind him and Hammer spoke softly. "He's *completely* sincere." She sounded awestruck.

After several long seconds, Toru looked up from his broken sword. "Until I have fulfilled my father's command, I am unworthy of an Iron Guard's blade."

"And when the Pathfinder's beaten?"

"In the unlikely event we both live, we will tend to our unfinished business. We will fight. One will die. You helped kill my father, so we must; to do otherwise would be shameful. However, I will not let my hatred for you and your wretched ways deter me from my obligation."

That actually sounded pretty fair. "Then what?"

"Then?" Toru obviously hadn't thought that far ahead. "Should I win, I will then return to my people and commit *seppuku* as I have been ordered." Sullivan tilted his head, confused at the word. "Suicide. When my mission is done, I must kill myself to cleanse my disgrace from my family. It is necessary."

He didn't need Hammer's Power to know that was the truth. That fact that he'd shown up here proved that Toru was a suicidal maniac. Sullivan could just hold the trigger down and hose the crazy bastard down with lead, throw the body in a ditch and call it a night. He wanted to do it *so* very badly. Instead, Sullivan took his finger off the trigger and put the safety on.

This was no trick. The emotion on Toru's face when he broke his sword in half wasn't faked. This man had just turned his back on his entire life in order to keep a promise to a dead man. The Enemy was real, and in Toru he had someone who actually knew how to fight it.

"You got a deal."

The former Iron Guard bowed deeply. Feeling awkward, Sullivan did the same. He looked up just in time to see Faye Vierra pop into existence right behind Toru. The Traveler was lifting a big revolver in one hand. With no time for finesse, Sullivan surged his Power and Spiked hard, bending gravity away just as Faye fired.

Toru tumbled across the dead grass. Faye's stray bullet shattered one of the farmhouse windows. She squeaked in surprise as gravity changed around her and she went flying through the air. Faye Traveled out of the effect and hit the ground right next to him. "Look out, Mr. Sullivan! They've got a Heavy!"

He caught her by the arm before she could try to shoot at Toru again. "Cease fire."

"Iron Guard! Right there!" she shouted. Toru had caught his club as it had gone spinning by, and was standing in a fighting position with it raised overhead. Brutes were *fast.* Toru was red-faced and furious, but he wasn't charging them. *Yet*.

"Remember that one time when we first met and you murdered me by accident?" Sullivan asked gently.

"Yeah?"

"This is kind of like that. Faye, meet Toru."

"Oh . . . Whoops." She lowered the revolver. "Gotcha. Sorry about that." She looked over at Toru. "He seems *really* upset."

"You better pop on out of here until he cools off." Faye gulped and Traveled away. Toru slowly lowered the club. "She gets a little excitable."

"Keep your *kichiku* ninja on a leash, Sullivan," Toru spat.

He shrugged. "With the rep you assholes have developed around here, we'll be lucky if that's not about the *friendliest* greeting you get. Put the meat tenderizer away. We've got a lot to talk about."

Hammer

Chapter 14

Awake. Aware . . . Feeling every pain, every wound. Never healing. The poor bastards just can't die. It's no wonder they all go mad eventually. And the screaming coming from the trenches all night long . . . I wished they'd quit screaming. That was the worst part. Always with the screaming. Zombie Kraut sons-a-bitches. Damn the Kaiser's eyes.

—Unknown survivor
of the First Volunteer Brigade (Active),
Army report on the second battle of the Somme, 1918

Miami, Florida

AS WAS TO BE EXPECTED, the temperature inside the morgue was kept chilly. The room smelled of formaldehyde and detergents. The two knights followed the attendant down the wall of small metal doors. It was obvious right away which door they were looking for. It was the only one with a padlock on its latch. The attendant looked both ways to confirm that they were alone, then pulled out a ring of keys. A moment later, he slid out a table containing a sheet-draped corpse. Even with the sheet in place hiding the evidence, it was obvious that the body was in two pieces, with the lump of the head being just a bit too far from the remainder.

Well done, Francis, John Moses Browning thought.

The morgue attendant looked at them expectantly. "Well, gentlemen?"

Donald Bryce removed his wallet from inside his suit jacket, pulled out five twenty-dollar silver certificates and handed them over. The attendant tried to pull them away, but Bryce wouldn't let go of the money. He scowled at the attendant and waited.

"Half now. Half when we're finished," Browning said.

The attendant looked hurt. "Okay . . . You got fifteen minutes. That's all I can promise. I don't want to get fired for letting reporters in here. We're under real strict orders."

"That'll be sufficient," Browning said as he nodded at his companion.

Bryce relaxed his grip and the attendant snatched the money away. "Fifteen minutes. Take your pictures quick. Don't fiddle with it," he said, indicating the dead man. "The doctors can always tell."

The bag in Browning's hand did in fact have a camera in it, but that was only in case any of the police officers or staff had bothered to check as they'd bribed their way in. No one had. Apparently they were not the first "newsmen" that had snuck illicit photographs of the assassin's body. None of the pictures had shown up in a legitimate newspaper yet, since a decapitation would never make it past the censors, but it made for a very plausible story.

The attendant hurried out of the room and locked the door behind him. Bryce pulled the sheet down to the corpse's waist. The darkly intense knight was entirely too comfortable around the dead for Browning's taste, but that was to be expected. One did not chose their particular Power, their Power chose them. So a man wielding a Power based in death would obviously be as at home with the dead as Browning was with metal and machines.

"Can you tell if anyone else has tried this on him?" Browning asked.

"No. It's clean . . . Not surprising. Even when I was with the NYPD nobody wanted to know about what I did. They were just happy to close all those murder cases." Bryce chuckled. "I'm a *rare* breed. Maybe a handful of us in the whole world."

There was an overhead lamp on a long arm. Browning brought it over and turned it on. The body had taken on a pallid, nearly blue shade. Incisions had been made to open the chest, and those lines cut directly through the intricate spell that had been carved there before. The neck ended in a jagged tear. The exposed flesh was the purple of old meat. The head was resting on its side, features limp. Giuseppe Zangara had been a plain man.

"Best hurry." Bryce casually took a handful of hair and hoisted the head from the table, so that the sunken face was pointing his way. It made Browning's skin crawl. Bryce's voice was raspy and cold. "No lungs to work with. Vocal cords, what's left of them, are mangled. But if I channel enough Power through him I can make him understandable."

Browning had never worked with a Lazarus before. "How?"

"Broadcasting. Sort of like how a Beastie can talk through an animal. The words are still there, even if the parts to make them aren't. . . . But the way the spine's been crushed and how much decay's set in, he'll be in extraordinary pain."

That afternoon had been spent surveying the scene where hundreds of innocent people had died. The fire department had been hosing down the streets to clean the dried blood. There was no compassion for one such as this. "Carry on, Mr. Bryce."

The other knight closed his eyes, concentrated, and exercised his Power. The air grew colder. It was as if the lights dimmed, but perhaps that was just a trick of the imagination. Browning did not know, but the Power of a Lazarus made him deeply uncomfortable. Browning looked toward the entrance. They were in the basement and door seemed solid. *Good.* There could be screaming.

While Bryce worked his magic, Browning studied the intricate spell that had been bound to the assassin's chest. It was far beyond anything he'd seen before, greater than anything the Society had ever discovered, more complex than any Soviet design, even better than the flowing Imperium kanji . . . This was a work of art. Even Browning, who had spent a lifetime studying such things, could only comprehend bits and pieces of it. Someone capable of creating a spell of such Power was very dangerous, indeed. They were tracking a worthy adversary.

The spell also matched the sketch that they'd received from their source in Washington. That was good news.

He'd been unsure if he could utilize that particular source, but this confirmed the infomant's trustworthiness. That source should prove valuable.

"Got him . . ." Bryce said simply, as if he'd just hooked a fish and was reeling it in, instead of the absolute horror of dragging a captive intelligence back from the spirit world. Intellectually, he knew it was unfair to judge a man's character by what type of Active he was, but Mr. Bryce seemed to enjoy this entirely too much.

This time Browning was certain that the lights did in fact flicker. Dead eyes opened, revealing milky orbs, and Zangara looked about in terror. The jaw unhinged as the zombie let out a terrible wail. It was a revolting sound.

Bryce held the head so that Zangara could see his own body. "See that? Look familiar? Yeah, you're dead. Get used to it." Bryce spun the head around. "Welcome back to the world of the living, you rotten son of a bitch. The faster you answer our questions, the faster I'll let you die again. Until I'm satisfied, I own you." He turned the head back to face Browning.

The eyes were blinking and twitching. The dead man seemed very frightened. A creaking hiss was their answer.

Browning folded his arms and glared at the severed head. "You have some explaining to do, Mr. Zangara. We shall start from the beginning."

"It hurts."

Bryce swung the head back to face him. "You heard me the first time. Quit messing around. Sooner you talk, sooner the pain stops. Do not waste my time. Got it?"

"Yessss."

"All yours." Bryce swung Zangara's head back around.

"Who put that spell on your chest?"

"The angel."

Browning was certain it was no angel that had bolstered the Power of this madman. "Did the angel have a name?"

"No names. Only angel. So beautiful."

"Did the angel tell you to kill Roosevelt?"

"Yes. Wanted to kill him before. The angel heard my dreams and made me strong enough to do it."

"What did the angel look like?"

"So beautiful. Eyes made of light."

"Eyes?" Browning played a hunch. "Tell me about the eyes?"

"Red light. Soooo pretty. Like Christmas lights. First there were two. Then it had four."

The two knights exchanged a glance. The angel had been a Summoned.

"The angel carved the spell on your chest by itself or did someone help it?"

"No! Only the angel!"

Bryce took the head and smashed it against the metal table. Zangara screamed. "Don't lie to me, zombie. Summoned aren't smart enough draw spells."

"It was the angel. It talked to me. It knew me. It made me strong. There were no helpers, only the angel."

Bryce lifted the head again, but before he could smack it against the table, Browning held up one hand. "You heard the report from Oklahoma."

"The bastard that killed George . . ." Bryce muttered.

"The most clever Summoned I've ever met was as intelligent as a good hunting dog." Browning gestured at the complicated spell. "That is the work of a talented wizard."

"When did you get the spell?" Bryce shouted.

"When? Time means nothing here . . ." Bryce whacked the head against the table again. *"Day before. Day before killing time."*

It was unknown how quickly Crow could travel in his demonic form, but he had been in Florida the same day in order to assault Francis at the police station. He very well could have been here the entire time. "Things are beginning to fall into place."

"We're treading on dangerous ground here . . ." Bryce said slowly. "You know what this means?"

"It means we're in greater danger than expected. Another question, Mr. Zangara. Before your death, did you ever speak with a man named Crow, or did you ever speak with any government entity, especially the Office of the Coordinator of Information— OCI—or with anyone else about your desire to murder the president?"

"No Crow. No office of things. No government run by filthy capitalists . . . Spoke to only one man."

"Tell me about the man you spoke to."

"The capitalist pigs had me arrested once. I lost my job because I was sick. I was mad. I threatened some of the capitalists. Said I would kill them. They said I was crazy. Wanted to lock me in crazy house. Doctor interviewed me. He knew about magic. I liked him. Told him truth. He told the capitalist judges I was not crazy. I was not danger to society." It took Browning a moment to realize that the horrible grinding noise was the severed head laughing. *"I told him everything. Friend agreed with me. He was good friend."*

"What was your friend's name?"

"Doctor Bradford. Not kind of doctor that could fix my guts. Kind that fixed heads. Kind of doctor for crazy people. He was expert on crazy people with magic. Good thing I'm not crazy." The head laughed again, and Browning had to resist the urge to draw his .45 and end its wretched existence.

"Name ringing any bells?"

"I've not heard of the man. If that's his real name, we should be able to discover something about him. Do you have anything to ask?"

"Got anything else you want to get off your chest?" Bryce asked the head, then he laughed when he realized he'd made a joke. "Heh . . . chest. I kill me sometimes. How about it, Giuseppe? I'm tempted to sneak your head out of here and keep you on my trophy wall. Thick skull like you, you could be up there screaming for years." Browning sincerely hoped that Bryce did not have such a wall, but it was difficult to tell with a Lazarus, even one that was supposedly trying to only use their Power for good. "Either that or you're about the right size for a football. . . . Help me out and I'll let you get back to the big sleep."

"The angel will stop you. The angel is too strong for you."

Bryce put the head down on the table. "Eh, he's done."

"Do not hurt my angel!" Zangara begged. Bryce shoved the tray back into the wall, and closed the door behind it. Zangara's wails could be heard coming from inside. Bryce simply walked over to the sink and began washing his hands.

"Shouldn't you . . ."

"Put him out of his misery?" Bryce laughed as he lathered up. "It don't work that way, John. He's stuck for a while. I can't just release him. They're going to have to crush him flat or burn him to free his spirit. That's the nasty part of what I do. You know Dead City?"

He had never been there, but he'd heard the tales, mostly from Heinrich. "Of course."

"You think the Kaiser herded them all into Berlin and put a wall around it just to be mean? Nope. He couldn't just shut them off." Bryce dried his hands on a towel. "We better get going. Next person to open that door is going to be in for a *nasty* surprise. That attendant looks healthy, so he shouldn't have a heart attack, but he sure is going to earn that bribe money!"

Browning was exceedingly glad to get back out into the sunlight.

Browning had dropped Bryce off at the library to do some research before returning to the hotel to prepare a mirror to report their findings to the others. The Lazarus would catch a cab back later. His company would not be missed. Though professional enough, there was always an awkward edge to all interactions with someone of his nature, as if you knew they would be much more comfortable talking to you if you were already dead.

They had set up shop in one of the less remarkable hotels in Miami to stage out of. The normal crowds of vacationers fleeing the cold had been replaced with newsmen from around the country hoping to interview victims of the carnage. He did not care for the reporters, since they behaved with all the manners of a flock of turkey buzzards. He had been told that in Miami, alligators actually wandered the streets. Perhaps they would do everyone a favor and eat some reporters.

Since he was thinking about reporters, Browning stopped at a newsstand on the way back to pick up the paper. With all of the recent turmoil, staying caught up on recent events seemed like an important thing to do. One of the headlines immediately caught his eye:

UBF HEIR FRANCIS STUYVESANT
IMPLICATED IN ACTIVE PLOT.

"Oh dear . . ." Browning muttered as he paid for two different papers. He read the first one on the walk back to his car, and the other as soon as he made it back to the hotel. According to the articles, Francis was wanted for questioning, but was missing, and was believed to have fled the country. A retired Marine general had come forward and said that a group of businessmen who purported to represent several wealthy Actives had approached him about leading a fascist coup against the government. The Hearst owned paper was calling it the Active Plot, while the other seemed to be gravitating toward the title Business Plot, which was not a surprise since Hearst's low opinion of Magicals was well known.

He prepared a communication spell. Browning prided himself on always doing meticulous work, and the spell was perfect as usual. While waiting for the response, he pondered their current predicament. All of this recent turmoil had been keeping him from his true passion, inventing. It was like his Cog mechanical genius was tugging at the reins, hoping for a chance to be free. Ideas were everywhere, and some of the Grimnoir's more recent struggles had brought a few of those ideas to the fore. He promised himself that as soon as this problem was dealt with, it was time to get back to making new weapons. Certainly, even when these nefarious plots were squashed, there was still the matter of this Pathfinder. The creature had made mincemeat of the Chairman's early group, but the Chairman had not had the greatest engineer of fighting implements of all time on his side . . . Perhaps, if he knew more about how the creature operated, he would be able to build something that might even their odds.

The spell connected. The first respondent was Jake Sullivan. Browning had not liked the Heavy when they'd first met. Sullivan was a former convict with a reputation for thuggery, but as usual, his old friend Black Jack had been a good judge of character. Sullivan had proven to be a man of integrity, a fearsome fighter, and a remarkably perceptive autodidactic individual. Browning had taken a real liking to him. Plus, it helped that Sullivan had excellent taste in firearms. It had been a pleasure to give him the Grimnoir oath.

"Good morning, Mr. Sullivan. How goes it?"

Sullivan had dark circles under his eyes, appearing as if he'd not slept well, if at all. "Busy. I know we were supposed to ask the higher-ups about recruiting first, but we've had a couple of folks just kind of show up and volunteer for duty."

"Really? Who?"

"An Iron Guard and an OCI bounty hunter."

Browning twitched. The most coherent response he could form was, "I see . . ."

A smile cracked Sullivan's unshaven face. "Yeah, I know. I'll have to catch you up. The Chairman's boy wants the Pathfinder gone. The OCI one seems to think that Heinrich is still alive and being held under their headquarters."

It would be wonderful if one of his men was still alive, but his natural cynicism kept him wary. "Can you trust him?"

"Her, and I don't yet, but she sure thinks Heinrich's a prisoner and they're going to execute him soon."

The Grimnoir were not in the habit of letting their people hang. "If that's the case, then we need to mount a rescue operation."

"Working on it. It could be a trap, but sometimes a trap works both ways."

Browning could only nod. When it came to issues of potential violence, he had to bow to Sullivan's mastery of the subject. "I trust your judgment, Mr. Sullivan."

"Thanks. And I almost forgot, we kidnapped J. Edgar Hoover yesterday. I think we're secretly allied with the Bureau of Investigation against the OCI."

If it had been anyone other than Sullivan, he would have been certain it was a joke, but the Heavy wasn't known for telling tales. "You jest."

"No, sir. I'm not pulling your leg. Like I said, we've been real busy."

"Recruiting Iron Guards *and* Hoover . . . Perhaps I should retract what I said about trusting your judgment."

"Hoover I don't know about. The others seem legit, but

I'm keeping an eye on them and Faye both. I don't want her killing anybody."

"Yes, that can be a full-time job . . . How did Faye—"

"I guess she got bored of driving and Traveled clear from Tennessee in one hop. The others are on the way."

Nothing about that girl could really surprise him at this point. "Did you see this morning's paper yet?" Sullivan shook his head. "It has more bad news. They've gone public about Francis and they say that he has fled. I'm trying to contact him now but have not gotten a response. Have you had any word from him?"

"Not since word came down about Ada. I'll see what I can find out. I sure hope they didn't roll him up. Any luck down there?"

"Possibly." Browning was hesitant to say how they'd gotten their information and had to choose his words carefully. Since Sullivan's young lady friend had suffered such a tragic end through Lazarus magic, the Heavy's feelings about such things were well known. "I believe the spell was bound to the assassin by a Summoned."

"That's impossible. A Summoned couldn't—no!" Sullivan's brow furrowed. "*Crow.*" As usual, the Heavy was remarkably perceptive. "That son of a bitch, excuse my language. It had to be him, unless there's somebody out there just like him, and that's one hell of a coincidence."

"I am inclined to agree. We are now searching for a Dr. Bradford that may have been Zangara's confidant. If we can come up with a link between the doctor and the OCI, we may have the evidence we need to clear our names."

"Speaking of evidence, I might know where to find some . . ."

Bell Farm, Virginia

DESPITE BEING SO TIRED that she could barely keep her eyes open, Faye continued watching the Iron Guard suspiciously. He just sat there, cross-legged, eyes closed, "mediating" he called it, looking innocent as could be . . . But she knew that he was up to no good. Iron Guards were evil, heathen, no-good, rotten, murdering scoundrels, and the only reason she hadn't killed this one already was because Mr. Sullivan had made her promise not to.

After having a long conversation with Mr. Sullivan, the Iron Guard had claimed the barn as his place to sleep. She figured it was so he could have someplace private to do whatever horrible things it was that Iron Guards did when nobody was looking. So Faye had volunteered to spy on the Iron Guard. It wasn't like she was going to be able to sleep with one of *them* around anyway. Sullivan had told her that spying was unnecessary and that she should get some rest.

She'd agreed, but as soon as the bedroom door was closed, she'd gathered up some warm clothing and Traveled outside to keep an eye on the Iron Guard. Of course Faye wasn't going to go sleep in a comfy bed, all unaware and vulnerable, while evil was lurking around doing who knew what. Not on her watch. So she had followed him, sneaky as possible, just knowing he'd do something awful right quick. However, the Iron Guard had just gone out to the barn, pulled a blanket out of his pack, and gone to sleep on the hard-packed dirt floor.

She'd Traveled up to the hay loft and picked a quiet spot to keep watch.

The most interesting part of the night was discovering that the barn had rats, big black ones, and she'd passed the time by identifying and naming them all. The Iron Guard didn't so much as roll over or even snore. Spying on him turned out to be completely uninteresting. Killing him in his sleep would have been super easy, if a little unsportsmanlike. It was still really tempting.

The long night in the drafty old barn gave Faye plenty of time to think. Despite all of the horrible things that were happening around her, her mind kept spinning back to a completely selfish issue. *Why was her magic getting stronger again?* Months had passed since the *Tokugawa* and she'd been relatively weak that whole time, with Power like a little stream, but all of a sudden she was doing better, and her Power had grown back into a small river. *How come?* She didn't pretend to understand this stuff like some of the other knights. Faye had always been a little different than everyone else, and she had just taken it for granted, but now those differences were really nagging at her.

The government demon, Crow, had known something. He'd danced around it, trying to get her to come peacefully. It could have been a trick, but she didn't think so. He knew something about her. How had he said it? "What if I could tell you exactly what you are?" He hadn't said "who," he'd said "what," and Faye didn't care for that one bit.

Would she keep on getting stronger like before? And if so, what would happen if she didn't use it all up in one great big burst like last time? Would it ever stop, or would the Power just keep on giving her more magic? How strong could she get? And if she got strong enough, could she maybe learn how to use other Powers? Could she become as powerful as the Chairman had been?

All those questions without answers made her head hurt.

The night was really cold, but she'd borrowed some of Jane's clothes and dressed extra warm, or so she'd thought. The predawn frost made life miserable, and she found herself wishing that he would hurry up and do something nefarious so she could kill him and then go warm herself by the wood stove. The only hay left in the loft was old, and since the roof leaked, it was moldy and smelly, so she couldn't even lay in that for extra warmth. Her grey eyes had always been extra good at seeing in the dark, so after she got done counting rats she counted the holes in the roof.

A few times she let her eyelids droop shut. Just for a second, she'd tell herself, only to realize what she was doing, panic, and then flinch back awake, expecting to see the Iron Guard leering over her, ready to slash her throat. However, each time she found the Iron Guard still sleeping peacefully below. Finally, after several hours of doing the blink-too-long-and-panic routine, she decided to check her head map to see if maybe playing with it for a time would help keep her awake.

And there was Mr. Sullivan, hidden fifty yards away, wide awake and smoking a cigarette, back against a tree, machine gun resting across his knees, watching the barn intently. He had probably been there all night, unmoving. He had just been trying to be nice when he'd told her to get some sleep. She should have known that of all people he wouldn't have trusted the Iron Guard either. Faye probably could have Traveled back to the house and gone to bed at that point, but it had now become a matter of pride to see her watch through to the end.

The next thing she knew she had woken up and it was daylight and somewhere nearby a rooster was crowing. Panicking, she scurried over to the edge of the hayloft, sure to discover that while she'd slept the Iron Guard had murdered everyone.

Instead of being on a rampage, he was just sitting there on the floor, legs crossed, hands on his knees, back perfectly straight. He didn't even bother to open his eyes. "Did you sleep well up there, Traveler?"

He knew? "I'm watching you, Iron Guard."

"Do not call me that." He opened his eyes. "I no longer have the honor of bearing that title."

"What are you then?"

"I do not know. That is why I'm meditating." And with that he closed his eyes again and ignored her.

Faye waited for him to do something else. She got bored. "Hey . . . Hey, jerk-face, I'm talking to you." When he didn't answer, she found a small scrap of wood and chucked it at him.

He caught it in one hand without opening his eyes. "Do not call me 'jerk-face.'"

"Why not? It fits . . ." He was a Brute. Faye decided that if she was going to pick a fight with him, she really should have struck when he was asleep. "What should I call you then?"

"My name is Toru."

"A likely story."

"Then I do not care what you call me." The Iron Guard got up, dusted off his pants, and folded the blanket. "You are beneath my notice. You are an insignificant bug."

"I'll just stick with jerk-face then."

"Very well, bug." Toru put his things back in his pack. Faye noticed that he was very careful to stow the broken sword pieces. He should be. Even with his Healing kanji, he still had a bandage wrapped around one hand from grabbing the sharp part last night.

"What're you keeping that busted thing for?"

"You would not understand."

"I know more about your kind than you think," Faye snapped.

Toru removed some wrapped food and closed the pack. "A blade can be reforged. A soul can be cleansed." He walked out of the barn, chewing on what looked like a ball of white rice.

Cleansed? Faye could agree with that sentiment in principle. People could make all sorts of things right, but she had a real hard time thinking of murderous Iron Guards as people.

She found Mr. Garrett in the kitchen, cooking bacon. Faye Traveled in right next to him. "Smells good."

Her sudden arrival startled him and he splashed bacon grease on his hand. "Don't do that!" He stuck his burned finger in his mouth.

"Well, somebody's jumpy."

"Can you blame me? You about give me a heart attack when you do that."

"Grumpy too."

"Sleeping with one eye open will do that to you," he answered as he forked a few cooked pieces onto a waiting plate. "I didn't know who was going to murder us in our sleep last night first—the Imperium or the OCI. Jake's lost his mind, joining up with these people."

"I haven't met the other one yet."

"Hammer. Don't trust her, Faye. She's a manipulator."

"Isn't that your job?"

"You bet, and that's why I can tell. Just because you can't lie to her doesn't mean she can't lie to us."

Faye snagged a piece of bacon and popped it into her mouth. "Don't worry, Mr. Garrett. I'm still the most dangerous person here."

"That you are. Well, I'll just have to trust you'll keep us safe." He chuckled, so Faye did too. She had always liked Mr. Garrett. He passed her the plate of bacon. "Here's my protection payment." Faye was starving. She wasn't about to turn that down, and immediately started wolfing down the food without even bothering to sit.

Mr. Sullivan joined them a moment later. He still had his BAR slung over one shoulder. It said a lot about the company that she kept, that his wearing a machine gun at breakfast didn't even strike her as odd.

"Sleep well?" he asked with a wink.

So much for being sneaky. It was like everybody knew she'd slept in the barn. "Oh, my bed was just *lovely*."

Mr. Garrett had boiled up a pot of coffee, and Mr. Sullivan poured himself a cup. He took it black. "I just got some bad news."

"Why are you looking at me like that?" Faye asked.

"'Cause I don't want you to fly off the handle and do something stupid when I tell you Francis is missing."

Faye went numb. The plate shattered on the floor. "We've got to do something!"

"We will." Mr. Sullivan was mulling over his coffee. "The others will be back soon. Sit tight. I got a plan."

John
Browning

Chapter 15

There will be some innocent victims in this fight against magical Fascists. We are launching a major attack on the enemy; let there be no resentment if we bump someone with an elbow. Better that ten innocent people should suffer than one enemy of the worker get away. When you chop wood, chips fly.

—Nikolai Yezhov,
Deputy People's Commissar for Special Affairs, comments related to the resettlement of Actives during the "Soviet Planned Population Transfer," 1930

OCI Headquarters

IT WAS LIKE WAKING UP from a two-day bender, only judging from the dungeonlike surroundings illuminated by the single flickering light bulb hanging from the ceiling, this certainly wasn't his old fraternity. Rust-colored water was dripping down the brick walls and the floor was poured concrete covered in half an inch of dust. There was a single door, no windows, and he was alone. The last thing he could remember was being clobbered by Crow.

He reached up to put one hand to his throbbing head, but a chain snapped tight against his wrist. "Ugh. Where am I?"

There was a noise, some movement, and a cough. "Francis?" The voice had come from the wall behind his back. "Is that you?"

"Yeah." Francis had to be hallucinating from the head injury. Was there such a thing as auditory hallucinations? He didn't rightly know. Getting hit so hard that you begin hearing dead people couldn't be good. "Heinrich?"

"*Mein Gott*, it is you!" There was a scraping noise and the clank of chains. "They got you too."

"You're alive?"

The laugh was bitter. "For now, though I don't know why."

He was very excited to discover that one of his best friends had cheated death, but the circumstances of their reunion left something to be desired. Francis managed to turn his head far enough to see that there were small holes cut in the wall. His chains led through them, so he couldn't fiddle with whatever they were tethered to. "You've got no idea how glad I am to find you. Where are we?"

Heinrich's voice was coming through the holes. "I believe we are under OCI headquarters."

"Hang on." Francis concentrated on the light bulb to see if he could make it swing. *Nothing.* They had to be under the influence of one of Buckminster Fuller's nullifiers. "Damn."

"Using your magic? It doesn't work here. A man named Crow said they have a device—"

"We've met. He's the reason I've got a splitting headache."

"A pleasant-enough sort, for a statist secret policeman. I believe he will kill us as soon as we are no longer of use."

"He's a demon," Francis said.

"Indeed. His kind always are."

"No. Literally. He's a Summoned."

Heinrich laughed. "You must have gotten hit very hard."

"I heard from one of the new knights that's with—"

The chains clanked. "Quiet! Speak of no one else. Do you think they put us where we can talk to each other by accident?"

Francis shut his mouth and studied the walls suspiciously. Heinrich was right. They were probably listening. "Sure . . . Never mind."

"I was wondering why they finally gave me food and water . . . They wanted me strong enough to have a conversation." Heinrich sounded very tired. "I'm sorry, Francis. It is too late for many. They made me talk. Drugs and magic. I don't even remember, but they stole names right out of my mind. I don't even know who for sure, but I've put them in danger. This Crow, demon or man, whatever he is, he's clever."

"Trust me. The bastard grows horns and can fly. How long have I been here anyway?"

"An hour, maybe, since I heard them drag you in and chain you up. Not too long."

There was a ring of metal on metal as his door was unlocked. "Shhhh."

The door swung open to reveal Crow. "Afternoon, Francis."

"Go to hell, demon."

"That's not fair," Crow said as he came into the room. The door was closed behind him and relocked by unseen staff. This bunch sure didn't take any chances. He walked over and stood under the lightbulb, the brim of his hat shadowing his face. "I'm a person too. Born in Cleveland. Dad was a foundry worker. Mom died when I was little. Real sob story, you can fill in the blanks. I'm as much a human being as you are. Well, part of me at least. See . . ." Crow squatted down so they could see eye to red eye. He leaned in so close that Francis could smell the tobacco on his breath. "I'm just not as limited as you. I got more than one body that I can use. When one gets broken, I just get a new one . . ." Crow placed one finger softly on Francis' cheek.

"Go fu—" And then Francis ground his teeth together as Crow slowly sliced his face open.

"You, on the other hand . . ." The demon rocked back on his haunches, examining his open hand. His fingers ended in black needle points. Crow licked the blood from one and smiled. ". . . are so *fragile*."

Francis' face burned. He could feel the heat of the blood dripping down his chin. "What do you want, asshole?"

"I knew you had some fire in you. Knew it from the beginning. What do I want? What was it again?" Crow cocked his head to the side until it was at an unnatural angle. "I want to drink your blood and eat your soul," he hissed with a voice that was unlike any Francis had ever heard before. It made him think of rusty nails and dried snakeskin.

This was no act. Crow was losing his mind. Francis cringed away.

Crow stood up. His hand returned to normal as he looked toward a sound that Francis couldn't hear yet. The metal bar clanked and the door opened again. A man stood there, tall and wide, with the broad shoulders of someone who'd been strong in his youth, but the muscle had long since turned to fat. Wearing a pinstriped suit and carrying an ornate cane, he appeared to be in his sixties, with a long white mustache and unfashionably large, old-fashioned sideburns. He came into the room and gave Crow a stern glance. "What are you doing here?"

Surprisingly, Crow dropped his head. "Questioning the prisoner, sir."

"Get out," the stranger ordered. He stepped out of the way and pointed his cane at the door. Crow strode from the room without another word. When he was gone, the stranger returned his attention to Francis. "My apologies, Mr. Stuyvesant. You see, Mr. Crow has been under a great deal of stress lately. I'm afraid it has been getting to him."

"He's insane."

The man shook his head. "Only sometimes, and that is entirely dependent on the nature of the body that his mind is currently inhabiting. I'm afraid some can be worse than others."

"He's insane *and* he's dangerous. You're playing with fire."

"Yes. Fire is dangerous, yet if man had never harnessed its power we would still be living in caves. Electricity is dangerous." He reached up with his cane and tapped the light, making it swing and cast wild shadows. "Yet, we harness it for all of our modern technological marvels. Why, Mr. Stuyvesant, should magic be any different?"

The odd fellow seemed vaguely familiar. "Do I know you?"

"We've met briefly, but it was a very long time ago." He rested his weight on the cane, and took a white handkerchief out of his suit to wipe the sweat from his face. "Excuse me. Far too many stairs for a man in my condition. I should have an elevator installed. Yes, we have met. You were but a child. I knew your father, was friends with one of your uncles, and an acquaintance of your grandfather." He started to put the handkerchief away, then took note of the cut on Francis' face. Clucking disapprovingly, he came over and gently pressed the cloth against the cut. "Oh, Mr. Crow . . . He's something of a project of mine. Here, keep pressure on that."

There was just enough slack in the chain for Francis to tilt his head and keep the handkerchief in place to stop the bleeding. He winced as the cut burned. "Who are you?"

"Bradford Carr. Do you remember now?"

Francis was drawing a blank. "*What* are you?"

He chuckled. "I've held a few titles in my day. In my military days it was only captain. For the longest time it was doctor, or professor of magical studies at the University of Chicago, briefly ambassador. Most recently, it has been senator, and since last summer when Herbert Hoover saw fit to the appointment, I have been the Coordinator of Information. I was, after all, the most qualified applicant for the position, since I have made the study of magic my life's work. However, since my current assignment is one of utmost secrecy, let's just keep that between ourselves." Carr smiled. "Does that answer your question, Mr. Stuyvesant?"

Now he remembered. Carr hadn't been as grey or as fat back when Francis' father had replaced him as ambassador to Japan. He too, had known about the Chairman's schools. "You dirty bastard. You were on the Imperium payroll, too."

Carr clucked disapprovingly. "You're smarter than that, Mr. Stuyvesant. Do not make the mistake of thinking that just because I studied the Imperium ways, meant that I was in their service. I had a friendly relationship with the Chairman, and of course many of the things I observed went unreported, but that was necessary to further my own research into the nature of magic. The Nipponese were merely unafraid to delve into mysteries that my own countrymen would not. As a scientist and a philosopher, I would have been foolish to ignore all of the valuable knowledge they'd gained."

"The Imperium schools are evil!" Francis shouted. He'd seen the horrors with his own eyes. There had been torturous ordeals to bind nonmagical people to the Power, and even worse experiments to create stronger Actives. His family hadn't cared, as long as the gold kept flowing, and that's what had driven Francis away from them and toward the Grimnoir, who were brave enough to do something about it. "Anyone who can't see that is a fool."

"The Imperium schools are a *necessary* evil. The Power must be studied, harnessed, and controlled for the good of all mankind. It is selfish to think otherwise. Power is a resource that must be properly managed, just like any other. If a nation cannot control its own resources, then it will fall into the dustbin of history."

"Those are people you're talking about, not some nebulous things."

"Exactly, my boy!" Carr wagged his cane at Francis. "And that's why the United States has lagged so far behind others in this regard. We, as a government, have lacked the will to take control for the greater good because of a naive faith in the individual. As it stands now, all of our useful magic is being squandered on foolish pursuits. Wasted by *individuals* who think only of themselves and not of the rest of society. Just imagine what could be accomplished if these resources were managed in a scientific way!"

"You mean slavery."

"An emotionally loaded choice of words."

"You take someone's freedom and tell them what to do. Sounds like slavery to me."

"I'm talking about the greater good, for both normal mortals." Carr touched one big hand to his chest, "and you! This is for your own protection. An individual with magic is capable of causing much harm. They are dangerous at worst and wasted at best. I have a vision for a greater tomorrow, where the miraculous Power is used for the betterment of all. My vision—"

"Like the Imperium? Like the Soviets? Are you going to cull the herd like them? Experiment on the weak? Breed the strong?" Francis was furious. "The unworthy go to the schools or the gulag? Fuck your vision."

Heinrich's voice came through the wall. "We had a

politician who preached eugenic nonsense like this in Germany; Hitler was the name, if I recall it right. We put him against a wall and gave him the firing squad. I'd suggest we take up that tradition here, Francis."

Francis looked Carr squarely in the eye. "That sounds like a fine idea, Heinrich."

Carr's face turned red. "I was hoping for the sake of your family name that you would listen to reason. Your father was a fine man. I felt I owed him enough to at least try."

Francis was no politician or philosopher, but he had a finely tuned sense when it came to detecting bullshit. "Your reason, science, whatever you want to call it, is a sham, a two-bit hustler's scheme. This is America. The government doesn't own the people. The people own the government."

"You would be surprised to learn how many very important men disagree with you on that point, Mr. Stuyvesant. Once my operations are complete, the rest will have no choice but to come around. They will come to understand that Actives must be controlled. It only takes one great visionary to change the course of a nation."

It all became clear. The assassin's ring, the mystery spell, the newspapers, the manhunt, everything. "You're the one who set us up . . . You're the one who tried to kill the president."

"If only that had been enough." Carr just smiled. "Recent events have forced me to expand my ambitions. It seems that this deadly Grimnoir terrorist group is not happy that they failed in their last attack. I have warned the cabinet that we believe they are plotting another attack sometime very soon. I'm sure it will end tragically."

"You bastard!"

"Would you like a preview of the newspapers a few days from now? I find I'm rather good at predicting these sorts of things." Carr cleared his throat. "Many innocents were murdered by mad Actives last night. Luckily, during the aftermath of the attack, two leaders of the foul Grimnoir organization were intercepted and killed by brave OCI operatives. One of them had a manifesto on his person detailing how they would continue to kill Normals until the Active race rises up, throws off the shackles of oppression, and takes their rightful place as world leaders, since they are the superior evolution of man. Everyone will be shocked and saddened to discover that this cabal is being led by a well known industrialist, Francis Cornelius Stuyvesant."

Francis was so angry he couldn't form coherent words and instead emitted a growling noise.

"The rich make such convenient villains, don't you think? Half of society already hates you for the station you were born into. Your peers will be embarrassed that you've endangered the status quo. Your name will become a symbol synonymous with tyranny. It is already in the papers how some of your *underlings* tried to enlist Smedly Butler's help in overthrowing the government."

"Who?"

"That's priceless," Carr chuckled. "A political opponent of mine, a retired general with far too much integrity to ever fall in with such a plot. Oh, but questions will remain. How deep do the roots of your cancerous organization grow? Everyone knows when you pull weeds, if you only take the top, they grow back. You must dig up the roots.

Drastic measures must be taken to find all of the Grimnoir sympathizers amongst the Active race. Controls will need to be put into place, for the greater good. Once it begins, it will not end."

Francis threw himself against the chains. They didn't budge. "You'll not get away with this! Someone will find out the truth."

"Who? If your allies come here they will be walking directly into a trap that Mr. Crow has very capably set, and I'll have more Grimnoir bodies to deposit at the scene. None of my men will talk. The majority of OCI's staff are simple recruits who know nothing of my plans. They are pawns that I will use to round up those that trouble me. The men I have stationed here are absolutely loyal, hand-picked because of their personal hatred for your kind, and they are as committed as I am. No one will talk. None of my colleagues know my plans, and even my political enemies would never guess how far I am willing to go . . . That's because they don't get the big picture."

"You're going to pay."

"You are in no position to make threats. I tire of this." Carr walked over and rapped his cane on the door. It was opened for him. "Goodbye, Mr. Stuyvesant. We will not meet again. You will be dead in a few days." He strolled out of view and the door slammed shut behind. The heavy latch fell into place.

Francis waited to make sure Carr was gone. "Heinrich?"

"We are in far more trouble than I thought, my friend."

Crow waited for his superior in the hall. He knew he was in trouble. The boss had seen him losing his cool. This was only a minor Summoned, but it was a mean one. The alien thoughts were pushed back to the rear of their shared mind, but they were all about stalking and killing prey. Back when this particular Summoned had its own form, it must have been quite the vicious little predator. That was completely unacceptable. If he got in any more trouble, the boss would yank the spell he'd been given. Crow was not ready to go back to being a nobody.

Fuming, the fat man hobbled down the hall on his cane, flanked by his two personal bodyguards, Sharps and Deych. They were Normals, but they were both bruisers and handy with gun or blade. Like the rest of the men stationed at headquarters, they were magic haters, recruited personally by the Coordinator from various militant anti-Active groups, like Humans Only or the League for a Magic-Free America. They hated Crow as much as they hated all Actives, but as long as he was seen as the Coordinator's tool, they left him alone. These men were scum, but they were reliable scum. They'd caught the Coordinator's vision for the future.

Crow didn't give a shit about anybody's grand dreams. He played a part, and in exchange got something that benefited him. Right now he was going to have to play the part of eating some humble pie.

"Sir, I'm—"

The Coordinator raised one bushy eyebrow suspiciously. "It's quite all right, Mr. Crow. I assume you were just putting the proper amount of fear into the boy—correct?"

That was a surprisingly opportune way out. Doctor Carr had to know the truth, he was way too smart not to, but for whatever reason he was letting it go. "Yes, sir." He looked over at the bodyguards. Even wearing the body of a lesser Summoned, he would have easily been able to whip them and get away. However, the Coordinator knew where his real body lived, and knowing the old man, he'd probably hedged his bets. This was his lucky day after all. "Just scaring him a little to get him ready for you."

"Excellent work. However, the Stuyvesant predilection for self-preservation must have skipped a generation. His forbears would have leapt at any out I offered to save their own skins. The boy is an obstinate fool. We'll use him as we discussed. Have you had any luck capturing any of the others?"

"Not yet, but I've baited the trap."

"Walk with me." The bodyguards fell in behind them. "You used the Justice?"

"I gave her just enough rope to hang herself. She plays like she's hard, but she's too much of a goody-two-shoes at heart. She knows about the German and she knows we've got exonerating evidence. She went off the reservation a little while ago, which means now they know too. The Grimnoir will try something. I guarantee it."

"Do we have enough nullifiers?"

"Four on site and the big one upstairs. The EGE packages were delivered this morning, and everything seems to be working fine"

"Excellent. When the time comes, send the men first. Those robots were expensive."

They paused at the stairs. The old man needed a breather before tackling them. Crow could smell the bodyguards' fear as they watched him. They were pathetic. Sure, they thought they were tough, but they were nothing.

The Coordinator's inner circle were all true believers, thinking they could control Actives. Sharps had been a prizefighter until a tiny Active had whipped him. Some of them, like Deych, had been Carr's students back when he was a professor, going on and on about how someday they would see his idealized world. It was tempting to just reach out and pluck their eyes out; then they wouldn't see shit, but Crow refrained.

"I want this expedited, Mr. Crow. I want to proceed with the next attack as scheduled. I have to keep up the pressure. If we do not strike while the iron is hot, then my political allies will lose their will and all this work will have been for nothing."

"I'll spread the word that we're going to start executing prisoners tomorrow. That ought to get their attention."

"Excellent idea as usual . . . Make it two days."

"If it feels too rushed, they might just chicken out."

"Exactly. Let them plan, but not for too long. Let them bring in reinforcements. I want *all* of these meddlers dead. The nail that sticks up must be hammered down. Remember, the only one I care about capturing alive is the Traveler girl. She is a valuable anomaly. If she truly inherited Warlock's magic, I can only imagine what I could learn from studying her."

Dissecting her, you mean, but Crow held his tongue. "My pleasure."

Hartwood, Virginia

IT WAS A SMALL TOWN, but that didn't mean it wasn't

being watched. Hammer drove around the country store once before coming back and parking near the telephone booth. She was still driving a stolen car, and the last thing she needed was to be picked up by the law for something stupid. Since the coast was clear, she got out and walked quickly to the payphone. If she was gone too long, Sullivan would get suspicious. The Grimnoir were extra jumpy since another one of their own had gone missing.

Her argument had made sense. If she kept checking in periodically with the OCI like she was supposed to, then they wouldn't get suspicious. If she went silent, then they'd assume she'd been killed or compromised. Surprisingly enough, Sullivan had agreed with her, and not even had anyone ride with her to make sure she wasn't selling them out. For someone in a rough line of work, he seemed remarkably trusting, but she wouldn't have been surprised to discover the farmhouse abandoned by the time she got back.

Hammer dropped in the coins, got the operator, and gave the number that Crow had supplied. The connection wasn't very good. She got a man that didn't identify himself, and when she asked for Crow, he told her to hold. Two minutes of background echo later, Crow answered. "Hammer? Are you all right?"

"I'm fine. I lost the trail for a while, but I've picked it back up."

"We found your car." *Truth.* "I was worried you'd been hurt." *Lie.*

"I thought they'd spotted me at one point, so I switched vehicles. I was wrong, though. It wasn't them."

For somebody with magic based in truth, she could be an extremely convincing liar.

"Where are you?"

She scanned the empty road and the quiet store. There were no witnesses, but he had a government agency full of professional investigators. Surely he'd have somebody talk to the operator to figure out where she'd connected from.

"Northern Virginia, but the trail's cold here. They're a day or two ahead of me and heading south. I'll check back in when I get closer."

"Fine. Try to wrap it up. We're about through with him. The German's been scheduled to die in forty-eight hours." *Truth.* "So new sources would be helpful."

"I'll do my best . . ."

There was a sudden thump against the glass. Hammer jumped. Somebody was right outside the booth and she had no idea how'd they'd gotten there. A pair of grey eyes were gleaming at her from under a gigantic straw hat. It was the Traveler girl. Excited, Faye jerked the door open and Hammer instinctively put her hand over the mouthpiece. Faye mouthed the word, *Wait!*

Crow was saying goodbye. She uncovered the mouthpiece. "Wait," Hammer said, then covered it back up.

"Ask about Francis!" the Traveler whispered.

"What is it?" Crow asked.

"One thing . . . Just thought of something. I saw in the papers about that rich guy in New York. Stuyvesant?"

"Yeah?"

"Was that one of our captures?" She liked the choice of the word *our*. It made her sound like a team player. "I mean, it identified him as Grimnoir. Did we get him, or do I need to be on the lookout for him too?"

"We got him," Crow said proudly. "He's downstairs with the German." *True.*

"Okay, good to know." Hammer looked at the Traveler, who was nervously biting her lip. "I'll be in touch." She hung up the phone. "They've got your friend. The German dies day after tomorrow."

"Gosh dang it." Faye wandered off, hands on her hips, and kicked the brick wall of the corner drugstore. "I told him not to do anything stupid. Now I have to go save him too."

"You followed me."

"Of course," Faye said indignantly. "I'm not dumb. I wanted to see if you were going to fink us out."

"And if I had?"

The Traveler just smiled, weird grey eyes narrowing. "Bad things would have happened."

"What are you, twelve? Are you threatening me, girl?"

"I'm eighteen . . . I'm pretty sure." Faye folded her arms indignantly. "Listen, lady. Mr. Sullivan said that your magic makes it so you can always tell when folks are lying, so try this one on for size. If you had told Crow where to find us, I would've killed you extra hard. I would have killed you so fast that you wouldn't have seen it coming. I'd have killed you and made it extra messy as a warning to anybody else that was hunting my friends, unless I decided to make it look like an accident, because then I'd have just Traveled you over in front of a truck and left you there . . . Basically, lady, you do *not* want to mess with me."

The terrifying little girl was absolutely telling the truth, and it didn't bother her in the least. "How many people have you *killed*?"

Faye shrugged. "I've lost count. Around a hundred or so, give or take twenty. It can get pretty confusing sometimes and I don't always stick around to see if they're all the way dead or only mostly. So, you mind if I ride back with you? Traveling to keep up with a speeding car is hard work and I didn't sleep much last night so I'm plumb tuckered out. Come on. Not magic tired, that's fine, I mean my body is tired." Faye began walking for Hammer's car. "What? Come on already. We've got a lot of work to do. It's going to be a super-busy day."

"You just threatened to kill me . . ."

"Only if you were a fink, but you didn't tell on us, which makes you okay far as I'm concerned, so now we can be friends. Hurry up, Pemberly. Can I call you that? Pemberly is a real pretty name." Faye opened the passenger door and climbed in. "Don't make me start honking the horn. I'm a fugitive, you know, and that's very embarrassing."

Hammer followed the strange girl and got into the car. "Back to the farm?"

"Nope. The others just got back, so some of us are going on a top secret mission. I think Washington is supposed to be that way." Faye pointed the wrong direction. Hammer pointed the other way. "Okay. Great. I've never seen Washington, D.C. before. We've got a jailbreak to plan!"

Bell Farm, Virginia

SHE WOKE UP RIDING *in the military truck. The*

rumble of the Big Fight was silent for the first time in days. Somewhere behind her, everyone she'd ever known was gone because of the killer with grey eyes. The man that saved her noticed she was awake."My name is Jacques Montand."

She tried to talk, but her voice didn't want to work. Finally, she was able to squeak out, "Are you a policeman?"

He could probably barely hear her over the loud engine, but he shook his head. "No. I lied to those American soldiers. My papers are forgeries. I am something different, though we also try to help people, just in a different way. Especially people with magic. I have magic and I can tell you do too. So now I'm going to try to help you. Do you have any other family, friends I can take you to?"

She shook her head no.

"I would offer to drop you off at your local church, but it appeared that a dirigible from the front has crash-landed on top of it."

"I have nobody," she whispered. "The monster took them."

"Yes, he was a monster. His name was Anand Sivaram. We called him the Warlock. He'd cursed himself with a terrible spell. It was that spell that made him what he was and you were very brave to face him. Very brave, indeed. He's gone now. . . . What is your name, child?"

"Coline," she answered softly.

"What? I'm sorry. I can't hear you. You will have to speak up."

She tried again, but her sadness caught up, and then she couldn't talk anymore.

"It's alright. You are very quiet. It is fine to be quiet if

that makes you more comfortable." He turned to her and tried to give a consoling smile. "How about for now, I simply call you Whisper?"

Her eyes opened. Sad memories of her seven-year-old self were replaced by her twenty-two-year old present. Whisper sat up in bed and listened. The decrepit farmhouse was silent. The second floor *felt* empty. Most of the others had left on a fool's errand. She had told them that she was exhausted from the drive and needed to rest, and that was mostly true, but there was also another matter she needed to attend to privately.

There was a mirror in the bedroom, but it had been cracked long ago. It didn't matter, though, since she found one corner that was large enough to work on. This particular door did not have a lock, so Whisper braced a chair against it. She had the glass shard prepared in a minute. The Grimnoir elder that had sent her on this mission appeared quickly.

"Whisper. Oh, thank God. I was worried."

"I'm fine, Jacques." She had to smile. He had always been quick to worry about her. "You taught me too well. It'll take more than one gigantic demon to do me in."

"You were a fine student and an even better knight," he said proudly. "But an old man is allowed to fret over our loved ones. That's what we do best." His manner turned grave. "Any new developments with the Spellbound?"

Whisper noted it was no longer Faye or even the Traveler, it was simply the Spellbound. "She's growing stronger again. She used a spell like the one we are using now to check ahead for danger and then Traveled several hundred miles in one jump."

"Unbelievable. I assume she was close by when George Bolander died?"

Whisper nodded. "He was a brave man, with a *very* strong connection to the Power. What did the other elders have to say about my report?"

"They believe that we should wait and observe. If she does not realize the extent of her abilities, then perhaps she will not be tempted to grow them to a dangerous level. Though she is cursed, she is also innocent of any wrongdoing, and they felt that any preemptive action was unconscionable."

"And what do *you* think?"

Jacques looked away. He was a just and decent man, but he alone among the elders knew what they were truly facing. He had spent much of his life studying the Warlock, tracking him down, and eventually destroying him. No one in the Society knew more about the dangers of that awful curse than Jacques. "I voted to eliminate the Spellbound immediately."

The answer was sad, but expected. "Do not call her that. She is more than her curse. She is a person. She has a name. Faye is a good girl. She is kind, generous, and brave. I am honored to call her my friend."

The man that raised her shook his head sadly. "So you agree with the elders then? Leave her be as she grows increasingly unstable and dangerous? I do not like it, but I will follow my oath and abide by the decision. I just did not expect you to agree so readily."

Whisper surprised him. "There is no agreement."

"I do not understand."

"If you are prepared to kill someone, you should at

least have the courage to call them by name. This choice should not be easy. I do not wish to make my decision lightly. Her name is Faye and she is good . . . but she is dangerous. When the natural progression of things was not quick enough, how many people died by Warlock's greedy hands?"

"There is no definite answer . . . Hundreds for certain. Perhaps more. India, Persia, Turkey, across North Africa, finally France . . . We followed him by the corpses left in his wake. How many others did I not see with my own eyes? Who can say?"

"And if you had not tracked him down at the cost of so many of *our* people," Whisper said, obviously meaning both her family and the knights that had been under Jacques' command. "If he had been able to soak up the million slaughtered at Second Somme . . ."

"He would have been unbeatable." Jacques was concerned, and he was right to be. "What are you suggesting?"

"How many lives could have been saved if the Society had known about Warlock's research earlier? What if they had moved against him sooner?"

"We did not know about him until it was too late," Jacques answered quickly. "I know what you are thinking, but the elders have spoken. Whisper, please—"

"How many orphans will the Society's inaction create this time?"

"You will do nothing!" Jacques shouted. "The decision has been made. She is not to be harmed."

Whisper turned away from the mirror. "Very well . . ."

"Whisper?"

"I will not harm Faye." She would not look at him. "My observation mission is done here, then. What would you have me do, *elder*?"

The use of his title stung. "Come home, please. Things are becoming too dangerous in America."

"Do you doubt my skill as a knight now, as well?"

"Of course not!"

"There is much to be done here, then. I would like to assist until the Society's name has been cleared of these crimes, and after that, I am convinced that the concern about this Enemy being is legitimate. I think my Power will be of more use here than at home."

"I . . ." He hung his head in shame. "You have always been a very headstrong, but brave girl. Very well. Be careful. Anything you need, please let me know."

"Goodbye, Jacques."

"I know this is difficult and it seems as if no one understands your loss, but I do," he said as the spell faded away. "Farewell, Whisper."

He was gone. *Wrong answer, Jacques. What do you know about loss?* She had been forced to lie to the man who raised her as his own child. Furious, Whisper tore out the corner of glass and dashed it against the floor. "No more orphans, Jacques. I will allow no more."

Chapter 16

We can argue all day whether they are one in a thousand or one in a hundred, but what about when they are one in ten? One in five? All the experts agree their numbers are growing. When is it going to be enough? When will they stop? How much is too much? You've all heard about the Active supremacists' plot. They think they're better than us. They won't be happy until they overthrow this great democracy and rule us with an iron fist! It is time to take a stand! Join me, brothers, as we converge on Washington. This week we are already ten thousand strong, but we need more. What have you done today to protect your country from them! *We need your help to resist magical tyranny. Together, we will make our voices heard!*

—Radio promotion for the League for a Magic-Free America march on Washington, 1933

Washington D.C.

THIRTY AGENTS from the Bureau of Investigation had been detailed to this operation by the Director. Extra agents were already in the city to keep an eye on the ever-growing numbers participating in the antimagic protest. They did not know the particulars of the case, only that J. Edgar Hoover insisted that it was of the utmost importance, and he was overseeing the operation personally.

Per Hoover's orders, an agent had left a large courier envelope under some bushes at a small park on the corner of two busy streets. Ten agents had eyes and telescopes on the package. They were undercover, sitting on nearby park benches, watching from windows or rooftops, or simply out for a stroll. The other agents were waiting in chase cars, ready to swoop in and grab whoever picked up the package.

The agents were in the dark. Was it a ransom payment? A foreign spy? Communist agitators trying to stir up trouble in the antimagic mob? Was it related to the Active Plot? All they knew was that Hoover was taking this case very seriously, and he'd warned them to be ready for anything. The director was pacing nervously in the command center, listening to the constant radio check-ins.

The package had been placed at noon on the dot. It was now just after two o'clock in the afternoon and nobody had so much as sniffed around. A dog entered the area and began exploring the bushes, looking for a place to do its business. The presence of a golden retriever was dutifully reported. Twenty seconds after entering the bushes, the dog reappeared, carrying the courier package in its mouth.

As soon as he heard, Hoover ordered his men to seize the dog.

The agents had not been prepared to chase a dog. The retriever fled up the street and into an alley where it was briefly out of visual contact. The first three agents on the scene grabbed the apparently confused dog, who bit one agent on the hand during the struggle. However, the package was gone.

On the opposite side of the alley, one of the chase cars called in a sighting of a suspicious, two-foot-tall *dough* creature. It waddled quickly along on two legs, cradling the package in its lumpy arms. Pedestrians screamed at the sight of the tiny Summoned and tried to get out of its way.

Hoover ordered all cars to arrest the demon.

The creature turned and walked through the door of a haberdashery shop. A crowd of agents pursued it inside, only to discover that the room was filled with a thick, dark smoke that quickly dissipated. The package was missing. The proprietor of the shop explained that the store had been empty except for a pleasant young lady in a straw hat and dark glasses that had been browsing the wares. She was nowhere to be found.

When the dejected agents returned outside, a small hand mirror had been left on the driver's seat of one of the chase cars. Surprisingly, the reflection in the mirror was that of a large, square-jawed, unshaven man. The mirror requested to speak directly to J. Edgar Hoover. It was brought back to the command center and turned over to the director, who promptly threw everyone one else out of the room.

"Was that supposed to be a test?" Jake Sullivan asked. "I'm assuming we passed."

"It wouldn't do to ally with a group of incompetents. The dog was a nice touch," Hoover responded, watching the magic mirror as if it might turn into a snake and bite him.

"Your people are as clever as you made them out to be."

Sullivan was already opening the package. "Is this intelligence current?"

"It is," Hoover assured him. "We at the Bureau like to stay informed. However, I was recently ordered to have no involvement whatsoever with the OCI. So I'm afraid I have no need of these files. I've been hearing some very troubling things about our mutual acquaintances. Ugly things. Anything reliable you find will enable me to start an official inquiry. Until then, any action I take will be looked upon as mere political vindictiveness. He's seen to that. Bradford Carr is a crafty one."

"Small world," Sullivan muttered as he read one of the linotyped sheets. "*Doctor* Bradford. Ain't that something? I've been in the library named after him. Very nice collection, though now I'm betting he was keeping the good stuff for himself."

"Do what is necessary, but I will not abide a complete disregard for the letter of the law."

"Uh huh . . ." Sullivan was studying one of the pages. "I bet you won't. I'll be in touch."

"There is something else, Mr. Sullivan. The OCI has released a bulletin that they are expecting another attack shortly. Time is of the essence. We have never spoken."

"Keep the mirror. It makes a nice souvenir."

Bell Farm, Virginia

THE GANG'S ALL HERE!

Well, except for the ones that were in prison, the ones

that had died, and the others that were far away, but it was most of the Grimnoir Faye knew, all in one place, and all, sort of, working together. The old farmhouse was packed. Faye Vierra, Jake Sullivan, Lance Talon, Dan and Jane Garrett, Whisper Giraudoux, Ian Wright, and the new lady, Pemberly Hammer, were all in the living room.

Faye thought Pemberly seemed nice, if a little frazzled. She was pretty too, in a straightforward sort of way, though she was no Whisper, who was constantly dolling herself up and putting cosmetics on her face and playing with her hair—Faye figured it was because she was French—and she was certainly not in the same league as Jane, who Faye still thought should be a movie star or something. Jane just woke up beautiful. All of the other women made Faye feel sort of plain in comparison. It was okay, she was used to it. Besides, Francis seemed to think she was pretty, but that wasn't the only reason she was going to go rescue him.

Toru was the only one on the farm missing from the meeting, but Lance was using a rat to watch the crazy Iron Guard. Lance said that he was just sitting there on the barn floor, *meditating* or whatever it was Iron Guards do.

Mr. Sullivan had only been a Grimnoir as long as she had, so he was supposedly still one of the junior members, but everybody knew that when it came to combat nobody knew as much as he did. There wasn't any pride about it, he just kind of came in and took over when the discussion turned to fighting. She was glad that Lance was smart enough not to let his pride get in the way. Mr. Sullivan had used a grease pencil to draw a map on the wall. He'd been going over the plan for the last hour. As had been pointed out repeatedly, it wasn't much of a plan, but the clock was ticking. It was Tuesday afternoon and sometime on Thursday morning, Heinrich was scheduled to die. They weren't about to let that happen.

Luckily, they weren't too far so they didn't have to worry about getting there in time, just about what to do when they got there. Some of the others knew right away where the secret OCI headquarters was just from the name. *Mason Island.* Faye had never heard of the place.

"It's a swampy chunk of dirt in the Potomac, just between D.C. and Arlington County." Sullivan kept on drawing as he spoke. "Half a mile long, quarter mile wide. One bridge crosses the southern end of the island"—he made a broad slash—"connecting it to land on both sides. Government bought the place right after the Great War. They started building it up to put a Peace Ray on it, but that was before scientists figured out that the rays turned the air around it to poison. Couldn't have that zipping a couple hundred yards over the city."

"The elevation is crap. Stupid place to put an energy weapon," Lance said.

"I think the idea was that it would make an impressive silhouette, looming over the Capitol. Symbolic and all that. Anyways, they finally gave up and built this region's Peace Ray over on Catoctin Mountain, but before that decision, they'd finished the bridge and a couple of buildings. Officially, there's nothing there, even though you can see the lights from the other shore. According to Hoover"—Sullivan drew a square above the bridge—"this is where the OCI has set up shop."

"Good place for a secret police force. No flash, nice

and secluded, out of sight, out of mind," Dan said, "but driving distance to where the action is."

"We can bet it's fortified and heavily guarded. With twenty good men I could hold a place like that from now 'till doomsday. This isn't going to be easy."

"Maybe there's another option," Ian insisted. "Why don't we go after this Carr and take him out of the picture instead?"

Sullivan sounded weary. "Thought of that. First, they'll still have our people. Second, Hoover said Carr hasn't left OCI headquarters since the assassination attempt. He's been working through intermediaries and telephone calls."

"He's scared of us," Lance suggested. "Damn well ought to be. That's what happens when you poke the wrong hornet's nest."

"You'll still need whatever evidence they've got inside there anyway." Pemberly hadn't spoken in a while. She knew she wasn't very popular.

"I don't recall asking you," Lance said, sounding distracted, but that was how he normally was when part of his brain was occupied somewhere else. "Yesterday you were working for the enemy."

Faye turned to him. "I think she's okay."

"You thought the same thing about Isaiah Rawls," Lance responded gently. "Right before that treacherous son of a bitch near killed us all."

Faye blushed. Lance had her there. She'd been the one that had spilled General Pershing's secrets. At the mention of his father-in-law's name, Ian visibly bristled, but didn't speak up. Lance had no way of knowing the relation, and since Ian was in a room full of people who'd suffered because of Rawls, keeping his big stupid mouth shut was smart. She could tell it was difficult for him. Ian sure did like to argue and always be right. Faye didn't hate Ian as much now that she understood why he was such a bitter know-it-all jerk, and he'd been brave in Ada, though she was still mad about being pushed out the window.

"Lance, is it?" Pemberly asked. "I'm risking my life by being here. If it wasn't for me, you wouldn't even know your friend was alive. So you can stuff it."

"Well, excuse me, missy."

Faye thought that Lance and Pemberly sounded kind of alike. Not their voices, because Lance sounded like all deep and grumpy and Pemberly sounded kind of light and pretty like she might sing real nice. It was more about *how* they talked, with an accent like they should be riding horses and branding steers and other cowboy type things. Some folks said Faye had an accent too, a country one, but she couldn't hear it, so she figured they didn't know what they were talking about.

Mr. Sullivan seemed to be ignoring them. He was too focused on that map to pay attention to little things like squabbles. He got that way sometimes. While Faye seemed to be at her best when her brain was bouncing around between topics a million miles an hour, Sullivan focused on one thing until it got done. "Biggest problem is going to be those magic nullifiers. Place is probably crawling with them and we don't have a clue how to stop them. Stealth is out. Faye could pop in and get stuck and we're missing our Fade. Without magic, we're just guns, and they're bound to have more of those too."

"They can't have too many men, though," Dan mused. "If they're as dirty as we think they are, they'd have to run a tight operation. Problem with conspiracies is the more people know, the more likely somebody will talk."

"I'd like to assume that, but I can't. I'd rather not shoot a bunch of know-nothing security guards just there trying to do their job that don't know any better."

"We might not have a choice," Dan said. "They've declared war on us."

"Maybe. Wouldn't be the first time I've killed a bunch of folks who didn't know no better . . . Keeps a man up at nights. I really don't want to do the same thing with my own countrymen if I don't have to."

"Me too, Jake, but how many of our kind are going to die if we don't?"

"Said I didn't like it, never said I couldn't do it . . ." Sullivan muttered, deep in thought, as he ran one finger down a line representing a wall.

"Mr. Sullivan, if I may?" Whisper lived up to her nickname. It seemed bigger groups made her a little bashful. "Mr. Sullivan?"

He broke away from the map. "Huh?"

"Do you still have this box? The Dymaxion, you called it?"

He rummaged through one pocket and came out with a small orange cube. "Right here."

"Could you turn it on? We can all try our Powers and see if perhaps any of us can work around it."

The orange lid hinged open to reveal a sparkly ball inside. "Good thinking." Sullivan touched it with one finger and gave it a shove. Faye thought it was rather pretty, the way it caught the light, and made bright spots swirl around the room. "Try it." Whisper held up her hands but there was no fire. Ian looked like he was thinking too hard. Faye checked her head map and got . . . *nothing.* It was terrifying.

"Hey, Hammer," Dan said. "I totally trust you a hundred percent and think that you're just swell and really look forward to working with you."

"Oh, now I know my Power is broken," she answered.

Lance held up one hand. "Jake, shut that thing off." Sullivan put a finger on the ball and the spinning stopped. Faye's head map came flooding back. "Interesting . . . Start it again. Okay. Stop."

"You got something, Lance?"

"Maybe. Ian, while it's down, bring in a spirit or something."

"Give me a minute."

Jane sounded perplexed. "Very strange. I can still see everyone's insides, just like I always have, but I can't feel my Power. I don't feel like I could Mend anyone, but shouldn't I see everyone like a normal person would?"

"That's too bad, honey. Then you'd finally be able to see just how ruggedly handsome I really am," Dan quipped while rubbing one hand through his thinning hair.

"Oh, Dan. I love you just the way you are." She took his hand. "Squishy and filled with juice . . ."

Whisper squealed and jumped as a gigantic barn rat scampered in front of her shoes. "Relax," the rat and Lance said simultaneously. "You got a critter yet, Ian?"

The curtains rustled as if there was a light breeze, but the windows were all closed. "Yes."

Sullivan spun the ball again. They all looked at the rodent expectantly. The rat turned to Sullivan. "I feel fine."

"You can't see it, but the spirit I called up is floating right over there," Ian said. "That ball only stops magic from happening, it doesn't banish something that's already in effect!"

The rat did a couple of back flips to prove the point. "Yep. Looking good."

"Neat! Can you make him dance?" Faye asked. Whisper was cringing. "You can toss fireballs at a super demon, but you're scared of a big mouse?"

Her "S" sounds were even more pronounced when she was upset. "Because it is disgusting. Yuck. Look at it. So vile." Faye had to wonder how much of that was an act. It was almost like Whisper wanted folks to think she was softer than she really was; she just did it automatically. It was as much a mask as her makeup. Faye had seen her standing in the middle of a raging firestorm ready to fight to the death, and that sure wasn't sissy behavior. Whisper was an odd one.

"Oh well. I grabbed the prettiest one in the bunch, too." Lance let go of his Power and the rat panicked and fled the room. Whisper stood on her chair and didn't get down until she was sure it was gone. Faye didn't mind rodents. They made decent enough company as long as they weren't eating your food or giving you plagues.

Sullivan put the nullifier box away. "We can work with that. We know Crow used one of these on Francis, so unless that was his real body, we can assume that's how Crow's magic works too."

"Good, but if we're gonna do this, we're gonna do it right. I'm tired of wasting my talents on puppies, vermin, and livestock," Lance said. "I'm in the mood to run something mean, something carnivorous."

"For the rescue, but in the meantime—"

"I know, I know. Rodents and birds . . ." Lance looked over at Ian. "Sounds like me and you are going on a little scouting mission, kid. We'll leave at sundown."

Ian looked pained at the idea. Serves him right, Faye thought. Ian liked to be bossy, but nobody could boss Lance. If Lance decided he respected you enough, like Mr. Sullivan for example, he'd listen, but anybody else who told him what to do was likely to get a punch in the mouth. Lance didn't take no guff off anyone. Working with him would be good for Ian's attitude.

"Well, that's two that aren't completely useless. What about the rest of us?" Dan asked.

Sullivan went back to staring at the map. "We'll figure something out. We always do. Any word back on our request for reinforcements?"

"Browning is on his way with one other knight. No idea what he can do. As for the other groups, not yet," Dan answered. "I think the elders are inclined to have everyone lay low."

"Damned cowards," Lance spat. "Fat lot of help they've ever been."

Ian's temper got the better of him. "Now hold on. They're anything but cowards. There are more battles going on than just the ones you know about."

"They got something more pressing than my friend getting hung? Maybe some party to attend? Let me check my social calendar." Lance folded his thick arms and glared at the younger knight. "We're going with or without them and they damn well know it. If they don't have the spine to help, that makes them yellow." Faye resisted the urge to clap. For once Ian had no response. The Summoner was surly, but he was *nothing* compared to Lance Talon. "They need to wake up and realize that if we fail here, everyone in the world is in big trouble. They pin this particular crime on us and get away with it, the whole Society is done forever. We need help and we need it now."

Whisper had returned to her chair and was straightening the dress she'd borrowed from Jane. It was baggy on her. She seemed to be intrigued by what Lance had just said. "What kind of help would you like to have them give, then?"

Lance looked to Sullivan. The big man shrugged. "Men. Weapons. Plenty of each. More Powers that we can use to take out these nullifiers, and more Powers we can use to fight our way in and then back out. Then resources so we can get away. It's hard to say when you don't know what you're facing and the whole thing might just be a trap."

"It isn't a trap!" Pemberly was exasperated. "I'm sick of telling you, I heard what I heard. He was telling me the truth."

"I didn't say you were in on it." Sullivan's voice was flat. "But you're assuming that you're smarter than this Crow fella. Don't underestimate the enemy."

Faye chimed in. "I'm just hoping he underestimated us!"

❧❧❧

This visit had been expected. Toru opened his eyes to see that Sullivan had entered the barn. He stayed seated on the dirt. The Heavy leaned against the pickup truck and studied him. "I need your help."

"Are you ready to learn more of the Pathfinder?"

"Believe me, nothing I'd like more, but I've got to handle some business first."

"Very well. Come and get me when you are ready to learn. Otherwise, leave me be," Toru closed his eyes and pretended to go back to his meditations. He was curious to see what the Heavy would do.

As expected, Sullivan was persistent. "You swore to help me."

"To help you defeat the Enemy in order to fulfill my father's final wish. I do not care about your petty Grimnoir struggles. If your government destroys the Grimnoir, so much the better for the Imperium. They have always been a small, but annoying, thorn in our side."

"I thought you weren't Imperium anymore?"

"There is a difference between a warrior without a master, and a traitor . . . I am no traitor."

"Neither am I. Accusation hurts though, don't it?"

An unexpected tack. Sullivan was more perceptive than he looked. "Yes."

"You've seen a lot of war, haven't you, Toru?"

"All Iron Guards know is war. It is what we . . . *They* do."

"Now some fraud has taken your honor away . . . Been there myself. Hurts."

We are not the same. "What do you know of honor?"

Sullivan did not respond. The truck springs creaked as the Heavy shifted his weight. A match was struck and Toru could smell the smoke from Sullivan's cigarette. He wasn't going anywhere.

"Nothing you do here makes a difference, Sullivan. Your troubles now are insignificant compared to what is coming."

"I know."

Curious. Toru opened his eyes. "Then why do you waste your time? We should be preparing for the war against the Pathfinder. We should be building a new Dark Ocean."

"With who?"

"Any one who is worthy, of course."

"A bunch of worthy folks are going to die if I don't help in this fight."

"Then they should be stronger!" Toru snapped. "Leave me be." He closed his eyes and bowed his head, feigning disinterest. This was not Toru's war. Sullivan was a fool to even think that Toru would lower himself to fighting the wretched Grimnoir's battles.

The cursed Heavy stuck around. "I got a question for you . . . Been nagging me since you got here. Why else did you leave the Iron Guard?"

"I told you. I have an obligation to Okubo Tokugawa."

"What else?"

"What do you mean 'what else?' That is all that matters."

"Before all this, how'd a Brute like you get put in the diplomatic corps? Strength, speed, damn hard to kill—Brutes are the top tier of combat-capable Actives. Why'd the Imperium take you off the front lines? You're still young enough, healthy enough, and you act like you're always looking to fight. The Imperium's fighting in how many countries right now?"

"Six," Toru answered sullenly. "If you count the Chinese and Thai rebels."

"Seems a waste to pull a fighter, with an Active talent that's practically born for war, off the line and send him to an embassy a couple thousand miles away from where the action is."

"If you are trying to get me to slip up and admit to knowledge of covert Imperium operations in the United States, I will not do so."

Sullivan chuckled. "Oh, of course not. I was just wondering how you fucked up bad enough to get kicked out of the meanest army in the world. Maybe you weren't tough enough . . . You bastards worship strength." Sullivan made a big show of reasoning it out. "But since you're a Brute, it couldn't have been physical toughness you lacked. Cowardice?"

"Go away."

"Incompetence?"

"I said *go away.*"

"Had to be something."

Manchukuo. The competitions, who could collect the most peasants' heads in an hour? Who could make the biggest pile of ears? He remembered watching the starving prisoners fight for the officers' amusement, the pleasure women with their blank expressions and eyes where the soul had long since fled, the Cogs and their infernal sculpting of flesh. Manchukuo had been a dark time. It had not been a war befitting the Imperium that he believed in. It had been madness. Toru had disapproved of the troops' bloodlust. His disgust was taken for weakness. His questions caused dishonor. His hesitation to obey his superior's orders had brought him shame.

"Maybe you just lacked the stomach for it—"

It was too much. Toru surged to his feet, covered the distance in a split second, and grabbed Sullivan roughly by the collar. "I will not be questioned by the likes of you!"

They stood eye to eye. The Heavy did not so much as blink as he rolled his cigarette from one side of his mouth to the other. "You talk about being worthy to fight the Pathfinder. How am I supposed to know that you really are?"

"I was Iron Guard, the finest warriors in history!"

"So you say. Why don't you prove it?"

"I can do so very easily." Toru tightened his grip on the Heavy's coat. It would be so easy to rip his heart out. Sullivan kept on staring him down, surely ready to fire his own Power. It would be such a satisfying fight. "Here and now."

The sound of an automatic pistol's slide being racked came from the loft. "Need a hand, Mr. Sullivan?"

The Heavy looked Toru in the eyes. "Naw, Faye. We're just talking is all."

"Okay. I'm gonna hang around for a minute if that's okay, though."

"Not like this, Toru," Sullivan lowered his voice. "I know you can fight. We're not going to brawl with the Pathfinder and we're sure as hell not going to beat it in a duel. Show me you're a *soldier*. You've pledged to help me. Prove it. Show me what you've got. There's a fight coming. Show me you can follow orders and function in a unit." Sullivan spit his cigarette on the ground and smashed it with his boot. "Prove it to me or walk the fuck away."

The temptation to rend him limb from limb was great, but the obligation was all that mattered. The Chairman's ghost had asked for this man among the multitude he could have requested among their American foes. He had not asked for a military leader or powerful politician. He had asked for Sullivan for a reason. It was not Toru's place to judge worthiness, when Okubo Tokugawa had already done so himself.

Fires of purity burn on a Dark Ocean.

Toru let go of Sullivan's coat. Sullivan shoved him away. The two men glared at each other, nostrils flaring, fists clenched, ready to fight. "I can see now why my father chose you for this mission, though I still do not understand how you could possibly have been strong enough to defeat him. . . ." Toru bowed his head slightly. "I will think about your words." Then Toru turned, snatched up his tetsubo, and walked quickly from the barn.

"That went well," Faye said.

Sullivan watched him go.

"About the whole thing with him not getting how come we could beat the Chairman and all . . ." Faye suddenly appeared at Sullivan's side. "Please don't mention that was mostly me, okay? He seems mad enough as it is."

Dan Garrett watched through one of the second-floor farmhouse windows as the Iron Guard stomped away from the barn, red-faced, angry, and with a spiked club in one hand."What're you doing?" Jane asked suspiciously.

"Keeping an eye on our friend, the Jap." The Iron Guard stopped in the middle of a barren field, took a wide stance, raised his club overhead, and then stood as still as a statue. "Right now I think he's trying to be a scarecrow."

Jane came over and stood beside him. The Iron Guard wasn't so much as twitching. "What do you think?" his wife asked nervously.

"About keeping that animal around? I think Jake's lost his damned mind."

Suddenly, the Iron Guard moved, striking out at imaginary opponents, moving in a circle, attacking in all directions. "What's he doing?"

"Practicing how he's going to cave our heads in when the moment of inevitable betrayal arrives."

The club came down, back around, and up again. lightning quick. The Iron Guard went through several intricate movements, lashing out, and then leveraging the club as if he was blocking an attack, before returning to the starting position. The constant footwork raised a cloud of dust. It was too far away to hear with the window closed, but from his face it looked as if he was shouting with every swing. Toru was far too graceful for such a muscle-bound hulk and faster than any human ought to be.

Dan was terrified of him, and he had never been kidnapped by an Iron Guard. He could only imagine how his wife was feeling. He reached over and took her hand.

The Iron Guard finished the complicated movements with the club extended in a blow that would pulverize half the bones in a man's body, and then returned to the same ready position he'd started from. He waited a few seconds and then launched into the exact same series of movements, only faster this time.

"I'm sorry about this, Jane," Dan muttered. "I know how you must be feeling."

"I'm fine."

"With all that happened last year, the very thought—"

"Dan. Look at me." He complied and stared into her perfect eyes. "What do you see?"

"The beautiful and completely wonderful love of my life?"

"Correct . . ." She gave him a mischievous smile. "And?"

"You're tougher than you look?"

"Yes. It's alright. Don't forget, I've been in the Society longer than you have. I grew up with this kind of stress." She gave his hand a squeeze. "Of course I'm scared of the Imperium elite. Only a fool wouldn't be."

"I'm not scared of him."

Jane cocked her head to the side. "I may not have Hammer's Power, but your blood pressure is elevated and the muscles around your left eye socket develop a nervous twitch when you're lying."

Dan unconsciously put one hand to his eye. "Okay, fine. You got me. I'm scared to death, but not for me. For *us*. Madi thought you were a valuable commodity, and now Jake is inviting the fox into the henhouse. What happens when Toru makes the same decision? Sure, he might be telling the truth with all that talk about honor and obligations, but what if he changes his mind and decides they'll take him back if he brings his masters a good enough present? Like maybe a perfectly good Healer and a sack of Grimnoir heads. I'm telling you, no good can come of this. Jake's lost his *damned* mind."

"Jake is afraid, desperate maybe, but not crazy. Judging from the physiological indicators, I'd say that Jake is the most rational one in our group, and you have no idea how much it pains me to say that, since I believe he's fully willing to throw his life away at the slightest provocation if he thinks it will make a difference. He's prepared to do whatever he has to in order to win. If that means making a deal with evil incarnate, so be it."

"Is it worth making a deal with the devil, to beat another, bigger devil?"

"I'm afraid your theological analogy sort of falls apart there, Dan. But if they are even half right about how dangerous the Pathfinder is, can we afford to find out?"

Toru finished yet another set of intricate movements and froze. He held still for what seemed like forever. Unyielding.

"I don't like it . . . but you're probably right."

"I usually am, dear," she said. Dan just grunted in agreement. Even a man who could magically win any argument wasn't going to touch that idea with a ten foot pole. One of the cars left the barn and set off down the lane in a cloud of dust. "Who's leaving?" she asked.

"Jake, Lance, and Ian are going to scout the OCI's island fortress."

"And they're simply leaving the women here alone with that crazy Iron Guard?"

"Hey, I'm here." To be fair, his Power hadn't proved

the most useful against Iron Guard level willpower, and he knew it. He wasn't offended. As far as protecting the *women folk* went, Faye by herself was more than a match for any old Brute, and the French girl was a Torch. It was difficult to be a male chauvinist when women were human flamethrowers or could outfight a platoon of Imperium marines.

"That's not what I meant." Jane sniffed. "Of course I know you'll protect us!"

"It's okay. I'm not offended. A wise man knows his limitations, though I thought you weren't worried about him?" He chuckled. "Never mind. I'll quit while I'm ahead. Don't worry. I asked for this." He removed the captured Dymaxion from his pocket. "Mr. Toru doesn't know this thing exists. If he tries any funny business, he won't be nearly so tough when he finds out he's not bulletproof anymore."

"Oh, Dan. You're so clever." She kissed him.

"That's why you married me, babe."

OCI Headquarters

FRANCIS TRIED TO REMEMBER exactly how Buckminster Fuller's drawing had looked before he'd been forced to eat it. *A square. A circle. Another circle. Got to get the intersections right. Three triangles stuck together in back. Two squiggly bits that connected all the points. Two? Or was it three? Shit. I haven't even gotten to the octagon yet.*

Frustrated, Francis wiped away the design, smoothed

the dust, and tried again. The dim flickering light made it difficult to see and his fingertip wasn't the most precise instrument, especially when it was attached to a hand that was shackled to a chain.

"What are you doing?" Heinrich asked through the wall.

"Nothing." *I can't talk about it or they'll hear us.*

"You know, I have been thinking about something."

Square. Circle. Circle. "Yeah?"

"The one nice thing about them using our bodies as evidence is that they can't torture us too obviously, plus they have to feed us, and let us use the latrine. To do otherwise would cause suspicion during the investigation."

Sure, they'd been given water, canned rations, and been unshackled, then handcuffed and taken to the toilet while being watched by five burly guards with clubs and a Dymaxion twice a day, but it wasn't like they had any opportunity to escape. Heinrich had tried last time, but had only managed to injure two of the guards before being wrestled down, and dragged back to his cell. "Your point?"

"No point. I'm just saying that this could be a lot worse. Starving and wallowing in our own filth before being murdered . . . now *that* would be unpleasant."

"Nobody likes annoying optimists," Francis said.

"And to think that a few days ago you called me a pessimist."

Francis went back to trying to draw the spell. If only he could get this thing to work, then Heinrich could fade through his chains. Fighting a Fade indoors was suicide. The guards wouldn't have a chance. All he had to do was perfectly re-create the most complicated spell that he'd ever seen, and then only for a minute, and they could blow up all the Dymaxions and waltz right out of here. *Squiggly bits. Octagon . . . Fuck.*

Heinrich started to say something but then stopped. The opposite chains rattled for a moment and then his friend was still. Francis could have sworen that he heard whispering. "Heinrich, you okay?"

"Couldn't be better."

Heinrich was a strange one, even for a German. Francis shrugged and went back to drawing. A few seconds later he heard a small ticking noise coming from inside the wall. A whisper came through the hole in the bricks. "Shhh, don't talk. Just listen."

Lance?

"They've got spy holes in the walls. You're being watched and listened to." He turned his head enough to see the black head of a rat perched on top of his chain. "Here's the deal. We're going to spring you tomorrow."

Yes! He should have known his friends wouldn't let him down. He hadn't given up hope, but he'd been getting close.

Francis urgently tapped his finger in the middle of the spell he was drawing.

"Interesting. What's that do?"

Francis wrote in the dust. *BLOWS UP DYMAXIONS.*

"That would be handy," Lance whispered. "Think you could do that on demand?"

SIGNAL?

"Explosions. Screaming. Gunfire. That kind of thing."

???

"Well, a maybe is better than nothing. How big do they blow up?"

GRENADE

"I'll tell Sullivan not to keep his in his pocket then. Anything else you can tell me?"

BRADFORD CARR

"Already know about him."

Francis smoothed the dust. *ATTACK COMING. KILL US. FRAME UP.*

The rat made a skittering noise. "Figured as much. Be ready to move quick. If that spell works, great. If not, we'll come get you boys the hard way."

FIND BUCKMINSTER FULLER N.Y. HIS SPELL.

"Not much time, but we'll try . . . Oh, and I can see what you're doing there. Draw the wavy lines first. Then put the solid shapes on top of them. Easier that way. I've been messing with some of the ones Sullivan's come up with, nothing like that beast, though."

Francis scowled at the design. *Why hadn't I thought of that?*

The rat moved around for a moment. There was a tinkle of metal against the floor. "Here's some pieces of wire and a nail I found. I did the same thing for Heinrich. Maybe you can pick your lock. I'll be back with the cavalry tomorrow. You boys hang in there." And then Lance was gone.

They were going to bust out of here, no matter what. With renewed determination, Francis cleared the dust and started over.

There was only so much he could tell by glassing a dark tree line over and over. The shapes of the buildings could barely be seen and there weren't very many exterior lights. He couldn't even pick out the guards. Sullivan finally gave up and lowered the spyglass.

Apparently their Beastie was finished scouting too, and Lance wandered over to join Sullivan on the shore. He had heard Lance's side of the conversations with Heinrich and Francis. "How bad is it?"

"Exterior wall is solid, and our targets are buttoned up tight in the main building. I counted eighteen heavily-armed men barracked there, our boys, and half a dozen other prisoners in another area. Guards patrol outside, working in pairs. Don't know how many, but twenty-five bunks in total, though they might sleep in shifts. We could cut the electricity and telephone lines easy enough, but they've got a radio transmitter so they'll still be able to call for help."

"Only one bridge across. Easy to block our escape, too."

"Too bad Pirate Bob's on the other side of the world. Being able to land an armored blimp right on top of them would be mighty convenient."

Sullivan shook his head. "The Navy's had their newest carrier tethered over the city since the attack. We come in by air and the *Lexington* will have fighters on our tail in no time."

"We're gonna have to work for this one."

It was cold on the Virginia side of the river; that humid, pierce-your-clothes kind of misery that made nights like this especially bitter. Sullivan jammed his hands into his pockets and waited for the young Summoner to finish up with his spirits.

Ian was sitting on the lowered tailgate of the truck, talking to thin air. "Good work, Molly. Tell me what's inside the loud room?" He listened intently as the invisible creature spoke in a way that only Summoners could hear. "You're so smart. Yes you are. Who's my good girl? Molly's my good girl."

"Are all of them like that?" Lance asked.

"Summoners? Believe it or not, this one seems a lot more squared away than most." Sullivan had worked with a few different Summoners over the years, from the scouts of the 1st Volunteer to friends he'd used for detective work. Compared to the rest, Ian could interact with society rather well. He was still young, though. Maybe Summoners just got crazier with age. "What've you got, Ian?"

He sounded smug. "Molly is one of the sharpest spirits I can bring in. She says there's a room at the top that's got an engine running inside of it. It's spinning a big ball. That's got to be a Dymaxion."

Sullivan was inclined to agree. The smaller one he'd found had a range of maybe fifty feet, but this one seemed to cover the whole island. They'd driven over the bridge to the D.C. side and back to test it out, and his Power hadn't responded at all while crossing the river.

"I heard the noise upstairs," Lance said. "I didn't spend too much time trying to get in. The room was solid concrete with a bank door on it. But if it's motorized, then there will be ventilation for that engine, and if there's ventilation a rat can get in and start chewing through wires."

"Might not be a bad idea."

"You got any idea how bad copper wire tastes?"

"Can't say that I do . . . I wonder how many of their men know what's really going on? You know we're going to end up having to kill some of them."

"I know." Lance was somber. "But if you sign up to take away innocent folks' freedom, you better be prepared to pay with your life. I saw something else while I was in there you need to know about. There's a command center on the main floor. Nobody's working this late, so I did some reading. They're making big plans."

"More attacks to blame us for, I bet."

"Francis tried to warn me that something's coming, but he had no details. That wasn't what got my attention. Bad things, Jake."

It wasn't like Lance to be this hesitant. "Spit it out."

"OCI is building prison camps big enough to hold tens of thousands. They're segregated by Active types. Places I've never heard of out west, Topaz and Gila River for physical Powers, Granada and Minidoka for mental. They're got lists of names. Pages and pages of them. Who's not a threat, who to round up, and who to exterminate."

"Aw hell . . ." This was worse than imagined.

"*Exterminate*, Jake. I didn't pick the word. I didn't make it up. It was on the title. *Extermination order for undesirable Actives*."

Ian just stared at the dark mass of Mason Island. "I can't believe that."

Lance hawked his throat and spit in the Potomac. "Believe it, kid. It was posted on the fucking bulletin board."

Sullivan took the spyglass out and put it back to his eye.

Had it really come to this? *What's your game, Senator?* But the trees held no clues.

Lance's laugh was bitter. "OCI's just gonna keep on pulling stunts like Miami 'til they get what they want."

"It's hard to believe they can hate us that much," Ian muttered.

Sullivan wasn't sure. Maybe it was hate for some, fear for others, but was there something more? Were Actives an excuse for a power grab? Were they pawns in some bigger game? Sullivan didn't know, but he was damn tired of being pushed.

It was a different time, different place, and it was right in his own nation's Capital, but Sullivan couldn't help but feel like he was back in the Great War, planning a raid across no-man's-land. He had a mission, he had an enemy, and that meant that he had a purpose. If the OCI wanted a war, then they'd get one. "Let's go home. Get a good night's sleep. Tomorrow, we attack."

"We've been scouted, sir," Crow reported to his superior.

Bradford Carr had been getting ready to turn in for the evening, and was dressed in his robe savoring a pipe. He'd claimed the general's officer's quarters of the old Peace Ray facility as his personal suite and paid a great deal of money to have the rooms properly decorated. The plain concrete of the bunker had been paneled over with fine wood. Ornate light fixtures had replaced the wire-covered emergency bulbs. All of the furniture was huge, dark, and expensive. Crow felt like he was sitting in the salon of some upper-crust intellectual, which technically, he was.

The room was decorated with trinkets and souvenirs from the Coordinator's travels around the world. There was a lion skin rug on the floor; the Coordinator had shot the beast himself. One wall had weapons—Zulu spears, Arabian scimitars, even an Amazonian blowgun complete with darts coated in a poison made from blue frogs. Two walls were covered in books that the Coordinator had shipped down from his private collection in Chicago. Most of those books, scrolls, and stacks of paper were about magic, personally gathered by Carr from every corner of the globe. The last wall was covered in plaques, diplomas, medals, and awards, all strategically arranged to show how much better he was than everyone else. It was the honorable Doctor Bradford Carr's display wall of personal arrogance.

"Scouted, eh? Grimnoir, I assume?" Carr leaned back in his plush chair. It creaked ominously under all that fat. Crow had to remind himself that if the chair broke and the Coordinator came tumbling out, he'd better not laugh. The Coordinator struck him as someone who would be sensitive to even the smallest slight.

"So it would appear. It was a minor spirit. I could sense it poking around."

"Any chance that it might have been sent by someone else?"

The Coordinator was more worried about his rival, J. Edgar Hoover, who at best might be able to put them in jail, than the ruthless Grimnoir that would certainly try to kill them. *Damned politicians. No sense of perspective.* "Hoover's got no trust of magic. I'd say it was the Grimnoir, which means they'll be coming soon."

"Very good. Speed up the timeline then." Carr smiled as he sucked on his pipe. "I want the next operation to begin as soon as the Grimnoir attack us. Move up the schedule. Have some of the men prepared to evacuate Stuyvesant and the German into the city. I want it to seem as if the two events, the attack on the city, and the Grimnoir assault against our headquarters were done simultaneously. It will make their group seem more capable of nefarious scheming in the papers, and it will position the OCI as the logical force to stop them."

It would also split his available resources and put all of them in more danger. The Coordinator didn't care, though. He would be safe in his bunker the whole time. "Of course, sir."

"Excellent, Mr. Crow . . . I'll bring the rest of the trustworthy men here to reinforce our numbers. The Grimnoir's little scout will not have known that . . . Here, let me show you something." He picked up a thick leather book from his reading table and held it out for Crow to take. Crow had to lean way forward in his chair to get the book. The wheels of his chair couldn't roll across that stupid lion rug. The book was battered, the cover was stained, and the writing on the pages was done by hand. "Do you know what that is?"

"No, sir. I do not." The writing was in a language Crow didn't recognize. He flipped through a few pages, noting the many intricately designed spells.

"I bought this book from a Romanian peddler back in '23 for thirty-five cents. The poor Gypsy had no idea of the astronomical value of such a tome. In fact, from the pages of that very book came the spell that I gave to you, and that you gave to Giuseppe Zangara, to drastically increase your abilities. What you hold in your hands is one of the personal research journals of Anand Sivaram, an absolutely brilliant mystic, driven insane in a quest for more Power. He was one of the first to figure out how to bind new forms of magic to his own body, including the single greatest design ever accomplished by the hand of man: a spell that worked as a collector of recently severed Power. A design that no one has been able to replicate since, yet it ruined his mind, and as a result, he did many unspeakable things."

Was this about the spell that the Coordinator had carved onto Crow's narrow chest? Crow fidgeted nervously. Did the boss know just how difficult it was getting to control the demons? Was he going to take it away? Crow would rather die than lose his freedom.

"In the west, Sivaram was referred to as the Warlock."

Crow had been briefed about the mad Traveler. "The Spellbound?"

"For many years, I'd thought he was a myth. You see, I've always been fascinated by magic. Ever since I was a child the mysteries of the Power intrigued me. Sadly, I was not born blessed with any miraculous abilities . . ." The Coordinator paused to stroke his huge mustache as he reminisced. "Yet, I was driven to dedicate my life, my considerable intellect, and my family's wealth to the study of such things."

Where was the old coot going with this? "You've accomplished great things."

"With more to come, I assure you, but I have gotten away from my point—Warlock. I'd thought he was a myth, this crazed mystic that murdered man, woman, and child in order to absorb their life-force to strengthen his own Power. At the time we all believed it was impossible to manipulate magic beyond what a tiny percentage of mankind was born with. All legitimate scholars thought so as well . . . until during my service during the Great War, when by fluke happenstance I came across the bullet-riddled corpse of the Warlock on a farm in France. I could positively feel the energy still smoldering in the designs carved upon the body. If he was real, the stories were true! Magic could be manipulated and molded for our use."

Crow could only nod along with the story. The boss had never talked about this before.

"It was an epiphany. As a man of science, I do not believe in gods or fate, but at that moment in time my future was laid clear before me. I would be the one who would control magic. I would tame its wild fury. I would harness it for the good of all." He held out his hand, and Crow had to struggle forward to give the strange book back. "For far too long, Actives have squandered their gifts through ignorance and selfishness. Magic does not belong to them alone. It belongs to all mankind. It will take a great man to correct this deficiency. History is defined and directed by the wills and vision of great men, Mr. Crow. Let us make history."

You self-righteous idealistic bastard. "Yes, sir."

"That will be all. I will have one of the men take you back to your quarters."

"If it would be alright, it would be safer if my real body wasn't near the battle."

The Coordinator sighed, as if insulted by Crow's cowardice. "Very well. I'll have the men take you across the river. Dismissed."

Even in the pathetically weak, very limited, human form he'd been born with, Crow found his dislike for the smug Coordinator growing. He'd liked the man up until a few days ago, and Crow wasn't sure if the feeling originated with him or was lingering hate left over from the demons he'd been sharing a mind with. It was a good thing he was not allowed in the inner sanctum in demon form, because he was beginning to doubt that his employer would survive the meeting.

Chapter 17

I have killed many Mexicans; I do not know how many, for frequently I did not count them. Some of them were not worth counting. They had attacked my camp, slain my aged mother, my young wife, and my three small children. The Mexicans paid for their malicious ways with their lives. I walked through the walls of their forts and spilled their sleeping blood. Their bullets passed through me as if I were mist. They called me a ghost, but I still lived. It was vengeance, not death, that had changed my form.

—Geronimo, *My Life: The Autobiography of Geronimo*, 1905

Bell Farm, Virginia

"CRY HAVOC and let slip the dogs of war," Dan Garrett said as he looked over Sullivan's final battle plan. The grease pencil map that covered one wall of the farmhouse living room was far more detailed today.

"I read Shakespeare in prison," Sullivan muttered. "Why don't you pick somebody who writes happy endings?"

"Only line I remember from a college production," Dan answered. "Seemed appropriate."

They'd spent the morning going over the details, filling in the blanks, and making assignments. Everyone was there, except for Whisper, who had gone to the airfield to pick up Browning. Their gear had been checked and their weapons cleaned. They'd go over the plan one last time with everybody present, have a good supper because it might be awhile before they had time to eat again, and then head north to Mason Island.

Sullivan hated this part, deciding who to use and how to use them. Just like the war, his decisions here would determine who was likely to live and who was likely to die. *How had General Pershing managed this with thousands of lives at a time?* There was no pride involved, just that when it came to fighting, Sullivan had seen by far the most, which meant he would be the one to make the call.

"Browning and Jane stay on the Virginia side of the river. That's the direction we're planning on retreating."

"John isn't going to like that," Lance pointed out. "He's a brave man."

"He's also an old one. Faye, Hammer, and the French girl will be here"—he thumped the wall—"On the D.C. side."

"No way!" Faye shouted.

"Uh, Jake . . . She is our most dangerous Active."

"And until those Dymaxions are shut off, she's only a teenage girl. If the OCI gets a call out for reinforcements, they'll likely come from that direction. The Torch can set the bridge on fire and slow them down. Besides, we all know the second Faye thinks it's clear, there ain't nothing that's going to stop her from popping over to the island and raising hell, regardless of what we tell her to do."

Faye blushed. "Well . . . obviously."

"That's fine, Faye. Once the nullifiers are off, your orders are to just *be yourself*."

"I can do that, Mr. Sullivan!"

"I figured you'd be okay with that."

"What about me?" Lance asked.

"You and Ian are with Browning."

Lance obviously didn't like that much. "That's an awful long way from the shooting."

"We've got two Powers that can cause some harm, and I'm not going to waste them. Besides, Lance, if it all goes to hell, you know how to use the mortar."

"Fine, but I'm stopping by the National Zoo on the way to *borrow* something worthwhile. Me and the kid can hang back."

"No can do," Ian interjected. "If I'm going to be bringing in a Summoned capable of fighting, I'll need to be closer than that or I could lose control of it."

The last thing they needed was another out-of-control demon on the rampage. "Fine. Me, you, and Dan are going in quiet from the north. There are plenty of boats around there that we can take. They'll be watching the bridge, but we didn't get any sign they were watching the forest. Wear your boots."

Hammer raised her hand. "Why is it that all of the women are on the shore?"

"Blame it on me being old-fashioned if it makes you feel better," Sullivan said.

"There's not much for me to do over there, and you're awfully thin on the island. I can shoot and I know how to handle myself in the woods. Better than the fat city boy, for sure." Hammer gestured at Dan. "No offense."

Jane bristled at the jab against her husband, but Dan just laughed it off. "None taken, though the fat part was unnecessary. Unless, of course, you just want to be on the island so you can warn your OCI buddies when we've arrived . . ."

"You tricky Mouth bastard!" Then Hammer shut up because she had no response to that particular accusation.

Sullivan had already thought about how to utilize her, but there wasn't much use for a Justice in combat, and he didn't want to get her killed. She wasn't a knight and Sullivan already felt like getting her mixed up in this whole plot was his fault to begin with.

"She's got a point, though, Jake. That's me and you with no Powers and Ian who's going to be busy concentrating, taking on at least twenty men. What are we supposed to do with only three of us?"

"Four." Every head in the room turned toward the new voice. Toru stood in the doorway. He surveyed the group, glaring, daring anyone to disagree. "As I said I would, I thought upon your request."

"Hell no!" Lance shouted as he stood up. "No way am I going with an Iron Guard." Some other voices rose in agreement. "I'm not working with the likes of him."

Sullivan had been afraid of this. Many had lost people to the Imperium, but Lance had lost his wife and child. Jane had been kidnapped by an Iron Guard. Faye's grandfather had been gunned down by the same man. Ian was red-faced and shouting, so he was probably in the same club.

"*Silence!*" The Iron Guard's bellow shook the farmhouse. Several hands moved to gun butts. "You have my most sincere apologies for the rudeness of my interruption. I have made a promise, and in order to fulfill that promise, I need this man"—he nodded toward Sullivan—"alive. If that means participating in your petty war in order to keep him alive, then I will do so. Whoever tries to stop me from fulfilling the promise I have made to my father," he looked directly at Lance, "will be considered my enemy."

Lance drew his revolver. "How about I send you to your father right now, you Imperium son of a bitch."

"However," Toru continued, voice completely even, "I have pledged my loyalty to Sullivan's cause. Anyone who stands with him against the Pathfinder is my ally, and my ally's fight becomes my fight." Then Toru surprised everyone by bowing deeply. He held it for a long time before rising. "I will be in the barn. Wake me when it is time to begin the slaughter." The Iron Guard turned and walked from the room.

"Well . . . shit . . ." Lance put his gun back in the holster. Dan Garrett had discreetly opened the Dymaxion box and had been ready to use the nullifier. "That your bright idea, Jake?"

"We've all fought the Imperium before. You know what they're capable of. The OCI won't know what hit them."

"They're evil," Ian stated with steel in his voice. "Flat out evil. He'll turn on us when he gets the chance."

"I don't think so," Sullivan said. "I'm playing a hunch."

Ian was furious. "Your hunch strong enough to keep us from getting stabbed in the back? Strong enough to keep him from carting off whoever he wants for the Chairman's Cogs to murder?"

"Yeah." Sullivan folded his arms. "It is."

Hammer surprised him by jumping in on his side. "I agree with Sullivan. Toru's a mean one, but my Power says he's telling the truth about this."

"A bunch of you are of the opinion that the OCI declared war on us. Well, in my experience, you want to win a war, you don't hold back nothing. If that means using an Iron Guard, then that's what it means."

Lance sure wasn't happy about that, but he threw up his hands in disgust. "Fine. You want to play with fire, I've got one condition—put that Iron Guard in *front*, because I sure as hell ain't turning my back on him."

Hammer sought Sullivan out afterwards. If she was going to do this, there was no halfway about it. Helping meant being where the action is, regardless of the danger. She figured it was because she was a woman, and this was Sullivan's misguided attempt to keep her safe, like the rules that kept her from becoming a peace officer, even though she was born with a Power that would make her perfect for that kind of work. She resented being treated like a weakling.

Sullivan was alone in one of the back rooms of the farmhouse. The Heavy had disassembled his machine gun and was cleaning it. The parts were spread all over a card table.

"Got a minute?"

"Sure," he answered as he inspected a spring carefully. Sullivan struck her as someone with single-minded attention to detail. "Thanks for backing me up on what the Iron Guard said."

"He was telling the truth, though I don't think your friends believed me."

"Most don't." Apparently satisfied, Sullivan put the spring back. "We're not the most trusting bunch. Come by it honestly." Sullivan looked uncomfortable, like he didn't know what to say. "But you already know that. Have a seat."

She pulled up a stool. "I just wanted to—"

"Why do you want to help us?"

The question caught her off guard. "They're going to kill your friend."

"And?"

"He's innocent!"

Sullivan nodded. "That don't answer why you're helping us."

She stood up. "If you don't want my help—"

"I didn't say that. Sit . . . please." The Heavy was embarrassed, so she returned to the stool. "Sorry. I meant no offense. I'm just curious."

"Saving an innocent man isn't enough for you?"

"In this world, innocent folks die every day. Why risk your neck to help somebody you don't even know?"

"How's that different than what the Grimnoir do?"

He shrugged. "You looking to join up?"

She'd never been one for causes. "Not really."

He went back to his chore, picked up the bolt, and wiped it down with a rag while he waited for her to talk.

Hammer had a feeling that if this conversation came down to a game of patience, Sullivan would win every time.

"All right. Don't laugh. Since I was a little girl, I've had a dream. I've wanted to be a lawman."

"Despite the fact I was a convict, I see lawman, in most cases, as a respectable profession."

"Not for a lady it's not. It's a fluke or a joke when it has happened, and it doesn't happen anymore. For me . . . . well, I was raised by the best marshal there's ever been."

"So I've heard."

"I wanted to be just like him. Only thing I ever wanted to do. Catch bad men, help folks, keep the peace. I was born for it. I thought maybe working for the OCI would give me that shot. Only they're doing terrible things, and I can't tolerate that. They're tyrants hiding behind the law. Maybe I'm naive, but I think that the law isn't about words on paper. It's about doing what's right, and the OCI is *not* right."

"No argument from me . . . Garrett told me something you need to know. Helping the Grimnoir is what got your father killed."

She was quiet for a long time. After Sullivan and Garrett's discussion she'd figured there was some history. "He was ambushed by a gang of train robbers."

"Led by an Active criminal. Some of our men wanted to stop them before that got out. Lee Hammer helped us. Garrett didn't know the details, though General Pershing told him that your father died bravely. Which is why I'm not turning down your help, but I'm putting you on the other side of the river with Faye and Whisper. The

Grimnoir already cost one Hammer his life. I don't want to be responsible for another."

"That's . . ."

"Selfish? I suppose. I've led men into battle enough times to recognize our odds, and without our magic, they ain't good."

Even though she disagreed with his logic, she could respect how he'd come up with it. Once again, Sullivan surprised her. "I thought it was because you didn't trust me, or maybe because I'm a woman."

"Even Faye thinks we can trust you now, and hell, far as trust goes, I'm taking an Iron Guard along, though Brutes get a pass 'cause they can punch out elephants, so they're handy for this sort of work. As for being a woman . . . yeah"—Sullivan looked back down at the gun parts—"That's kind of hard to miss. You're quite the woman."

"Why, Mr. Sullivan." She used the same flirtatious voice as the first time they'd met. "Whatever do you mean?"

"You know what I mean."

She didn't need her magic to tell that he was attracted to her. "Maybe when this is over . . ."

"For me, this will never be over." Sullivan chuckled bitterly as he began putting the machine gun back together. "Sorry, Hammer. You're a smart girl. In another time, another world maybe . . . Now I'm bad luck and bad news. I've got a tough road ahead, and it's only going to get worse. I've known a lot of women, but only ever loved one. She had a dream too. Delilah just wanted a life that wasn't awful, but I ruined that. Now she's dead because I wasn't good enough to save her."

"I'm sorry."

"Naw, Hammer. No need." When the machine gun was reassembled, he gently set it on the table and looked at her. There was far too much sadness in those eyes. "You can do a lot better than the likes of this broken-down Heavy."

And the tragic part was that Sullivan believed that to be absolutely true.

Faye picked up the automobiles with her head map before anyone else heard them coming. The first one was easy enough to recognize. Whisper was coming back from the airfield, but she didn't recognize the second car. She warned everyone else, grabbed one of the Tommy guns off of the big pile of guns in the kitchen, and Traveled into the bushes to wait.

The gun turned out to be unnecessary. Whisper, Mr. Browning, and Mr. Bryce got out of the first car, and the second car was filled with strangers. She Traveled over to see what was going on and caught Whisper just as she was explaining to Lance and Mr. Sullivan, who were the first ones out of the house.

"These knights are from another group, though for secrecy's sake they are not supposed to share from where they come nor to whom they answer. Their flight arrived before Mr. Browning's. They are here to help us."

Suspicious, Lance studied the four men getting out of the second car. "You know that for certain?"

"Yes. I am friends with some of them, as is Ian. He can vouch for their integrity."

Mr. Browning came over and shook Sullivan's hand. "I

too know some of these knights. They are legitimate. My request for help was acknowledged."

"We can use them," Sullivan said.

"It appears as if the elders felt the same way," Whisper said with a bright smile.

"Really?" Lance was taken aback. "I didn't think—"

"No. Of course you didn't think, because you were far too busy telling us how cowardly everyone else was to have time for *thinking*." Whisper could be very mean while seeming perfectly charming about it. Faye marveled at how she could do that so well. "The elders know how important this is, and they do not want to see your friends perish anymore than you do."

The others came outside. Several gun cases were removed from the trunk of the second car and stacked on the ground as introductions were made. Their leader was a thin, bespectacled man who introduced himself as Steve Diamond, Mover.

Diamond seemed too young and too soft-spoken to be the boss, and Faye figured that for sure that his name was some kind of Grimnoir alias, but she'd already learned to never underestimate any of her fellow knights. Then he proceeded to introduce his team: Dan Mottl who was an Icebox, and Adam Simmons, Torch. They all shook Faye's hand like she was a man, and even seemed a little deferential. She wasn't used to that, but apparently word of her exploits had spread.

The last of the new knights was an olive-skinned young man wearing a neatly trimmed beard, and a very expensive suit and silk vest. Diamond introduced that one as Nicholas Dianatkhah, which Faye thought sounded suspiciously foreign, but he talked familiar enough. In fact, he was a little too familiar, as he took Faye's hand and kissed the back of it. "Miss Faye, the marvelous Traveler that defeated the dastardly Chairman. Your reputation precedes you, even in the distant lands I hail from . . . Though, no one told me that you would be this lovely in person."

That made Faye blush.

"Distant lands . . . We were in *Pittsburgh* when we heard about the Chairman." said Diamond, shaking his head. Apparently he was used to that kind of behavior from his companion. "Please excuse him. Dianatkhah here is a Healer."

Even Sullivan seemed impressed by that. Healers were the rarest of the rare, and now they had *two* here. The elders had sure sent some powerful Actives to help them. Faye looked over at Lance, but he was still being all stuffy and grumpy. She sort of liked this Dianatkhah, as he was kind of exotically handsome, but Francis was being held prisoner, so she reminded herself to try extra hard not to be flirtatious. People might get the wrong idea.

Faye had already met the glowering Mr. Bryce, and she was interested to note that of all of them, he was the only one that did not say what his Power was. Mr. Browning didn't seem to be in a hurry to talk about it either, so she didn't bring it up.

"We were told Pershing's knights could use a hand. These knights are capable." Diamond gestured at his men. "What do you need to us to do?"

"Attack the headquarters of the secret police," Sullivan said.

"Sounds crazy."

"Yeah. Mostly."

Sullivan's words didn't seem to bother the young Grimnoir. "George Bolander was one of ours. I'm assuming that we're dealing with the group responsible for his death?" When Sullivan nodded, Diamond smiled and rubbed his hands together. "Wonderful! Let's get to it then."

While the other knights were speaking, Whisper caught Faye's eye and motioned for her to step aside. "Take a walk with me, Faye."

Whisper was acting funny, like she was nervous about something. Whisper picked a path toward the fields and set out, so Faye followed along. The trees along the trail were old and gnarled. They were missing their leaves now, but Faye could only imagine that in the summertime they would make for nice shade. She waited until the others were out of earshot. "What's wrong?"

It was like Whisper didn't want to look at her. She just kept her eyes on the path. "Have you heard of Anand Sivaram?"

"That's an odd name."

"He was from India. They say that he was one of the greatest Actives that has ever lived. Before he died, some said that he might have even been like unto the Chairman. They had other names for him too. The Mad Traveler, Warlock, the Spellbound . . ."

"A Traveler? Well, huh. There aren't very many of us. Sorry, Whisper. I haven't had time to learn much history yet."

"Not many know of this history. It is a secret." Whisper kicked a stone across the lane. "They do not speak of him, lest someone else would be prideful enough to delude themselves into thinking that they could succeed where even one as brilliant as Sivaram had fallen. They are scared that his form of evil could begin anew."

"He sounds bad."

"Oh, yes. Very. The man that raised me knows more about the Warlock than anyone else alive. Jacques Montand had to study him in order to catch him. About his strengths, his weaknesses . . . his curse . . ."

Faye was intrigued. "What curse?"

"A terrible spell, one that he created himself and carved into his own body. Awful beyond imagining. He tried to grow stronger than any man ought to, and it ruined him. It twisted his mind until he did unspeakable things." Whisper stopped in the middle of the lane and wiped her eyes. *Was she crying?*

"Are you okay?"

"I am fine . . ." Whisper was lying. Faye put one hand on her arm, but Whisper jerked away. "No." She began walking again. "Warlock was a vulture. A carrion feeder. And when that wasn't enough, he became a predator. He killed hundreds, perhaps thousands. Men. Women. Children. Always needing more, and at a rapidly increasing rate. If he hadn't been stopped, it would only have gotten worse."

"Why are you telling me about this?"

"Because Jacques told me that the Warlock did not start out as a monster. He was once a kind man, motivated by pure intentions." Whisper still had her back to her, but

Faye could see that she'd extended one hand. A tiny ball of fire appeared in her open palm. She held it there, floating just above her skin. "He was innocent too, once." Whisper laughed bitterly. "So naive. Like unto the children that he massacred."

Faye was growing concerned. "I don't understand."

Whisper was letting the fire curl between her fingers. It moved like a snake as it curled around Whisper's bare forearm. Her head was down, and Faye could see that she was shaking. "I always promised myself that if I had the opportunity to stop someone like the Warlock, I would do so without hesitation."

"Of course you would. That's the right thing to do. Heck, I've killed oodles of evil folks."

"But what about before he turned evil? What about before he had turned to spilling innocent blood? Wouldn't I be a fool if I lacked the courage to strike down a child if I knew that child would someday become a monster?"

"Of course not." Now Faye was just confused. "Not unless your Power is telling the future . . . Because how would you know?"

Whisper straightened up and sniffed. The fire snake curled around her hands froze.

"I'm not one for all that philosophy and stuff some folks like to quote so they seem smart and all, but come on. I mean, you're talking about a person, not gophers or rattlesnakes. This one's easy. I mean, if you killed a kid just 'cause of what the kid *might* turn into, then you wouldn't be any better than this Warlock fellow and all his massacring. Then who's the real bad guy?"

Whisper stood still for a real long time. Faye hadn't

known that fire could just be still like that, but then it just sort of drifted away and disappeared into thin air. Whisper still didn't turn around though.

Somebody shouted her name. They needed to get ready. "Sounds like we better get going."

Whisper finally turned. "I'll be along." Her makeup was running. She had been crying.

"You sure you're okay?"

"Not really." Whisper gave her a sad smile. "But I will be eventually."

Faye just shrugged. "You can be really weird sometimes, I swear. Let's go."

Chapter 18

When I began my career, I was told that there was no longer a need for stage magicians in a world with real magic. Yet I knew, as everyone knows, that the easiest way to attract a crowd is to let it be known that at a given time and a given place someone is going to attempt something that in the event of failure will mean sudden death. That's what attracts us to the man who paints the flagstaff on the tall building, or to the "human fly" who scales the walls of the same building. Bury a Fade alive and there is no wonderment when he escapes, because nothing can hold a Fade. Bury a normal man, such as myself, and the crowds will gather to see if I may die. That, my friends, is showmanship.

—Harry Houdini,
Interview, 1931

Mason Island

LIGHTS COULD BE SEEN down both sides of the Potomac, but the island was only a blacker shadow on the river ahead. Luckily for them, it was a particularly dark night, moonless and cloudy. It smelled like rain. Their oars dipped quietly as Toru steered their tiny boat toward the island. Twenty feet behind, the water could be heard lapping gently against the second rowboat.

Sullivan was in the front, bullpup BAR pointed in the general direction of the island. There was a Maxim sound silencer screwed onto the muzzle. If a sentry spotted them, he'd need to shoot them down before the alarm could be raised. "Ian?"

Their Summoner was at the back of the boat, listening intently. "Molly doesn't see anybody close to the shore," Ian whispered. "I'll have her go further south."

He'd learned in the Great War that spirits were good scouts, but they often missed things. They weren't that smart and could be easily distracted. Just because Molly didn't see any guards . . . didn't mean there weren't any there. He went back to scanning the shore.

The first boat carried him, Dan, Ian, and Toru. The second held Diamond and his three knights. All of them had smeared grease on their faces and were dressed in dark, rugged clothing, from Sullivan's beat-up dock worker's coat and skull cap to Ian's brown getup that was straight out of a safari outfitter's catalog. Everyone was armed with a long gun, extra ammo, a sidearm, and other gear. Under Sullivan's coat were three canvas BAR gunner's belts improvised into a sort of crossed bandoleer, one over each shoulder, roped to the one around his waist, and each one was weighed down with spare magazines. That load was nothing compared to the Iron Guard though. He'd lost track of how many weapons Toru had thrown on, including that absurd spiked club riding on his back.

He just hoped the Brute wasn't overestimating how much stamina he would have once the nullifiers blocked his Power.

The island was closer now. Toru lifted the oars from the water and they all listened. Crickets and frogs, and the water lapping against a felled tree, but nothing that suggested they were drifting into an ambush.

It was cold, and even the brief ride in the rowboat had coated them with a fine mist that left their clothing damp. Moving through the forest, even if it was walking into a fight, would be a welcome relief, because at least it would generate some heat. The bottom of their boat thumped against something unseen, and the noise made Sullivan flinch. The frogs fell silent. They drifted for a moment, waiting . . . Then the frogs began croaking again.

Toru stowed the oars and rolled silently over the side. He entered the water without hardly making a splash. It was shallow here, barely coming up to Toru's waist. Sullivan tossed the Iron Guard a rope and he pulled them forward until the boat was stuck in the mud. Toru tied the rope to a tree while the other three climbed out.

Diamond's boat kept drifting to the east. They'd agreed to make landfall at two separate points and then converge as they got closer to the compound. Lance's surprise had simply swum across the river before them and would be waiting somewhere ahead.

Dan and Ian weren't nearly as quiet as he'd hoped. There was just something about moving in the woods that could only be learned through practice. Dan's real value was if the nullifiers could get knocked out. At that point he could probably just ask real nice and the OCI would surrender and hand over all of their evidence. Until then, he was clumsy and loud. *Maybe I should have brought Hammer.* He kept his voice low so it wouldn't carry. "You two . . . stay back and get your Summoned ready." They'd discussed it earlier—anything Ian was capable of bringing in that would be much use in a fight sure wouldn't be very stealthy. "Then stay a hundred feet behind us. Toru, you're with me."

Walking in a crouch, Sullivan made his way forward. The woods were thick, but he took his time to keep from making too much noise. The ground was nice and soft, which meant that his boots gained clinging mud with every step, but at least he didn't have to worry about dry leaves and branches cracking. Stalking through no-man's-land had been a thousand times worse, because you had to do that on your belly, crawling over the dead bodies and the barbed wire, and a carelessly raised head would get you popped by a German rifleman. For Sullivan, this felt more like the deer hunting he'd done as a kid than the deadly stalking he'd learned in France.

Walking into the nullifers range was like walking into a wall. The Power just stopped. The spells he'd carved on his body felt lifeless and dull. Suddenly everything felt *heavy*.

Toru moved to the side, silent as one of Ian's spirits. He'd brought that big Jap machine gun, but even without his Brute strength, it didn't seem to be bothering him any. They had just shy of half a mile to travel. They made good time, trying to stay far enough ahead of the louder two. Sullivan was so used to subconsciously manipulating gravity that he'd forgotten just how weighty a BAR and two hundred rounds of ammunition were. Despite the cold, he began to sweat beneath his coat.

Five minutes in, Toru froze. The lack of movement in his peripheral vision was enough to make Sullivan unconsciously take a knee. The Iron Guard had sensed something. Sullivan's nose caught it a second later. Cigarette smoke.

There was a noise up ahead and Sullivan pulled tight against a tree. There was a game path, and two shapes were making their way down it. The men were talking quietly, nervous. The long things in their hands could only be rifles. He looked to where Toru had been, but the Iron Guard was already gone, crawling forward, his machine gun left leaning against a log. Sullivan slung his BAR, drew his trench knife, and followed.

It was almost too easy. Just like old times, like silencing the German city boys who didn't know how to listen to the night. The guards never even saw them coming. Toru took the left side of the game trail and Sullivan took the right. Palms covered mouths as heads were jerked back. Boot to the back of their knee, the blade goes in under the ear, then ride them down, nice and quiet. You only had to keep them still for a few seconds that way. The smart ones would at least try to pull a trigger to warn their friends, but Sullivan had found that most folks couldn't think that far ahead with six inches of steel in their neck.

Sullivan dragged the corpse back into the bushes and wiped his blade on the guard's shirt before putting it back in the sheath. His hands weren't even shaking. There was only the emotional blankness hard earned in the trenches of France. The earlier reservations about taking these men's lives had been dismissed after Lance's discovery of the extermination order. If human life was that cheap to them, then Sullivan figured this was all they deserved.

He joined Toru at the edge of the trail. The Iron Guard gestured to the south and held up two fingers. More guards. They had to hurry. Dan and Ian were blundering along behind, and were sure to get spotted. Sullivan put his hand down to begin crawling, but froze. His palm had come to rest in something that felt suspiciously like an animal track. A *huge* animal track.

Damn, Lance. Did you get something big enough this time?

He signaled for Toru to intercept Dan and Ian. Toru moved off, and Sullivan waited. A moment later the second half of the patrol came into view. They'd left far too much room between themselves to be effective. Sullivan disapproved of their lack of professionalism.

These two were warier than the first, but it didn't matter. There was a flash of shadow, a thump, and the guard bringing up the rear simply disappeared from view. The lead man turned, confused, as the shape in the bushes rose soundlessly, bounded back across the trail, leapt, and took down the other. This time Sullivan could hear the snap of bone as they disappeared.

The bushes shook as the predator made its way toward him. Every instinct in Sullivan's body told him to either run for his life or start shooting, but he held perfectly still. He couldn't actually see the animal until it was almost on top of him. You wouldn't think that orange and black stripes would be effective camouflage, but it really was.

The tiger came out of the brush and strolled down the trail toward him.

"Hey, Jake. We're clear from here to the wall. Couple guards on top of it and more in a tower behind the perimeter. Bad news though. I can smell a lot more men inside than when we were here earlier. I'd say at least double, maybe more."

He swallowed hard. Up close, the tiger was even more terrifying than he'd imagined. Sullivan prided himself on being a tough guy, afraid of nothing, but this was a little too close for comfort. "You're making me nervous."

"Aw, this little thing." The tiger made a show of turning its head and looking at itself. "Now *this* is more like it."

"Is it safe?"

"Safe as a six-hundred-pound Siberian tiger can be. The National Zoo is gonna be right angry when they find her missing."

"You have to put it back."

"Aw, come on. Can't I keep her? Heh . . . just kidding. You know how much this thing would cost to feed? Look, I got to concentrate. I'm trying to get word to Heinrich, trying to break the generator with another rat, and keeping this girl from eating you. I'm going to park her here and put her to sleep, so I can't talk for a minute."

Sullivan watched the tiger as it seemed to study him back. "Anything I can help with?"

"Just don't try to pet the big kitty, Sullivan. I don't think I could handle that."

I think I've got it!

Francis was giddy with excitement, or maybe it was just

the exhaustion, since he'd been working on Fuller's design nonstop for an unknown number of hours. It was hard to tell time in a prison cell with no windows or clocks. The design finally looked, and more importantly, felt right.

So now what?

It just kind of sat there, a gigantic conglomeration of squiggles, shapes, and lines drawn in the dust, utterly lifeless.

Since he had proved incompetent at lock-picking, the wire that Lance's rat had snuck to him had been used as a drawing implement instead. Between the finer lines, and dozens of agonizing attempts, the spell was finally done; it seemed to be correct, but it wasn't doing anything. It had to work just like any other spell. He had to concentrate on it, had to make it connect to his own Power. Until then, it was just a drawing in the dust. But how was he supposed to touch it with magic with the nullifier messing him up? He concentrated on the design, like he normally would, but felt nothing at all. "Damn it all to hell!"

"Huh?" The chains rattled. "What?" Heinrich sounded like he'd been sleeping.

"Nothing . . ." Francis couldn't even tell his friend why he was frustrated because the stupid guards were probably listening. "How're you doing?"

"I am doing rather well, believe it or not," Heinrich answered. "I am looking forward to getting this over with." Which probably meant that he'd had more luck picking his locks than Francis had. It didn't seem fair at all. You wouldn't think that a Fade would have ever bothered to learn a skill like lock-picking when he could just walk through walls, but Heinrich was just so damned crafty that he'd probably learned how for fun. As a very talented Mover, all Francis had to do to open a lock was think about bouncing tumblers until something clicked. It turned out to be a whole lot harder with one hand and a piece of wire. "How are you, Francis?"

"Not as good as you apparently."

"I see. Well, I think we are going to have a busy day tomorrow. Try to get some rest then."

Easy for Heinrich to say. He'd learned how to sleep while dangling from ledges and rain gutters to keep from being eaten by zombies. Francis much preferred a nice, civilized bed. His idea of roughing it was a three-star hotel.

There was another noise from inside the wall, skittering right behind his head, and it made Francis jump. "Don't say anything," Lance's voice whispered from a space far too small for a human to fit. "This is it. We're right outside. If you can make that spell work, Francis, now's the time. Nod your head if you got that." He did. "Good. Gotta run." There was a rattle of a pipe and Lance was gone as quickly as he'd appeared.

Desperate, Francis turned his attention back to the spell. Time was up. He had to make this damned thing work or else.

The rat scurried up the conduit, forced its head through a tiny crack in the wall, and then pulled its body through behind. Lance knew that anything its skull could fit through, the body could be forced to follow. All of God's creatures, even the utterly disgusting ones, were amazing. He was tracking the gasoline stink of the engine.

The generator was close. He could feel the vibration through his feet. More twists and turns took him through walls and behind panels.

The generator room was illuminated by a single light. There was no smell of danger, though the corners were cloaked in shadows. The rodent tumbled through the last hole, dropped several feet to hit the hard floor, and immediately scampered toward the engine. *Pick some wires. Chew till something breaks. Get the hell out of here.*

The rat didn't even hear the tiny demon until it was too late. A black claw pierced the rat's body and pinned it to the floor.

Crow's modest apartment overlooked the Potomac. Though he couldn't even see Mason Island from here, he'd parked his chair right next to the window anyway. A smile creased his face as his distant minor Summoned destroyed the intruder in the generator room. He'd figured they'd try to kill the main Dymaxion somehow.

He released the demon from his control and let it fade from reality. By the time the demon had drifted into smoke, Crow was entirely back in his own body. The little ones didn't take much consciousness to control, so within seconds he was in full possession of his limited human faculties and could again feel all the weakness and fragility of the body he'd been born with. Since he'd received the Doctor's spell, he'd been spending less and less time in that body every day, just returning to it often enough to keep it fed and cleaned. Returning to his real body always seemed like such a waste.

The telephone was waiting on the stand next to him.

The line had already been prepared to go directly to OCI headquarters and all he had to do was push a button to be patched through. Someone picked up on the other end immediately. "This is Crow. Intruders are on the island. Lock it down. Prep Stuyvesant and Koenig for transport. I'll be there in a minute." He returned the handset to the cradle.

This was a special occasion. It was almost like picking which tie to wear before that special date with a sweet young thing you really wanted to impress. He was eager to kill these Grimnoir, so only one of his finest demons would do. The one that he'd used in Oklahoma was the strongest he'd ever attempted to control, and that had turned out dicey. He'd lost control and embarrassed the OCI last time. Since the boss was going to be at the scene, he'd better play it low key and Summon something a little tamer.

But Crow hesitated. Something was eating at the back of his mind. *Screw Doc Carr. I know what I'm doing.* He'd Summon the same demon that he'd used in Oklahoma. If the Traveler girl was going to be there, the ram-horned demon deserved another shot at her. Its spirit had been out here sulking since it had been defeated last time. It was only fair.

The ram-horned demon wasn't the greatest that Crow had ever found, just the greatest that he'd ever attempted to bring over to the real world. He'd sensed a few others out there, floating in the between place that only Finders and Summoners could reach. Those were bigger, older, even stronger, just waiting to be given form. Their spirits dwarfed all the others, so epic that he hadn't even been able to recognize them as actual entities before the Doctor had magnified his Power. These things had been the top of the food chain on the dead world that the Summoned originally hailed from. It was really tempting to try one of those on for size. To be able to have a body like that . . .

Better safe than sorry. Ram-horn will do for now. I'll work up to one of those big boys eventually. Crow reached deep inside, fired up his Power, and called for his servant.

The tiger's sudden roar caused Sullivan to fall over on his backside into the mud. The gigantic feline took a step toward him. Surprised, he jerked the BAR up and got ready to shred the cat.

"Lance! What're you doing?" Sullivan hissed.

"Got speared by a demon." The tiger rapidly shook its head as if it were distracted by pain. "They know we're here." The tiger leapt away and disappeared into the trees.

Sullivan got out of the mud and hurried for the compound. Active or not, it was now or never. Ahead, the shape of the wall appeared ahead through the trees. The only gate was on the south side facing the bridge. There was no entrance here on the north side, so they'd planned on making their own. Hoover's intel said that it was twelve feet tall, made of bricks, with a single tower overlooking it, and there was an open space of about fifty feet where the trees had been cut away for visibility. All of that was good useful information.

However, the intel hadn't specified that there was a walkway on the other side, so that men could peer over the top to shoot at them.

He'd almost reached the clearing when brilliant floodlights switched on, bathing the trees in light. "Everybody down!" Sullivan shouted as he slid behind a fallen log. He shouldered the BAR and the front sight appeared as a gigantic black triangle before the light. The Maxim silencer absorbed most of the noise, and he was rewarded with shattering glass and darkness. He swept over and took out another one of the floodlights before someone on the wall returned fire. Sullivan calmly got as low as he could as machine gun fire ripped the log to splinters above his head.

Toru dove into the bushes off to the side and crawled behind a mound of solid dirt. He leaned out and worked his machine gun across the top of the wall. Somewhere inside the OCI compound a man cried out in pain and another light went out. A Thompson roared far to the left as Diamond's men joined the attack. Within seconds, seven automatic weapons were peppering the fortifications and smashing brick into dust.

"Ian!" Sullivan bellowed at the top of his lungs. The plan hadn't changed, they just had to do it while getting shot at was all. "Make us a door!" Then he went over the log and emptied the rest of his magazine into the watchtower. "Toru, hit that tower."

Between the two of them, the wooden structure was absolutely riddled with bullets. The guards' shadows jerked and twitched. A red mist hung in front of the watchtower's spotlight for an instant before it too was broken. Gun empty, Sullivan ducked back down. He barely had time to see a body sag against the railing, flip over the edge, and tumble from sight. The tower was out of the picture.

Deprived of targets, the fire from Diamond's side tapered off. Toru pulled back behind cover to reload. The Iron Guard's teeth were visible in the dark as he smiled. "It seems they did not expect that level of response."

"Too easy."

"Agreed. Expect trouble."

He raised his voice. "Anyone hit?" Sullivan counted the shouts back. Nobody was down. If there were more OCI on the wall, they were staying concealed. "Hurry it up, Ian."

"On the way."

A pale glow appeared in the forest back the way they'd come from. The soft ground began to rumble with ponderous footsteps as the glow grew brighter and brighter. Ian's Summoned was coming. "Cover that monster!" Sullivan's command was echoed a moment later as Diamond repeated the order to his men.

BAR reloaded, Sullivan watched the wall, but no targets appeared. A dark spot that could only be an arm dangled limply over the side, but other than that there was no sign of the OCI. The rhythmic rumble increased as the Summoned neared. It crashed haphazardly through the brush, breaking smaller trees and pushing medium-sized ones over. The Summoned was only a few yards away when it passed by, the color of the full moon, vast, four eyes glowing red. It looked clumsy, with a great big body, oversized arms, and stubby little legs driving it relentlessly forward, but it was gaining speed as it charged the wall.

Someone in the OCI realized what was coming and shouts could be heard on the other side. Shadows appeared as a few guards risked peeks over the wall. The Grimnoir immediately began shooting at anything that moved. A few of the OCI got shots off before they were driven out of sight. Bullets puckered through the Summoned's doughy flesh, hissing smoke, but it wasn't nearly enough to slow the mighty beast.

The Summoned lowered its formless head, ducked a shoulder, and hit the wall with a terrible crash. The bricks cracked, split, and the whole wall shuddered. Men cried out as they were flung from the walkway. The Summoned kept on pushing, stubby legs throwing up plumes of dirt, and the wall began to fall apart. The pale glow momentarily disappeared in a cloud of red dust as stones crashed and broke.

The Grimnoir began to cheer.

When the dust cleared, the Summoned was standing before a huge gash in the wall.

They had their entrance. "Follow me." Sullivan shouted as he vaulted over the log.

"Halt," the Iron Guard ordered. "Incoming."

Sullivan froze at the sound of leathery wings. Something passed overhead and blocked the stars, then the wings folded in and a bolt of black fell from the sky, whistling through the air. It hit the ground next to Ian's Summoned in an explosion of soft earth. Sullivan covered his eyes as he was pelted with dirt and bits of brick.

Something massive shot from the hole toward Ian's creature. The pale Summoned spun toward the new arrival, only to have four awful lacerations rip through its chest in an explosion of ink. It crashed backwards, tearing down an even wider chunk of wall, and was quickly covered in tumbling bricks.

Lowering the gigantic claw that it had used to

effortlessly tear through the Summoned, the new demon slowly turned to face them. It was humanoid, mostly, blacker than the night and nearly as tall as what was left of the crumbling compound wall. A bank of four red eyes watched them from under a heavy brow of bone. Ram's horns curled around each side of the misshapen skull.

It was the most impressive demon Sullivan had ever seen. Bigger than the one that had killed General Roosevelt in the war, bigger than the Bull King from Mar Pacifica, and that one had soaked up a burst from a .50 caliber like it was nothing. Sure, bullets would kill a greater Summoned eventually, but without magic, they wouldn't have a chance in hell of beating this thing without taking heavy causalities.

The demon grinned with a mouth full needles. "Heavy Jake Sullivan, I presume . . ." The horns dipped in recognition.

"Yep." Sullivan said flatly. This had to be Crow. There was no use talking to this asshole. "And you must be—*Open fire!*"

Francis could barely hear the gunfire through the thick walls of his prison cell. He was focusing so hard on the spell that he'd drawn that it was making his eyes hurt, but he still couldn't access his Power.

There was a clank and a clatter in the hall. They were unlocking his door.

Come on. Come on. Come on.

He could hear them now. "—and Griffin, take the rich guy first. He's soft. The rest of us grab the German. That bastard's a handful."

The heavy door creaked open.

Francis swore at the design and cursed Buckminster Fuller to hell. *Why won't you work? Damn it*! The OCI men came quickly into the room, but Francis was too busy to look at them. It was all there, bits and pieces, shapes and lines. Why did the Power have to be so damn complicated?

Rough hands grabbed hold of him. "Come quiet, Stuyvesant, or we'll have to bust you up." A key was inserted into one shackle and the lock clicked open. Pain flooded through his cramped arm, but Francis was still trying to figure out what he'd done wrong. The other wrist was freed and he was hauled to his feet.

From this angle the spell looked a little different. Obviously, he'd been stuck looking at it the same way the entire time, plus, from standing, Francis could see what he'd done wrong. Two of the lines hadn't met completely!

"Come on—" The goon choked on the words as Francis slammed his elbow back hard. The other men standing in the doorway were taken by surprise. Francis shook free long enough to slug the second one in the mouth before he was tackled and dog-piled to the ground.

Don't mess it up. Please, don't mess it up. Despite the weight on top of him, Francis struggled forward, got one hand free, stretched, and tried to complete the intersection. Then somebody had his legs and he was pulled across the floor on his face. *Did I get it?* He couldn't see anymore, as he was now completely surrounded by OCI thugs. His hands were yanked behind his back and tied with cord. "Get off me, you rat bastards!"

Somebody punched him in the mouth. Someone else kicked hard in the stomach.

"Watch it, idiot. Can't have him too beat up."

"Thought you said he was soft," gasped one man.

"Get them, Francis!" Heinrich shouted through the wall.

"Shut up, Kraut! Get him out of here. We'll deal with that damned German."

The last thing Francis heard was Heinrich shouting, "Come and try me, *Scheisskopf!*" before he was dragged into the hall with one man clamped onto each elbow. Four other OCI men followed them out into the hall, but they turned and went toward Heinrich's door. Despite his thrashing, both of the guards were far bigger and stronger than he was and they merely pulled Francis along like an unruly child.

As they started up the stairs, Francis managed to crane his neck enough for one last look. The others were focused on Heinrich's door, and they didn't notice the shift in the shadows as some new source of light flickered through the open door of Francis' cell.

Francis experienced a momentary flash of excitement.

But nothing happened.

Then the OCI thugs pulled him up the stairs and his hopes were dashed.

Heinrich was ready as he could be. The unlocked shackles were resting on his freed wrists. Outnumbered and against an enemy prepared for a scrap, he would be at a disadvantage, but they would not be expecting him to have freed himself. The nails that Lance had slipped him were squeezed in one fist, just their points sticking past his knuckles. An advantage, any advantage, could be utilized to great effect, and surprise was one of Heinrich's favorites.

When he'd struggled against the OCI before, he'd discovered that they were a hardy lot, but it didn't matter how tough you were with your eye gouged out or your throat crushed in the first few seconds of an engagement. He reasoned that he could take one, maybe two of them quickly, then it would be a struggle to defeat the remainder.

The room was only ten by ten, slightly more spacious than fighting inside an elevator car. There would be little room for maneuvering, another advantage to the numerically superior side. There was a single light source in the room. If he could put it out, the darkness could add to the confusion. It was a useful possibility.

However, even if he made it past these men, there would be many more, and he was unarmed, had no Power, and did not know the layout of the facility at all. He would more than likely be gunned down, but it would be worth it if he could cause a distraction to aid his fellow knights.

Most men would have been frightened, but not Heinrich Koenig. It was about time he'd finally be able to have some excitement around here. Being a prisoner had proven to be terribly monotonous. Worst case scenario, the OCI would damage his body to the extent that they would no longer be able to utilize his corpse in their secret scheme. Sometimes, spite alone was worth dying for.

He could hear the men unlatching the door, but there was something faint in the background . . . *What is that noise?* It was like . . . wind? But it was coming through the chain hole leading to the cell that Francis had occupied.

Interesting. There had never been a breeze any other time that door had been opened, though it wasn't quite right, as there was something other than simply the whistling of wind . . . It was almost a *suction* noise.

But there was no more time to ponder on the sound. The door opened.

"Time to go," said the leader. Heinrich recognized him from the split lip. He had been one of the guards Heinrich had fought on his last escape attempt. The leader and two other burly types entered the cell while a fourth stayed in the hall. That one had a small orange box in hand, and stroked it as nervously as an old nun with a rosary. Of course, there was a large nullification field over the entire prison, but they would have to be bringing along some smaller ones to keep him and Francis under control while they were transported. "Let's get you to the scene of your crime. It's gonna be a bloody night."

"You disgust me. You filth would murder your own people to advance your cause?"

"Literally, our own people," said the man on Heinrich's right. "Buddy, you got no idea."

Heinrich didn't know what he was talking about. *Who was the target?*

"Shut up, Deych. The Coordinator's plans are solid. Sometimes you've got to break some eggs." The chief OCI man was a thick-necked, dark-haired slab of meat, with a nose that looked like it had been broken a few times. "Grab him."

"Alright, Sharps. Never mind I said anything." Deych took one of Heinrich's arms. The second pulled a ring of keys from his coat and reached for the shackles.

"What's that noise?" asked Sharps, hearing the whistling wind for the first time. He put one hand to a cauliflowered ear. "You boys hear that?"

"Yeah—" But the man didn't get to finish, since Heinrich punched him in the throat with two rusty nails. He kicked Deych in the knee, and as he lurched away, the open shackles fell to the floor. Heinrich scrambled to his feet.

"What the fuck?" Sharps took in his men, one hopping on one leg and the other clutching his bleeding throat. "How'd you get loose?"

Heinrich charged, but Sharps surprised him. The OCI man was remarkably quick on his feet. He sidestepped and threw a hook into Heinrich's ribs. The blow was fearsome, and Sharps followed that up with a nasty punch to the side of his head. Heinrich tried to hit back, but Sharps simply blocked the shot and put one of his fists into Heinrich's eye. Heinrich realized as he crashed into the far wall that he'd drastically underestimated the fighting skills of this particular OCI agent.

The man in the hallway drew a pistol.

"Stay out of this. The German is mine," Sharps ordered. "Well, shit . . . Look at that. I messed up his face. Look what you made me do."

"He can't look too roughed up," Deych said. "The Coordinator will be pissed."

"The Coordinator didn't think he'd have already escaped either. I'll try not to mess up that pretty face, otherwise Stuyvesant will have to do. Stand back, boys, and Greg, see if you can't get Tom's neck to stop bleeding all over."

Blood was running down Heinrich's face. He'd cut his

scalp against the rough wall. Hopefully it made him look more injured than he really was.

Sharps cracked his knuckles. "You're a clever Jerry, but you picked the wrong man to tussle with. Nick Sharps. Heard the name?"

Heinrich pulled himself up. His ribs were on fire. The big man was only a few feet away. "Can't say that I've had the pleasure."

"Heavyweight contender few a years back, until some tiny little Active punk near killed me in an exhibition bout. You know what that does to a man's fighting career? It's like losing to a kangaroo. Embarrassing regular folks just 'cause you can. Your kind ain't shit without fancy magic tricks to back you up." Sharps lifted his scarred fists. "You got no idea how much I'm gonna enjoy this. Let's see how good you Actives are in a fair fight."

Heinrich had lost the nails. Which was rather unfortunate, since Heinrich was of average size while his opponent was nearly the size of Jake Sullivan, but Heinrich had grown up fighting zombies, and thus had no concept of the words *fair fight*. Heinrich mirrored Sharps' boxing stance, though he had no intent of duking it out with this monster.

Sharps stepped up to swing, but Heinrich immediately dove at his legs, wrapped his arms tight around the bigger man's ankles and drove all of his weight against the knees. The OCI man bellowed as they crashed into the dust. Heinrich rose enough to punch him in the crotch a few times, then rolled away, managed to get up first, and kicked Sharps in the back of the neck.

"Lumbering oaf!" Heinrich shouted as Sharps tried to

get up. He stabbed one thumb into Sharps' eye and used his other hand to try to rip his ear off. "I'll show you how we do it in Berlin!"

"Get him off!" the OCI man cried.

So much for fair. The other two rushed him. One was still bleeding badly from the neck punctures, so Heinrich concentrated on him first, and managed to strike him repeatedly on the face before Deych caught a handful of Heinrich's shirt. So Heinrich bit a chunk out of Deych's forearm. Then Sharps got up and joined in. It was a blur of motion as the three of them crashed and blundered about the tiny cell. The Fade was dwarfed by his opponents, but he fought like a cornered animal. Something hit the light and sent it swinging. Wild shadows added to the confusion.

They had not been expecting this level of savagery. Heinrich mentally congratulated himself for that as he jerked a knee into someone's face, but then a flailing fist smashed his nose flat. He managed to hook his finger into a snarling mouth and fish-hooked Sharps until the man's face split open. There was an incoherent cry of pain, and that just spurred Heinrich on. Each one of these men was larger than him, and all of them were tough, but he never quit moving, striking, punching, and kicking. He'd been hoping that one of them had been stupid enough to bring a gun into reach, but they'd not given him that opportunity.

Thirty seconds later, Heinrich was in one corner, back to the wall, bruised knuckles raised before him. His shirt was hanging in tatters, one eye was swollen shut, and he could taste blood and feel the grit of broken teeth. Heinrich was not sure if the noise he was hearing was from all the severe blows to his head or if the whistling noise had actually turned into an obvious howl.

The OCI men were standing at the far end, bleeding and shaking. The room was so small that one step would put them back into striking range. The OCI with the new neck piercings leaned against the wall, then took a slow, dazed seat on the floor. He was done.

"So much for not damaging the merchandise. Kid's a scrapper. Forget this . . ." Sharps gasped. He may have maintained some of his striking abilities, but he no longer had a fighter's wind. "Shoot him, Clark."

The man in the hall coldly lifted his gun, pointed it at Heinrich's face, and *exploded*.

The concussion smashed Heinrich against the wall.

It took him a moment to blink himself back to coherence. *What was that?* The hall was painted with blood. The gunman, now flat on his back, raised one arm that now ended in a stump and began to scream.

The explosive hadn't been very large, so it must have been on the OCI man's person . . . There wasn't time to think it through. His opponents had been knocked down as well, but Sharps was already getting back up. Then Heinrich noticed that the light bulb had been knocked out, but somehow he could still see, though the illumination was very odd. The white of Sharps' shirt glowed bright, as did his teeth and eyes, but everything else was lit by some sort of black light that was coming from . . .

"Scheiss!" A small bit of crackling black light had appeared in the bottom of the wall that separated them from Francis' cell. Dust motes were swirling around the strange spot as if it was some sort of vortex. Inside the

strange light was *nothing*, and the nothing was *growing*. The circle inched forward, and as it did so, the bricks around it crumbled into dust and disappeared into the vortex.

Heinrich had no idea what that was, but the way it was devouring the bricks made him very uncomfortable. It was time to *go*. He leapt for the exit.

Again, Sharps was too quick. He caught Heinrich and threw him violently back. Heinrich bounced off the far wall and slid to the floor.

"Fool. Look at that!" Heinrich pointed desperately at the slowly growing . . . *whatever* it was. "Run!"

"Stinkin' Fade." Sharps had his fists up again. "No more of your tricks."

"What is that?" Deych, too, had seen the anomaly. "We gotta get out of here." The blackness had now taken up the bottom half of the wall and a few feet of the floor.

"Not now, Greg. Not 'til he's dead," Sharps growled as Heinrich pushed himself back up. The OCI man had wised up this time, and his approach was methodical. When Heinrich rushed him, the gigantic fists fell like rain. Heinrich managed to latch onto Sharps' coat, but the big man just kept punching him in the side. Heinrich's knees buckled, but before he could fall, Sharps cocked back one arm and smashed a mighty overhand right into Heinrich's skull. The hard floor rushed up to meet him.

"Sharps! We've got to go!" Deych shouted again, the fear obvious.

The OCI man that Heinrich struck in the neck had passed out from blood loss and was slumped on the floor. As the edge of the darkness touched one of his outstretched hands, he was simply pulled into the vortex without a sound, almost as if something had taken hold and dragged him inside. Within a second, his feet disappeared into the black light and he was gone. Deych swore and ran for it. Heinrich tried to crawl for the door, but Sharps kicked him in the side hard enough to lift him off the ground.

The howl turned into a scream as their air was consumed by the void. Heinrich could hardly see the devouring blob through his swollen eyes, but now he could feel it. The void was fueled by magic, and the OCI's nullifiers were pushing against it. Only this thing was so powerful that it laughed at the dampening effect and pushed back. This time the explosion came from above, and it was far stronger. The entire building shook to its foundation. Boards broke and dust rained from the ceiling. It was like being at the receiving end of an artillery bombardment.

It all came flooding back. For the first time in days, Heinrich could feel his Power burning hot, and despite his injuries, he felt very *good.* He had never been deprived of his magic before, and very much hoped that he would never have to do without it again. *Oh, how I have missed you.*

"What was that?" Sharps shouted, confused. Then he noticed the spreading nothingness and froze.

Filled with magic and anger, Heinrich stood up and spit out a wad of blood. "Now it is my turn."

Sharps turned, surprised to see Heinrich still moving. He swung, but lurched as his fist flew cleanly through his target as if Heinrich was made of smoke. He struck again, but it was like attacking the shadows. Sharps' eyes grew wide. "Oh shit."

Heinrich was a Fade, and as such, could make his body insubstantial enough to pass through solid objects for a brief time. He could also take someone else with him. He made himself solid again, reached out, grabbed Sharps by the throat, then Faded them both. Sharps thrashed as they began to sink into the floor. Heinrich let go, and then altered himself just enough to step out of the ground before becoming solid again.

Sharps screamed as the molecules of his feet and ankles fused with the earth.

It was a terrible way to go, with all of those severed nerve endings screaming, trapped, while some horrific darkness came to eat you, but Heinrich wasn't feeling particularly charitable. "Good day, sir," and then he hobbled out the door.

Deych had barely made it into the hall before the explosion had gone off overhead. It appeared that a large chunk of the ceiling had fallen and struck him down. He was stunned, but alive. Heinrich grabbed Deych by the collar and dragged him away. Sharps kept on screaming incoherently, jerking his frozen legs, and windmilling his arms helplessly.

Heinrich got Deych ten feet down the hall, then slapped him until he began to stir. Deych had been hit pretty hard by the debris and it took a moment for his eyelids to flutter awake.

Talking was very painful and Heinrich wondered if they'd managed to crack his jaw. "The attack you are framing us for. Where is it?" Deych looked back at the darkness. It had consumed most of the cell and its edge was spilling into the hall behind them. It was growing faster now. Sharps' screams grew more desperate. "Where? Or I feed you to it!"

"There's a gathering on the mall. Antimagic people are camped out there for a big protest," Deych stammered, unable to take his eyes off the darkness. "There's a truck bomb on the other side of the river. We're going to blow them up."

Heinrich's face hurt too much to smile. It made a sick sort of sense. If the Grimnoir were truly as evil as Bradford Carr was portraying them as, then obviously they would strike directly at their political foes in the most craven and cowardly way possible. The backlash against Actives would be terrible.

"I told you! Let me go! Let me go!"

Heinrich stood up and took another look at the vortex. Now that it was free of the cell he could see that it was uniformly round, with a center that must have begun in the other cell, and it was getting bigger by the second. Francis must have created some sort of spell to destroy the nullifiers, but he wondered if creating a black hole had been part of the plan. It would be interesting to see when it would stop growing . . . Maybe a better question would be *if* it would stop growing.

Sharps' screams stopped abruptly as the nothingness reached him.

"Flee, you fool," Heinrich spat at Deych.

Sullivan Spellbound

Chapter 19

I speak to the just people of the South. You charge that we stir up insurrection among your slaves, and more insidiously, amongst your slaves with dangerous magics. We deny it. Where is your proof? Harper's Ferry! The mad wizard John Brown was no Republican. Despite this slander, we will strive to keep harmony in the Republic. Yet if our sense of duty forbids this, then let us stand firm. Let us have faith that right makes might, and in that faith, let us, to the end, dare to do our duty as we understand it.

—Abraham Lincoln,
Speech at the Cooper Institute, 1860

Mason Island

FAYE COULD HEAR the gunfire and see the occasional flash through the trees. She checked her head map for the fiftieth time and found that her magic still wouldn't work against the island's defenses. Faye, Whisper, and Hammer were sitting in a car parked just north of where the bridge reached land, watching the island.

"We'd best get ready," Whisper said as she glanced up and down the Washington side of the shore. Lights were now on in many windows and people were coming outside to see what the commotion was. Soon the police would arrive, so Whisper would set the bridge on fire to make a mess of things and then they'd have to skulk away.

That was really making Faye mad. Somewhere on that island, Francis and a bunch of her friends were in danger, and she couldn't do a darn thing about it. Here she was, one of the most powerful Actives anybody knew of, with a perfectly good automatic shotgun, bandoleers full of buckshot, a .45, and a great big stag-handled stabbing knife, but with nobody to use any of this useful stuff on. Since Sullivan had said the island was muddy, she'd even worn *pants*. Faye was ready to get to work.

Suddenly there was a huge flash of light on the island. It was so bright that it was almost like looking into a photographer's pan of flash powder when it went off. It took a second before they heard the loud *whump* that was then followed by an ominous rumble. An orange glow began to grow behind the trees, obviously a fire, and Faye could see the smoke curling slowly in front of it.

"What in the world was that?" Hammer exclaimed.

"I don't know." Faye checked for the fifty-first time . . . only this time her map could actually reach the island. There were a few smaller bits that were all blurry on the periphery where some of the other little Dymaxions were still working, but the great big one was off. There was something else really weird going on, a confusing circle that seemed to poke a hole in her head map, but other than that, she was good to go. "All right!"

"Faye, can you—" Whisper turned, but Faye was already gone.

Crow was thoroughly enjoying himself. He couldn't remember the last time he'd had this much fun. The Grimnoir had shot him hundreds of times, but it didn't matter. A Summoned was given form in this world by gathering up stray matter and coalescing it into a physical body. The smoking substance that most referred to as demon's ink bound the creature's essence to this world, and in order to banish the creature, the created body had to be battered to the point until most of that essence had escaped. On a form as resilient as this one, that was a very difficult task.

Sure, this wasn't exactly what the Summoned had looked like back when it had been a real, living, breathing being on its own world. With some effort he could make the bodies appear completely human, or he could set them free, to take on a more familiar form. Crow knew that the Summoner's subconscious played a role in how the creatures appeared here. He didn't want to think too hard about why his always tended to look so *evil*. He figured it had something to do with all those hellfire-and-brimstone sermons he'd had to endure as a child.

The bullets felt like beestings. The Grimnoir were falling back through the trees, each one pausing in turn to stop and futilely shoot at him as their friends ran by. *Let them run*. It made the chase more rewarding.

However, one of them wasn't the running type. "Get to the boats," Sullivan ordered the others. The Heavy stood in the middle of a path, slamming another magazine into a funny looking rifle. "I'll slow him down."

"How do you figure you're going to do that?" Crow laughed. The monster in the back of his shared mind was screaming for blood, but he told it to shut up. This stupid Heavy had embarrassed him, made his life difficult, and was one of the backbone members of his enemy's Society. He had a reputation for being especially tough, so Sullivan's death would demoralize the rest. Crow wanted to enjoy this.

Sullivan didn't waste time with talking, he just shouldered the machine gun and fired. Crow felt the pulsing impacts as the bullets tracked up his torso and into his face. There were no organs inside a Summoned, no bones to break, no weak spots to exploit, just a shell filled with hate, but Sullivan's bullets were spilling precious ink. The flaming blood set the brush on fire and Crow's body was wreathed in smoke. Every drop spilled made the body weaker, and though he still had plenty to spare, it was time to end this nonsense before any of them escaped. So Crow covered the ground in a few huge steps, swung a claw, and knocked the gun away. Sullivan jumped back and scrambled to draw his sidearm. *Pathetic.* It was like human beings moved in slow motion. Crow simply lifted one gigantic foot, placed it on Sullivan's chest, and shoved him back. Crow didn't even push hard, but the mortal still flew ten feet through the air to splash into a puddle.

"This isn't even fair," Crow said. "You know, some of my men are taking your buddies over to the Capitol for a little show right now. Maybe I should keep you in one piece? Use you the same way? What do you think?"

Sullivan got to his knees, lifted his pistol, and shot Crow in the mouth. "Ah, never mind then." Crow leaned over and backhanded him.

Sullivan slid through the mud until he hit a tree. That stopped him solid and the Heavy cried out as something broke inside of him. Playtime was over. Crow reached down, stuck a claw through Sullivan's bandoleers and hoisted him into the air. He had never tasted the blood of a Heavy before, and as he pulled Sullivan's throat toward his mouth, he wondered idly what it would taste like.

THWACK!

One of Crow's legs went out from under him and he was falling. Something had hit him on the back of the knee and levered him right down. Sullivan went rolling away as Crow tore through the branches and landed in the mud.

A man was standing there, holding some sort of metal club. He raised it overhead and shouted a war cry in a foreign language. *Japanese?* Crow lifted one gigantic forearm and easily blocked the club, but the spikes ripped holes in his shell to let out the precious smoke. He was fast, but no normal human was as fast as a Greater Summoned, and Crow easily knocked the man across the trail. "You Grimnoir don't know when to quit."

The Oriental hit the ground hard, but he got right back up. Crow could admire the tenacity. "I am no Grimnoir!" He lifted the club, roared, "*TOKUGAWA!*" and charged.

Imperium? Sullivan was making all sorts of strange new friends. *No matter.* This guy could be First Iron Guard, but he wasn't shit without magic against a demon of this caliber. Crow spread his claws wide and prepared to eviscerate the Jap, and then for a split second, it was as bright as day.

The explosion startled him as it seemed to rock the whole island. Crow instinctively turned in time to see orange flames boiling up over the OCI compound. The air pressure seemed to change and he felt his own connection to the Summoned's body strengthen. *The Dymaxion!*

Crow turned to finish the Jap, but he wasn't there. Instead, the Jap had leapt high into the air and was on the way back down. *Brute!* Crow tried to get out of the way, but it was too late. The spiked club slammed into his shoulder with a blow that would have pulverized bones if he'd had any. He managed to slash his claws across the Jap's chest as the club came back around. The spikes pierced Crow's chest and sent him reeling, but the Jap spun away in a spray of blood. Crow went after him. A Brute could not be underestimated. He had to eliminate the Jap quickly.

Only Crow couldn't move. It was like trying to walk into a tidal wave. He couldn't lift his arms. His feet sunk into the soft ground. The smoke pouring from his wounds suddenly came shooting out in pressurized jets and for the first time Crow felt the demon's pain.

Sullivan! The Heavy appeared before him, covered in dirt, a grimace of concentration on his face as he hammered Crow with a multitude of extra gravities. The other Grimnoir were coming out of the trees behind Sullivan, guns blazing. Crow was frozen in a storm of lead. He realized they had a Mover as well, as rocks turned into missiles and tree branches struck like spears. A multitude of lacerations ripped through the demon's skin, showering flaming ink everywhere. Crow tried to roar, but smoke poured from his mouth instead of sound.

The demon was screaming inside of its head, furious and confused at the treatment. Crow tried to force it back, but it was much harder that time, and he started to panic. *What would happen if the demon took over while he was still inside? No. Focus. Get back!* Luckily, the demon retreated before Crow's Power.

The waves of gravity kept on crashing. The Heavy couldn't possibly keep up that level of Power for long, and the second it let off, Crow would kill them all. Sullivan was wobbling. He'd been hit hard earlier and was feeling the injury now. Crow could sense the gravity weakening, and he managed to take a step forward.

Another Grimnoir rushed to Sullivan's side and laid a glowing hand on him. Sullivan stood a little straighter and the pressure coming down on Crow increased. *The Grimnoir had a Healer!*

"On my mark, cut your Power!" The Jap was back. His shirt was hanging open and several deep lacerations were dripping blood, but a few of the Imperium kanji spells were visible on his skin, burning bright. The Jap hoisted the ink-soaked club as he gathered all of this awful Brute magic for a single shot. He closed his eyes and waited as the magic forces built until Crow could *see* the Power.

"NO!" Crow and the Summoned shrieked at the same time.

The Brute opened his eyes. "Now." He bellowed as he swung, the steel club moving through the air with an inhuman speed. The crushing gravities fell away and Crow could move, but only for an instant before the impact.

Crow's torso exploded into a black mist.

There was no brain inside the Summoned's form, its intelligence was spread throughout the entire being. Crow's consciousness was ripped into multiple pieces, but for a brief moment he could still see through the demon's eyes as the horned head went flipping through the air. Then the Summoned's connection to this world was broken and its spirit was sent hurtling back into the ether from which it had come.

Several miles away, Crow slammed back into his real body, pieces at a time. It was like a brilliant, jagged shaft of lightning drove through his skull and twisted. Crow screamed and convulsed, as he fell from his chair to lay twitching on the floor.

Crow was delirious from pain, but it was almost as if some of the savagery of the demon had returned with him. He wanted to kill these Grimnoir. He needed to taste their blood and snap their bones. His Power was burnt and scattered. It would take a minute to gather up enough to Summon again, but he'd destroy them if it was the last thing he did.

Desperate and delusional, Crow reached out for the greatest Summoned he had ever discovered.

The smoke gradually cleared. The forest was on fire; everybody had been splattered with burning demon bits, but Crow was gone.

Sullivan thanked the new Healer and pushed him away. Crow had pulverized him, but Dianatkhah had got him stabilized enough for the spells carved on Sullivan's chest to handle the rest. "I'm fine. Save your Power for somebody who needs it more." Toru was looking rough. He too had kanji engraved on him, and they were emitting heat and light as they pulled in Power to keep him alive. Crow had tagged him good, and the Iron Guard's chest looked like somebody had slashed him with a pair of butcher knives. "Fix him," Sullivan said, gesturing at Toru.

To his credit, Dianatkhah only hesitated for a second before moving over to put his hands on the Iron Guard. They might not like him, nor trust him, but Toru had just proved that he was mighty useful in a fight.

Diamond came running up. At some point one lens of his glasses had been cracked. "The compound's burning. I sent Simmons and Mottl forward to secure the breach."

"Good." Sullivan did a quick head count. The rest of the knights were present. Ian wasn't looking so good, but that was probably from the drain of having one of his Summoned destroyed rather than from any physical injuries. With the Dymaxion down, the tables had just turned in their favor. Dan Garrett had found Sullivan's BAR and tossed it over. Sullivan caught the massive gun in one hand. "Let's go."

The knights moved forward. Sullivan paused long enough to pick up one bent half of Toru's spiked club. He'd broken the solid steel bar against the demon. The one piece in Sullivan's hand weighed twenty pounds. He held it up to show the Iron Guard. "Nice shot."

The Iron Guard gave him a small nod. He seemed a little misty-eyed. "That was my favorite tetsubo. They will pay for that. Come. Let us kill these dogs."

The broken chunk of steel landed in the puddle with a splash. Sullivan turned toward the burning compound. He figured that if the OCI knew what was good for them, they'd surrender now.

Francis had been dragged, kicking and fighting, up the stairs, down a corridor, to where someone else had pulled a burlap sack over his head, and then he'd been carried outside. He could tell it was outside because it was colder, stunk of smoke, and the gunfire was louder. There'd been some shouting between the OCI men to not wait for Heinrich, and then he was tossed onto something that, from the rocking and the sound of the water, could only be a small boat. An outboard motor had started, and then they were heading across the river. Francis didn't even know which direction they were going.

He had struggled against the cords on his wrist, but an OCI man sitting right across from him had growled at him to stop. They probably didn't want any rope burns to show up during the autopsy. Francis had tried to be more discreet when he went back to struggling. That had earned him a smack over the top of his head. "I got a .38 on you. Try anything stupid and I'll gut-shoot you and roll you over the side."

They'd been on the river for only a few seconds when a horrendous noise came from behind. Francis could even see the flash of light through the rough fibers of the hood. The boat rocked wildly as somebody fell against the motor.

"What was that?"

"Headquarters blew up! Look out."

There were slaps and splashes as debris fell out of the sky. Francis unconsciously scrunched lower against the wooden seat.

"Hell. That had to have taken out the big Dymaxion. We should head back."

Francis hurried and checked his Power, but there was still nothing.

"Proceed with the plan. They've still got the portable units, same as I'd—"

CRACK!

This explosion was much closer—so close in fact that the impact knocked Francis off his seat and pelted him with stinging bits. The boat shuddered and lurched. Cold water came washing over the side. Francis felt a moment of terrible panic about going in the water with his hands tied behind him, but the boat stayed upright.

His ears were ringing, but somewhere behind that he could hear screaming; then there was a loud splash as that man fell overboard.

"What the *hell*!" There was creaking and banging as the men tried to take cover. "Where'd that come from? Are we under fire?"

"No. Griffin's chest just *popped*! What was that?"

"I don't know. What are you waiting for?" the man closest to Francis shouted. "Get us out of here!"

"Shouldn't we pull him out?"

"Water that red? He's dead. Go already!" The motor roared and they were moving, bouncing against the current.

Fuller had said that when that spell hit them, the Dymaxions would blow up. Francis checked again, and almost couldn't believe it. His magic was back. *Yes! Buckminster Fuller, whatever Ray paid you wasn't nearly enough.*

First things first. He was sick of being tied up. Francis focused on the cords around his wrist. He didn't even need to see them. Being a Mover was like having a bunch of invisible extra hands, and he could feel the shape of the knot in his mind. It had been tied fast, simple and sloppy. Francis started picking it apart. A few seconds later the ropes fell away.

He'd only heard three voices, and one of those had the misfortune of having a Dymaxion in his pocket. That left two. Piece of cake, but for this, he'd need to be able to see. Francis concentrated on the burlap sack and it flew off.

The OCI man sitting across from him had a revolver in his hand. He saw the bag go flying and realized what was happening. The muzzle moved toward Francis as the trigger was pulled, but Francis was already concentrating on stopping the cylinder from turning. Just like using your hands: if you want to stop a revolver that hasn't been cocked, just grab the cylinder.

The G-man's eyes widened as Francis threw a bunch of extra Power against the gun. Might as well, he'd been saving it up for days and felt like he had plenty to spare. The man fought, but the revolver gradually turned in his sweaty hands until the muzzle was pointing back at his face, then Francis let go of the cylinder and concentrated on the trigger. "No! *No*!" *BLAM.*

One down.

Francis turned just as the man at the motor realized what was going on and went for his gun, but it was too late for him too. The first agent's revolver leapt into Francis' outstretched hand, and he managed to fire twice before the last OCI goon tumbled over the side to disappear into the Potomac.

The shore was near and the lights of Washington were behind it. The boat had been pointed at this particular patch of shoreline for a reason. A big delivery truck was parked there, and he saw a shape pass in front of the headlights. Francis concentrated his Power on the motor, grabbed the stick, and kept them on course. That truck was probably OCI and related to Carr's mystery attack. He sure as hell wasn't going to let that happen on his watch. There were certainly going to be more gunmen there, but Francis had three bullets and a whole lot of Power. This was about to get ugly.

Faye's job was simple. Mr. Sullivan had told her to be herself.

So that meant causing lots of trouble.

Unable to spot Francis or Heinrich amidst the confusion and the swirling magical oddity at the bottom of the main building, she picked the room that had the most people in it. From the way Lance had described the place, this was the OCI's command center. That seemed like a relatively safe place to raise a ruckus. Sure, there were a bunch of folks in it who wanted to shoot her or send her to prison, but none of them were actively launching bullets at the moment.

Traveling to the back of the command center, Faye found herself in a confused scene. The room was filled with so much smoke and dust it was hard to breathe. There was a bank of radios on one wall, but they were wrecked and dripping sparks, and a big piece of the roof had caved in. She was a couple floors under where the big Dymaxion had been, but Faye could smell it burning with a sort of noxious chemical stink.

A few of the people in this room had been injured in the blast, but several of them were still up and scurrying about. Some were shouting orders, others had guns and were watching out the broken windows or guarding the door, a few were pulling papers out of some filing cabinets and throwing them into a fire that had been started inside a garbage can.

"Grims are in the courtyard, sir."

"What happened to that fool Crow?" asked a fat old man who was holding a handkerchief over his face. "I swear he's failed me for the last time. The robots are prepped? Very well. Send them in." One of the men picked up a phone, cranked a charge handle, and started giving orders. The fat man turned to the ones at the burn barrel. "Make it snappy. I'm going to sue Dymaxion into the poorhouse for their faulty workmanship! Years of work ruined . . . I was mad to ever listen to Crow's ideas, luring these damned wizards here. I want everything sensitive eliminated, including the experiments in building two."

That made one of the burners pause from his shoveling of papers. "But . . . those are—"

"People?" The fat man strode over to loom over his subordinate. "They're science projects! Nothing more!"

"Sorry, Dr. Carr." The OCI man bowed his head and went back to throwing papers in the fire.

Science projects? Lance had said there were other prisoners. Were they doing things to them like they did in the Imperium? The possibility made Faye extra mad.

Nobody had seen her yet, but she was fed up with listening to these jerks, so Faye lifted her shotgun and pointed it at the nearest enemy. She hadn't really thought this part through. She was extremely good at killing folks, but these had information that could clear her friends' names, so just shooting them, especially the fat one, was out of the question. "Reach for the sky!" Faye shouted, because that was what they said on the cowboy radio serials when they captured outlaws, and it seemed as reasonable as anything else.

It didn't work nearly as well for her as it did on the radio, though.

"Traveler!" Carr shouted, and ten men all decided to shoot her. Faye pulled the trigger. She was so close that the buckshot didn't even separate. She simply blasted a big hole through the first man, then she Traveled to the opposite side of the room. She'd killed a second one before any of them managed to get a shot off, and that was aimed at the spot she'd just left. Faye ran to the side, jerking the trigger on her automatic shotgun, and as soon as they focused on her and her head map screamed danger incoming, she instinctively Traveled away before bullets filled the air where she'd been standing. Glass shattered and lead ricocheted off metal.

Faye hit the ground and rolled under a desk. She waited a moment and let the bad guys do her job for her. Panicked, confused by the smoke and the flickering lights, with their imaginations filling in grey-eyed killers popping into existence everywhere, they began to shoot at anything moving, which was mostly their friends. Faye grinned as she pulled shells off her bandoleer and stuffed them into her shotgun. She loved her job.

Seeing a pair of legs coming close, she blew his knees off, and then she shot him in the chest when he got to her level. Then she Traveled out from under the desk to the far wall, where she shot another man in the back, jumped to the other corner and had to fire several times to finally get enough lead to go through a filing cabinet to hit a fellow that thought he could hide from her. Shotgun empty, she pulled her .45 with one hand while stepping through space, appeared behind somebody who was shouting profanities, and put a single bullet in the back of his neck. His buddy turned toward her and she shot him in the chest four times before he could even lift his pistol.

Faye paused to check her head map. There were bodies strewn everywhere. That's what they got for not reaching for the sky like she'd told them to! Except for the crackling flames, the room was deathly quiet. *Did I kill everybody already? So much for confessions.* But happily, her head map told her that the fat doctor in charge was limping down the stairs. Her head map also said that whatever the oddness was below, it was getting bigger, right quick, and it wasn't like anything she'd ever felt before. Instinct told her that if she Traveled next to that thing, there would be no coming back.

She'd deal with the doctor in a minute. It wasn't like anybody could outrun her. Faye went over to the filing cabinet and pulled out some of the papers that they'd been trying to destroy. There was lots of writing and it seemed to be in code, which meant it must be super important, so Faye gathered up as much as she could possibly carry in both arms and Traveled away.

"What the hell are those?" Dan asked as he risked a glance around Sullivan's shoulder.

Grey metal forms were marching out of the main building and across the hard-packed dirt of the OCI compound. These machines were similar to the one that Sullivan had met at the EGE factory, with rounded bodies and ungainly limbs, only these were slightly bigger and each one had a single glowing blue eye in the center of their rectangular heads. It reminded him of an illustration from a *Popular Mechanics* article about the future of warfare, only this was right now, and these things belonged to the secret police rather than the Army.

"Mechanical men," he muttered, then he raised his voice so the rest could hear. "Take cover!"

The knights had come through the hole in the wall and used the outbuildings and parked vehicles to cover their approach, but the robots were blocking their way. The roof of the main building was on fire, and it provided enough illumination to see at least half a dozen of the things. The automatons all froze in place at the same time. A beam of light, bright as the headlamps on a car, erupted from each mechanical man's eye, and the heads slowly began to turn side to side like a searchlight.

Toru crouched off to the side. "So you Americans have *gakutensoku* of your own? I was not aware of this." Before Sullivan could respond, Toru stepped out from behind cover, held his machine gun at his hip, and fired as he ran to the side. Bullets sparked against one of the robots.

Three of the blue headlights locked onto the Iron Guard and three arms rose simultaneously, returning fire just as Toru dove behind the corner of another building. "Ours are faster"—Toru shouted as a bullet punctured the wall next to his face—"and more accurate."

The robots let loose a torrent of machine gun fire, working their flashing arms back and forth, piercing the knights' meager cover. A bullet went through a car door and Simmons' leg went out from under him. The Torch seemed surprised as he hit the ground and a torrent of blood spilled from the jagged exit wound. Heedless of the danger, Dianatkhah crawled to Simmons and went about trying to save his friend's life.

"Cover the Healer!" Sullivan picked a robot and the slow thunder of his BAR began. He worked the gun across the metal body, burning just a bit of Power to make the gun heavier and more controllable. Sullivan was an artist with a machine gun and he picked different spots—legs, arms, joints, neck, the head—looking for a weakness. The light of the single eye went out just as it was able to swivel over to shoot back. Bullets ripped a line up the dirt several feet away. "The eyes are how they aim," Sullivan shouted as he pulled back to reload. It sounded rather simple when he said it that way, but you never knew until you tried.

Off to the left, three of the blue lights went out simultaneously as Diamond used his Power to hurl debris against them. They continued shooting, but wildly, flinging bullets everywhere.

One of the blinded robots lifted its other arm. With a roar, a gout of flame rolled past, forcing Sullivan to retreat to avoid being engulfed. "Flamethrower!" The robot turned, casting a wide arc of destruction, igniting vehicles and buildings.

But not men. Their wounded Torch lifted one bloody hand from his ruined leg and extended it toward the fire, which recoiled, stopped, grew, and then was forced back against the pressurized jet. The fire climbed back into the robot's arm and ignited the fuel stored inside.

The explosion rocked the courtyard. Fire washed over several of the other mechanical men. One of them ignited, wobbled a few steps on its duck feet before it too exploded into a cloud of shrapnel and bolts. The others must not have been packing flamethrowers, since they caught fire, but didn't burst. A flaming robot charged Sullivan, the rounds for its machine gun popping as they cooked off inside its arm. Sullivan hit it with a wave of gravity and sent it tumbling away.

Mottl used his Ice magic and hit a few of the robots with a burst of extreme cold. The humid air froze and clung to them in a sparkling sheen. These seemed to grow sluggish and confused. Apparently, robots weren't that resilient against temperature extremes, but before Sullivan could yell encouragement to Mottl, the Icebox caught a bullet in the stomach. On the right, the robot that had shot him lurched as Ian's latest Summoned collided with it, took it down, and hammered its gigantic fists against the robot's head. A line ruptured and hydraulic fluid sprayed across the Summoned's pale flesh.

The Summoned was knocked over by the impact of an explosive shell. Another robot had clanked its way through the drifting smoke, and this one had a recoilless rifle mounted on one shoulder. As it turned his way, Sullivan shot at it; Diamond put out its eye with a brick, but it still got off a blind shot. The wall next to Sullivan turned into an expanding cloud of shrapnel and he went rolling through the dirt. The Healing spells on his body were burning, trying to keep up with the cuts and abrasions. By the time he lifted his face out of the mud, Toru had knocked the robot down and was beating it savagely with what appeared to be a bumper torn off a car. Dianatkhah was dragging Mottl away.

It was chaos.

Dan appeared next to Sullivan and shouted between bursts from his Thompson, "Times like this . . . can make a Mouth . . . feel a little inadequate!"

"So let's go find you some bad guys made outta meat." Sullivan slammed in a fresh mag as he got up. "I'm heading for the command center. Cover me." He ran for it while Dan emptied the remainder of the Thompson's drum. Sullivan slid in behind a disabled, ice-crusted robot just as a blue targeting light swept overhead. The freezing cold of the metal could be felt through the rough fabric of his coat. He waited for the light to pass, then sprang up and continued on.

A robot lumbered out from behind a burning truck. Sullivan ripped gravity to the side, and the top-heavy thing toppled onto its back, only to be immediately engulfed in magical fire. The next robot that appeared through the smoke was speared by a steel bar that Diamond had hurled across the compound, and as it stumbled back, a blast of ice struck it in the head.

Sullivan reached the mechanical man, grabbed the

steel bar protruding from its chest and ripped it free in a spray of hydraulic fluid. He swung hard, and the iced-over head shattered like glass.

The robots were outmaneuvered, outfought, outwitted, and their numbers were dwindling rapidly. They were no match for the combined Powers of the knights. They shouldn't have sent a machine to do a man's job. Ian's Summoned tackled the last visible mechanical man and began to pummel it into scrap. "Diamond, see to your wounded and clear this compound. I'm going in."

As he reached the large door the robots had filed out of, Sullivan took cover to one side and risked a peek. Inside was a wide-open, pitch-black space. He went around the corner and— *Wham!*

Tasting blood, he hit the ground hard. The robot had been just on the other side of the entrance and it had nailed him with one big metal arm. Dazed, Sullivan gathered his Power to knock the robot aside, but the machine gun arm was already coming up. A terrible blue light scalded his eyes.

The machine gun roared. Sullivan flinched, but death didn't come. There was a horrendous racket as metal was shredded by bullets. The blue headlight turned away enough that he could see again. Partially blinded, it took Sullivan a second to realize that the robot's gun arm had been twisted back against its own torso. A figure, dwarfed by the immense robot, was shoving it back. "Get up, Heavy!" Toru shouted.

The Brute slammed his fist against the robot's chest, and the huge dent indicated that he was burning his Power hard. The robot crashed back into the warehouse, and Toru immediately clambered up its side and drove one hand through the narrow gap between spindly neck and armored chest. His fist came out clutching a handful of wires and a hose squirting oil. The robot's legs collapsed and it toppled over, but Toru wasn't finished. He grabbed the rectangular head in both hands and wrenched it around backwards. Metal tore and rivets popped, until the head was hanging loose and useless. The light flickered and went out.

Toru stepped off the dead robot. "You call this garbage a mechanical man? Cumbersome, slow, poorly balanced . . . The Tanaka Engineering Works' *gakutensoku* is superior in every way. Your Cogs should be ashamed of this inferior design." Reaching down, he took hold of the machine gun arm and pried open the metal casing. "I need this more than you do, my metal foe. Hmmm . . ." Toru tore out the Browning 1919 machine gun and a long belt of ammunition. "Though, I must admit that you Americans gave yours a bigger gun," he admitted begrudgingly.

The Healing spells on his chest were certainly earning their keep tonight. Sullivan got to his feet. The lack of noise from the courtyard indicated that his team gotten all the mechanical men. "Thanks."

Toru just grunted a noncommittal response as he lifted the feed tray to check the condition of his borrowed machine gun. They didn't see the final robot inside until it turned on its eye and illuminated the Iron Guard in blue light.

Sullivan's Spike reversed gravity, and the gigantic machine fell upward to hit the steel beams in the ceiling.

Sullivan cut his Power and the robot dropped. It crashed hard into the floor where it lay twitching and kicking. The two of them riddled the mechanical man with bullets until the light died and it lay still in a spreading puddle of oil.

"Normally, this would be the part where you thank me for returning the favor and saving your life."

"Yes. Normally . . . If we were court ladies instead of warriors," Toru answered. "Shall we continue onward or do you wish to stop and discuss your feelings over tea?"

Sullivan looked forward to the day that the two of them would be able to finish their fight. "Let's go."

The only other passenger still aboard had a .38-caliber hole right between the eyes, so Francis used his mind to steer the rudder while he hid in the front of the boat. There was a tarp, so Francis covered himself, got low, and waited to hit land. The OCI on shore had more than likely heard the gunshots. If he was lucky, they would come running to investigate when they didn't see their friends, and even luckier if they didn't have a Dymaxion.

Behind him, Mason Island was on fire and there was so much gunfire it sounded like Fourth of July firecrackers. As he got closer to shore, he saw that to the south the Washington side of the bridge was burning. It was quite a ways off, but the sirens of the police cars stuck there could be heard. Closer now, he pulled the tarp over his head and waited.

He was terribly nervous, but his Power felt ready, which meant that there was probably no Dymaxion here, or at least if there was, they hadn't turned it on yet. There was a crack of wood against rock, and the whole craft shuddered hard. The boat slowly turned sideways and ground against solid earth.

Footsteps. Somebody was running this way. There was swearing, and Francis could only assume that they were playing a hand torch over the boat. The boat shifted as some weight landed in the middle of it. Francis pulled down the tarp just enough to see. A man in work clothes stood over the body of the thug Francis had shot in the face. Francis hesitated, because he had no way of knowing if this man was OCI or not.

Keeping his light on the dead man, the stranger grabbed a handful of hair and lifted. He swore again, then turned and shouted back toward the truck. "It's Pete. They shot Pete!"

That'll do. Francis shot him through the tarp. It wasn't like he could use the sights that way, but they were nice and close. The first bullet hit him low in the back. He grunted in surprise and stood straight up. So Francis adjusted the muzzle upwards and fired again. That one got him right between the shoulder blades, but instead of falling over, he started climbing out of the boat. This was a perfect example of why Francis preferred a .45 to a .38. The man landed on the rocks, shouting that it was an ambush while reaching into his pocket. He came out with a little pistol and popped off a couple of wild shots at the boat before turning and running. Francis sat up, and since he couldn't see the sights in the dark, pointed and squeezed off his last shot. That time the OCI man threw his arms wide and fell on his face.

There was more shouting from the truck. Francis could easily hunker down here and wait for help . . . But that truck was part of a bigger plot, and the way Bradford Carr had talked about it, innocent people were going to die if he didn't stop them. "Time to be heroic."

Francis clambered over the side. Water splashed up to his knees, but he quickly moved up the rocks. He was out of ammo and needed to find items that could be weapons with his Power. The more something weighed, the harder it was to manipulate. The further away it was, the harder it was to control, and if something was more than forty feet away, it was pretty safe. Sure, he could throw something further than that, but good luck hitting anything.

Sadly, the truck was parked nearly twice that far away and there was absolutely nothing between him and it worth hiding behind. He concentrated on the downed man's dropped pistol and it zipped over to him. Francis snatched it out of midair and ran for the truck. Somebody moved in front of the headlights and a gun boomed. The shot was so close that he could hear the bullet whine past his ear. Francis raised the unfamiliar pistol and fired wildly. He had to get closer.

Suddenly, Francis was falling and couldn't figure out why. He landed hard on his face, and then he felt a searing flash of heat in his thigh. He'd been shot. *The son of a bitch shot me!*

He had to get up. These men were about to do something terrible and he was the only one that could stop them. Francis was far more furious than scared, and he shoved himself right back up. Pain flared through him when his foot hit the ground, but it didn't matter. He had to get closer to use his magic. Limping forward, another bullet clipped him. This time the pain radiated up his arm, and Francis looked down, astonished, to see a hole right through his left wrist. Then it was as if somebody had taken a spear and driven it through his chest.

Shit. I've been shot in the chest. But he was still alive. Good thing it was too dark for proper aiming or that one might have been in his heart. He kept on limping, raised the little pistol and cranked off the rest of the magazine in the general direction of the truck. There was a clang of metal and one of the headlights went out. The shadow in front of the truck seemed to be reloading while the door of the cab opened and another person leapt out.

It was close enough. The cheap little pistol clicked when Francis pulled the trigger on an empty chamber. Francis opened his hand and let it fall, but he reached out and took hold of it with his Power. It floated in the air while he concentrated on the shadow in front of the truck, then Francis shoved it with all his might. It wasn't nearly as aerodynamic as a serving tray, but the pistol blurred through the air, guided precisely, and Francis steered it directly into the OCI man's face. Teeth shattered and the gun hit so hard that the slide broke off and the recoil spring shot out the side.

Francis limped closer. He was having a hard time breathing. It was too dark to spot anything else to throw. The ground was just grass. Everything seemed *blurry*. The rocks at the shore were too big to lift. The truck driver had pulled a gun. Desperate, Francis reached out with his Power and slapped it down. It was too far to hit the driver very hard, but the gun discharged into the ground at his feet. *Closer.* The process repeated, only this time Francis hit him a little bit harder and the next round struck the dirt. *Closer.* Francis was losing blood, but he'd never been this mad before. The gun came up again, and Francis surged his Power desperately. There was no subtlety, and instead of a careful invisible hand, this was a mighty fist. A wave of telekinetic force slammed into the OCI man's hands so hard that Francis could hear bones break across the beach. He'd never done anything like that before. The gun fell from ruined hands. *Closer.*

His lungs ached. It was like breathing fire. The first one was getting up, spitting out mouthfuls of blood and reaching for his gun. Anger filled Francis, and this time his invisible hands reached out, took hold of the man's eyeballs, and *squeezed.* He screamed, so Francis gave his Power one extra shove and was rewarded with two sickening pops.

He stumbled. He had to stop the bleeding soon or he was going to die. *Closer.* He was next to the truck. Both of the OCI men were screaming their heads off. One blind, one with ruined hands. Francis spotted a pistol on the ground, tugged on it, and it flew over. The driver tried to run, but Francis shot him in the back and he fell. Then he turned and shot the blind one in the head.

Blood was pumping out of his leg. He'd seen enough combat to know that a leg wound bleeding that much was really bad, but he couldn't stop to look at it yet. There might be more men. Francis made it to the back of the truck. Whatever was back there was heavy, and the big truck was sitting low under its load. The bed was covered in canvas tied shut with ropes. He ripped apart the knots and flung the canvas open with his mind before spinning around the edge. There was nobody back there. He'd gotten them all.

Woozy, Francis slowly lowered the pistol. The truck was packed full of barrels and the whole thing reeked of chemicals. A length of cannon fuse led into one of the barrels.

There had to be a couple thousand pounds of explosives in the truck. It was a bomb. A really *big* bomb.

He found himself facedown. Francis was unsure how he'd gotten there, but the grass was cool and damp against his cheek. Everything else was going numb. *Good work, Francis. You saved the day,* he told himself before passing out from blood loss.

Chapter 20

If you want a picture of the future, imagine a boot stamping on the human face—forever.

—Eric Arthur Blair,
Editorial in G.K.'s Weekly. 1927

OCI Headquarters

THE UNITED STATES Coordinator of Information, Bradford Carr, Ph.D., was trapped in his office. He was against one wall, back pressed against a multitude of plaques and awards, nervously sweating, while a Siberian tiger sat on its haunches in the middle of the room, watching him carefully. Carr had inched toward some of the display weapons, but a low growl from the tiger had informed him of what a terrible idea that would be.

"Nice catch, Lance," Sullivan said as he entered the office.

"Thanks. Big as he is, it would be like eating a water buffalo, which is very tempting right now, you have no idea, but I figured we'd want him alive."

The esoteric weapons were neat and all, but Sullivan

marveled at all of the books. From what he knew about the Coordinator, this place was a treasure trove of information on magic. Hell, he would have done this job just to loot this library, let alone rescue his friends, but first things first.

"Let me go or you'll regret this," Carr sneered. "I've got a force of robots that will—"

"We already broke them. Your men are either dead or swimming, and we destroyed your pet demon too. So save your breath." Sullivan turned to Lance. "It looks like Whisper blocked the bridge for now, but we need to get a move on."

"Francis and Heinrich?" There was dried blood all over the tiger's face, but none of it appeared to be from the tiger.

There was a rasp from the door. "I am here." Sullivan turned to see a very battered Heinrich Koenig. His face was swollen with bruises and cuts and his shirt was hanging in blood-stained tatters. He'd found a pump shotgun somewhere. "But they took Francis away."

It was good to see the Fade had made it. Sullivan had taken a real liking to the tough German. Sullivan strode over and punched Carr in his ample stomach. Sullivan took it easy, but only because he didn't want to accidently kill the man. Carr sank to the carpet, purple-faced and gagging. "Where'd you take him?"

"Go to hell, Active rabble," Carr gasped.

"We should question him somewhere else," Heinrich suggested.

"Yeah, cops are going to be on the—"

"No. There is a black hole growing in the basement

of the main building. It is devouring everything and expanding rapidly. We only have a few minutes."

"A black hole?" It could never be simple.

"I've got to get her out of here. I'm about out of Power, and I don't think you're going to want her around when I lose control," Lance said through the tiger. "Catch you boys later." The animal turned and bounded from the room.

Heinrich calmly stepped out of the way to let the predator pass. "I cannot emphasize this enough. We really must be going as well."

That meant it was seriously bad. Heinrich certainly wasn't the dramatic type. Diamond had secured the building that Lance had said housed the other prisoners. There was nothing else keeping them here. Sullivan looked sadly at the shelves of books. Sometimes life just wasn't fair.

Toru appeared behind Heinrich so silently that he even made the Fade jump, and that was saying something. "Sullivan, your prisoners have been freed and are being taken to the boats, but something strange is happening at the main building—"

"Told you," Heinrich said as he studied Toru suspiciously. "Who are you?"

"That's our new Iron Guard," Sullivan said. "He's okay. I'll explain later."

"I am imprisoned for a brief time and everything goes to hell." Heinrich shrugged. "Very well. I am Heinrich Koenig."

"Toru." The Iron Guard nodded. "You seem more accepting than the others of your kind."

"Oh, I despise all Imperium scum, but I have had a very difficult day. I will worry about it when we are not being sucked into a magical vortex, which will be happening very shortly. Speaking of which . . ."

Sullivan grabbed Carr by the neck and hoisted him to his feet. He gave a quick pat-down but the Coordinator seemed to be unarmed.

"You're Heavy Jake Sullivan, aren't you?"

"Yep."

"I was afraid of that," Carr muttered. "You have a considerable reputation in some circles."

"You picked the wrong man to slander. Come on."

"Wait, Mr. Sullivan. I know you're a student of magic. If he is telling the truth about our impending destruction, there is something priceless we must take with us. I have in my possession here the singlemost valuable magical tome in existence. To lose its knowledge would be a tragedy for the entire human race."

It went against his better judgment, but Sullivan let go long enough for the Coordinator to pick up a large book off of his desk. If he'd so much as made a move for a drawer that could conceal a gun, he'd have gotten himself Spiked to the roof. "Give me that." Sullivan snatched the book away. Flipping through the pages, he didn't recognize the language, but it was absolutely *filled* with complicated spells. They looked legit. "My God."

"I knew you would understand. If you didn't have such a reputation for stubbornness, you are exactly the kind of man that I would have approached concerning my grand vision."

Vision? Sullivan snorted. Just like the visionaries of the

Imperium, the Kaiser, the Soviets, Carr's vision was just another group of assholes wanting to control everybody else. Sullivan was sick and tired of visionaries. "Shut up."

Toru had moved to the wall of weapons and picked out a long Japanese sword. He set the 1919 down long enough to draw it from its black scabbard. It was a foot longer than the other Iron Guard swords that Sullivan had seen. "Magnificent."

"And very valuable. That nodachi is said to have belonged to Sasaki Kojiro," Carr said. "It was restored and given to me as a gift by Chairman Tokugawa personally."

That seemed to surprise the Iron Guard. "One of my father's blades? This is no accident." Toru had to blink away tears of emotion. He smiled as he slid the blade back into the sheath. "Even now he guides my steps."

"Well . . ." Carr had been ambassador. Of course he had souvenirs. It was obvious from the walls that he loved them. The big sword just seemed like a coincidence to Sullivan, but he'd actually talked to the dead man in question on the spirit phone. Who was he to judge things like signs of approval from beyond the grave? "Good, I suppose."

"The Tokugawa family is reclaiming this blade, Doctor." Toru ripped a strip of silk from a robe in Carr's display and used that to quickly tie both ends of the scabbard so he could throw it over his shoulder. Carr cringed at the defacement of one of his artifacts. "Attempt to stop me and I will spill your bowels with it."

Sullivan shoved Carr toward the exit. "Walk."

"Do you intend to kill me?"

"If you don't tell me where you took Francis, you're gonna wish I had."

"I can cut off his feet," Toru offered. "I have found that makes men talkative . . . briefly."

Carr's lip quivered beneath his gigantic mustache, but he didn't speak.

As they hurried toward the outside, a trembling could be felt through the floor. This bunker had been meant for the command staff of the old Peace Ray project, so it had been built solid, but the whole place was shaking like it was about to fall down. Heinrich had talked about some sort of hole, but Sullivan really didn't know if that could be causing an earthquake. He got his answer when they made it out into the courtyard.

The main building was gone. In its place was the top half of an expanding ball of black. It cast off an eerie light that seemed to make light colors glow. It was forty feet tall and lightning played back and forth across its curved surface. Wind howled past them as it was gobbled up. On one side, the darkness reached the outer wall of the bunker and the bricks immediately began to dissolve into it, while on the other it reached one of the ruined trucks. The front end lifted into the air as the rear dropped into space. Within seconds it had consumed the entire truck.

"Is this your doing?" Sullivan grabbed Carr by the jacket and shook him hard.

"I don't know what that is!" the Coordinator gaped at the blackness. "All my work . . . All of my research was in there. It's all been ruined."

More like all of the evidence of your wrongdoing's been erased. They especially had to keep Carr alive now. Without physical evidence to turn over to J. Edgar Hoover, they were still in hot water, probably more so now since they'd just attacked a government facility and killed a mess of government employees.

"I believe Francis may have been responsible for this one," Heinrich said.

The dome of death had expanded another few feet while they were standing there gawking at it. It was time to go. Sullivan said, "Me and that boy are gonna have a talk."

They ran for it. Carr walked with a bad limp, so Sullivan used his Power to make the Coordinator lighter and dragged him along. He didn't want to help the man. He wanted to toss him into the black hole, but he needed the fool's testimony.

Faye popped into existence ahead of them. "Mr. Sullivan! Over here!"

They reached the gap in the wall. "Is everybody else out?" he shouted to be heard over the wind.

"Yes. We've already filled up one boat and sent it toward Mr. Browning," Faye responded. "Oh, Heinrich! I'm so glad to see you! Where's Francis?"

"We don't know, but he does." Sullivan pushed Carr to the ground. "You know about me, Coordinator, so I'm assuming you know about Traveling Faye here, and no, the rumors haven't been exaggerated."

Carr's eyes grew large. Apparently he had heard about her exploits. It was sad when a teenage girl had more intimidation power than an ex-con Heavy or an Iron Guard.

"What do you mean, he knows where Francis is?" Faye stepped toward Carr, grey eyes gleaming. She reached behind her and pulled out a Bowie knife. "What did you do with my boyfriend?"

He couldn't have planned it better if they'd rehearsed it, only Faye certainly wasn't acting. She was about the single nicest human being he'd ever met, but she'd kill anybody she considered a bad man faster than a farmwife would wring the neck of a chicken. With Faye, once you crossed a certain line, your life was worth nothing.

"Talk, Coordinator, or I leave you with her." It was a bluff, but Carr had no way of knowing Sullivan's deal with Hoover.

Faye reached down and grabbed Carr's tie. "Let's toss him in the big sucking thing. I want to see what happens when you put a person in it."

"It is rather unnerving," Heinrich stated.

"Fine! I'll talk. Just give me your word you won't hurt me."

Sullivan looked back toward the dome. They'd better hurry. "We won't kill you." *But I sure hope you enjoy prison.*

"Stuyvesant was taken across the river in a boat. There is a truck bomb there. It is to be detonated in the marchers' camp."

"The antimagic march?" Sullivan asked, shocked at the barbarity. "Those are your allies."

"Useful idiots." Carr ground his teeth together. "Their deaths will be the final catalyst for ensuring that magic is properly controlled in this nation forever."

Faye shrieked. "That's it! He goes in the sucking thing!" Sullivan reached and blocked her with one hand.

She was the only one that could get there in time. "Get Francis," Sullivan ordered. "Stop the bomb."

The Traveler pointed at Carr. "I ain't done with you!" Then she disappeared.

"Stop staring at me. If those marchers knew what their deaths will cause they'd be glad to make the sacrifice. I'm doing you people a favor. Your way, magical *freedom*"—Carr practically sneered the word—"leads only to chaos and anarchy. My way leads to order and prosperity for all. Every man has a place in the order of things. Actives subvert that natural order." Sullivan was too disgusted to respond. He dragged Carr to his feet and set out for the boat. "You have gifts and it is selfish for you to do only what you want with them. You people must be utilized properly. Actives must be given order, they must be controlled. You must be used where you are most valuable to the collective."

"Specialization is for insects."

"Exactly! The anthill can only have one queen. The drones and the warriors must know their place! To allow people with such uncontrollable Power absolute freedom is to invite disaster for us all."

Sullivan swore to himself that if Hoover couldn't get this man convicted, then he'd personally see to it that Carr didn't live a day past the trial, and if he got a short sentence, he'd be there waiting the day the warden let Carr out the gate. "Shut up or I'll break your fucking face."

But Carr was too antagonistic and proud of his philosophical bullshit to close his stupid yap. "Your man in Oklahoma, Bolander, through his actions, he's set the stage to become a folk hero to the common people. As news of those events spread, they threatened to counter the effects of the assassination attempt in Florida. The spectacular nature of his death is what forced me to raise the stakes. If Actives could be capable of such heroics, then I also had to display the depths of their depravity. Do not blame me for this bombing. You brought this on yourselves."

They started down the trail. "Save your bullshit for the judge."

"Judge?" Carr shouted. "You still don't grasp the enormity of the situation. This is bigger than any judge, bigger than any simple laws. Are you such a fool that you think this stops with me? This is about more than just one man's vision, Mr. Sullivan. I answer to a higher authority. This is far bigger! Do you really think something as capable as the OCI can operate without sufficient clearance and oversight? I am not alone! Your kind will be controlled!"

Sullivan slugged the old man in the mouth. He pulled his punch to keep from breaking anything, but it was still intensely satisfying. Carr collapsed into the mud. Sullivan yanked him right back up. "Warned you." Carr was dazed, but Sullivan dragged his bulk along like he weighed nothing.

Since they were running away from the vortex, they were running into the wind, and it was getting worse. The blackness was gaining on them. The bigger it got, the faster it seemed to grow. Sullivan glanced back and noticed that the anomaly had doubled in height since he'd first seen it. It had to be visible on both sides of the river now. How big was this damn thing going to get?

They reached the north shore. Diamond had already taken the bigger boat, but he'd also evacuated the mystery prisoners. The mud was so churned up that it told him a lot of feet had gone through here already. Dan Garrett and Ian Wright were waiting at the remaining boat. "About time!" Ian shouted.

"Heinrich!" Dan exclaimed at the sight of his closest friend. He ran over and clasped his friend by the arms. "What did they do to you?"

"I was the winner. You should see the other fellows."

"Nothing Jane can't fix. Hurry up and get in."

Something hit the ground hard far behind them. Tree trunks cracked and mud came raining down. A demonic roar pierced them all to the soul and sent shivers down their spines. "Crow's back!" Sullivan shouted.

Toru hoisted the 1919 and immediately ran to the side. Sullivan unceremoniously tossed Carr into the boat, then turned back and unslung his BAR. He was about to order Dan and Heinrich to get the Coordinator out of here, but there wasn't time. The demon was coming too quickly. Trees were being pushed over, and the noise of splintering trunks was closing too fast.

Crow had Summoned something *nasty* this time.

"Fan out!" Sullivan ordered. Toru was already out of sight. Dan, Ian, and Heinrich hurried down the shore. Sullivan tested his Power, felt it there, reliable and true, and got ready to face down the demon. They'd come too far to die now.

From the noise; he was expecting something massive, but instead, it was only a normal-sized figure running through the trees. Yet, it was as if he was drawing a mass of smoke around him, and as he passed down the trail, the smoke was smashing the trees flat or tearing their roots right out of the ground like it massed the same as a herd of elephants.

Crow stopped twenty feet away, appearing to be a normal man in a black suit, but he was surrounded by the seething cloud of evil smoke. It seemed to coalesce around him in a vague animal shape. "I'm back, Heavy," he hissed, "and this time, I'm wearing the greatest demon of them all."

In the distance behind him, the void was growing larger. If the demon didn't get them, then the black hole would.

Oh, Francis! Faye found him lying on the grass behind the back of a truck on the Washington side of the river. He'd been shot several times and from the dead bodies, it was obvious who'd done it. Luckily, Pemberly Hammer and Whisper had gotten there first.

Hammer had looked up long enough to say, "Tourniquet isn't stopping the bleeding."

"We must get him to the hospital," Whisper said. "Too bad I had to use our car to block the bridge."

"He needs a Healer or he's dead."

"Healer's on the other side of the river."

"Out of my way!" Faye shouted.

"Faye?" Hammer asked. "Where—"

She was glad that her friends had tried to save him, but everybody else was just too darned *slow*. Faye took Francis by the hand. It was cold. Her grey eyes could see well enough in the dark to tell that he was deathly pale. "Hang on, Francis. I've got you."

She didn't know where the handsome Healer was, and Jane was clear on the other side. That was a heck of a long jump with carrying the weight of another person, and it would take a much larger burst of Power, but she was feeling especially feisty tonight and figured she could do it. She checked her Power and was excited to discover that it had grown since the night had begun. It was counterintuitive, but her magic was getting stronger again. She could probably get Francis over there in one hop, but the island was still a safer waypoint first. Faye subconsciously ran the math in her head in the time it took anybody else to blink. She studied her head map, only to realize there was only a hundred yards or so left of the island that wasn't dangerously close to the sucking void, picked a spot, and Traveled.

She and Francis appeared an inch above the ground and landed in the mud. It was better safe than sorry. To the north, the other knights were fighting something, and she recognized the human form of that no-good Crow. There was no time to help though. She'd come back for them once she saved Francis. Her head map picked out the spot on the west side of the river where Jane and Mr. Browning were, so she focused, looking for a safe spot, and . . . *Clear.*

Jane Garrett was only ten feet away and had her back to where Faye landed. She was watching an incoming boat, filled with knights and bedraggled, scared prisoners. "Jane! Jane! I need you!"

The Healer's reactions were honed. When somebody called her name like that, she responded immediately. Grimnoir Healers were used to being needed in a real hurry. "Francis! Oh no . . ." Jane got on her knees and studied her angle of attack. "Three entrance holes. Two exits. Some fragmentation and multiple wound channels.

Lung damage. Liver damage. Femoral artery is severed. Blood pressure dropping." She put her hands on Francis' chest. "Heart will stop in forty seconds."

"Fix him!" Faye cried.

"Shhhh." Jane closed her eyes and her hands began to glow. "I've got this."

"Don't let him die, Jane. I love him," Faye blurted out.

Jane was exasperated. "Do I tell you how to teleport? No. I don't think so. So go do whatever it is you do and quit fussing at me so I can concentrate." The hole in Francis' chest made a sizzling noise and he moaned.

Faye stood up. Jane was right, and she was the very best Healer ever. There was nothing else she could do for Francis . . .

Except punish the organization that had hurt him.

Crow was pleased. This new body was amazing. He couldn't believe that he'd waited so long to try it out. He'd been foolish to be so scared of the greatest of all Summoned. It hadn't even taken much coaxing to bring it to Earth. It had been eager. No Summoner had ever dared call on it before. They'd been too frightened. Only Crow had the nerves to tame the fiercest beast that had ever existed on a very fearsome world.

It hadn't even fought him for control. He'd expected more of a struggle, but it had simply accepted his demand and let him take charge of its body. It had been surprisingly accommodating, and had gone obediently to the back of its mind. Crow could sense the savage brutality of the creature, but it was also cunning, it might not have understood humanity, but it understood that its master had a need for strategy and discretion.

He was only allowing a tiny percentage of its true physical form to manifest, but even then, Crow had never felt so mighty. He forced it to look like his regular, chosen, human shape, but its abilities and strength were off the charts. It was sorely tempting to let the true form free, but he was afraid. Not of another embarrassment like what had happened in Oklahoma, but rather that once he started, he would not be able to stop. Crow didn't know if he, or the demon, could handle that much freedom.

In fact, he was far more worried about the growing darkness behind him than the Grimnoir in front of him. He did not understand what it was, but it was all-consuming. There was only death inside the darkness. He did not know if even the great one would be able to pull itself out of the darkness should it get too close.

The Grimnoir attacked. They were powerful, but they were nothing compared to this form. The Heavy struck him with waves of crushing gravity, but he simply shrugged them off. Up became down and down became up, but the Greatest Summoned did not care, and it willed itself to stay connected to the ground. The Iron Guard hosed them down with bullets from a belt-fed machine gun, but it was like being pelted with handfuls of sand.

They had a Mouth. He hurled words at Crow. The words were filled with magic, but they were feeble human words, and they made no sense. In fact, he was having a very hard time understanding any of the words the Grimnoir were saying. That gave Crow pause . . . Was the demon affecting him more than he'd thought? If it was, it was very subtle, and as Crow thought about that, the words began to make sense again and the garbled nonsense the Grimnoir were shouting turned back into English. That was better.

I apologize, master. I was only trying to protect us.

Don't let it happen again. Crow thought that was interesting. He'd never had a Summoned that could communicate so clearly before. He should have been afraid, but instead he felt strangely relaxed. This form was very comforting.

He tried to swat the Grimnoir, but even in his great form, they were annoyingly difficult to kill. The Heavy increased the mass of his body and withstood a blow that should have crushed him. Interesting, this Heavy also possessed some of the capabilities of a Massive. *The creatures of this world are able to connect to more than one aspect of the Power . . . This is different than the home world. Perhaps, if we had been able to do such a thing, then the Predator would not have been able to consume us.*

Crow was confused. The memories were odd, filled with strange colors and unfamiliar smells, cluttered with overwhelming sadness, bitter regret, and an all-consuming desire for conquest. He forced the demon back down. *I'm in charge here. Not you.*

The Fade was elusive. He disappeared as Crow tried to strike him down, but re-formed on the other side, and managed to make both of their forms indistinct. Crow's pathetic human form sunk deep into the rock before the Fade leapt away. The Heavy began to congratulate the Fade, but Crow simply jerked his stuck limbs out of the ground, dragging the foreign matter with him.

These enemies are robust. Some of them have bound more Power to their bodies. This world has advanced much in the ways of magic.

A sword cleaved down through one arm, sending it spiraling away, then came back up quickly to remove the Summoned's head. The head went bouncing off into the forest.

Crow's severed head laughed. He gathered up some of the excess essence of the mighty Summoned and reformed the body. The Brute seemed surprised when Crow simply grew a new head.

This form is too clumsy. Set me free.

No. Crow knew there was too much danger in that.

Let me free and we will rule this world.

It was tempting.

A Traveler appeared. The demon recognized right away that this was the most dangerous of them all. Her personal magic was astounding, and her spirit was bound with a diagram of Power beyond anything ever created in the old world. Crow began to tell the demon what to do, but the demon shoved him aside. The human did not understand just how fearsome the Traveler really was. She was possibly his equal and obviously one of the rulers of this world.

Free me or she will destroy us. I do not want to return to the cold place.

She folded space, attacking over and over, moving from spot to spot quicker than their divided mind could follow. Crow fought the demon while the Traveler fought them both.

❖❖❖

Faye was Traveling like mad. Crow was much faster than before, and even though he looked like a man, he was moving with unbelievable quickness. It was like there were walls of force around his hands, and when he swung, great big patches of ground were torn apart. Whole trees were sent flying into the air. He'd strike, so she'd move and stab him. They kept on repeating the little dance, and Faye couldn't figure out why he'd not managed to kill her yet. It was like he was distracted or something.

The others had hit Crow with everything they had, and it hadn't done a thing. The big sucking thing was getting closer. There was only about fifty yards of island left. They were shoving the boat into the river and trying to escape while Faye kept Crow occupied.

Faye had fought demons before. She'd helped beat the Bull King by finding its Summoner and blowing his brains out. Only, how could she kill a Summoner when he was inside his own demon? They'd already killed him before, and he'd just come right back. That didn't hardly seem fair. She needed to kill his real body once and for all. That way he'd never come back again. She needed to kill his body good and dead—for George and for everybody else this awful man had hurt.

Ian sent his Summoned in on a suicide charge. Crow simply uppercut the creature. It flew a hundred yards through the air, plummeted down, and hit the river with a huge splash. Ian had been trying to help Fay, but he'd only gotten in the way. Ian cried out in pain as his Summoned was banished. Summoners definitely had a connection to their creatures—maybe Ian had helped in a different way: Crow had to have some kind of connection as well.

Faye checked her head map and pushed it out further than she ever had before. Her Power was burning so hot, and she was Traveling so fast, that she could easily do both things at once. Where would Crow be? For all she knew he could be hundreds of miles away. Yet he was connected to the demon somehow. When they'd killed him before, his spirit had figured out how to get back home. He hadn't gotten lost. So Faye reasoned that there had to be some sort of link between the two; she just had to figure out how to find it.

When she'd brought Jake Sullivan back from the land where the dead went to dream, she'd followed his connection to the Power. Everybody had one, even the really faint ones that belonged to Normals from when the Power had tested them when they were young, but decided not to bond permanently. Her head map had spotted those before—she'd just had to adjust how she perceived the world. Would a Summoner's trail be any different?

Faye pushed her head map even harder. She didn't need to see further, she needed to see finer . . . Faye was stunned as her head map showed her what she was really fighting. If Crow knew what he'd brought here, he was an even bigger fool than she'd thought. It was *vast*. This was no regular Summoned. This was one of their gods.

She had to find the trail . . . Look beyond the terror of the monster. It had to be there somewhere. And sure enough, she found it. Through the noxious smoke were what looked like chains encircling the Summoned, and they pointed in a straight line to the east. Faye forced her map to follow the chains. Crow's real body wasn't very far away at all.

Crow screamed when he realized what she was doing, but it was too late. She was already gone.

Faye landed in the middle of a plain living room, still holding a Bowie knife that was dripping demon ink to burn black spots into the floor. The furniture was dusty. Dirty dishes sat rotting and forgotten in the sink. There were pictures on the wall. She recognized Crow in a few of them, only these were very old tintypes, and in some he was wearing an old-fashioned Army uniform. These had to be pictures of his father or something.

The apartment was small and quiet. It smelled like decay. Her head map told her the only other living thing here was in the bedroom. Faye wiped her knife off on the tablecloth, put it back in the sheath, and drew her .45. Alert for danger, she turned the knob, and let the door creak open.

There was a shape in front of the window, sitting in a chair, staring off into space. Faye went to the lamp in the corner and turned it on. Crow's back was to her, and it took Faye a moment to realize that he was sitting in a wheelchair.

Reaching out, Faye took one handle of the wheelchair and pulled it so that he faced her. She gasped in surprise. Crow was *ancient*. His real body was all shriveled up. His head was more of a skull than anything, and his paper-thin skin barely hid big purple veins. From the tiny diameter of his legs beneath his flannel pajamas, he had not walked in a long time. He smelled bad, and his gooey eyes were staring off into space.

Faye checked again. Sure enough, this was where the chains led. This was the mighty demon that she'd fought.

This was the man who had killed or hurt her friends. His shirt was hanging open, and on his bony chest was carved an intricate spell. His ribs were slowly moving up and down as he breathed.

Crow blinked. Some of his consciousness had returned. "Please . . . Don't." He raised one palsied hand. "Please. I'm begging you."

"Why?" It was all she could ask.

"I'm scared of dying." He touched the spell on his chest. "I want to live."

She'd wondered how an Active could be so eager to enslave other Actives. Now she had her answer.

Faye lifted the 1911 and shot him in the chest. Crow jerked and spasmodically grabbed onto the wheels of his chair. Then she shot him again and again. She shot him until the magazine was empty and the slide locked back. Faye slowly lowered the smoking gun. Crow was already so dry and dead inside that hardly any blood came out of the holes.

Crow

Chapter 21

There comes a time in the life of every warrior when he must face a clearly superior foe. A proud warrior lives for such moments, for there is no shame in defeat and great glory in victory. I prefer to let such proud warriors lead the charge against these superior foes, and while that superior foe is distracted, I use that to my advantage to destroy them. Honor is defined by the winner.

—Baron Okubo Tokugawa,
Chairman of the Imperial Council, My Story, 1922

Mason Island

THEY GOT THE BOAT into the river in a hurry. Dan was yanking on the cord to get the motor started. Mason Island was almost completely gone.

Crow was standing on the edge of the shore, screaming incoherently at volumes unachievable to human lungs. Faye was gone. The rest of them had gotten aboard, but it wasn't going to do them much good. If Crow came after them, they'd be swimming, and Sullivan didn't think that any of them would be outswimming the black hole. Even as he thought that, the blackness reached the river and water began to thunder into it as if it were a waterfall.

He had no idea why Crow hadn't gone after them. Faye had disappeared, and ever since then, Crow had just been twitching and yelling, but not chasing them. Whatever she was up to, it seemed to be working.

Dan got the engine started, but with the water below them rushing into the darkness and the nearly hurricane force winds buffeting them, they'd be lucky if they didn't capsize anyway. Already waves taller than the boat were tossing them about. Having always figured he'd end up shot to death, he'd never considered drowning a serious possibility. It just went to show that life could be full of surprises.

Carr was holding on to the side of the boat for dear life. The Grimnoir were a little more stoic, until Ian threw up. Toru was just glaring at Sullivan with his arms folded. "When the Pathfinder destroys the world because you died badly on this fool's errand, I hope you will be happy."

"Hey, you said your father wanted you to have that sword," Sullivan shouted back over the wind, "so apparently we're supposed to drown here."

"I said when *you* die badly. *I* am an excellent swimmer."

Whatever internal struggle that was keeping Crow stuck in one spot must have ended, because he started wading out into the river. As the smoke around him struck the water, it was blasted aside, and Crow walked after them.

"Like Moses parting the Red Sea," Heinrich said.

"Too bad this guy's on Pharaoh's side!" Dan shouted back.

"You had better set me free before my associate gets here, Mr. Sullivan," Carr demanded.

Sullivan took a good look at the animal insanity on Crow's twisting face. "I figure he's more likely to eat you than rescue you, Doc."

The darkness consumed the last bit of beach. Mason Island was completely gone. Crow was headed right for them, and their boat was being sucked his way fast. Their engine was helpless against the brutal new current.

Suddenly, Faye appeared in the air over Crow's head. He turned to meet the new threat, but Faye dropped straight out of the sky and landed on him. They both disappeared and the water came smashing back into the empty space.

"What's she doing?"

"There!" Ian pointed high into the air.

It was difficult to see them because of the darkness and the distance, but two figures materialized in the air over the top of the crackling black hole. They fell, tumbling, toward the center of the vortex. There was a flash of lightning right before they hit and Sullivan lost sight of them.

"Faye!" Dan cried.

"*Mein Gott,* she killed herself!"

"She killed herself to kill Crow." Ian was awestruck. "I can't believe it."

Sullivan wasn't so sure. Faye was crazy, but not suicidal crazy. A moment later something appeared in the air, then splashed into the water next to them, but disappeared beneath the waves before he could see what it was. Toru left his sword in the boat and immediately dove over the side.

"He better have been telling the truth about being a good swimmer, or he's fish food," Sullivan muttered. Toru came up thirty seconds later, with a limp form under one arm. There was a mass of blonde hair floating. "Damn it." Sullivan hoisted her out of the water while Heinrich and Ian pulled in the Iron Guard. Thankfully, she began to cough and spit. "What the hell was that, Faye?"

"I don't swim good," she gasped. "Quit yelling at me!"

"Good work, girl. Good work." Sullivan pulled her close, hugged her tight, and began to laugh.

Awkwardly, she joined in a moment later, and everybody except Toru did as well. The Iron Guard just put his sword back over his shoulder and glared sullenly at them. "I am wet," he complained. That just made Sullivan laugh harder.

There was still the issue of the expanding darkness to deal with, and their boat's motor just wasn't cutting it. "Hate to interrupt, but could you be a love and Travel us to land before we all die?" Ian asked Faye. She nodded. "Oh, thank goodness."

Sullivan figured she'd pop them back and forth, one by one, like she'd done on a few other desperate occasions. So he was rather surprised when the entire boat suddenly appeared a foot in the air over solid earth, and then crashed hard into the ground. Several boards broke and Ian went spilling over the edge.

"Good work, kid." Sullivan let go of Faye and stepped out onto dry land. "Damn near bit my tongue off, though. Warn me next time before you do something like that."

"Show-off," Heinrich chided. Then Faye came over and hugged him. "Yes, dear. I missed you as well."

"I cried when they told me you'd got blown up," Faye said, embarrassed.

"Do not fret. I cried when I heard that as well."

She'd dropped them on the Virginia side. Lance had picked a home that had been foreclosed on back when the economy had fallen apart. There had been plenty to choose from. It had a small dock, and it had made a good staging area. Dan dragged the Coordinator out of the boat at gunpoint. They'd gone through a lot of work to bag him, and it wasn't about to go to waste. Though knowing Dan, a few minutes of conversation and he and the good doctor would be best buds.

Faye Traveled off to check on Francis, and Sullivan walked over to the shore where John Browning was watching the commotion over Mason Island. "Mr. Sullivan," he tipped his hat in greeting. "It appears that all of us except for Miss Giraudoux and Miss Hammer wound up on this side of the river. I have been in communication with them."

"They okay?"

"Miss Giraudoux said that they were securing a very large truck filled with explosives. Apparently everyone in the city has come out to watch this . . . disturbance. She says it is rather chaotic. With your arrival, I do believe that everyone is accounted for. You will be very interested to hear what the other Active prisoners have to say about their treatment at the hands of the OCI, and it appears that you brought along another guest. Excellent work as usual, Mr. Sullivan."

"Except for that thing." He pointed at the vortex. It was as tall as a high-rise. The whole island was gone, most of the bridge was gone, and it was stretching toward the shore on both sides. "Is it going to eat the Capitol?"

Browning was calm. "I do not believe so. I have heard rumors of such a thing once before. It is an extremely rare type of magic. The last Active I know of that manifested this Power took his own life after he accidentally killed his entire village and everyone he loved. Luckily for us, that occurrence was in a very remote area in the jungle. The knights involved with that case took to calling him a Nixie, and so did some scientists when they heard rumors of the event. The largest area he ever affected was about half a mile across. I believe that it has already slowed and should be collapsing on itself soon."

"Where does it lead?"

"I have no idea." Browning folded his arms behind his back. "I just hope that I'm correct in my assessment."

"I don't know . . . If it ate all those politicians, would that really be so bad?" Sullivan asked. Browning chuckled.

The darkness stopped growing. A few minutes passed while it seemed to fill out until it was a perfect dome. "Just as I expected," Browning said. And then the darkness instantly vanished, leaving a staggering hole in the earth. Sheer walls of water stood on both sides for the briefest instant, and then it all came crashing down. The noise was deafening. Every one of the knights had gathered along the shore to watch the spectacle. Sullivan had been to Niagara Falls before. This was like that, only deeper and in a circle.

It seemed like the spell had been round, and that meant that it had also devoured untold tons of dirt from below. Sullivan had absolutely no idea how deep the river was, but he figured that the Potomac had just gotten one heck of a deep spot. It was now very early morning, so hopefully there hadn't been anybody out boating . . .

It took a surprisingly short time for the hole to fill in. Despite the muddy color and the turbulent waves, a few minutes later it was almost as if it had never been there at all.

"What's going to happen when all the people that were already scared of magic find out that an eighty-acre island, walking distance from Washington, D.C., just magically disappeared?"

"I do not know the answer to that, Mr. Sullivan," Browning said, "but the possibilities terrify me."

Sullivan had no response to that. By trying to fix things, had they just made them a whole lot worse? In stopping Carr's schemes, had they given their enemies even better ammunition to use against Actives?

Faye appeared at Sullivan's arm. "Francis is going to be okay. Jane's the best. She said that he needs to rest because he's missing so much blood, but he should be better in no time. He got shot while defusing a bomb that was supposed to blow up the White House."

"That's not what happened, my dear," Browning corrected. "He told me so himself."

Faye didn't care. She seemed to prefer her version where Francis was extra heroic. "He's so brave."

"Yep," Sullivan agreed. "That sounds like Francis all right."

Two biplanes flew down the river and the spotlights of the aircraft carrier *Lexington* could be seen sweeping down over the city. There would probably be hell to pay tomorrow, but for better or worse, this mission was complete. Dan would interrogate Carr before they turned him over to Hoover. Maybe combined with the testimony of the other prisoners, they might be able to clear themselves. They wouldn't know the aftermath until the sun rose anyway. It was time to call it a night.

Suddenly, Faye jerked. Sullivan turned to see her weird eyes darting back and forth rapidly. She was normally twitchy, but this was abnormal even for her. "What is it?"

"Something's wrong . . . bad wrong. In my head map. I can see . . . something . . . It's in the river. In the hole. Oh no. He's alive. He's getting bigger! He must have gotten out of the sucking thing somehow. He was too strong to get sucked away! He's growing. He's climbing out!"

"Who? What are you talking about?"

The girl was absolutely terrified. "The god of demons is coming."

Death had come for him, but he'd found a way out. It was a great deal. All he had to do was sell his soul.

Crow. It was his only name now. He couldn't remember the one he'd been born with. Those memories wouldn't come to him. For almost a hundred years he'd lived a life of debauchery and murder. He had no morals, no sense of right or wrong, no conscience. He lived by the sword and figured he'd die by the sword. That hadn't scared him back then, but that's because he'd been young and stupid. When the magic had come to him, he became a lot more valuable, a lot more deadly, and even less compassionate . . . as if that was possible.

He'd sold his demons to the highest bidder. He'd

performed sickening tasks and never asked why, as long as the money was good. As he got older, he knew that his time was coming, and unlike when he was young, the thought of dying terrified him. He could get glimpses of the plane the Summoned came from, and he'd developed an intense fear that if there was life after death, that's all there was in store for him. Floating in a haze, to be dragged in at some alien Summoner's whim, only to be cast back into the darkness when the Summoner was done. Crow couldn't bear the thought.

Money could buy Healers, but not even a Healer could make you immortal. As his body broke down, the specter of mortality had hung over him. As he'd aged, his body had become a prison. The Coordinator had given him a way out with the possibility of using his Power to use new bodies. It had been liberating to have a strong body again, but even then the solutions were only temporary.

The Traveler had shot his real body full of holes. There was nothing left to go back to. The part of him that was still inside the greatest of all demons was all that was left. When that link was severed, his life would be over.

It does not have to be that way. Set me free, human. Become one with me. Together, we will own this world. This world must fear me. I cannot tolerate being unknown. Their fear will make me strong.

Crow knew that he would not die, but he would be consumed by the demon, and that was almost scarier than the thought of dying. While they struggled, the Traveler had dropped them into the darkness. The great one latched onto the edge of this reality and barely managed to hold on.

Serve me, human. Death is cold and silent. You do not wish to die. Give me what I want and I will save us both from this fate. You will be perfected in me. Serve, and live forever.

The darkness stretched on into infinity, and so did Crow's fear. He gave in.

Freedom.

Crow's soul began to unravel, and as the nothingness consumed him, he begged for mercy, screaming that the demon had promised him eternal life.

I lied.

And Crow was no more.

Faye watched in horror as the god of demons came out of the river.

The cascade of bubbles was visible clear from the other shore. It erupted from the water on the Washington side, rising from the river like a new island, dark and glistening, bristling with spines and bony plates. It was crouched near the shore, partially submerged, but even then, it was taller than any of the homes along the river. It slithered downstream, jutting bones and horrible angles breaking the surface, then it turned toward the city. First came one hand, as big as an automobile. It hit the ground, and the monster pulled itself out of the water.

It was *huge*.

Of course they couldn't hear the screaming of the witnesses from such a distance, but Faye could only imagine.

It was hard to see details in the dark from half a mile away. It was vaguely man-shaped, but wrong: four arms, two legs—all bending with extra joints—creaking and clacking as animated earth ripped from the river bed and filled with demonic smoke meshed together into the semblance of a body. It had taken on the color of the void it had torn itself from, with skin an empty black that seemed hungry to absorb the light. It stood, spread its arms wide, and roared at the city, nearly as loud as the crashing of the temporary waterfall from a few minutes before. Despite its vast size, it was quick, and it lurched over to where the bridge was still burning. A police car was tossed through the air and another was kicked into the river.

Faye rubbed her eyes. It was incomprehensible. Nothing alive could be that big without squishing itself under its own weight. Except Summoned weren't really alive like we thought of living, now were they? How could it even move? She didn't know that either, but it was over there tossing police cars like baseballs. Despite what some folks said, she knew she wasn't crazy. This thing was real. She just couldn't wrap her brain around it, and her brain was extra good at wrapping around strange concepts.

Sullivan spoke up first. "I'd say seventy feet tall." As usual, he seemed calm, and Faye was surprised just how much that helped her stay calm.

All the other knights were shocked, standing there with their mouths open as they watched the spectacle across the Potomac. John Browning turned to their Summoner. "Your estimate, Mr. Wright?"

"There's nothing like that out there. That thing can't exist."

"Apparently it can. Is size always proportionate to the difficulty in banishing a Summoned?"

"As far as I'm aware, yes."

"So, how difficult will it be to defeat such a beast?" Browning snapped. Ian mumbled an inaudible response. "Spit it out, man."

"It would be impossible. The bigger they are, the more smoke they hold, and the harder they are to hurt. That thing? Christ . . . I don't know. If you killed its Summoner, it would weaken it; eventually it would just fall apart and dissipate on its own."

"I already killed him," Faye said. "Except Crow's different. What would happen if the Summoner couldn't die, like if he was stuck inside his own monster?"

Ian was clearly in over his head. "I've got absolutely no idea."

"What can we do then?"

"Let the Army handle it," Ian answered sheepishly.

Faye knew that the Army was in the city already. They'd been called up just in case the antimagic marchers turned into rioters, though Mr. Sullivan said they were keeping a low profile because of how awful they'd looked last year when they'd dispatched the Bonus March. She really doubted that the Army would be ready for anything like this.

Gunfire echoed across the river as the police shot at the monster, but it didn't show any reaction. The knights were silent as they watched the demon attack the homes along the river. It just ripped through houses like they were made of paper. It was nearly three times as tall as the two-story homes along the riverfront. It hadn't turned so they could see its face yet, but it paused and crouched for a moment, hands moving from the ground to what she could only assume was its mouth. It repeated that process several times, snatching things up from the torn apart houses as it went. "What's it doing?"

"Oh, dear Lord," Jane whispered. "It's *eating* people."

The demon lifted its head, and they were finally able to see a face straight out of nightmares. There were two eyes on each side of its head, glowing red as the fires of hell. Two long horizontal gashes bleeding smoke bisected the head, one on top of the other, that had to be mouths. It noticed the lights of the Lincoln Memorial, opened both sets of jaws, roared a challenge, and thundered toward the south.

"Knights," Mr. Browning raised his voice, "we must act. There are tens of thousands of men, women, and children camped on the mall tonight. We must help kill this thing or distract it until they can evacuate."

"Those ten thousand came here to protest *us*," Ian snapped. "I don't think you understand what a Summoned that size should be capable of. Fighting it is suicide!"

Browning ignored him. "Faye, do you have the strength to ferry individuals across?"

She checked. Even with Traveling a motor boat full of people a quarter mile in one hop, her Power felt great, not as strong as it had gotten aboard the *Tokugawa*, but much better than it had been. "Sure thing."

"Good. Start with the most combat capable first and work your way down. The rest of us with magic not suited for fighting can still fire a gun. Someone tell Dan to interrogate the Coordinator quickly. He may have information that we can use against this thing." Browning was good at taking charge. "Any other ideas?"

Sullivan tossed his partially finished cigarette in the river. "If you're on speaking terms with the Almighty, start calling in favors. Take me across first, Faye. Toru, you in?"

The Iron Guard was standing apart and had not yet spoken. "You would die defending those that wish only to destroy you?"

"Among others."

"You are a fool. Such compassion for the stupid is a waste of righteous Power."

"Fine. Be a chicken."

"Never question my courage," Toru growled. "I did not say I would not slay this demon, only that you are a fool. Of course I will fight." The sword he'd found was so long that Toru had to pull the scabbard off of his back in order to unsheathe it. "And since I am the strongest, I *demand* the honor of striking first."

"Knock yourself out."

Faye walked over and touched the Iron Guard on the shoulder. "Ready?"

He took the sword hilt in both hands. *"Hai!"*

She'd take that as a yes. It was tempting to drop the pushy Iron Guard right into one of the demon's mouths and be done with him, but she reckoned they'd need all the help they could get.

Chapter 22

We've got a great show for you tonight. We've got dancing. We've got singing. We've got magic like you wouldn't believe. Displays of superstrength, deadly stunts, risking life and limb, all for your enjoyment. We have got it all. Ladies and gentlemen, you ain't seen nothin' yet!

—Al Jolson,
Sinbad's Vaudeville Theater, 1911

USS *Lexington*
Over Washington, D.C.

THE AIRSHIP HAD SOUNDED the alert as soon as the electrical anomaly had been spotted at the abandoned Peace Ray facility just west of the city. The crew of the aircraft carrier *Lexington* had reacted like a well-oiled machine. They'd dropped two of their complement of sixteen Curtiss Raptors to investigate within five minutes of the first alarm, and then they'd waited.

The radio call that came in next had been simply unbelievable.

"A giant monster came out of the river?" The captain

had just been roused from his bunk and it was taking him a moment to digest the news. "And it's heading for the Lincoln Memorial?"

"Yes, Captain," confirmed the radioman. It sounded insane, but that was the word.

"Is this some kind of joke, Lieutenant Heinlein?"

"No, sir. It appears to be some sort of creature, like something a Summoner would have, only bigger."

Tensions had been high ever since the assassination attempt, but nobody had expected that there would actually be anything for the Navy's most advanced airship to do over the Capitol other than be a sign of strength and stability to the people. They'd been wrong.

"Damned wizards. Ought to hang the lot of them . . . Bring us around to engage with the main guns and drop the fighters."

Washington, D.C.

SULLIVAN'S BOOTS hit the pavement hard. Faye always seemed to like appearing a little above the ground for safety's sake, and a lot above it when she was carrying somebody with her. Traveling was terribly disorienting, so it took him a moment to regain his bearings. He had no idea how the girl was able to do it so quickly and always keep herself pointed in the right direction. The reflecting pool was in front of them. They were near the Roosevelt Memorial. The Washington Monument rose in the distance to their left. To the right was the Lincoln Memorial, and standing next to it was one big demon.

The police were shooting futilely at the demon. An awful roar filled the air and the ground shook as it assaulted the memorial. Each footfall was like thunder and the police had no choice but to scatter. It wrapped three of its arms around one of the Greek columns and tore it from the building. The pillar broke in half and the monster flung the first piece at a passing biplane. It missed, but the massive chunk of stone flew off to crash in the distance.

"Holy shit . . ." Sullivan trailed off. He prided himself on always being cool in a fight, but this was overwhelming, even for him. It was a whole lot scarier being on the same side of the river as this thing. "Either I'm bad at estimating size or it's still growing."

"It's sucking in the air around it and turning it into Summoned smoke. When it gets thick enough, it turns that into ink and it stretches its body even bigger," Faye explained. He did not know how she could see that. It had to be that head map of hers that she was always talking about. "Want me to take you back?" Faye asked, terrified herself.

"Tempting, but naw. I got this."

Faye nodded and then she was gone.

The Roosevelt Memorial was at his back. The familiar bronze of Teddy on his rearing stallion rose behind the trees, rifle lifted overhead in a dramatic pose that had never actually occurred during the Great War, since there hadn't been much use for horses in the trenches. Many of the antimagic marchers had camped in the open space east of the Roosevelt Monument, and they were running for their lives now. He couldn't rightly blame them, since the demon was still scooping up people and stuffing its face, not even bothering to chew. It was a demon, living on alien essence and magic. It couldn't possibly need the nourishment. It seemed to be eating them out of spite.

Most of the figures around the Lincoln Memorial were running away, but one had somehow managed to climb onto the creature's back and was moving between the spines, swinging what could only have been a sword. That had to be Toru. Maybe he'd climbed up its leg. Maybe he'd jumped from the top of the Memorial onto its back, but it didn't matter, since the demon jerked violently and slapped at its back with one claw. It was like the motion a man might make when stung by a wasp. The Iron Guard was knocked off and fell into the trees.

Sullivan steeled himself. He had absolutely no idea how to hurt this thing. His Power had already been used hard during the night's events, but even at full strength he wouldn't have been able to squish something that big. There was no time to dwell on it, though, since the demon was heading his way. Four glowing eyes tilted as its head swelled, like it was testing the air, and somehow Sullivan understood that it sensed the thousands of defenseless lives trapped in the open to the east. The marchers would just be waking up and fleeing now. The demon roared.

He fired the BAR without consciously thinking about it. The bullets did nothing. Sullivan pointed it right at the creature's eyes, but those were vast empty pools of fire. It didn't so much as twitch as it got closer. Reloading, hand a blur between gun and vest, Sullivan tried again. The second magazine was as useless as the first. The demon was closer now, and it was like trying to stand during an earthquake. Stumbling, he turned and ran for the cover of the Roosevelt Memorial. He dove behind a concrete flowerbed as one of the demon's huge feet kicked the iron bars of the perimeter fence overhead.

The demon had an overpowering stink to it, like damp ground and ozone. Sullivan crawled forward as another foot landed only twenty feet away, bouncing him across the grass. The foot was shaped like a monkey's paw, with toes like fingers, each as long as a tall man, with an obsidian nail on the end like a shovel head. The limb was covered with plates like broken asphalt chunks, while the skin beneath was black as oil and appeared slick and moist.

Tracer bullets splashed across the reflecting pool, tore up clumps of dirt, and ripped into the demon. A sleek Curtiss biplane banked away, engine buzzing. The demon roared with a noise that threatened to make Sullivan's ears bleed. There was a terrible sound as the bronze statue of Teddy Roosevelt and his horse was ripped from its base and hurled after the speeding plane. This time the demon connected, and the statue tore one set of wings off. The Curtiss went spiraling downward in a cloud of wood splinters and aluminum shrapnel.

Sullivan gathered enough Power for a brutal Spike, rose, and concentrated on the nearest foot. He brought gravity down on it, sloppy, but hard and fast as he possibly could. A visible depression appeared in the oily skin and the plates cracked. A cloud of demon smoke spilled forth as the foot jerked into the sky. Summoned oil fell on him like rain. *It can be damaged!*

Then the massive foot came down right on top of him.

The Power use was instinctive, and he flared it hard, increasing his density as everything went black. He was driven deep into the ground, flat on his back, stomped like a bug.

There was no light. There was no air. No sound. There was dirt in his eyes, filling his ears and mouth. He was buried alive beneath the black oily heel of the demon. His Power was burning hot, dwindling quickly, but he was alive. Alive and crushed beneath the incalculable weight of a god.

This had to be how he'd survived the year before when he'd fallen from a blimp and through a train car. There was no calculation to this magic, only a pure desire to live. Even seconds from death, in a race between what would run out first, his air or his magic, Sullivan's analytical mind was making notes of this surprising use of his Power. *Fascinating.*

The wounded foot rose, leaving Sullivan at the bottom of a footprint in the grass. His mass returned to normal and he could move again. His lungs filled with air. Desperate, he scrambled upward, drawing himself out into the night. The demon was moving on. Sullivan had to hurry and strike with whatever he had left.

But before Sullivan could do anything else, the beast spun, tearing one leg through the Memorial. The landscape seemed to curl into a wave of approaching earth. An uprooted tree spun his way and he barely had time to increase his density before impact.

He found himself sailing through the air. Water came rushing up to meet him, but not nearly deep enough to cushion the impact. The splash was far too brief and his shoulder cracked the concrete beneath. Sullivan sat up in the middle of the reflecting pool, gasping and choking.

The injured foot came down, still mangled and bleeding smoke, but the demon just contorted its unnatural body and used one of its spare hands to steady itself. It must not have realized where that attack had come from, or he'd be dead for sure. It knew that something in the area had severely injured it though, and that something had to be eliminated. Both mouths opened wide and emitted a blast of pure fire in an arc that stretched for hundreds of feet. It swept its head across the mall, side to side, immolating everything. Trees exploded into flame. Innocent people were burned to ash. Sullivan ducked back under the lifesaving water as the fire tore across the pool.

The son of a bitch breathes fire, too? he thought as he hugged the bottom. It was very shallow, and much of his back was still exposed to the intense heat. He rolled quickly to put himself out. *This keeps getting worse.*

Holding his breath as long as he could, it finally felt as if the worst of the heat had passed. The water was scalding as he sprang up and gasped for breath. The air was filled with smoke. Being crushed had left him dizzy and weak. It took quite some time to collect himself.

Sullivan wiped his eyes and watched as the demon went on to attack the Washington Monument. It covered a football field's worth of ground every couple of steps and reached the monolith in no time. Even as big as the demon was, the monument was far taller still, and that just seemed to make it mad. The creature struck it several times, angry that anything else might upstage it, but after clawing away several chunks of stone it seemed to realize that the monument was no threat to its superiority. Instead it scrambled effortlessly up the side of the monument, climbing to a higher vantage point so that it could survey its new kingdom.

A pair of biplanes did a strafing run against the demon. This time it simply turned and engulfed the incoming planes in a stream of fire. One was struck and exploded in midair. The other managed to dodge under the flames, only to cut too close to the monument and was swatted from the sky by one of the demon's extra arms. It would accept no challenges to its rule.

Sullivan waded across the pool. He had to follow this thing before it was too late. His Healing spells were working like mad. His own Power was battered and weak. He still had his gun, and the only reason it hadn't been destroyed beneath the demon's foot was because John Browning had enchanted it with runes of durability. He didn't know what he was going to do when he reached the monster, but he had to try something.

The demon's eyes turned to the east, toward the lights of the Capitol and the field of screaming, fleeing humans. It climbed down and lumbered onward.

Faye stepped through space and found herself back on the west side of the river at the Grimnoir staging grounds. "Next!"

She'd just dropped Lance Talon off behind one of the museums. He had insisted on taking the Stokes mortar from the back of his truck. Between Lance, the mortar and its shells—it had been quite a bit of weight—and it had forced her to make a couple of quick hops to get him in place. Before that had been Diamond armed with one of those Goddard rocket launchers. She'd stuck around long enough to watch him shoot one of the explosive rockets into the demon's back, but their only reward on impact had been a puff of smoke. It had flicked off the Iron Guard, stepped on Mr. Sullivan, and was swatting down fighter planes like hornets. She was beginning to fear that nothing they could do could hurt this thing.

The knights had actually formed a line like they were waiting for a turn on a Ferris wheel. Heinrich stepped up next. He hadn't been Mended yet, but he had one of Mr. Sullivan's Healing spells carved on him so he was hanging in there, and he'd found a pickax in the tool shed. "Drop me right on its head."

"Are you sure?"

"It should prove fun," Heinrich said as he put the pickax over one shoulder. He gave her a battered grin. "What is the worst that could happen?"

And people say I'm crazy. Faye took him by the arm.

Her Power was burning hot. Though she'd jumped far and often over the last few hours, she seemed to be getting stronger and stronger as the night went on. Her greatest limitation right now was her physical body, which was completely exhausted. One mistake because she was not thinking clearly would get her, and even worse, anybody she was carrying, killed. Her magic was feeling nearly as strong as it had been aboard the *Tokugawa* and she had no idea why, but she was thankful for it. Even then, it was taking her a couple of shorter hops to get back to the demon. She had a passenger and it was getting further away. By herself, she figured she should be able to make the return trip in one jump.

They landed near the Washington Monument. It was

scored with several deep claw marks. A biplane had crashed on its side nearby. The area was in complete pandemonium. There were hundreds of people present, some running away, some stumbling about injured, others trying to help. Fires were burning everywhere. The demon was busy tearing apart the big museum on the north side of the lawn while it ignored the flock of biplanes that were taking turns swooping down to shoot at it. The monster had to be a hundred feet tall now.

"Still want to do this?" she asked Heinrich.

"I do. But before you put me on that thing, I just want to say again that I am very sorry for that time that I shot you in the heart."

"Oh, Heinrich. Don't go talking like that!"

"Like what?"

"Like you're saying goodbyes."

"Why would I do that?" This smile was a sad one. "Of course I'm not, Faye. Let's go."

Despite Traveling onto a moving target, her head map had no trouble keeping up with the mad thrashings of the gigantic beast. The spot that she picked was in what seemed like a forest of spines, each one several feet long, a foot in diameter, and ending in a brutal point. It was like being in a stinky living forest. Heinrich let go of her, balanced himself against a spine, lifted the pickax overhead, and embedded it deep into the monster's flesh. Smoke boiled out of the puncture. The whole world tilted. Heinrich grabbed onto a spine and held on for dear life. Faye Traveled out of there just as the demon tried to scrape the new interloper off against the marble facade of the museum.

She landed a hundred feet away and watched as the demon smashed its way through the building. Heinrich must have Faded through the debris; he reappeared, swinging the pickax again and taunting the demon in German. A flashbulb popped as a nearby reporter took a photograph. Faye figured that guy was even crazier than Heinrich. Everybody with any sense was running. At least the knights had magic, so they had some excuse for sticking it out.

Back on the Virginia side, she had to pause to catch her breath. Her Power was still growing and it was making her a bit giddy. She caught Mr. Browning in the process of telling Mr. Bryce that his Powers were "unsuitable" for their situation, and forbidding him from going. His tone was rather stern and as Bryce sulked away, Mr. Browning turned to face her. Apparently he was next. "But you're—"

"Old. Yes. Now get a move on, young lady."

She took him to the front of the Capitol and deposited him next to where the Army was gathering. There were only a handful of small vehicles there, but from the engine noise more were coming. They had been prepared to disperse marchers, not for a situation like this. The evacuating crowd was dense, surging past the soldiers that were trying to get ready to stage a last-ditch defense. The protestors had abandoned all of their antimagic signs and banners. Faye knew she shouldn't have hated them so much for being here, but she did.

The Summoned was disengaging itself from the museum, which meant that Heinrich was probably gone. It moved into the middle of the open space, placed two of its hands on the ground, lowered its head, and breathed fire down the mall. It wasn't close enough to burn the protestors yet, but Faye could feel the temperature rise dramatically.

One of the military men was standing on the roof of a truck, giving orders and waving his arms as other vehicles arrived. Faye didn't know the difference between the various ranks, but this fellow had the fanciest hat and the most embroidery on his sleeves, so that probably made him the boss. He was shouting that they were going to hold this position or else.

Faye, having gotten a pretty good idea of what this particular Summoned was capable of, figured that it was going to end up being *or else*.

There was one larger green vehicle with tracks on the back and wheels on the front. It wasn't quite a tank, but it was certainly no tractor, and it did have some sort of big gun on top. A soldier was standing behind it, wrestling with the gun, seemingly unfamiliar with how to operate it.

Mr. Browning saw the soldier having a hard time, so he pushed his way to the back of the tracked vehicle. Another frightened soldier tried to stop him. "What're you doing, you old coot? You need to scram."

"That boy has no idea how to use that." He gestured at the gun. "I do. Let me up there."

"How would you know?"

"That's a Browning 30mm auto-cannon. I know because I designed the blasted thing! Now stand aside!" That caught the first solider flat-footed long enough for Mr. Browning to climb up the ladder. Exasperated, he pushed the other soldier out of the way. "What are you doing? It isn't that complicated." He pulled a big lever back and opened the tray on top. "Faye, get Dan. See if he's learned anything from the Coordinator about how to banish this creature." He slammed the tray down, worked the charging handle back and forth, took up the spade grips and pulled the trigger. The auto-cannon belched a column of flame over the heads of the evacuating masses. The recoil shook the vehicle and the muzzle blast made Mr. Browning's long coat flap behind him.

There was a chain of small explosions across the demon's chest. Chunks of plate were knocked off and fell to crush some of the screaming marchers below. Browning stopped shooting long enough to yell at her, "Fly, Faye!" Then he returned to blasting the demon.

"Mr. Garrett!" Faye hit the Virginia side running. Her ears were ringing from the cannon. "Where's Dan?"

"Over here," Dan Garrett shouted back. He came around the side of the abandoned house carrying a fat leather book. "Get me to Sullivan, quick."

That she could certainly do, provided Mr. Sullivan was still alive. It took her two hops to get her head map close enough to find their Heavy. Not surprisingly, he was running along the Mall, between the craters created by monstrous footsteps, trying to catch up with the demon, which was now a few hundred yards ahead of them.

"Jake!" Mr. Garrett shouted, before he fell, dizzy, into the mud. Some folks just didn't have the constitution to Travel well. "Over here!"

Sullivan slid to a halt, turned, and ran back to them. The Heavy looked like death warmed over. He was almost unrecognizable beneath the coating of dirt and blood. "What've you got?"

Dan had used a chunk of newspaper as a bookmark. He flipped the book open to show a complicated spell. "The Coordinator said this was the only antidemon spell he knew of in here. He'd learned it as insurance in case Crow ever got out of hand."

The demon leapt high into the air to swing at a biplane. The landing shook the whole city and knocked most of them off their feet. "I'd say he's out of hand now!" Faye exclaimed.

The demon had missed the biplane, and it was buzzing their way. Both mouths opened wide after it, revealing a swirling red light emanating from deep within the monster's core. Sullivan bellowed, "Get down!"

The demon's fiery breath streaked their way in a blazing wall of hot death. Faye's mind was moving quickly, running complex calculations on instinct—the weight of her companions, the approach speed of the jet of flame, the distance her head map told her that she'd have to move all of them to be safe . . . In a tenth of a second she understood that she would only be able to move one of her friends in time and none of the other injured stragglers trapped beneath the fire.

But she was saved from having to choose at the last instant. The fire broke before them, rushing upward and away. It was a miracle they weren't consumed. The air was unbearably hot, and Faye was forced to cover her face as the heat threatened to suck the moisture from her eyes.

Whisper stood some distance behind Sullivan, both palms open, as if she was shoving the fire away with her bare hands. Her hair was whipping wildly around her and her eyes were glowing with unnatural light. "Find your own tricks." With a snarl of rage, Whisper pushed back, and the vast fire arced up and back, curled in on itself, forming into a huge cloud, which then raced back to strike the demon. It roared in confusion as it was engulfed. "Fire belongs to me!"

Whisper fell to her knees. The heat broke, leaving all of them dehydrated and red. Faye got up and ran to her. "You're alive!"

"For the moment," Whisper responded weakly. "What manner of beast is this?"

"It's an old god from the Summoned's world. It's real bitter and wants to eat everybody on our planet . . ."

The demon had shrugged off the flames and was once again heading toward the Capitol. Explosions were rippling continuously across the creature as more military guns joined in. Some of those were coming from the mortar shells that Lance was tossing over the ruined museum. The searchlights could be seen beaming down from the aircraft carrier that had been patrolling over the city. It was maneuvering against the wind to use its main guns as well. A mass of panicked humanity was still in front of the monster, though, and it was doubtful anything would be able to save those people in time.

Sullivan took the spell book from Dan and started analyzing the page, dark eyes flying back and forth rapidly. The main writing looked like gibberish to Faye. Tightly packed notes had been scribbled in the margins, and luckily those were in English. "Yeah, I should be able to draw this . . . What's it do?"

"It's a shield of some kind. Summoned can't get in, no matter how hard they try."

Sullivan studied the demon for a moment. "Faye, get us in front of that thing."

She took Sullivan first, dropping him off near where she'd left Mr. Browning, who was busy ordering young soldiers to hand up more heavy cans of ammunition. Since Mr. Sullivan was so unnaturally heavy, nearly twice what he looked like, she had to be extra careful when she picked a spot. Several soldiers and marchers leapt out of the way as Sullivan suddenly came barreling through them. Normally the sudden magical appearance of a mud-covered Heavy would have startled them more, but he was nothing compared to the spectacle of the oncoming god of demons. Sullivan had already opened up the book and was looking for a spot to work by the time she'd gone back for Whisper and Mr. Garrett.

Even with Mr. Garrett's pudginess, the two of them together weighed less than Sullivan, so she took the both of them in one hop. She realized as she touched down that she probably wasn't doing them any favors, since they had been on the west side of an eastbound demon, and now she'd dumped them right into the shadow of its next target.

"Dan! How big a shield does it make?" Sullivan asked as soon as they'd arrived.

"The more Power the creator puts into it, the bigger it should be."

"Shit . . ." Sullivan muttered.

Faye knew right away what was wrong. Mr. Sullivan was by far the best of them at making spells. He just had an artist's knack for it. However, he'd already burned his Power hard and there was no way he'd had time to recuperate. If you pushed too hard you risked killing yourself. The others hadn't made that connection yet, but Sullivan caught her looking at him, and he just shook his head. He was going to do it anyway.

"I've got plenty of Power!" Faye exclaimed.

Sullivan held up the open book. "Could you bind this?" It was terribly complex. She was still struggling with the most basic communication spells, and there wasn't normally a giant demon coming to kill her if she messed those up. Her hesitancy was obvious. "Didn't think so. This one's on me."

Near them, a tank fired its main gun. The shock wave sent her reeling. Sullivan just hunched his shoulders and walked ahead of the line of military vehicles. Hundreds of soldiers had arrived, and they were going to hold this line or die trying. He picked an open spot of sidewalk and knelt down. People were still fleeing past, but the bodies parted around him like waves against a rock. Mr. Sullivan took a knife from his belt, used it to slice open the tip of one fingertip, and began to write on the sidewalk with his own blood.

The demon was charging toward them. There would be only one chance to get it right.

"Jake, what're you doing?" Mr. Browning shouted.

"If this works, don't leave the circle," Sullivan responded.

"I see . . . Would it be all right if my bullets leave the circle?"

Sullivan drew another line. "I don't see why not." Browning went back to shooting.

A hand landed on Faye's arm and pulled her around

hard. It was Whisper. Her eyes were wide, terrified. "Listen to me. There is something I must tell you. It is about who you are."

Faye didn't understand. She turned back around. The demon was closing fast. "Can't it wait?"

"No! Listen to me, Faye. Remember what we spoke about before?"

"Of course, but I—"

Whisper was desperate. "You must listen to me. You are the one."

What?

Faye didn't have time to think about Whisper's words. The blood magic design Sullivan was drawing had caught someone's attention. Several soldiers were running toward the Heavy. "Stop that, wizard!" shouted an officer.

"His kind brought the wrath of God upon us!" screamed one of the marchers. "Kill him!"

It was understandable. A man drawing obviously magical markings with his own blood, with a great big demon nearby, was pretty suspicious-looking. Rifles were raised in Sullivan's direction. "Back off. I'm busy," he growled.

"Shoot him!" ordered the terrified officer.

"*Stand down!*" The voice that came next seemed to drown out the entire world. "You heard the man," Dan Garrett said, angry magic seething from every word. "*Back off.*" The soldiers lowered their rifles. The Mouth was pushing so hard that even Faye wanted to surrender, and she was already on his side. "That big fellow is going to save your life." The Mouth decided to take it up a notch and put his new allies to work. "Protect this man. Fix bayonets and keep these idiots out of his way."

"Yes, sir!" the soldiers shouted in unison, and formed a protective circle around Sullivan.

"Faye, listen to me," Whisper pleaded. "I was sent to watch you, even to kill you if necessary."

But Whisper was her friend. "Kill me?"

"Because you are the Spellbound."

Faye didn't know what to say. She recalled Whisper's strange story, but it didn't make any sense. "The murderer?"

"You have no idea how much I wanted to simply murder you and be done, at first . . . But I was wrong. The last Spellbound was evil. You are not like him, you are nothing like that grey-eyed monster, but you could become like him. The possibility was there, and that was enough."

Faye looked away from Whisper. Sullivan had finished the spell from the Coordinator's book. Now he was concentrating on the small design, binding it to the ground, connecting it to his own Power.

"That was his spell! That was his curse! You inherited it when Jacques killed him. Can't you feel it? All of that death? Every time someone dies near you, you grow stronger, don't you?" Whisper had gone crazy. She didn't know what she was talking about.

Except she was stronger, like before, like when she'd fought against the Chairman.

Where so many had died.

"The Power bonds to us, lives through us, and when we die, it takes that bit of itself back, larger than before. The Spellbound subverts the order of things. That energy, instead of going back to the Power, it goes to the

Spellbound for a time. It isn't like your regular magic that will regrow. When you use this stolen Power up, it returns home, and that leaves you hungry for more. That's how the first Spellbound became evil. He needed more and more magic, so he began to take it. That's how he became a monster, and the same thing will happen to you."

Faye's mind had always moved rapidly, and now it was spinning through the implications of Whisper's words. The first time she'd had a jump in Power had been when Grandpa had died. After stabbing a kanji-bound man in the heart, she'd had enough Power to beat Delilah in a fight. She'd grown stronger again during Mar Pacifica amidst the dying Iron Guards, and then even greater aboard the *Tokugawa,* and all of that extra Power that she'd been granted had been burned up in one epic Travel, when she'd dragged the entire *Tempest* a thousand miles through the walls of space. And it had started again with the sudden death of George Bolander. He'd died fighting Crow . . . and Faye had *taken* his connection to the Power.

Faye was different from other Actives. She'd just never understood how different. It made sense. She was *stealing* magic when people died. That was horrible. Whisper was right. Only a monster would steal somebody's magic.

She snapped back to reality. Why had Whisper decided to tell her all this now when there was other important stuff going on? The strain was going to kill Mr. Sullivan. Veins stood out on his neck. Sweat poured down his filthy face. He gathered up every last bit of Power he had and shoved it into that design and then he went back for more. They only had seconds left.

"When a Normal dies, it isn't much. Just the little connection that was there from when the Power first checked to see if it could bond to them, but with all of those poor people . . ." Whisper trailed off as she looked across the mall. "Are they enough? Could they ever possibly be enough?"

But Faye didn't know what to do.

The god of demons' rampage was almost upon them. Its footfalls were shaking the tanks. Shells were exploding across it with no effect. Soldiers and marchers flinched away, prepared to die.

The air seemed to shimmer around Mr. Sullivan. He lifted one hand, and with a roar, slammed it down into the middle of his spell. The sidewalk cracked. The world seemed to flex in an expanding blue wave out from Mr. Sullivan's hand. It washed over the soldiers, over the refugees, and over her. The wave passed them by and the world behind seemed to return to normal, except for an electric hum audible just beneath the ringing in her ears.

Mr. Sullivan collapsed, seemingly lifeless, onto the broken sidewalk.

The wall of blue surged outward until it collided with the unnatural bulk of the Summoned. The demon recoiled as if it had driven itself into a mountain. It drew back and crashed into the wall again. The spell did not budge. Furious mouths opened and the demon hurled fire against the shield. The heat that came through was brutal, but the flames washed over the blue wall, leaving them all in what felt like a hollow dome of fire.

He did it! He'd saved them! Dan went to try and help Mr. Sullivan.

The *Lexington* had gotten into firing range, and the next shells that struck were the biggest of all, the biggest Faye had ever felt. The demon rocked back under the mighty impacts. Shrapnel whistled through the air and the spell did nothing to stop it. Soldiers and marchers died all around her. A mighty strip of flesh was ripped from the demon's side and flaming ink poured across the ruined lawn.

Angry at being unable to break through Sullivan's spell, and finally being challenged by something that could actually injure it, the demon took two mighty steps back, roared at the airship, and—

"Wings?" Faye shouted. "It can't grow *wings!*"

The black smoke that was pouring from the thousands of wounds on the Summoned was coalescing into two vast shapes across its back. Sullivan's sacrifice had been for nothing. The wall had only saved the lives of those assembled in one spot. The god of demons was simply going to continue past them. It would tear the *Lexington* from the sky; then there would be nothing nearby that could hurt it. It would find a place to hide, maybe in the depths of the ocean, while it grew stronger. Even her head map couldn't fathom just how big the god of demons would get on this world if given enough time.

The wings became solid.

"Faye!" Whisper said. "Look at me!"

She turned to face the young woman that she'd thought had been her friend. This whole time Whisper had been prepared to take her life, and it seemed that in these final desperate moments, Whisper had decided to fulfill her mission. There was a small black pistol in the French girl's hand. "What're you doing, Whisper?"

"All of those Normal deaths aren't enough for you. It is the connection of a Powerful Active that you need." She was crying, tears cutting through the soot on her cheeks. "No one else can stop this demon. Only you. You're this city's only hope . . ." Whisper seemed to grow more determined. "Promise me you'll stay good, Faye."

"I don't—"

"Promise me!"

"I promise to stay good."

"You must always. Find a way to kill this beast. There are children here, and they are hiding, scared, in the dark. They need someone to come and save them. When this is over, find Jacques Montand of the elders. He will know how to help you . . . Stay close to me, and do not waste my Power." Whisper lifted the pistol and put it next to her temple, then thought better of it, and moved the muzzle down against her chest. "I would like to make a pretty corpse at my funeral."

"No!" Faye reached for her but Whisper pulled the trigger and shot herself in the heart.

Time came shuddering to a violent stop. Faye could see the slide traveling back and forth and the single gleaming brass case spinning out. Whisper's eyes were wide, earnest, with just a hint of mischief and sadness, but that changed, and for an instant there was only hurt and fear and doubt, and then that too was gone, and so was Whisper.

Time returned to normal.

Whisper's eyes rolled back into her head and she began to fall.

Faye caught her friend. At best, she only had seconds

to get Whisper to Jane or the other Healer. "Whisper, don't die! Don't die!"

But it was too late. She was already gone.

It wasn't fair.

Faye knelt there, crying, another dead friend in her arms, in a field filled with smoke, blood, and exploding bombs, under a shimmering dome of magic, beneath the spreading wings of an angry god, as she grew . . . *furious*.

Had Whisper been right? She'd certainly thought she'd been telling the truth. But why? Why choose Faye? Why did it have to be her? Was Whisper a noble sacrifice or a selfish, deluded fool? And Faye hated herself for even asking. Was Whisper right? Had her death fed the furnace of Faye's magic? Fearful, Faye peeked inside.

The connection to the Power had grown. Faye could feel new magic humming through every bit of her body.

Whisper had been right. She was the Spellbound. All this time, she'd thought she was special, but she was just a thief robbing the dead. She was a monster.

And it would take a monster to beat a monster.

The demon roared and leapt into the sky. Powerful wings beat and wind struck them like the edge of a tornado. Faye looked toward it, a great black shape blocking out the sky, as it surged toward the *Lexington*. She let go of Whisper's body.

Faye reached the demon in one effortless hop, landing precariously between the spines on its back. It didn't even notice her. She may as well have been a flea. The air whistled around her. They were climbing fast. Below was the city, people shrinking into flailing dots and tanks looking like toys. A desperate biplane flew past, so close that

Faye could see the pilot's mouth open in astonishment. Above, the searchlights of the aircraft carrier illuminated them. The main gun fired and Faye's heightened senses actually watched the gigantic shell pass between the massive, flapping wings to explode far below.

Even with all her Power, Faye didn't know what she could do against this thing. Hot smoke was pouring through thousands of wounds. She knew that she could tear up bits of the creature and Travel them away, but it was so very strong that it would take hours before she could break it down, if that would even work since it seemed to be growing so quickly, absorbing matter from this world to feed its body. And she knew it wasn't stupid. It would find a way to adapt against her attacks. She needed to destroy the demon quickly or not at all.

Her head map said that the god of demons was a shell. Inside was ink, smoke, and evil. There was no heart to stop, no lungs to pierce, no brain to destroy. They were poking holes in it, but it simply fixed itself and moved on. Faye's mind was quick, quicker than anyone else that she'd ever met, but she didn't have time to figure this problem out before the *Lexington* would be torn from the sky. She needed to buy time.

Faye spied one of the wings and that gave her an idea.

Where the wing intersected with the body, it was only as big around as a stout tree. Traveling directly to the base, Faye picked a hot gash in the unnatural flesh and drove her hand deep inside. It burned. The airship was only a few hundred yards away and the body beneath her seemed to swell as the demon sucked in oxygen, ignited it, and prepared to spray deadly fire across the *Lexington*.

Faye concentrated on the base of the wing, gathered up a harsh burst of magic, and Traveled away with as much mass as she could tear free.

She did not need to go far. Appearing in the air, Faye yanked her injured hand away from the thousands of pounds of unnatural flesh she'd ripped from the demon's hide. One wing tore away, and, surprised, the god began to fall. Fire that had been meant for the airship escaped, boiling out the hole toward her.

Calm, Faye faced the fire. Her head map expanded outward, heedless of the fact she was falling, clothes and hair whipping hard against her frame, and she searched for another weapon. She found what she was looking for one quarter of a second before the flames would have incinerated her.

Faye hit the grass too hard. She'd been in the air just long enough to build up some speed. The truck that Francis had intercepted was parked before her. The back was absolutely packed with barrels of explosives, and it was a *very big* truck. Behind her, the demon was spiraling toward the ground. Even from here it was making a noise like a broken kite fluttering. Her head map showed her where it was going to hit, how fast it was going to be moving, and she was already running the calculations as she Traveled into the bed of the truck.

There was a single black cord that was tied into a bunch of other black lines, and those were spread to all of the other barrels. It was cannon fuse. There was quite a bit, since the OCI men who were meant to set it weren't suicidal. She tore most of the fuse away, just leaving a short stub.

Faye pulled her matchbook from her pocket, struck one on a barrel, and held it to the end of the coarse black line. It caught fire with a sizzle, burning rapidly, sputtering toward the flash point.

Even a mile away, the demon's landing was so hard that it shook the truck springs. Her head map told her that it had created a crater in the city, but even that wouldn't be enough to stop it. She needed to release all of the demon's smoke at once.

The truck was heavy, but she'd done heavier . . . though that single time had been physically too much, and had knocked her out and nearly killed her. This wasn't even near that far, but Faye was going to do something very difficult. She was going to Travel *inside* a demon.

She had no idea if she would be able to make it back out.

Gathering up her magic and placing her palms flat against the truck bed, she took in the entire thing and Traveled into the core of a god.

It was so very dark.

She was floating, not falling, not flying, merely hanging suspended in a void of infinite blackness. Pressure and heat touched her skin and alien feelings touched her mind. Faye let go of the truck, and—

Nothing.

You could not think it would be that easy.

The demon's quiet thoughts hit Faye in the face. Frantic, she tried to escape, but she was trapped, encircled by the demon. Her head map was only a single spark of light in an ocean of smoke.

You are mine.

The cannon fuse ceased to burn. The demon had extinguished the fire.

I will take your Power and make it my own.

She couldn't even scream, because to do so would mean opening her mouth and breathing in the alien smoke, but Faye was furious. This stupid demon thought it was so clever. Well, she'd show it.

Faye reached deep inside, gathering up all of her Power, and then she pulled harder, gathering up all the Power she'd stolen from the hundreds that had died that night, but rather than throwing it all at once like she'd done with the *Tempest,* she focused it as tight and hard and mean as she could. The spark of her head map grew into a beam, bright and straight as a Tesla ray. It pierced the darkness, and Faye saw her way out.

The demon screeched in agony. *How dare you deny me!*

But it wasn't enough to escape. She'd come to *win.*

Only seconds had passed inside the gullet of the demon. If she stayed here long enough to light another match, which instinct told her wouldn't work anyway, she would surely die. She needed to do something else and she needed to do it fast.

The blinding beam of her head map pushed outward, toward the Power itself, and she looked and beheld that bit that she'd temporarily stolen—Whisper's sacrifice. Faye grabbed hold of that bit of Power, pulled it toward her, and . . .

All of the bomb fuses burst to life with a cleansing fire.

Thanks, Whisper.

And Faye stepped into the night.

⁂

The god of demons rose from the hole it had made on the Washington Mall, surveyed its new kingdom, and roared defiantly. The impact and the loss of one wing had cost it much precious mass, but it was growing again, and would continue to do so, until it devoured all who dared threaten it.

The sound coming from the demon wasn't in any language they could comprehend, but Sullivan understood the meaning anyway. *Run, mortals. Run, and hide, because I'm coming for you.*

Jake Sullivan was being supported by Dan Garrett on one side and John Browning on the other. Sullivan was so weak he could barely stand. He'd fully expected to die when he'd activated the shield spell. It was only that last spell he'd managed to carve and bind to himself months ago, the one based on the geometry of the Gravity Spiker, that had given him the energy sufficient to fuel the demon shield. But the shield spell was wearing off. They were retreating along with the bedraggled crowd. Soldier, marcher, Active, it didn't matter, now they were all just trying to get away, same as everyone else. The troops that had arrived to protect the Capitol had burned through their meager allotment of ammunition. The Grimnoir were beat, and he had no idea where the others had wound up.

Two familiar figures pushed their way through the mob. Lance Talon was covered in ash and limping worse than usual, while it looked like Iron Guard Toru had been set on fire at some point. His shirt was gone and the Imperium healing kanji were glowing bright on his skin.

One advantage of his terrifying appearance was that the evacuees gave him a wide berth. Toru asked, "Status?"

"We lost," Sullivan muttered.

"We gave the city time to begin an evacuation," Browning said. "That is worth something."

Sullivan didn't care for losing. "We have to think of something else."

"Anybody seen what Faye's up to?" Lance asked.

"Why? Do you need her to help you escape?" Toru asked coldly.

"Your Chairman underestimated her once, too. Look where that got him."

Toru's hand tightened around the hilt of his sword.

"Faye's the strongest Active we've got left," Sullivan said. "If I draw that spell again, and she uses her Power on it, maybe we can trap the demon *inside* for a while." It was a desperate idea, but it was all that he could come up with besides running away, and he didn't like running away any more than he liked losing.

The roaring and crashing of the demon had been so continuous that its sudden silence froze them all in their tracks. They all turned to look at the now quiet beast. It had stopped mid-rampage, through another of the great marble buildings. Struggling human figures were clutched in its hands, and it had been interrupted before it could shove them into its mouths. The four cavernous eyes narrowed. If something so hideously ugly could be said to have an expression, Sullivan would've had to guess that it seemed puzzled.

Then it exploded.

The demon seemed to stretch, bulging like an

overinflated tire, and then it simply erupted into a million pieces. Animated flesh was sprayed in every direction, much of it dissipating before it hit the ground. Thousands of gallons of demon ink spilled, like a dam had burst, and it rushed across the ruined Mall, washing the stragglers away, collecting in the craters, and pouring down the cracks.

"I think we found Faye." Lance said. "Told you."

The body was destroyed, its spirit banished. The Mall had been transformed into a scene from Hell. Everything was black, either from ash or ink. A pile of dissolving meat was spread over acres. Burning trees and spotlights from the *Lexington* provided just enough light to see the carnage. The air was choked with a stinking toxic haze. A thick plume of smoke stretched upward until it disappeared into the night sky.

The mob had stopped, staring in shocked disbelief at the destruction. Then there arose a ragged cheer. It was the sound of thousands, thankful to live another day. Sullivan knew from experience that after the elation passed, then there would be the anger and grief over the ones that hadn't been so lucky.

Dan studied the ragged crowd. He was thinking the same thing. "Let's get out of here before they recall what brought them here in the first place. . . ."

Chapter 23

Dearest Devika. Much time has passed since I have written. I have been consumed by my work. I write this letter in a brief moment of lucidity. I do not know how many more I will have, as they are becoming fewer by the day. Do not let my sons listen to the rumors of what I have become. The rumors are true but they must never know of the evil created by my hand. I was blinded by pride. One does not steal from the Power without paying a price. It is more intelligent than I suspected and it is learning. Though I thought I was using it, I was truly the one being used. Human emotions are not sufficient to describe the Power, but it was not upset when it discovered my theft. My resourcefulness gave it hope. The Power tried to prepare me for a task, but I was unworthy of its gifts. I have failed the test. Now all that remains is the hunger.

—Anand Sivaram,
Personal correspondence,
never posted, discovered in Paris,
France, 1918

Arlington, Virginia

FRANCIS WOKE UP GROGGY. He was in a small, plain room, completely empty of furnishings except for a wool blanket somebody had wrapped him in. There was no window covering, and from the fuzzy light, he guessed it was just before sunrise. The house was quiet as he took in the humble surroundings. It was a hell of a lot better than a prison cell.

The last thing he remembered was getting shot several times while trying to reach the OCI truck. Everything after that was a blur. Since he was alive, and it didn't feel like there were any extra holes in him, he could safely assume that he'd gotten to a Healer somehow. Sitting up took some effort. Being Mended would keep you alive, but the soreness had a way of lingering.

"Francis?"

It hurt to turn his head. "Faye?" She had appeared in the middle of the room. Her sudden arrivals no longer startled him like they used to. He started to ask her what had happened, but then he saw the terrible state she was in. Clothing tattered, splattered in dried blood and ink, with scratches on her face, and a hand that was blistered and red, Faye just stood there, wobbling like she was about to collapse. "Faye!" Francis heaved himself to his feet, tossed aside the blanket, and went to her. He caught her as she fell into his arms and gently lowered her to the floor. He brushed the matted hair away from her face. "What's wrong?"

She pulled his head down and kissed him on the lips. The intensity surprised him. When she finally let go, Faye gave him the saddest smile he'd ever seen on her face. "Nothing's wrong now."

When Francis woke up again, strong daylight was beaming through the windows. Hours had passed. The air smelled like smoke and he didn't know why. Voices could be heard outside. Browning was giving orders. It sounded like it was time to clear out.

He rolled over and reached out, but the blanket was empty. Faye was gone. Not surprising, considering her seemingly boundless energy, she had probably Traveled away to go do something useful or heroic. That was simply how she was, and he loved her for it. Her absence made him sad, but it was good in one way, because things had just become a lot more complicated between the two of them and it would be nice to at least have a chance to think things over before she popped back in.

What was there to think about though? This was Faye . . . She was a force of nature. Francis knew that he was a handsome, talented, sought-after bachelor—not to mention incredibly rich—but here he was . . . wondering what *she* saw in *him*. Funny how things work out sometimes.

His fingers brushed against a piece of paper so he dragged it over. Still flat on his back, he unfolded the note. Faye's handwriting was horrible, but reading and writing had never been very important in her life before the Grimnoir, so it was to be expected.

Dear Francis

I am real sorry. I have to go away for a while. I learned some things about how come my magic is different from everybody else. There is a curse on me and I do not want to become a monster. I got to figure out what to do about it. There is someone I have to find. Please do not look for me. It is better this way.

Some of the elders were so scared of what I am that they sent Whisper to kill me. From what I know now they were probably right to. But Whisper died to help me instead. She was very brave. I made her a promise so now I have to figure out how to keep it.

Please do not tell the others that I am alive. It is safer that way.

When I thought you were gone I wanted to die inside. I was so scared. No matter what happens I am glad that I found you. I come from nothing and you come from everything but I love you Francis and I want to marry you and be your wife. But first there are monsters outside and monsters inside and I have to figure out how to beat both kinds. More bad things are coming. I know it. And I have to be ready.

I do not know how long I will be gone but I will be back. If I do not come back it is because I messed up and died. If I die I want you to go and be happy without me. So I need you to be brave for me.

Love

Faye

There were soft spots on the paper that were still damp. Francis thought that they might have come from tears.

The bag was removed from his head, revealing that they were in the kitchen of an average home. A large recording device had been set before him. The man who had removed the bag paused to turn on the audio recorder before taking a seat.

The Coordinator of Information, Doctor Bradford Carr, found himself sitting across the table from two dangerous Actives. The Grimnoir had finally decided to interrogate him. Very well . . . He had nothing to hide, and wouldn't have been able to hide anything from the likes of these anyway. He recognized both of them from the OCI files: Daniel Garrett, former radio celebrity and Mouth, and Pemberly Hammer, former asset of Mr. Crow, a Justice. One could convince him of anything and the other could detect any falsehood.

"So, I take it you intend to make me talk and then murder me?"

"No," Garrett replied. "Though that would be rather easy. We're recording this conversation to give to the Bureau of Investigation in order to clear the Grimnoir Society of any wrongdoing. Then you're free to go. You have my word."

Carr laughed. "You take me for an imbecile?"

"Not at all. We want the courts to deal with you publicly. It'll be quite the scandal. The nation needs to know what you were up to. They need to hear the truth.

They won't get that truth if we were to just bury you in a ditch, now would they?"

He looked at the spinning wheels of the recording device with disdain. If the Grimnoir thought that would work, then they were bigger fools that he'd thought. No testimony coerced, nor evidence gathered, through magical means was admissible in any court of law. "Well, Mr. Garrett, Miss Hammer . . ." He was careful to state their names for the record, assuring that the tapes would be thrown out, because after all, how could he, a mere Normal man, resist the persuasions of mind-controlling Actives? He would simply say that he'd been forced to repeat whatever Garrett had wanted him to. "I would be completely unable to resist your magical persuasion anyway; so we may as well continue."

"Was the OCI involved with the attack on Franklin Roosevelt?"

He did not sense any overt presence in his mind from the Mouth's magic, but it was certainly there. "Yes."

"In what capacity?"

It actually felt good to talk about it. "I had Giuseppe Zangara recruited for the task."

"And?" Hammer prodded.

A half truth wasn't much better than a lie to a Justice. "One of my men created a spell to augment Zangara's natural Power and then we provided him with a Grimnoir ring." Even if an investigator followed up on that, they would never be able to prove anything with Crow gone. "The purpose was to pin the crime on the Grimnoir Society."

"Why?" Garrett asked.

"I needed an enemy for the people to unite against—an antagonist, if you will. And since you were the types that would stand in the way of magical registration anyway, I could eliminate—"

"No . . ." Garrett held up a hand. "Not about us. Why Roosevelt? Why try to kill him? Isn't he in favor of registering Actives too?"

Carr laughed. "Of course he is. Registration will happen regardless. Oh, no, Mr. Garrett. Roosevelt had to go simply because I knew he intended to *replace* me! You see, the two of us have never gotten along. Franklin believes in the gradual and incremental increasing of controls over the Active race. I believe that time is of the essence and they must be controlled *now*. Rumor was that he intended to appoint someone else as Coordinator. I certainly did not put that much effort into building my dream only to have it stolen from me. Strike while the iron is hot I say!"

Garrett looked to Hammer. She nodded. Of course he was telling the truth. Garrett's file had said that he was extremely subtle. Carr was impressed. It actually felt good to get this off of his chest.

"And the demon that tore through Washington?" Hammer asked.

"One of mine that slipped the leash. And a further example of why Actives need to be controlled at all costs." Carr laughed.

"What's so funny?"

"I should be saddened by the destruction of my headquarters and the ruination of my plans, but this worked out so much better. Crow's rampage inspired far more terror in the hearts of the populace than anything I could have dreamed of. I was only trying to convince the Normals, but now Actives themselves will come begging us for protection. It was worth the sacrifice of my research—"

"By research, you mean those poor Actives that you were torturing on Mason Island?"

"Torture?" Carr snorted. "A small price to pay for knowledge. They were science experiments, nothing more."

"Innocent people, taken from their homes, and carved on, poisoned, manipulated, drugged . . . I've seen similar experiments conducted in the Imperium."

"And the Nipponese are wise to do so! We have entered an arms race. The first nation to fully harness magic to its fullest will rule the world. As long as people like you are running free, squandering your gifts, we will lag behind!"

"So what do you intend to do about it, Doctor?" Hammer asked.

"Me? Nothing. My job is done. The tipping point has been reached. The masses will speak, first with words, then with force. Actives will be regulated, studied, quantified, and organized. You will be commodities, resources, your skills going to where they are most needed for the greater good. Our way of life will be preserved. We will reach for the stars. We will—"

"And for those of us that don't want to go along?"

"This is America. Everyone has a right to choose—"

Hammer was blunt. "He's lying."

"Fine! To the trash bin of history with you! Collect the

troublemakers and use them as breeding stock. Take the children born with gifts and raise them to be obedient. The next generation will serve admirably. And for the very worst of the worst, like you"—Carr sneered—"we could learn a thing or two from the Imperium schools."

The Actives were silent for a very long time. Hammer was unreadable. Garrett seemed angry. Perhaps he'd said too much? But it could not be helped, not with a Mouth pressing his thoughts and a Justice testing his every word.

"What happens next?" Garrett asked.

"Plans have been made. Big plans."

"Who else knows about these plans?"

The door swung open. "That'll be enough." Two tall men in suits entered, then quickly stepped to the side. The Actives looked up, not surprised in the least by the interruption. One of the new arrivals shut off the recording device and deftly wound and removed the tapes. Another man entered the room behind them, and the Coordinator gasped in surprise when he recognized the round face.

"Director Hoover?"

J. Edgar Hoover tipped his hat. "Coordinator Carr . . ."

What was the Director of the Bureau of Investigation doing here? "These people kidnapped me! They're Actives!"

"Yes, I am aware," Hoover said. "I recently accepted Miss Hammer's application to be a BI *special agent*. She will be working for me now."

Hammer beamed with pride. "Thank you, Director. I suppose that makes it official."

That news seemed to surprise Garrett. "Really? I didn't think you hired women or Actives."

"Times are changing, Mr. Garrett, and the BI stays at the forefront of change. Recently, I've decided to reexamine some of the applications that were rejected in the past. Perhaps if I had more *gifted* agents on the payroll, heinous plotters, such as our good Doctor here, would not prosper."

"This one is a Mouth." Carr knew he had to think fast. "He forced me to say all sorts of terrible lies."

Garrett leaned back in his chair. "You know how we Mouths can be."

Hoover nodded. "I'm familiar with Mr. Garrett's tricks." He reached into his suit coat, removed a small orange box, and opened the lid. The sphere in the center was spinning. The Dymaxion nullifier was placed in the center of the table for him to gawk at. "I believe this belonged to you."

Carr felt all of the blood drain from his face. "No . . . It can't be."

"I was on the other side of that door. This device was running the entire time. However clever Mr. Garrett thinks he is"—Hoover explained as Garrett grinned and rested his hands on his ample belly—"there was no magical influence during the recording of your conversation."

The Coordinator tried to respond, but couldn't find his voice.

"In addition, we have some very questionable documents with your handwriting on them that were gathered up by a Traveler before your office was swallowed, not to mention several people who are willing to testify that you kidnapped and tortured them. We shall continue this discussion at BI headquarters."

"But you can't—"

"You made too many mistakes." Hoover's voice grew cold and dangerous, "But most of all, you shouldn't have tried to embarrass me in the papers. Nobody gets away with that. Take him away, boys."

Faye
Spellbound

Epilogue

I hope your committee will not permit doubts as to constitutionality, however reasonable, to block the suggested legislation.

—Franklin Delano Roosevelt,
Discussing the Active Registration Act, 1933

San Francisco, California
Three Months Later

THE FRONT PAGE OF THE NEWSPAPER was just as frustrating as usual. Roosevelt's Hundred Days were continuing, rolling out program after program. Only one of which really interested Jake Sullivan, and even though they knew about him, he'd be damned if he was going to obey any Active Registration Act on principle, and he sure as hell wasn't going to wear an armband in public with the floating anvil logo that identified him as a Heavy.

In other news, the OCI hearings were still going on, despite Bradford Carr managing to hang himself to death with a shoelace in his jail cell. The Grimnoir were in the clear, but most of the Society was very uncomfortable being icons to a large section of the population. George Bolander's legend had grown faster than the plant life in Oklahoma, and the now famous photograph of Heinrich Koenig bounding across the god of demons' back wielding a pickax had helped catch the public's imagination as well. Heinrich was rather proud of that photo. For a group that had fought in secrecy its entire existence, becoming public heroes took a bit of getting used to.

"Mr. Sullivan! Mr. Sullivan! A moment of your time, sir?"

He lowered the paper, scowling at the reporter. Sullivan wasn't used to being well known either. Even though he'd only been Public Enemy Number One for a few days before the warrant had been rescinded, it was hard to shake off that level of infamy. Plus, he was one of only a handful of people who had been identified in the newspapers as a knight of the Grimnoir, which meant that no matter how much he hated the idea, or how uncomfortable it made him, he was now one of the public faces of the Society. Most of the others were lucky enough not to have been identified by the OCI, which meant that they didn't have great big targets painted on them for the Imperium or any of the many other groups that the Grimnoir had pissed off over the years.

"Please, Mr. Sullivan, just a few words with you?"

There was no use beating around the bush. He had never been good at keeping a low profile anyway, and the reporter's shrill voice had got the attention of everyone else sitting in the lobby of the UBF station. Now folks were looking at him. "What do you want?"

The reporter stood there with a notepad and a pencil.

"A quote on what you think of the President's latest proposal."

"For the *needs of a nation*? Sounds like horseshit to me."

"We can't print that, Mr. Sullivan."

He checked his watch. It was about time to go anyway. He had a flight to catch. Standing up, he towered over the reporter. "What do you want me to say?"

"Well, our readers want to know what the reaction to the ARA is—"

Sullivan held up one big hand. He didn't like being seen as a spokesman. Nobody had voted him in. If they wanted somebody who could say something well reasoned and eloquent, they could talk to Dan who was serving as their voice in D.C., or if they wanted something impassioned they could talk to Francis who was back running UBF. All Sullivan was good for was honesty. "I'll tell you what I think of the Active Registration Act."

The reporter got ready to scribble furious notes. All of the other passengers waiting for dirigibles were watching him now too. Some of them kindly, others suspiciously, and a few with outright hatred on their faces. "Go ahead, sir."

"FDR can go to hell. I'm a man. Not a type, not a number, and sure as hell not something that can be summed up as a logo to wear on my sleeve. A *man*. And I ain't registering *nothing*."

"The President says that having Actives identify their Powers in public will keep everyone safer. What do you think of that?"

Sullivan picked up his bags, over two hundred pounds in each hand, and tried to walk away.

"Where are you going?"

"On a trip."

The reporter followed him. "Do you really intend to flaut the law, Mr. Sullivan?"

"Yes, I do."

"But the penalties are steep. Fines, imprisonment, they're even talking about—"

Sullivan stepped into the elevator. "I'll deal with that when I get back, but right now I got bigger fish to fry."

The doors began to close, but the reporter shouted one last question. "And what could possibly be more important?"

Sullivan didn't answer until the elevator doors had slid shut and he was alone. "Saving the world."

The cargo was almost loaded. The last of the crew had arrived. The brand new airship docked at the private section of the air station was the most advanced craft ever built by United Blimp & Freight. They were ready to depart.

"Jake Sullivan reporting for duty, Captain."

Bob Southunder was standing on the catwalk, hands clasped behind his back, inspecting his new ship. "Good morning, Sullivan." They'd needed an experienced captain and crew, and there was nobody who knew the business better than Pirate Bob and his marauders. "The last of Browning's crates has been delivered."

Sullivan had already said his goodbyes to Browning. The Cog had spent the last couple of months building some new weapons systems for this mission, and he'd kept Sullivan busy testing them out. Sullivan was rather excited to try the Spiker armor in action. Some of the defensive gadgets and improvements that Buckminster Fuller had come up with though . . . now *those* made him nervous.

Southunder went back to critically examining the airship. "What do you think of her?"

The *Traveler* was a twin-hulled dirigible with lots of horsepower and guns. "Francis said she's fast and packs one hell of a punch."

"I still miss my zeppelin, but I do believe she'll do nicely. I'm not so sure about the crew, though. They don't have to like each other, but they do need to trust each other. Otherwise *accidents* can happen up in the sky. In my experience I've found that the judgmental ones tend to fall overboard; must be their swollen heads throwing off their balance."

Everyone aboard was a volunteer who knew the risks. Southunder was like a father to his pirates, and Sullivan trusted the knights that were accompanying them. Heinrich had seen to the recruiting, and Sullivan knew that the Fade had put together a solid bunch. So there was only one person whom Southunder could be talking about. "He'll do what he's supposed to."

"We can't have one bad apple always looking for trouble."

"Looking for trouble is our mission . . . I'll go talk to him."

"Thank you, Sullivan. I'll get us in the air."

As expected, Toru was in his quarters, sharpening his sword. The former Iron Guard did not bother to look up when Sullivan entered. "Are we ready yet? I feel my ancestors grow impatient."

"Your ancestor murdered half of this crew's ancestors."

"I see." Toru replied as he examined the blade. "Then their ancestors should have ducked."

"You going to pick any more fights?"

"Only with the Enemy, and should we live through that . . . the two of us have one to finish."

"As long as you keep them in that order, fine with me. But where we're going, the Imperium will try to stop us. These men need to know which side you're gonna be on if that happens."

"Do you wish me to give them *my word?* It is said that a warrior does not make promises, for everything we speak is a promise. If a warrior says he will do something, then it will be done. If a warrior speaks, it is a vow. I have already said why I am here. We will fulfill the duty of the Dark Ocean." Toru finally put the sword down and glared at Sullivan. "Tell your men the entirety of the Imperium would not stand in the way of fulfilling the final command of Okubo Tokugawa. The Imperium will come to understand the coming danger or they will perish. I will *make* them understand the truth of this."

In Toru's head were the memories of a man who had fought the Enemy before and lived to tell about it. They needed him, whether they liked it or not. "You'd damn well better."

Toru bowed in response.

Sullivan went forward, deep in thought. One small group of men were going to try to do a job that the Chairman had built the whole Imperium for. The Grimnoir were loved by few, feared by many, and hated by more. No one in authority would listen to them about the Enemy, and even some of the elders doubted his sanity. No one had seen Faye since the god of demons had been banished, so it could be safely assumed their strongest Active was dead. Half of his friends were staying in the States to fight a war of propaganda and diplomacy, while the rest of them were embarking on a suicide mission against an alien threat.

General Roosevelt had once told the 1st Volunteers that a leader fights a war with the resources he had, not the ones he wished he had. Now it was Jake Sullivan's turn to be the leader, and his resources were a hundred men, a fancy blimp, guns, magic, and a whole lot of guts.

The view out the window shifted. The *Traveler* had lifted off.

The search for the Pathfinder had begun.

END

Glossary of Magical Terms

From the notes of Jake Sullivan, 1932
Active Icons created by the
Otis Institue for Magical Studies

A

Active—The catchall term for people with magical abilities, specifically those who have strong enough connections to the Power to utilize their ability at will and with a greater degree of control than a Passive. Actives vary in the amount of Power available to them, with some being more naturally gifted than others. The conventional wisdom has always been that Actives are only able to use one type of Power.

Actively Magical—Old-fashioned term for Active.

Angel of Death—(see Pale Horse)

B

Babel—Rare type of Active capable of understanding, deciphering, and communicating in any language.

Burner—(see Torch)

Beastie—Similar to Dolittle, but stronger, with the added ability to control animals telepathically. Extreme cases can actually put part of their consciousness into the creature and fully control it, including broadcasting the Beastie's speech, etc. There have been some rumors of Beasties capable of controlling human beings, but that may be anti-magic propaganda.

Beastman—(see Beastie)

Boomer—Unknown type of Active. The Special Prisoners' Wing guards at Rockville mentioned holding one of these in solitary confinement in a special lead-lined chamber.

Brute—One of the most common of all Magicals. Brutes channel Power through their bodies, increasing their physical strength and toughness. They must work up to greater feats of strength. If too much Power is used too quickly, severe injuries or death can occur. They have been banned from professional sports in most countries, but there is always work available for a Brute.

Beastie Boomer

Brute Cog

Crackler

C

Cog—The second most popular of all Actives. Cogs are able to tap their Power to fuel their intelligence, and to receive strokes of magical brilliance. They usually only have one area that they are gifted in; for example, Ferdinand von Zeppelin was a Cog when it came to airships. If it weren't for his bursts of magical ideas, who knows what we would be riding. I do not know if all Cogs are already intelligent, but I've never heard of a dumb one.

Crackler—Capable of channeling, harnessing, and controlling electrical current. They are a relatively common type, and most make their living as electricians or in industry. The more powerful Cracklers can draw energy from the air and generate their own lightning.

D

Demon—(see Summoned)

Dymaxion nullifier—A device created by the Cog Buckminster Fuller that Suppresses Actives' connection to the Power behind their abilities

Dolittle—Active with the ability to communicate with animals. Extreme cases that can actually take control of the animal's body are usually referred to as Beastmen or

Beasties. A series of popular children's books have been written about a fictional veterinarian with this ability, so it has become one of the more socially acceptable types of magic.

E

Edison—(see Crackler) I have been told this is considered the polite term now.

Elder—Member of the Grimnoir Society leadership.

Enemy—Unknown predatory creature that is pursuing the Power, according to Chairman Okubo Tokugawa.

F

Fade—Capable of walking through solid objects. Perhaps they do this through modifying their density so that other matter fits between their molecules. They are the opposite of the Massive, yet both of them originate from the same Density-related section of the Power. Fades are universally loathed for their reputation as thieves, cutthroats, and peeping toms.

Finder—Related to the Summoner, but dealing more with disembodied spirits rather than physical beings. Finders are primarily used as scouts, and their sensitivity varies greatly. It is possible that Finders and Summoners are using the same region of the Power, with Summoners simply being more powerful.

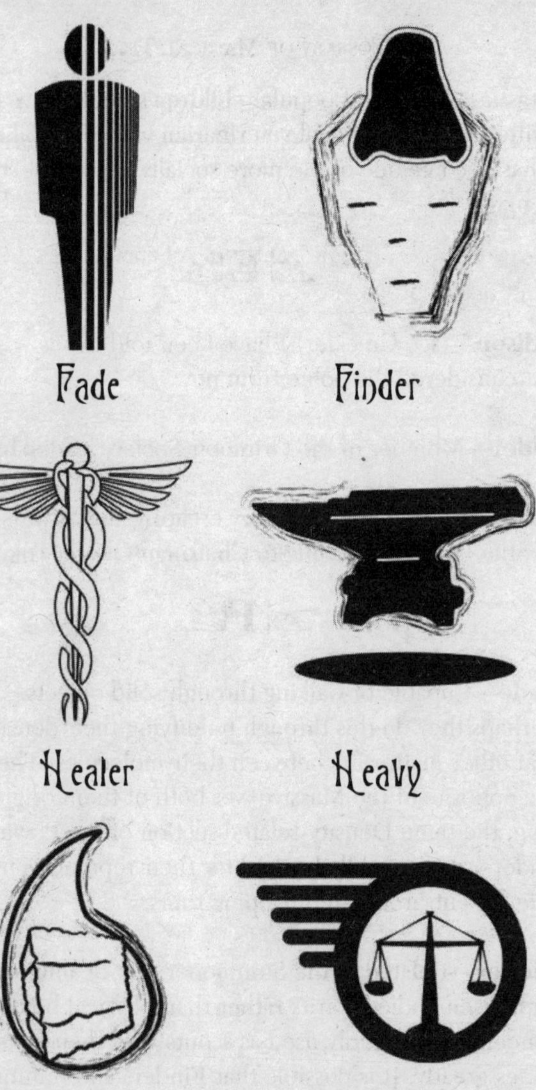
Fade
Finder
Healer
Heavy
Icebox
Justice

Fixer—(see Cog) Usually a term reserved for lower-level Cogs, who are better at repairing than inventing.

Fortune Teller—Charlatans who pretend to have magic and know the future to rip off suckers. There is no proof of any precognitive Active.

G

Gravity Spiker—(see Heavy) The much more dignified term for an Active Heavy.

Grey Eye—(see Traveler) All known Travelers have strange grey eyes.

Grim Reaper—(see Pale Horse)

Grimnoir Society—A combination of the French words Grimoire, for book of spells, and Noir, for black, because at the time the origins of magic were shrouded in mystery. The Society was founded to protect Actives from the Normals and to protect the Normals from the Actives. Their primary operatives are known as knights, and their leaders are referred to as elders. They work in secrecy.

H

Head Case—(see Reader)

Healer—One of the rarest and most popular of all Actives. They are capable of accelerating the natural healing process. Even the weakest Passive Healer is worth a fortune. Strong Healers can fix most wounds almost instantaneously. I have been led to understand that even without using their Power, they can always see a person's insides. I suppose it's a good thing they're paid so well, because that would make me ill.

Heavy—(see Gravity Spiker)A very common type of Active. Most Heavies are limited to changing the gravitational pull in a very limited area. Strong Heavies can change the pull and also the direction in a larger area. Heavies are one of the few types of Actives that all tend to fall into the same physical category; most of them being large of stature. There is an undeserved stereotype that Heavies are dumb.

I

Icebox—Always handy to have around when you want some ice in your drink, the Icebox is able to lower temperatures. Stronger Actives can freeze water or even blood and tissue instantly. There have been stories of Iceboxes who could produce ice walls or spikes out of thin air, but these may be the result of a popular radio program, the Adventures of Captain Johnny Freeze. As a physical benefit, Iceboxes cannot be harmed by frostbite or extreme cold.

J

Justice—This type of Active supposedly can always tell truth from lies. They also posses a tracking ability, being able to follow a "true path."

K

kanji—(see Spells) The Japanese term for physical spells. Their kanji tends to be more stylized and artistic than the Western European-style markings of the Grimnoir, but is very effective at channeling Power.

knight—An operative of the Grimnoir Society.

L

Lazarus—An Active capable of chaining the spirits of the recently dead to their bodies, creating tortured undead. This is the worst of all, sheer magic scum, and the only good Lazarus is a dead Lazarus.

Lightning Bug—(see Crackler)

Lucky—I had heard about these for years, and thought they were a fairytale to explain people who cheated at cards. They use their magical ability to alter probability. The term used by Dr. Fort to explain this ability to influence chance was psychokinesis.

M

Machine Head—(see Cog) Usually a Cog who is in tune with physical machines rather than theory or science.

Magicals—A common term for people with Power, which can include both Actives and Passives.

Massive—An extremely rare type of Active, capable of increasing their physical density until they are almost invulnerable. I believe they are related to Fades, but at the opposite end of the spectrum.

Mender—(see Healer)

Mover—The scientific term is telekinetic, which means moving things with your mind. They are very rare, and very few are capable of moving more than a small number of small objects at a time. As a Mover's Power increases they are able to lift more weight, lift more individual items at once, move them to higher velocities, and most difficult of all, exercise a finer degree of control over the controlled objects.

Mouth—The most hated or most loved Actives, depending on if they are in charge or not. Mouths are able to Influence anyone listening to their voice. Passive Mouths can alter moods and emotions, while a powerful Active can directly control your thoughts and feelings. The smarter you are, the harder it is for a Mouth to steer you. Mouths tend to gravitate toward politics.

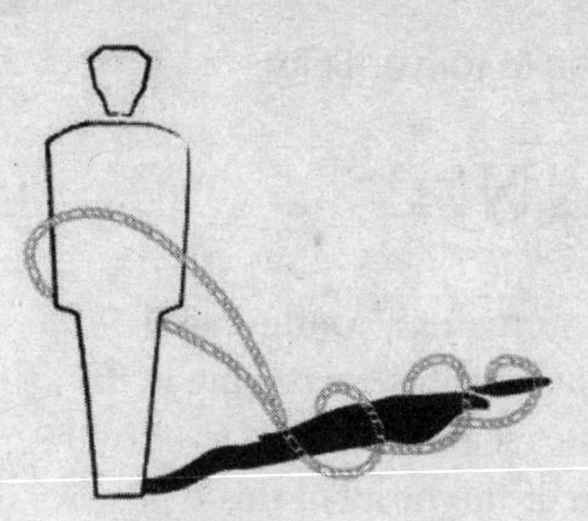

Lazarus

Lucky

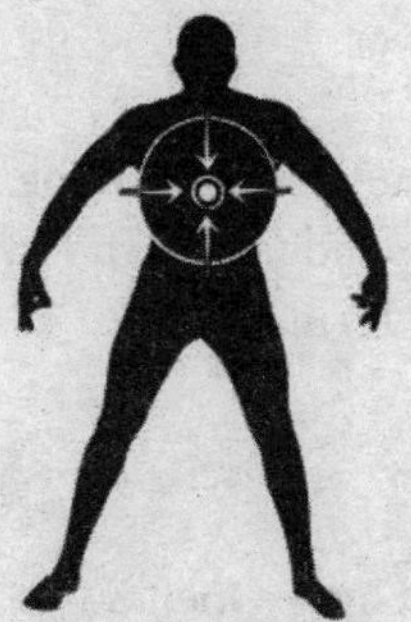

Massive

Mouth

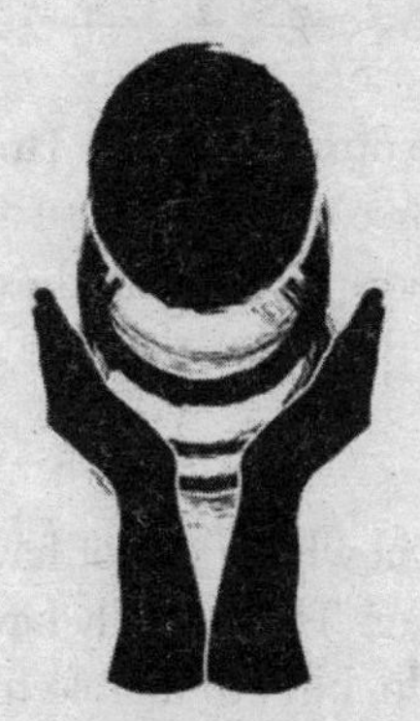

Mover

N

Nixie—One whose ability creates a continuously growing sphere that annihilates everything in its path. The area of effect seems to be set at a fixed distance, but because of the rarity of this type, I can't confirm. There have only been a few known cases. The Mason Island Incident was caused by a spellbinding of the Nixie's Power.

Normals—Term used mostly by Actives to describe people without any magic. Depending on who is using it, it can be a derogatory term.

O

Opener—(see Lazarus) short for Grave Opener.

P

Pale Horse—The opposite of the Healer, the touch of the Pale Horse causes disease and sickness. No Active is more hated than these. Luckily for us, most Normals think that they are a story used to scare children.

Passive—A Magical who does not have active control over their Power. They usually have one small trick that they can do, but are unable for whatever reason to grow their ability. For example, Passive

Heavies are instinctively able to pick up heavy things. Passive Healers can accelerate the natural healing process just by their presence but cannot target specific areas or wounds. Passive Readers can pick up snatches of other people's thoughts but often go insane from being unable to control the input.

Pipes—Unknown type of Active. Intelligence reports during the Great War showed that the Germans held one of these in reserve, but it is uncertain if we ever encountered him.

Power—a. The energy that all Magicals possess. As the energy is used, our reserves are depleted. The rate that it recharges and the total amount that can be stored depend on the individual's natural gifts and practice. It is currently unknown if a Magical is born connected to the Power, or if the connection forms at some point during their early life.

Power—b. The living being that all magical energy originates from.Its origin is a mystery. I believe it to be a symbiotic parasite. It grants magical abilities to some humans, and as we develop those abilities, the magical energy that we carry grows. When we die, the Power "digests" this energy and feeds. The process is then repeated. The growth of the being explains the increase in our numbers over time.

Pale Horse

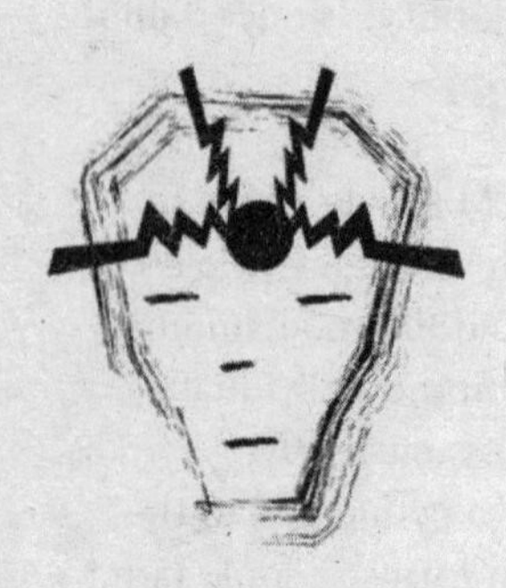

Reader

Ringer

Shard

R

Reader—Someone possessing the magical ability to Read another's mind, sometimes called telepathy. Weak Readers can get general feelings from their target, while a strong Reader can crack your head open and watch your memories like a motion picture. Readers can also broadcast thoughts and memories. The stronger their target's will or intelligence, the more difficult they are to Read, and the more likely they are to sense the intrusion.

Ringer—An extremely rare type of Active who can change their appearance and voice to perfectly mimic another. It is unknown if they actually physically change, or if they just create the illusion in other people's minds. I met one once in Rockville but he escaped within 24 hours of arrival.

Rune Arcanium—A book of spells collected by the Grimnoir Society.

S

Scales—(see Justice)

Slinger (see Lucky)

Shadow Walker (see Fade)

Shard—A rare type of Active that can modify their bone structure at will. I had one start a fight with me in Rockville. They still squish just like everyone else.

Shifter—(see Ringer) It is believed in some circles that there is a type of Active that can actually change their physical form, but my personal belief is that these are just talented Ringers.

Spellbound—A term used for when you've connected a person or thing to some area of the Power through the use of a spell.

spells—Through creating a representation of one of the coordinate sections of the Power, specific magical energies can be channeled into, and connected to, those markings. Grimnoir-designed spells tend to look like old European-style writing, while Imperium kanji are more artistic.

Summoned—A being brought into our reality by a Summoner. The strength of the creature is dependent upon the Summoner's skill. Summoned only communicate at a rudimentary level, though they do have some language. It is unknown where they originate from and they will never communicate on that subject except in the vaguest terms. Summoned remain in this world until destroyed or dismissed.

Summoner—An Active that can bring in creatures

from another world to serve their bidding. It is unknown where these beings come from. The personal beliefs of the Summoner seem to affect what the Summoned looks like. Extremely powerful Summoners can bring in drastically strong creatures. The more forceful the creature, the more Power and attention it takes to keep it under control.

T

Teleporter (see Traveler)—A scientific term that has recently comeinto common usage.

Torch—The singlemost common type of magical ability, Torches control fire. Passives are usually limited to very small flames, while a powerful Active can put out a flaming hydrogen dirigible. Unlike the Icebox who can't be harmed by cold, Torches can still be burned just like any other human.

Trap—(see Mouth) Usually used with a dual meaning, as in, "That politician is a Trap."

Traveler—One of the only Actives that can be spotted by a physical trait. All known Travelers have grey eyes. They are one of the rarest types, but not by birth, but rather because so few of them live long enough to control their ability. Travelers are able to move instantly between two places. The stronger the Traveler, the further they can go, and the more they can carry.

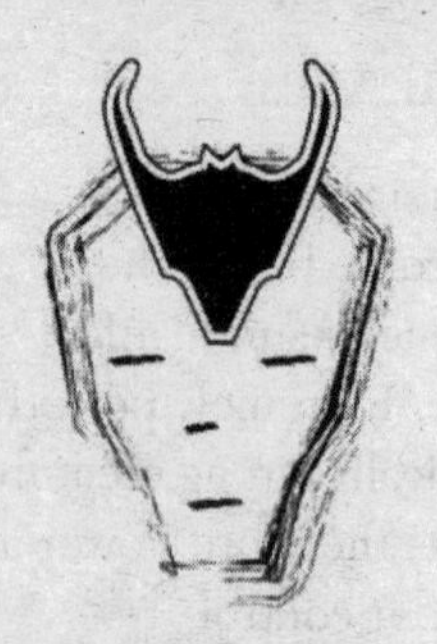

Summoner

Tinker

Torch

Traveler

Weatherma

U

Undead—A being created by a Lazarus.
Physical death has occurred but the body remains animated. Consciousness and intelligence remains but so does the pain of whatever killed them. Undead possess no natural healing abilities and only continue to deteriorate. They cannot be magically Mended. Very few undead remain sane for any length of time and they tend to grow increasingly violent and erratic. They do not truly die until their body is utterly destroyed. There is a special place in hell for anyone who would curse someone to being undead.

W

Weatherman—A Magical with the ability to influence the weather. Strong Actives can actually stop or start storms and change wind patterns, sometimes even up to hurricane force.
Too harsh use of this skill can cause severe side effects, such as the great dustbowl of 1927.

Words (see Mouth)

Y

Yap (see Mouth)

Z

zombies—(see Undead). The first known Lazarus originated in Haiti. It is believed that is where the term zombie originated from.

The Following is an excerpt from:

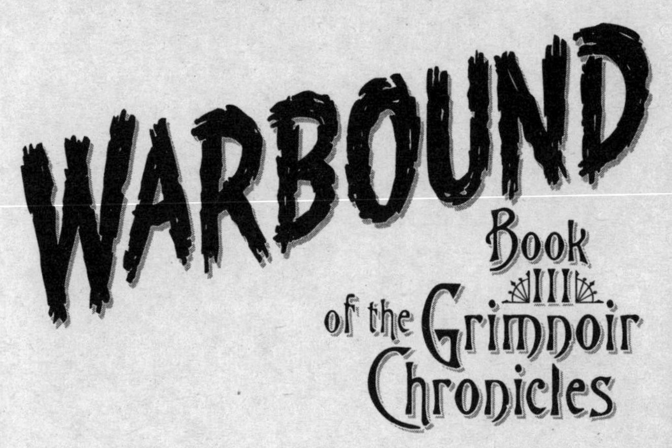

LARRY CORREIA

Available from Baen Books
August 2013
hardcover

Chapter 1

It was not so many years after magic first manifested in this world that the first members of the society gathered. We were to be a shield against injustice. We were motivated by righteousness. We become Grimnoir in order to become heroes, to sacrifice our lives in the pursuit of a higher cause, to defend the defenseless . . . I've found that means attending a lot of funerals.

—Toyotomi Makoto,
knight of the Grimnoir,
testimony to the elders' council, 1908

Paris, France
1933

FAYE THOUGHT that Whisper's funeral was very nice. Even though it was a rainy afternoon, there was a huge turnout, which was still to be expected since Whisper had been such a friendly girl. It made sense that she'd been popular. There had to be a hundred people down there all dressed in black. Faye hoped that when she died, she'd have a funeral this nice too, with all sorts of people coming from all over to say pleasant things about her before they stuck her in the ground. Dwelling on that thought gave Faye a touch of melancholy, since her friends probably already did think she was dead, blown to bits along with the God of Demons in Washington, D.C. Only Francis knew that Faye was still alive, and she was counting on him to keep her secret.

For all she knew, they'd already held her funeral and she'd missed it. Hopefully it had been well attended.

She couldn't make out the carving from this far away with the spyglass, but the tombstone would have the name Colleen Giraudoux carved on it. Nobody Faye knew had ever called her Colleen, it had always been Whisper. It had been months since Whisper had died, but she'd died far across the Atlantic Ocean, and Washington had been in a terrible state at the time, what with a big chunk of it being ruined or set on fire. Sadly, there had also been a lot of other bodies to sort out, so Whisper's corpse had been stacked in one of the overflowing morgues along with thousands of others for weeks before Ian Wright had identified her and had her remains shipped back to her home in France for a proper burial like Whisper would've wanted.

Faye had made a solemn promise to Whisper right before she'd died. So Faye had crossed the ocean, stowed away with the coffin in order to make sure that promise was fulfilled. The long journey across the sea had given Faye time to ponder on what Whisper's sacrifice had meant. Whisper had taken her own life in order to save the city from the big demon's rampage. Whisper had given up her magic in order to make Faye's stronger.

Faye was special, even by Active standards. She had known that for quite some time now. Her connection to the

Power seemed positively endless when compared to anybody else. Blessed with what she figured was the best kind of magic ever, she was maybe the strongest Active around, especially after she'd managed to kill the Chairman and he wasn't competition anymore. Everybody had said that Okubo Tokugawa had been the strongest in the world, but she'd shown him. *Greatest wizard ever, I don't think so.* Faye snorted as she thought about it. The Chairman wasn't so tough after she'd Traveled his hands off.

Faye was unique. The problem was thats he had never realized just how come she was that way, and why her magical abilities had grown so quickly, but Whisper had told her the secret. A long time ago, a terrible spell had been created, one that stole people's connection to the Power as they died. The man the spell had been bound to gobbled up more and more magic until it had made him crazy. They called him the Spellbound, and he had done some horrible things to make his magic better. The Grimnoir had finally killed him, only the terrible spell hadn't died along with its creator. It had simply moved on and found a new home.

For some reason, it had picked her. She really wished that it hadn't.

Faye was the new Spellbound. There was no way she could have known it at the time, but it was the spell that had enabled her to defeat the Chairman and save the *Tempest,* just as it was the spell that had let her defeat the big super-demon Mr. Crow had turned into. It seemed like she'd inherited a gift, but Whisper had made it sound like a curse. The fella that had created the spell had started out as a good man with noble intentions, but the more he used it, the more evil he'd turned.

The Grimnoir elders were so scared of what a new Spellbound might do that they'd been ready to murder her. It probably didn't help that they already thought she was kind of crazy anyway, so she figured she was already halfway there in their eyes. They'd even secretly sent Whisper to keep an eye on her and to kill her if she turned bad. Instead, Whisper had made Faye promise to stay good, and then shot herself in the heart to save a city.

Faye had held a bunch of very complicated one-sided conversations with Whisper's coffin on the trip over. Now they were lowering that coffin into the ground, and Faye had hidden herself several stories up on the rooftop of a fancy old church between some very ugly gargoyles. She was studying the mourners through a spyglass, trying to decide which one of them was supposed to become her teacher.

Jacques Montand was the expert on the Spellbound, and Whisper had asked her to seek him out. Jacques was one of the Grimnoir elders, one of the seven leaders of their secret society. Faye was proud to be a member, a knight as they called themselves, since they did a whole lot of good heroic stuff, but she did object to the part about preemptively murdering her just in case she decided to turn evil. That made it sorely tempting to teach them all a lesson . . .

Faye refocused on watching the funeral. Those kinds of murderous thoughts were probably the evil sort that she should be trying to avoid. It was hard not to think that way, though, because she was just so very talented when it came to killing folks. She'd *borrowed* the spyglass from the ship she'd stowed away on. She moved her focus from face to face around the coffin, studying each one, trying to figure out who was the secret magical warrior who had trained Whisper to be a Grimnoir knight, and which ones where just friends from Whisper's normal, not-secret life. It was hard to tell, especially with all of those darn umbrellas. Plus, on half of the people, she could only see the backs of their heads, but Faye didn't dare go down there. She had to stay hidden. The only way this was going to work was if the elders still thought she was dead.

Which did raise another question. What if, after she talked to Jacques, he decided to rat her out to the other elders? Then she'd either have to kill him to keep him from blabbing, or let the same folks who'd sent Whisper to kill her know that they needed to try again harder. She knew which one made more sense, but that sure seemed to go against her promise to Whisper to stay good, and she really didn't want to get into the habit of murdering other good guys, even if it was in self-defense.

This sure is complicated.

Being picked to be one of Grimnoir elders didn't mean you were old, just that you were supposed to be wise; but Jacques had to be older. Old enough to have beat the last Spellbound when Faye was still a baby, but there were several grey-haired men in that crowd. Faye knew from meeting a couple of the others that the elders were crafty and tended to keep a lot of protection around, which was understandable since the Imperium, the Soviets, and who knew who else was always gunning for them. So she tried looking for people who looked like bodyguards. There were a few tough-looking fellows, but for all she knew, they were just some of Whisper's multitude of boyfriends. And besides, in Grimnoir circles, you didn't have to be a side of beef like Jake

Sullivan or Lance Talon to be dangerous. Faye, being skinny and unremarkably plain, was a perfect example of that.

One nice thing about her particular Power was that she was able to see the world around her so much better than everyone else. It was basically like a big map inside her head. It wasn't like Faye could see through walls with her eyeballs, but she instinctively knew perfectly well what was on the other side of those walls. For example, this big church, or cathedral, she supposed it should be called, had fifteen people moving around inside of it, and she could even get a feel of what was in the first level of tunnels beneath it. *Rats and bones mostly.* She could sense danger or any objects large enough to hurt her if she should Travel into them.

Faye hadn't known too many other Travelers in her life, as they were the rarest of the rare. Grandpa hadn't known how to do the trick with the head map like she could, none of the Grimnoir books knew anything about it either, and the few Imperium Travelers' she'd met, well, they'd been too busy trying to kill each other to talk about how their Powers worked.

Her head map could sense life, and she could pick out magic. If she tried really hard, she could even sort of trace the individual links back to the Power. Faye concentrated, drew in the width of her head map, and focused on the people at the grave site. Sure enough, there was magic in that crowd, several different kinds in fact. And a few the Actives had connections to the Power that were quite strong.

Was this how the last Spellbound turned evil? Since he was a Traveler too, did he have a head map of his own that could show him who had Power and who didn't? And was that what tempted him to kill folks and steal it? Though Faye could sort of understand the appeal of gaining even more magic, the thought sickened her.

She had to pause to wipe the raindrops off the lens. The spyglass blew up the faces of the magical folks, and she studied each one. It was easy to pick out the Grimnoir. Sure, they were sad, just like everybody else. The difference was that they all shared this same look of resignation, like they'd been to way too many funerals already. She supposed that was to be expected, since members of the society were getting themselves killed all the time. Those had to be Whisper's fellow knights.

The spring rain shower was annoying, and you can't exactly sneak around spying on folks while carrying an umbrella. Plus the rain had softened up the years of pigeon poop on the roof so everything was slick and her traveling dress was a mess. *Come on, Jacques . . . Which one are you?*

Faye had focused her head map so intently on the mourners that she hadn't even sensed the danger until it was almost on top of her. *There was somebody else on the roof!*

She hadn't heard him approach, which was saying something since the top of the cathedral was slick as a milk-barn floor and anything you could stand on was at an obnoxious angle. She'd simply Traveled up this vantage point, but the newcomer was climbing up the tiles behind her and slinking along around a gargoyle. He'd scaled the side of the cathedral and wasn't even breathing hard. If it hadn't been for her head map, he would easily have been able to creep right up next to her.

Well, this mysterious fellow had picked the wrong girl to try and sneak up on. She carefully collapsed the stolen—

borrowed—spyglass and stuck it into a pocket so as not to accidentally scratch it. Faye picked out a narrow ledge just to the side of where the stranger had crawled onto the roof. Her head map confirmed that it was safe to Travel there. Rain drops were soft and easily pushed aside by her passage, so she focused on the spot and Traveled.

Faye appeared out of thin air and landed easily on the ledge. She didn't even need to put out one hand to correct her balance. Faye was rightfully proud of her Traveling skills. The science types had taken to calling her form of magic with the much fancier name of Teleportation, but she still preferred to think of it as Traveling. That name had been good enough for her adopted grandpa, Traveling Joe, God rest his soul, so it was good enough for her.

The climber was still focused on her last position. Faye studied him for a moment. It was hard to tell since he was all crouched over behind a gargoyle, but he seemed to be a tall, thick fella, gone soft around the middle. He must have lost his hat on the climb, because all men wear hats, and he didn't have one on. It was hard to tell his age, because though he looked old, he wasn't moving like an old fella. He was magic all right, she just couldn't tell what kind yet. His hair was stark white, thin, and plastered to his head by the rain. He was wearing what appeared to be a nice, dark-colored suit, but it was now smeared grey because of the stupid pigeons. *Well, serves him right for skulking around like an Imperium ninja.*

Still unaware of Faye's new position, he collected himself, reached inside his suit coat and came out with a small black pistol. Faye had a gun too, though hers was a much bigger .45 automatic, but she figured she wouldn't even need it. She watched, bemused, as the stranger rose from behind the gargoyle and pointed his pistol at nothing.

She Traveled, appearing only a few inches behind the man and shouted, "Boo!"

Startled, the man turned toward her with lightning speed. Faye had figured he'd be some sort of physical Active in order to have made his way up here so easily, so she was ready. The gun turned in her direction, but she was already gone, appearing effortlessly now in front of him. Even if he was a mighty Brute, he was in a rather bad position, what with being so close to the side of a really tall building, and so Faye simply reached out and gave him a shove.

Arms windmilling, his dress shoes squeaked on the rain- and pigeon-shit-slick roof as he tried not to fall over the edge. He almost would have made it too, but the tiles cracked and gave under his heels, and, top-heavy, he started going over the edge. "*Merde!*"

She knew a similar word in Portuguese, since Grandpa had used it a lot on all things relating to dairy cows, and apparently the exclamation translated over in French.

Before he could fall, Faye reached out and snagged his skinny tie with her right hand and a gargoyle's wing with her left, managing just enough of a grip to stop them both from tumbling to the street below. Of course, since she could Travel, only one of them would be going splat if she let go of that gargoyle.

"Whoa there, mister." She loosened up on the tie for a split second, just to demonstrate who was in charge. She snagged it again and kept him from falling. He grabbed her arm with both hands, nearly crushing it, though she could tell he was holding back—he was probably a Brute. Only his toes were still touching the edge of the roof and even Faye was mostly hanging over open space.She hoped he spoke English. "Don't do anything stupid. Let go of my arm."

He shook his head, then spoke with a light French accent. "If I fall, we both fall."

She'd been right to begin with. He was older, probably in his fifties, maybe sixties, but age was hard to tell with some folks. Eyes wide, the man looked first at the ground, then back at Faye, and then back at the ground. He was leaning back way too far to do much of anything except fall. A sufficiently skilled Brute might survive a fall like that, but it probably wouldn't be much fun. He'd dropped his pistol in a vain attempt to grab the gargoyle. He looked forlornly at the gun sitting in the rain gutter. "I did not see you coming."

"They never do."

Faye realized that the old man was studying her face, specifically her odd grey eyes. All Travelers had grey eyes, and there weren't very many Travelers. "You must be Sally Faye Vierra."

"That's me."

He looked around. *Faye. Ground. Gun.* Then, realizing that he was in a very bad way, he settled on looking at Faye. "Please pull me up?"

"Maybe." Faye answered, noting the black-and-gold Grimnoir ring on his gun hand. "Why'd you try to sneak up on me?"

After the initial shock of almost falling, the old fellow had regained his composure. "Why were you spying on us?"

That was a fair question, though she was rather

disappointed that her spying skills weren't turning out to be very good. "I'm looking for somebody in particular. He was a friend of Whisper's."

He was a distinguished-looking man, well dressed, despite the pigeon poop and new tears that he'd put into his clothing trying to sneak up on her. He probably would have been rather handsome in his youth. It was hard to tell if he had the commanding presence of a Grimnoir elder, since nobody really had much of a commanding presence when the only thing keeping them from falling off a roof was a little girl holding onto their tie. He was old enough to have fought the last Spellbound. "Are you Jacques Montand?"

"I am . . . You've come to kill me, then?"

Not really, but he didn't need to know that yet. "I'm thinking it over."

"So you know what you really are?"

"The Spellbound. Whisper told me before she died."

"I see . . ." Jacques sighed. They both knew there wasn't a whole lot he could do right then if Faye decided to just let go of the gargoyle. She could easily Travel to safety before hitting the ground and Jacques knew it. He slowly released the death grip on her arm. "I do not know everything she told you, but I would ask you to leave the other members of the Grimnoir leadership out of this. They voted to leave you alone. Our last instructions to Whisper were to observe you but to take no action. The majority of the elders thought that though you had been cursed, you yourself were innocent of any wrongdoing."

"Uh huh . . . On this vote, how close was it?"

"Five against two."

Well, she was even more popular than she expected. "How'd you vote?"

He looked her square in the eye as his shoes slipped a little further. "I understand more about the threat of the Spellbound than the others. I voted to have you eliminated immediately."

"I didn't ask for this!" Faye exclaimed. It would have been so easy to just let go of him. That big of a fall might've even killed a Brute as tough as Delilah or Toru. Then Faye could simply take Jacques' link to the Power and make it her own. But then again, that was probably just the mean side talking. Faye had made a promise, and Faye always kept her promises. "I should drop you, jerk."

"It was nothing personal. I have seen what the spell will eventually cause, and I have evidence which makes me believe this will happen again. I do not regret my decision." He closed his eyes and waited for her to let go. "Do it. I am not afraid."

Faye was impressed. The Frenchman had guts. "I didn't come all this way to kill you, Jacques." Faye pulled hard. It was enough to shift both of their centers of gravity back over the edge, and he stumbled forward onto more solid tile. It was also hard enough for the tie to choke the heck out of him, and he had to stop and adjust it before he could breathe a sigh of relief. Jacques stood there on trembling legs. He may have been a Brute, but he didn't have near as much physical Power as some of the others Faye had met. By the time he opened his eyes, Faye was ten feet away, sitting on a gargoyle's head, just in case he tried to do something stupid and heroic. "I came here so you could teach me."

Billings, Montana

ROCKVILLE WAS JUST AS UGLY and godforsaken as he remembered it.

The Special Prisoners' Wing was separate from the rest of the prison, and from the road it looked like one massive, windowless concrete cube. The ugly fortress sat in the middle of an open area that seemed unnecessarily big, but was that size to make sure that an escaping Fade would run out of Power or have to come up for air before he could reach the perimeter. Around the yard was a brick wall tall enough that even a Brute would have a hard time hopping it and thick enough that it would be tough to crash through. The wall was topped with concertina wire and had a guard tower on every corner. It had been said that the riflemen in those towers were all expert shots, and not of a hesitating nature. He'd never been in one of the towers, but he'd been told that, in addition to the thirty-caliber machine guns, they also had elephant rifles and even bazookas in case one of the tougher prisoners decided to take a stroll.

There had been two dozen escape attempts since the Special Prisoners' Wing had been built. There had been only one success that anyone knew of. The rest had ended up back in their cells or in the facility's crematorium.

Rockville was simply ugly. Rockville was a monument to ugliness. It served the ugly purpose of keeping dangerous criminal Actives away from the world. Its name served as a warning to any Active who thought about using magic to break the law. Rockville was a synonym for hard time. If any normal person ever passed by they would have to stop and gawk at the sheer *ugly* of the place. Good thing it was in the middle of nowhere.

But no matter how nasty Rockville looked on the outside, it was nothing compared to the monotonous hard-labor hell that was life on the inside.

Been a long time. He'd never thought he'd be back here, certainly not as a free man.

At least this time he wasn't here as a convict. He was here as a recruiter.

Jake Sullivan parked the car before the gatehouse and waited, feeling the eyes on him. The Special Prisoners' Wing of the Rockville State Penitentiary didn't get very many visitors. Cautious guards approached from both sides, polite enough, but carrying Thompsons and ready for anything. There was no such thing as a complacent guard at a facility where the average prisoner could have super strength or set you on fire with his mind. From what Sullivan knew, at least one of the gatehouse men would be deaf, and therefore immune to the manipulations of any Mouth trying to con his way through.

Papers presented, he waited while they triple-checked everything. It only took a few minutes. Of course they'd known to expect him. The Warden was thorough like that.

The gate was built solid enough to stop a bulldozer, and it took a good five minutes to get it open wide enough for his car to make it through. There was a second fence inside the first, this one made of wire, and he had to wait for that gate to be pulled aside as well. Originally they had kept attack dogs inside the wire, but had been forced to get rid of them after a Beastie had used them to maul some of the guards.

After that they'd electrified the wire, until one day a Crackler had sucked up the extra voltage and used it to blow a hole in the main wall during an escape attempt. So now it was just a fence.

That was the thing about containing criminal Actives. You just never knew what they were going to come up with next. Rockville collected the worst of the worst, the most violent, dangerous, magically capable hard cases that a judge couldn't come up with a good enough reason to just execute.

There was a loud clank as the main gate began to close behind him. A cold lump of dread settled in his stomach. He took a deep breath and waited for the guard to wave him through the secondary fence. He wasn't the sort to get rattled easily, but Jake Sullivan had served six long years inside that wall. Just over there was the rock quarry where he'd spent thousands of hours doing backbreaking manual labor. He'd killed a lot of men inside these walls, all in self defense, but regardless, that sort of thing lingers with a man.

The gate closed like the lid on his coffin.

The Warden's office was exactly as he remembered it, dusty and old-fashioned. Every flat surface held stacks of books and papers, most of which were about magic, all taken from the prison's extensive library. Sullivan had read them all at one point or another. Since the Special Prisoners' Wing was dedicated to holding Active felons, no expense had been spared in the collection of information about magic. The Warden was a scholarly man, not out of any sort of innate curiosity, but rather because his job required it. It took a keen mind to come up with defenses for all of the various ways his special prisoners could cause trouble, but the Warden took his job very seriously and was now something of an expert on the topic.

The last time Sullivan had been in this room was when he'd been offered J. Edgar Hoover's deal for an early release, his freedom in exchange for using his own Power to help capture wanted Active criminals. Sullivan had jumped at the chance. Some of the other cons had called it selling out, but they were just jealous. Anything beat breaking rocks.

The Warden had greeted him warmly and waved the escort guards away. After all, the Warden had known Sullivan had enough respect for law and order to not be scared of him trying anything while he'd been a prisoner. So he certainly wasn't about to worry about him doing anything now that he was a free man. Sullivan took a seat in a chair meant for a normal man, and it creaked dangerously under his extra mass.

"You've been busy since we last met," the Warden said from across his wide desk. He was a squat, thick-necked, wild-haired fellow who always seemed to have the stub of a cigar clamped in one side of his mouth. In his six years here, Sullivan had never actually seen the Warden with a *lit* cigar.

"Yes, sir." There was no need to be so deferential anymore, but old habits were hard to break. "It's been eventful."

"In addition to what I've read in the papers, I've heard a few rumors. They're saying you're responsible for exposing the OCI conspiracy and catching the bastards who tried to kill Roosevelt."

He couldn't exactly tell the Warden about how he was now part of a secret society that had saved the entire east coast from a Tesla superweapon. "I played a small part is all."

The Warden leaned way back in his chair and chewed on his cigar. "Then that would mean my arranging your release was a good idea."

It had been the Warden who had suggested to Hoover that Sullivan could be of some use in helping capture criminal Actives. He wouldn't go so far as to say that they were friends, since the Warden was the man responsible for keeping him caged like an animal in a prison full of violent madmen, but once he'd understood Sullivan's nature, there had been a certain level of respect. Plus, if the Warden had not allowed him access to the library, Sullivan would've gone crazy a long time ago. "I personally think it was a good idea. Can't speak for anyone else."

"Well, I do suppose it depends on who you ask. Some seem to think you're a national hero while the rest say you're a menace to society. I was a little worried about keeping my job when that whole Public Enemy Number One thing happened." The Warden chuckled. "Luckily, nobody in their right mind would want my job."

"Yeah, that was real amusing." Being framed for an attempted presidential assassination and becoming the most wanted man in the country hadn't exactly been a picnic.

"I imagine," the Warden agreed. "For a few days there I was under the impression I might once again be able to enjoy your sunny company here at beautiful Rockville."

There was no way the OCI could have taken him alive, but that went unsaid. Sullivan merely gave a noncommittal grunt.

"It isn't often that I get to speak to one of our rehabilitated fellows. So, what brings you back to my fine establishment, Mr. Sullivan?"

"I made a request to the Bureau of Investigation."

"Yes, I received the letter from Director Hoover. It was rather cryptic, but gave me the impression that you are working on a rather important project. He was clear that it wasn't one of his projects, but something that could prove to be vitally important nonetheless."

"It is." Sullivan didn't think that Hoover was entirely convinced as to the reality of the Enemy's existence, but after his political victory over the OCI, Hoover had felt like he'd owed Sullivan enough to at least humor his request. Not to mention that the BI director was happy to have the volatile and now infamous Heavy Jake Sullivan go off someplace where he wouldn't be able to talk to reporters anymore.

"I'll admit, I am curious. So what's the nature of this mysterious project of yours?"

Track down a horrible monster from outer space before it can send a message home to its daddy to come and destroy the whole Earth. "I can't really say."

"Hoover said you'd say that." The Warden leaned forward suspiciously. "So what do you want from me?"

"Not what. Who." Sullivan reached into his coat, pulled out the paperwork, already signed by a federal judge, and passed it over.

The Warden took it and read, disbelief growing on his face. "You can't possibly be serious? This prisoner . . . Released? Why—"

"There's an important job that needs doing. I'm putting together a team to do it. Real talented bunch, if you get what I mean. In fact, there ain't much we can't do. However, this particular fella's got some rare skills I need."

"He's dangerous."

"Which means he'll fit right in."

"You know about . . ."

"Heard about him. He got here after I left."

"Don't think you can control him, Sullivan. He'll get inside your head."

"He ain't a Reader."

"Might as well be." The Warden rolled his cigar to the other side of his mouth. "He's not like you, Sullivan. Letting you out was one thing. Anybody who has studied the law could look at your case and see you were railroaded. You were a war hero who stomped a crooked sheriff in a crooked town, and because you were a scary Active, you were made into an example. I just wish I'd read your file sooner. The vast majority of the rest of my convicts, on the other hand, are in here for damn good reasons. This man Wells, for example. He's a killer, nothing but a mad-dog killer."

"Sorry, Warden. I'm afraid where I'm going, mad-dog killers are exactly what I'm gonna need."

Solitary confinement was by the gravel pit. Sullivan had spent quite a bit of time in solitary. It was where you got put automatically after a fight. Didn't matter if you started it or not. Get in a fight, go in the hole. And Sullivan, having had the reputation of being the toughest man inside Rockville, had no shortage of upstart punks who'd wanted a shot at the title, so Sullivan had spent a lot of time in the hole. Usually, he hadn't minded. The quiet had helped him think.

The holes lived up to their name. They were just shafts that had been dug ten feet straight down into the solid rock with a four-hundred-pound iron plate stuck on top for a roof. The holes weren't even wide enough for a tall man like Sullivan to lie all the way down. Inside was just enough room for the prisoner, a bucket to shit in, and a whole bunch of rock. Once a day they'd send down a clean bucket with food and a can of water in it, and pull up the old bucket to hose out to send back with your rations in it the next day. Once they'd decided you had enough they'd roll down the rope ladder. It hadn't been too awful in the summer, but being in a hole during the Montana winter was miserable. There tended to be fewer fights during the winter months.

The Warden had telephoned ahead, so there were ten guards waiting around one hole in particular. Some were carrying nets, and the rest were armed with strange Bakelite batons with metal prongs sticking out the ends.

"What're those?" Sullivan asked, gesturing at the unfamiliar weapons.

The guard patted the big square end of his baton. "Electrified cattle prod. Gotta have something. Bullets just bounce off this guy."

"It won't be necessary. Stand back while I talk to him."

"Warden said you'd want it that way. Your funeral, pal." The lead guard shrugged. "Stand away, boys."

The guards complied, a few of them giving him dirty looks that suggested they remembered him from the old days. Even cleaned up and without the striped prisoner suit and the ball and chain clamped around his ankle, he was still an easy man to recognize. He'd never given the guards any trouble. They were just men doing a hard job, so Sullivan held no grudge, but to them, once a convict, always a convict, and only a sucker trusted a convict.

Waiting until the guards were safely away, Sullivan walked up to the hole and kicked the iron plate a couple of times to announce his presence. "Morning."

The voice was muffled through the plate. "What do you want?"

"I want to talk, Doctor."

There was a long pause. "So it's doctor now, huh?"

"You got a medical degree and you're an alienist, so that's your title, ain't it?"

"I suppose I've rather gotten used to my title being 'Convict.'"

Sullivan remembered his own stays in the hole, how only the tiniest bit of light could creep through the air slots cut in the iron plate, and the painful blindness that came with freedom. "Cover your eyes. It's bright today." Then Sullivan used a tiny bit of his Power to effortlessly lift the rusting iron slab and toss it to the side.

Sunlight filled the hole. "Aw. That really stings."

"Warned you." Sullivan kicked the waiting rope ladder down into the pit. "Come on up."

"Give me a minute to make myself presentable."

"Take your time." Sullivan waited patiently as the prisoner rubbed the feeling back into his limbs then struggled to make his way up the ladder. He didn't offer to help pull him up, since the man was filthy after several days in the hole, and Sullivan didn't particularly feel like getting his suit dirty, or worse, ending up in a wrestling match with a Massive who had a reputation for violence.

Like I got room to talk. Sullivan didn't just have a reputation for violence, he'd gained national notoriety for it. *Still ain't getting my new suit dirty though.* He folded his arms and waited for the prisoner to pull himself over the side. For being able to alter his density, and being so good at it that he could even make the Rockville guard contingent nervous, the prisoner didn't look like much. He was of average height and thin build, not particularly remarkable at all. Sullivan was half a foot taller and twice as wide in the shoulders.

Wells blinked for a moment, adjusting to the sunlight, then the two men stood there, sizing each other up. It was hard to guess the age of someone that dirty, but the OCI's file had said that Doctor Wells was thirty-five, so fairly close to the same age as Sullivan. Though right then the convict looked about ten years older. The hole had that effect on a man. The doctor had a widow's peak, and rubbed one hand through his thinning hair, seemingly bemused when he discovered how matted with dried blood it was. "Please, excuse my appearance. The facilities leave something to be desired."

For some reason Sullivan expected the convict to be a twitchy one, since his OCI file had repeatedly used the term *erratic genius*, but instead Wells seemed cool, almost *too* collected. Sullivan nodded politely. "Let me introduce my—"

"Wait." Wells held up one hand, which was still scraped and raw from the altercation that had landed him in the hole in the first place. "Don't tell me. I've had nothing new to keep my mind occupied for three days now. Allow me to deduce why you're here."

Sullivan was in no hurry. The *Traveler* was on its maiden voyage, and Captain Southunder was still shaking her down and checking systems. She wouldn't be ready to leave the

Billings airfield for another hour or two. "Knock yourself out."

"I take it you don't work here?"

"Nope."

Wells glanced over to where the squad of guards were fidgeting. "You're talking to me by yourself, and the Warden is far too thorough to not have informed a visitor of my capabilities, which suggests you're not afraid of me, nor do you seem even the slightest bit nervous."

Sullivan let him have his fun. "Should I be?"

"That depends." Wells saw the discarded iron plate. Normally it would take three or four strong men to move it into place. "You're obviously a Brute . . ."

"An interesting hypothesis."

He went back to studying Sullivan. "No. Not a Brute . . . You have the morphology of a Heavy. All known Heavies are physically robust, big-framed specimens."

Sullivan nodded. "I prefer the term Gravity Spiker. It's more dignified."

"And I prefer the term *psychologist* over the term *alienist*; however, most Heavies wouldn't care. Statistically, Heavies tend to score rather low on the Stanford-Binet intelligence scales. They're *slow*. You're an oddity. More than likely a self-taught man . . . Don't look at me like that. Your pronunciation of *hypothesis* suggests that you've read the word, but not heard it spoken very often, which means you've not attended school. It isn't hypo-thesis . . . It's *hýpothésis*."

Sullivan shrugged. "I'll have to remember that." He hadn't had much schooling, and frankly, some of the dumbest sons of bitches he'd ever met had been the ones with the fanciest educations and the most degrees framed on the wall. Despite that, you'd be hard pressed to find anyone who'd read more books in their life than Sullivan had. It helped that he could put down a fat tome in the time it took most men to read a newspaper.

Wells talked fast. His brain ran faster. "Your clothing is new, expensive, but you seem unused to it. It would suggest that you make a good salary, but that isn't right. Nice suit, but you didn't care enough to shave today, nor does your hair reaching your collar suggest you care much for grooming. But I have been out of circulation for a year, so I may have fallen behind on what is fashionable. You strike me as a man too busy to care about his appearance. The clothing was purchased for you so you'd look presentable, perhaps by an employer?"

"Close, but no cigar." Francis Stuyvesant, knowing that Sullivan was going to be doing a lot of recruiting for his mission, had ordered one of his legion of functionaries to hook Sullivan up with a good suit. It was nice to have something tailored and not bought from a secondhand store.

"But I'm close. It was a gift. Your shoes were not. Your shoes are too sturdy, picked for comfort and durability rather than style."

"A man never knows when he's gonna have to chase somebody down."

"Chase, rather than run from . . . The choice of words demonstrates your mindset. Either way, they don't match your suit." Wells' eyes darted back and forth, then he took a few steps to the side. "Though you don't have it on you now, your coat has been tailored to hide a firearm on your right hip. Something rather large apparently. So you are in the habit of carrying a large handgun, not a little gentleman's pistol, but a serious working weapon. The clothing is too nice for a policeman's salary."

"Maybe I got a rich uncle?"

"You don't talk like a man with an inheritance. You have less-refined enunciation. You don't strike me as *nouveau riche.* You have the face of a boxer."

"I've stopped a few fists with my nose."

"A fighter then. Your knuckles are scarred." Sullivan unconsciously clenched his fists. "And you are a former soldier. You can always tell by how they stand when they are being made uncomfortable . . ."

"I'm starting to see how you end up in so many fights around here."

"Yes. It's a good thing I'm indestructible."

"*Virtually* indestructible," Sullivan responded. "Everybody dies, Doc. Some folks, you just got to try a little harder."

"Great War, judging by your age . . . The most likely use for the common Heavy during the Great War was as manual labor. Heavies are a dime a dozen."

"Yeah. Lots of us around. Not so many of your kind."

"Odds are you've never met another like me," Wells said with a bit of false modesty.

He resisted the urge to smile. Wells was a smart man, just not as smart as he thought he was. Sullivan was one of the only Actives alive who'd learned how to blur the lines between different types of magic. He was no stranger to manipulating his own mass. "Naw. I met a Massive once. No big deal. They squish like anybody else."

"*However*," Wells said sharply, "you were no laborer

during the Great War. Your combative stance suggests the second most likely statistical probability for a Heavy, which was mobile automatic rifleman."

Wells was as astute in his deductions as the OCI file had suggested. "Machine gunner," Sullivan corrected.

"First Volunteer then," Wells said, noting Sullivan's surprise. He waved one filthy hand dismissively. "AEF used different terminology. Machine gunner there would suggest having worked on a crew-served weapon, but nobody would waste a Heavy in that role when they could be used as walking fire support on their own. General Roosevelt used Heavies as machine gunners. I'd wager you were no stranger to a suit of armor either."

"I should've said I was a blimp mechanic, just to see what you'd say then."

"Lying, and the types of lies the subject chooses, only help me understand the subject's thought processes." Wells was circling him now. "You're not a Rockville employee, but you don't have the nervousness that an outsider to Rockville would normally have. No . . . You're used to this place, but for reasons—*Convict!*" Wells suddenly bellowed, using a command voice like a guard would have.

Sullivan raised an eyebrow.

"Hmmm . . . A slight reaction. Maybe I was wrong, or maybe you are just not the sort given to dramatic reactions. But I'm never wrong . . . I know who you are . . . Mr. Heavy Jake Sullivan."

That was impressive. "Very good, Doc. You do that trick at parties?"

Wells gave a little bow. "It's nothing. You're a legend in Rockville."

"Beating a dozen men to death will do that."

"Only a dozen over six years?" Wells' smile was utterly without emotion. "Why, I'm halfway to your record in only one."

It was only an estimate. In actuality, he'd hadn't really kept track. "Congratulations?"

"So, Mr. Sullivan, would you like me to figure out what brings you all the way back here to beautiful scenic Montana to speak with me? I will admit, I was expecting to reason out the why of this visit long before I reasoned out the who. I wasn't expecting a celebrity."

"Save your parlor tricks. I've got a job to do and I think I might need somebody like you on my crew."

"A Massive? My type of Power *is* incredibly scarce."

"That could come in handy, but no. I need an alienist."

"Psychologist," Wells corrected.

"As long as you keep calling me a Heavy I'll keep calling you an alienist."

"Why pick me, Mr. Sullivan? Sure, I'm the best, but I have many capable peers who aren't incarcerated for the next twenty years. That could pose a logistical problem."

"You think you know about me? Well, I know a bit about you, too. I know you got bored, screwed over a bunch of gullible patients, and lost your medical license. Then somehow you wound up making a million bucks running cheap Mexican hooch across the border before you got caught. According to the Rockville doctors, you're what they call a sociopath. I know you don't give a shit about anyone other than yourself. I know that you'll kill somebody the minute it's convenient for you. You think life's a game and everybody else is just pieces on a board. Normally, none of those things would sound like attractive qualities to an employer.

"But the important thing, is I know you're a genius at predicting folks' behavior. Word is, as long as you think it's a challenge, nobody is better at guessing an opponent's moves than you. You come highly recommended in that regard."

"By whom?" Wells asked suspiciously.

"A former colleague of yours had a file on you a quarter-inch thick." That was an exaggeration, but there had been a few pages in the armful of evidence Faye had snatched before Mason Island had been sucked into a black hole. "Dr. Bradford Carr."

For the very first time, Sullivan was pretty sure he caught a genuine display of emotion from Wells, and it wasn't a pleasant one. Wells quickly contained the hate and managed to give a pleasant smile instead. "So . . . how is the *good* doctor?"

"Dead . . . Oh, that's right. You boys don't get to read the papers in here. Me and my friends ruined him. That's how I got my hands on his files, and how I know that you're one of the only men he ever actually feared. He committed suicide. Hung himself with a shoelace in his prison cell a little while ago."

"How delightful. *Now* I'm slightly intrigued. What is it you're proposing, Mr. Sullivan?"

"I've got paperwork from a federal judge releasing you into my custody. Each week you work for me knocks six months off of your sentence."

"I see." Wells seemed to be mulling that deal over, but Sullivan knew that was just an affectation he'd adopted to make normal people feel more comfortable around someone whose mind worked too fast. Brain like that? Wells had already run the numbers. "And despite what you read about me in Doctor Carr's files, you trust me not to betray you?"

Sullivan snorted. "Compared to some of the folks I've got on this, not particularly. Look, I'll save us both the time with the pointless threats. If you do anything to sabotage my mission, we both know I'll kill you, or one of my extremely dangerous pals will kill you. You can make the same threat to me, but then we'd just waste a bunch of time, and we're both too busy for all that posturing nonsense."

"Refreshing. And what happens if I try to escape?"

"You won't. You'll stick around till we're done, and after that I don't particularly care what you do."

"Why would you possibly expect me to do that?"

"A man who thinks life is all a big game needs a big challenge. Hell, you're probably enjoying Rockville because at least surviving here takes some cunning."

"I'll admit, it can be thrilling at times." Wells looked down at his striped clothing. "Though it does leave something to be desired in the style and hygiene departments. Despite that, your offer of freedom isn't as interesting as you'd think." Wells glanced over at the nervous guards. "I'm confident that when I tire of this place, my next challenge will be figuring out a way to escape."

"I only know of one person that's ever made it out of Rockville alive, and he was a Ringer."

Wells chuckled. "If any old schlub could do it, then it wouldn't be much of a challenge."

"If you want a challenge, I've got a challenge like nothing you've ever seen before. I've got an opponent that even somebody as smart as you will have a hard time getting ahead of." *A little flattery never hurt.*

Now Wells did appear to have to roll that one over for a moment, and since he seemed to have a brain like a Turing machine, that was saying something. "And what would this challenge be?"

"Saving the world."

Wells chuckled. "You must have mistaken me for an idealist, Mr. Sullivan. I don't give a damn about the world. The world is filled with small-minded fools. If you've brought me some war or conflict or another, whether starting it or preventing it, that's simply boring. I'd rather live out my days as a Rockville gladiator. If there's some warlord or politician that needs killing, save your breath, that's the sort of pointless manipulations Bradford Carr used that animal Crow for."

"Crow's dead too. Long story."

"A deserving death, I'm sure . . . Best of luck, Mr. Sullivan, but I am not particularly interested in subjugating myself to the whims of another again. I'm going back in my hole now. The sunshine was nice, but solitary is where I like to recite poetry."

Sullivan had used his time in the hole to ponder on gravity. Turns out it had been time well spent. "Suit yourself, Doc."

"I'm sure you'll be able to find a Reader or some other mentalist to outwit this opponent of yours."

"Hell, I've got a Reader, but I don't know if their magic will work on a thing like this. If I wait until it acts, then I'm already too late. I need someone who can figure out how it thinks so that we can get ahead of it."

Wells paused at the top of the ladder. "It?"

"Too bad even with all your fancy deductions you assumed the Enemy was *human.*"

That got his attention. "I am now slightly more intrigued," Wells admitted.

"Our opponent isn't from Earth."

"Another super-demon then? Even in here, I heard about what happened to Washington."

"Hardly. This thing is why demons exist. It eats magic and leaves dead worlds behind. It's an entity that's pursued the Power across the universe, and the ghost of the Chairman told me it's on the way. If it ain't here yet, it'll be here any day now. We're gonna stop it."

The doctor gave a low whistle. "And they called me crazy . . ."

"The challenge is for you to help figure out how to track down this thing so we can kill it. The most advanced airship in the world is waiting for us in town. Once our captain's feeling confident our experimental dirigible won't just explode, we're going to invade the Imperium. Want to come?"

Wells let go of the ladder. "I'd like my own private cabin."

"Space is tight on the dirigible. You get a bunk like everybody else."

"Top bunk?"

"Deal."

PRAISE FOR LOIS McMASTER BUJOLD

What the critics say:

The Warrior's Apprentice: "Now here's a fun romp through the spaceways—not so much a space opera as space ballet… It has all the 'right stuff.' A lot of thought and thoughtfulness stand behind the all-too-human characters. Enjoy this one, and look forward to the next."
—Dean Lambe, *SF Reviews*

"The pace is breathless, the characterization thoughtful and emotionally powerful, and the author's narrative technique and command of language compelling. Highly recommended." —*Booklist*

Brothers in Arms: "…she gives it a genuine depth of character, while reveling in the wild turnings of her tale… Bujold is as audacious as her favorite hero, and as brilliantly (if sneakily) successful."
—*Locus*

"Miles Vorkosigan is such a great character that I'll read anything Lois wants to write about him… a book to re-read on cold rainy days."
—Robert Coulson, *Comics Buyers Guide*

Borders of Infinity: "Bujold's series hero Miles Vokosigan may be a lord by birth and an admiral by rank, but a bone disease that has left him hobbled and in frequent pain has sensitized him to the suffering of outcasts in her very hierarchical era…. Playing off of Miles's reserve and cleverness, Bujold draws outrageous and outlandish foils to color her high-minded adventures."
—*Publishers Weekly*

Falling Free: "In *Falling Free* Lois McMaster Bujold has written her fourth straight superb novel…. How to break down a talent like Bujold's into analyzable components? Best not to try. Best to say: 'Read, or you will be missing something extraordinary.'"
—Roland Green, *Chicago Sun-Times*

The Vor Game: "The chronicles of Miles Vokosigan are far too witty to be literary junk food, but they rouse the kind of craving that makes popcorn magically vanish during a double feature."
—Faren Miller, *Locus*

MORE PRAISE FOR LOIS McMASTER BUJOLD

What the readers say:

"My copy of *Shards of Honor* is falling apart I've reread it so often.... I'll read whatever you write. You've certainly proved yourself a grand storyteller.

—Lisa Kolbe, Colorado Springs, CO

"I experience the stories of Miles Vorkosigan as almost viscerally uplifting... But certainly, even the weightiest theme would have less impact than a cinder on snow were it not for a rousing good story, and good story-telling with it. This is the second thing I want to thank you for... I suppose if you boiled down all I've said to its simplest expression, it would be that I immensely enjoy and admire your work. I submit that, as literature, your work raises the overall level of the science fiction genre, and spiritually, you work cannot avoid positively influencing all who read it."

—Glen Stonebreaker, Gaithersburg, MD

"'The Mountains of Mourning' [in *Borders of Infinity*] was one of the best-crafted, and simply best, works I'd ever read. When I finished it, I immediately turned back to the beginning and read it again, and I can't remember the last time I did that."

—Betsy Bizot, Lisle, IL

"I can only hope that you will continue to write, so that I can continue to read (and of course buy) your books, for they make me laugh and cry and think ... rare indeed."

—Steven Knott, Major, USAF

What do you say?

Cordelia's Honor
pb • 0-671-57828-6 • $7.99
Contains *Shards of Honor* and Hugo-award winner *Barrayar* in one volume.

Young Miles
pb • 0-7434-3616-4 • $7.99
Contains *The Warrior's Apprentice*, Hugo-award winner *The Vor Game*, and Hugo-award winner "The Mountains of Mourning" in one volume.

Cetaganda
0-671-87744-5 • $7.99

Miles, Mystery and Mayhem
pb • 0-7434-3618-0 • $7.99
Contains *Cetaganda, Ethan of Athos* and "Labyrinth" in one volume.

Brothers in Arms
pb • 1-4165-5544-7 • $7.99

Miles Errant
trade pb • 0-7434-3558-3 • $15.00
Contains "The Borders of Infinity," *Brothers in Arms* and *Mirror Dance* in one volume.

Mirror Dance
pb • 0-671-87646-5 • $7.99

Memory
pb • 0-671-87845-X • $7.99

1634: The Galileo Affair
by Eric Flint & Andrew Dennis
0-7434-9919-0 ✦ $7.99
New York Times bestseller!

1635: Cannon Law
by Eric Flint & Andrew Dennis
1-4165-5536-6 ✦ $7.99

1634: The Ram Rebellion
by Eric Flint with Virginia DeMarce
1-4165-7382-8 ✦ 7.99

1634: The Bavarian Crisis
by Eric Flint with Virginia DeMarce
978-1-4391-3276-0 ✦ $7.99

1635: The Dreeson Incident
by Eric Flint with Virginia DeMarce
978-1-4391-3367-5 ✦ $7.99

1635: The Tangled Web
by Virginia DeMarce
978-1-4391-3276-0 ✦ $7.99

1635: The Eastern Front
by Eric Flint
978-1-4516-3764-9 ✦ $7.99

1635: The Papal Stakes
by Eric Flint & Charles E. Gannon
978-1-4516-3839-4 ✦ $25.00

1635: The Saxon Uprising
by Eric Flint
978-1-4516-3821-9 ✦ $7.99